Red stood, and watched, and waited, dread roiling beneath her ribs.

Her blood touched the white trunk, hesitated. Then the tree *absorbed* it, took it in like water to parched soil.

Tripping over leaves, Red backed away from the tree until she collided with another, this one also thin and pale, also twisted with black rot. Underbrush tangled in her skirts, and Red tore herself away, the rip unnaturally loud in the silent forest.

That sound again, reverberating up from the forest floor, rustling leaves and stretching vines and clattering twigs cobbling themselves into something like a voice, something she didn't so much hear as *feel*. It boiled up from her center, from the shard of magic she kept lashed down through white-knuckle effort.

Finally.

It's been only one for so long.

FOR *the* WOLF

Book One of The Wilderwood

HANNAH WHITTEN

orbit

orbitbooks.net

Cover design by Lisa Marie Pompilio
Cover illustrations by Arcangel and Shutterstock

Author photograph by Caleb Whitten

Orbit
Hachette Book Group
1290 Avenue of the Americas
New York, NY 10104
orbitbooks.net

First Edition: June 2021
Simultaneously published in Great Britain by Orbit

Orbit is an imprint of Hachette Book Group.
The Orbit name and logo are trademarks of Little, Brown Book Group Limited.

Quote on p. vii excerpted from Rainer Maria Rilke, *Rilke's Book of Hours*, trans. Anita Barrows and Joanna Macy. New York: Riverhead Books (Berkley), 1996.

Library of Congress Cataloging-in-Publication Data
Names: Whitten, Hannah, author.
Title: For the wolf / Hannah Whitten.
Description: First edition. | New York, NY : Orbit, 2021. | Series: The wilderwood ; book 1
Identifiers: LCCN 2020044439 | ISBN 9780316592789 (trade paperback) | ISBN 9780316592802 (ebook)
Subjects: GSAFD: Fantasy fiction.
Classification: LCC PS3623.H5864 F67 2021 | DDC 813/.6—dc23
LC record available at https://lccn.loc.gov/2020044439

ISBNs: 978-0-316-59278-9 (trade paperback), 978-0-316-59279-6 (ebook)

Printed in the United States of America

LSC-C

Printing 5, 2022

To those who hold anger too deep to extricate, to those who feel too knife-edged to hold something soft, to those who are tired of holding up worlds.

You run like a herd of luminous deer,
and I am dark,
I am forest.

—Rainer Maria Rilke

To escape the will of the Kings, they fled into the far reaches of the Wilderwood. They pledged that were the forest to offer them shelter, they would give all they had for as long as their line continued, let it grow within their bones, and offer it succor. This they pledged through blood, willingly given, their sacrifice and bond.

The Wilderwood accepted their bargain, and they stayed within its border, to guard it and hold it fast against the things bound beneath. And every Second Daughter and every Wolf to come after would adhere to the bargain and the call and the Mark.

Upon the tree where they made their pledge, these words appeared, and I have saved the bark on which it is written:

> The First Daughter is for the throne.
> The Second Daughter is for the Wolf.
> And the Wolves are for the Wilderwood.

—Tiernan Niryea Andraline, of House Andraline,
First Daughter of Valleyda, Year One of the Binding

Chapter One

Two nights before she was sent to the Wolf, Red wore a dress the color of blood.

It cast Neve's face in crimson behind her as she straightened her twin's train. The smile her sister summoned was tentative and thin. "You look lovely, Red."

Red's lips were raw from biting, and when she tried to return the smile, her skin pulled. Copper tasted sharp on her tongue.

Neve didn't notice her bleeding. She wore white, like everyone else would tonight, the band of silver marking her as the First Daughter holding back her black hair. Emotions flickered across her pale features as she fussed with the folds of Red's gown—apprehension, anger, bone-deep sadness. Red could read each one. Always could, with Neve. She'd been an easy cipher since the womb they'd shared.

Finally, Neve settled on a blankly pleasant expression designed to reveal nothing at all. She picked up the half-full wine bottle on the floor, tilted it toward Red. "Might as well finish it off."

Red drank directly from the neck. Crimson lip paint smeared the back of her hand when she wiped her mouth.

"Good?" Neve took back the bottle, voice bright even as she rolled it nervously in her palms. "It's Meducian. A gift for the Temple from Raffe's father, a little extra on top of the prayer-tax for good sailing weather. Raffe filched it, said he thought the regular tax should be more than enough for pleasant seas." A halfhearted laugh, brittle and dry. "He said if anything would get you through tonight, this will."

Red's skirt crinkled as she sank into one of the chairs by the window, propping her head on her fist. "There's not enough wine in the world for this."

Neve's false mask of brightness splintered, fell. They sat in silence.

"You could still run," Neve whispered, lips barely moving, eyes on the empty bottle. "We'll cover for you, Raffe and I. Tonight, while everyone—"

"I can't." Red said it quick, and she said it sharp, hand falling to slap against the armrest. Endless repetition had worn all the polish off her voice.

"Of course you can." Neve's fingers tightened on the bottle. "You don't even have the Mark yet, and your birthday is the day after tomorrow."

Red's hand strayed to her scarlet sleeve, hiding white, unblemished skin. Every day since she turned nineteen, she'd checked her arms for the Mark. Kaldenore's had come immediately after her birthday, Sayetha's halfway through her nineteenth year, Merra's merely days before she turned twenty. Red's had yet to appear, but she was a Second Daughter—bound to the Wilderwood, bound to the Wolf, bound to an ancient bargain. Mark or no Mark, in two days, she was gone.

"Is it the monster stories? Really, Red, those are fairy tales to frighten children, no matter what the Order says." Neve's voice had edges now, going from cajoling to something sharper. "They're nonsense. No one has seen them in nearly two hundred years—there were none before Sayetha, none before Merra."

"But there were before Kaldenore." There was no heat in Red's voice, no ice, either. Neutral and expressionless. She was so tired of this fight.

"Yes, two damn centuries ago, a storm of monsters left the Wilderwood and terrorized the northern territories for ten years, until

Kaldenore entered and they disappeared. Monsters we have no real historical record of, monsters that seemed to take whatever shape pleased the person telling the tale." If Red's voice had been placid autumn, Neve's was wrecking winter, all cold and jagged. "But even if they were real, there's been *nothing* since, Red. No hint of anything coming from the forest, not for any of the other Second Daughters, and not for you." A pause, words gathered from a deep place neither of them touched. "If there were monsters in the woods, we would've seen them when we—"

"Neve." Red sat still, eyes on the swipe of wound-lurid lip paint across her knuckles, but her voice knifed through the room.

The plea for silence went ignored. "Once you go to him, it's over. He won't let you back out. You can never leave the forest again, not like... not like last time."

"I don't want to talk about that." Neutrality lost its footing, slipping into something hoarse and desperate. "Please, Neve."

For a moment, she thought Neve might ignore her again, might keep pushing this conversation past the careful parameters Red allowed for it. Instead she sighed, eyes shining as bright as the silver in her hair. "You could at least pretend," she murmured, turning to the window. "You could at least pretend to care."

"I care." Red's fingers tensed on her knees. "It just doesn't make a difference."

She'd done her screaming, her railing, her rebellion. She'd done all of it, everything Neve wanted from her now, back before she turned sixteen. Four years ago, when everything changed, when she realized the Wilderwood was the only place for her.

That feeling was mounting in her middle again. Something blooming, climbing up through her bones. Something *growing*.

A fern sat on the windowsill, incongruously verdant against the backdrop of frost. The leaves shuddered, tendrils stretching gently toward Red's shoulder, movements too deft and deliberate to be caused by a passing breeze. Beneath her sleeve, green brushed the network of veins in her wrist, made them stand out against her pale skin like branches. Her mouth tasted of earth.

No. Red clenched her fists until her knuckles blanched. Gradually, that *growing* feeling faded, a vine cut loose and coiling back into its hiding place. The dirt taste left her tongue, but she still grabbed the wine bottle again, tipping up the last of the dregs. "It's not just the monsters," she said when the wine was gone. "There's the matter of me being enough to convince the Wolf to release the Kings."

Alcohol made her bold, bold enough that she didn't try to hide the sneer in her voice. If there was ever going to be a sacrifice worthy enough to placate the Wolf and make him free the Five Kings from wherever he'd hidden them for centuries, it wasn't going to be her.

Not that she believed any of that, anyway.

"The Kings aren't coming back," Neve said, giving voice to their mutual nonbelief. "The Order has sent three Second Daughters to the Wolf, and he's never let them go before. He won't now." She crossed her arms tightly over her white gown, staring at the window glass as if her eyes could bore a hole into it. "I don't think the Kings *can* come back."

Neither did Red. Red thought it was likely that their gods were dead. Her dedication to her path into the forest had nothing to do with belief in Kings or monsters or anything else that might come out of it.

"It doesn't matter." They'd rehearsed this to perfection by now. Red flexed her fingers back and forth, now blue-veined, counting the beats of this endless, circling conversation. "I'm going to the Wilderwood, Neve. It's done. Just...let it be done."

Mouth a resolute line, Neve stepped forward, closing the distance between them with a whisper of silk across marble. Red didn't look up, angling her head so a fall of honey-colored hair hid her face.

"Red," Neve breathed, and Red flinched at her tone, the same she'd use with a frightened animal. "I *wanted* to go with you, that day we went to the Wilderwood. It wasn't your fault that—"

The door creaked open. For the first time in a long time, Red was happy to see her mother.

While white and silver suited Neve, it made Queen Isla look frozen, cold as the frost on the windowpane. Dark brows drew over darker eyes, the only feature she had in common with both her daughters. No servants followed as she stepped into the room, closing the heavy wooden door behind her. "Neverah." She inclined her head to Neve before turning those dark, unreadable eyes on Red. "Redarys."

Neither of them returned a greeting. For a moment that seemed hours, the three of them were mired in silence.

Isla turned to Neve. "Guests are arriving. Greet them, please."

Neve's fists closed on her skirts. She stared at Isla under lowered brows, her dark eyes fierce and simmering. But a fight was pointless, and everyone in this room knew it. As she moved toward the door, Neve glanced at Red over her shoulder, a command in her gaze—*Courage.*

Courageous was the last thing Red felt in the presence of her mother.

She didn't bother to stand as Isla took stock of her. The careful curls coaxed into Red's hair were already falling out, her dress wrinkled. Isla's eyes hesitated a moment on the smear of lip color marking the back of her hand, but even that wasn't enough to elicit a response. This was more proof of sacrifice than a ball, an event for dignitaries from all over the continent to attend and see the woman meant for the Wolf. Maybe it was fitting she looked half feral.

"That shade suits you." The Queen nodded to Red's skirts. "Red for Redarys."

A quip, but it made Red's teeth clench halfway to cracking. Neve used to say that when they were young. Before they both realized the implications. By then, her nickname had already stuck, and Red wouldn't have changed it anyway. There was a fierceness in it, a claiming of who and what she was.

"Haven't heard that one since I was a child," she said instead, and saw Isla's lips flatten. Mention of Red's childhood—that she'd been a child, once, that she was *her* child, that she was sending her child to the forest—always seemed to unsettle her mother.

Red gestured to her skirt. "Scarlet for a sacrifice."

A moment, then Isla cleared her throat. "The Florish delegation arrived this afternoon, and the Karseckan Re's emissary. The Meducian Prime Councilor sends her regrets, but a number of other Councilors are making an appearance. Order priestesses from all over the continent have been arriving throughout the day, praying in the Shrine in shifts." All this in a prim, quiet voice, a recitation of a rather boring list. "The Three Dukes of Alpera and their retinues should arrive before the procession—"

"Oh, good." Red addressed her hands, still and white as a corpse's. "They wouldn't want to miss that."

Isla's fingers twitched. Her tone, though strained, remained queenly. "The High Priestess is hopeful," she said, eyes everywhere but on her daughter. "Since there's been a longer stretch between you and...and the others, she thinks the Wolf might finally return the Kings."

"I'm sure she does. How embarrassing for her when I go into that forest and absolutely nothing happens."

"Keep your blasphemies to yourself," Isla chided, but it was mild. Red never quite managed to wring emotion from her mother. She'd tried, when she was younger—giving gifts, picking flowers. As she got older, she'd pulled down curtains and wrecked dinners with drunkenness, trying for anger if she couldn't have something warmer. Even that earned her nothing more than a sigh or an eye roll.

You had to be a whole person to be worth mourning. She'd never been that to her mother. Never been anything more than a relic.

"Do *you* think they'll come back?" A bald question, one she wouldn't dare ask if she didn't have one foot in the Wilderwood already. Still, Red couldn't quite make it sound sincere, couldn't quite smooth the barb from her voice. "Do you think if the Wolf finds me *acceptable*, he'll return the Kings to you?"

Silence in the room, colder than the air outside. Red had nothing like faith, but she wanted that answer like it could be absolution. For her mother. For *her*.

Isla held her gaze for a moment that stretched, spun into strange proportions. There were years in it, and years' worth of things unsaid. But when she spoke, her dark eyes turned away. "I hardly see how it matters."

And that was that.

Red stood, shaking back the heavy curtain of her loose hair, wiping the lip paint from her hand onto her skirt. "Then by all means, Your Majesty, let's show everyone their sacrifice is bound and ready."

Red made quick calculations in her head as she swept toward the ballroom. Her presence needed to be marked—all those visiting dignitaries weren't just here for dancing and wine. They wanted to see *her*, scarlet proof that Valleyda was prepared to send its sacrificial Second Daughter.

The Order priestesses were taking turns in the Shrine, praying to the shards of the white trees allegedly cut from the Wilderwood itself. For those from out of the country, this was a religious pilgrimage, a once-in-many-lifetimes chance not only to pray in the famed Valleydan Shrine but also to see a Second Daughter sent to the Wolf.

They might be praying, but they'd have eyes here. Eyes measuring her up, seeing if they agreed with the Valleydan High Priestess. If they, too, thought her *acceptable*.

A dance or two, a glass of wine or four. Red could stay long enough for everyone to judge the mettle of their sacrifice, and then she'd leave.

Technically, it was very early summertime, but Valleydan temperatures never rose much past freezing in any season. Hearths lined the ballroom, flickering orange and yellow light. Courtiers spun in a panoply of different cuts and styles from kingdoms all over the continent, every scrap of fabric lunar-pale. As Red stepped into the ballroom, all those myriad gazes fixed on her, a drop of blood in a snowdrift.

She froze like a rabbit in a fox's eye. For a moment, they all stared at one another, the gathered faithful and their prepared offering.

Jaw set tight, Red sank into a deep, exaggerated curtsy.

A brief stutter in the dance's rhythm. Then the courtiers started up again, sweeping past her without making eye contact.

Small favors.

A familiar form stood in the corner, next to a profusion of hothouse roses and casks of wine. Raffe ran a hand over close-shorn black hair, his fingers the color of mahogany against the gold of his goblet. For the moment, he stood alone, but it wouldn't be that way for long. The son of a Meducian Councilor and a rather accomplished dancer, Raffe never wanted for attention at balls.

Red slid beside him, taking his goblet and draining it with practiced efficiency. Raffe's lip quirked. "Hello to you, too."

"There's plenty where that came from." Red handed back the goblet and crossed her arms, staring resolutely at the wall rather than the crowd. Their gazes needled the back of her neck.

"Quite true." Raffe refilled his glass. "I'm surprised you're staying, honestly. The people who needed to see you certainly have."

She chewed the corner of her lip. "*I'm* hoping to see someone." It was an admittance to herself as much as to Raffe. She shouldn't *want* to see Arick. She should let this be a clean break, let him go easily…

But Red was a selfish creature at heart.

Raffe nodded once, understanding in the bare lift of his brow. He handed her the full wineglass before getting another for himself.

She'd known Raffe since she was fourteen—when his father took the position as a Councilor, he had to pass on his booming wine trade to his son, and there was no better place to learn about trade routes than with Valleydan tutors. Not much grew here, a tiny, cold country at the very top of the continent, notable only for the Wilderwood on its northern border and its occasional tithe of Second Daughters. Valleyda relied almost entirely on imports to keep the people fed, imports and prayer-taxes to their Temple, where the most potent entreaties to the Kings could be made.

They'd all grown up together, these past six years, years full of realizing just how different Red was from the rest of them. Years spent realizing her time was swiftly running out. But as long as she'd known him, Raffe had never treated her as anything more than a friend—not a martyr, not an effigy to burn.

Raffe's eyes softened, gaze pitched over her head. Red followed it to Neve, sitting alone on a raised dais at the front of the room, eyes slightly bloodshot. Isla's seat was still empty. Red didn't have one.

Red tipped her wine toward her twin. "Ask her to dance, Raffe."

"Can't." The answer came quick and clipped from behind his glass. He drained it in one swallow.

Red didn't press.

A tap on her shoulder sent her whirling. The young lord behind her took a quick step away, eyes wide and fearful. "Uh, my... my lady—no, Princess—"

He clearly expected sharpness, but Red was suddenly too tired to give it to him. It was exhausting, keeping those knife-edges. "Redarys."

"Redarys." He nodded nervously. A blush crept up his white neck, making the spots on his face stand out. "Would you dance with me?"

Red found herself shrugging, Meducian wine muddling her thoughts into shapeless warmth. This wasn't who she was hoping to see, but why not dance with someone brave enough to ask? She wasn't dead yet.

The lordling swept her up into a waltz, barely touching the curve of her waist. Red could've laughed if her throat didn't feel so raw. They were all so afraid to touch something that belonged to the Wolf.

"You're to meet him in the alcove," he whispered, voice wavering on the edge of a break. "The First Daughter said so."

Red snapped out of wine-warmth, eyes narrowing on the young lord's face. Her stomach churned, alcohol and shining hope. "Meet who?"

"The Consort Elect," the boy stammered. "Lord Arick."

He was here. He'd come.

The waltz ended with her and her unlikely partner near the alcove he'd referenced, the train of her gown almost touching the brocade curtain. "Thank you." Red curtsied to the lordling, scarlet now from the roots of his hair to the back of his neck. He stammered something incomprehensible and took off, coltish legs a second away from running.

She took a moment to steady her hands. This was Neve's doing, and Red knew her sister well enough to guess what she intended. Neve couldn't convince her to run, and thought maybe Arick could.

Red would let him try.

She slipped through the curtain, and his arms were around her waist before the ball was gone from view.

"Red," he murmured into her hair. His lips moved to hers, fingers tightening on her hips to pull her closer. "Red, I've missed you."

Her mouth was too occupied to say it back, though she made it clear she shared the sentiment. Arick's duties as the Consort Elect and Duke of Floriane kept him often out of court. He was only here now because of Neve.

Neve had been as shocked as Red when Arick was announced as Neve's future husband, cementing the fragile treaty that made Floriane a Valleydan province. She knew what lay between Arick and Red, but they never talked about it, unable to find the right words for one more small tragedy. Arick was a blade that drew blood two different ways, and the wounds left were best tended to alone.

Red broke away, resting her forehead against Arick's shoulder. He smelled the same, like mint and expensive tobacco. She breathed it in until her lungs ached.

Arick held her there a moment, hands in her hair. "I love you," he whispered against her ear.

He always said it. She never said it back. Once, she'd thought it was because she was doing him a favor, denying herself to make it easier on him when her twenty years were up and the forest's tithe came due. But that wasn't quite right. Red never said it because she didn't feel it. She loved Arick, in a way, but not a way that matched his love for her. It was simpler to let the words pass without remark.

He'd never seemed upset about it before, but tonight, she could feel the way his muscles tensed beneath her cheek, hear the clench of teeth in his jaw. "Still, Red?" It came quiet, in a way that seemed like he already knew the answer.

She stayed silent.

A moment, then he tilted a pale finger under her chin, tipped it up to search her face. No candles burned in the alcove, but the moonlight through the window reflected in his eyes, as green as the ferns on the sill. "You know why I'm here."

"And you know what I'll say."

"Neve was asking the wrong question," he breathed, desperation feathering at the edges. "Just wanting you to run, not thinking about what comes next. I have. It's *all* I've thought of." He paused, hand tightening in her hair. "Run away *with* me, Red."

Her eyes, half closed by kissing and moonlight, opened wide. Red pulled away, quickly enough to leave strands of gold woven around his fingers. "What?"

Arick gathered her hands, pulled her close again. "Run away with me," he repeated, chafing his thumbs over her palms. "We'll go south, to Karsecka or Elkyrath, find some backwater town where no one cares about religion or the Kings coming back, too far away from the forest to worry about any monsters. I'll find work doing... doing *something*, and—"

"We can't do that." Red tugged out of his grip. The pleasant numbness of wine was rapidly giving over to a dull ache, and she pressed her fingers into her temples as she turned away. "You have responsibilities. To Floriane, to Neve..."

"None of that matters." His hands framed her waist. "Red, I can't let you go to the Wilderwood."

She felt it again, the awakening in her veins. The ferns shuddered on the sill.

For a moment, she thought about telling him.

Telling him about the stray splinter of magic the Wilderwood left in her the night she and Neve ran to the forest's edge. Telling him of the destruction it wrought, the blood and the violence. Telling him how every day was an exercise in fighting it down, keeping it contained, making sure it never hurt anyone again.

But the words wouldn't come.

Red wasn't going to the Wilderwood to bring back gods. She wasn't going as insurance against monsters. It was an ancient and esoteric web she'd been born tangled in, but her reasons for not fighting free of it had nothing to do with piety, nothing to do with a religion she'd never truly believed in.

She was going to the Wilderwood to save everyone she loved from *herself*.

"It doesn't have to be this way." Arick gripped her shoulders. "We could have a *life*, Red. We could be just *us*."

"I'm the Second Daughter. You're the Consort Elect." Red shook her head. "*That* is who we are."

Silence. "I could make you go."

Red's eyes narrowed, half confusion and half wariness.

His hands slid from her shoulders, closed around her wrists. "I could take you somewhere he couldn't get to you." A pause, laden with sharp hurt. "Where *you* couldn't get to *him*."

Arick's grip was just shy of bruising, and with an angry surge like leaves caught in a cyclone, Red's shard of magic broke free.

It clawed its way out of her bones, unspooling from the spaces between her ribs like ivy climbing ruins. The ferns on the sill arched toward her, called by some strange magnetism, and she felt the quickening of earth beneath her feet even through layers of marble, roots running like currents, *reaching* for her—

Red wrestled the power under control just before the ferns touched Arick's shoulder, the fronds grown long and jagged in seconds. She shoved him away instead, harder than she meant to. Arick stumbled as the ferns retracted, slinking back to normal shapes.

"You can't *make* me do anything, Arick." Her hands trembled; her voice was thin. "I can't stay here."

"Why?" All fire, angry and low.

Red turned, picking up the edge of the brocaded curtain in a hand she hoped didn't shake. Her mouth worked, but no words seemed right, so the quiet grew heavy and was her answer.

"This is about what happened with Neve, isn't it?" It was an accusation, and he threw it like one. "When you went to the Wilderwood?"

Red's heart slammed against her ribs. She ducked under the curtain and dropped it behind her, muffling Arick's words, hiding his face. Her gown whispered over the marble as she walked down the corridor, toward the double doors of the north-facing balcony. Distantly, she wondered what the priestesses' informants might make of her mussed hair and swollen lips.

Well. If they wanted an untouched sacrifice, that ship had long since sailed.

The cold was bracing after the hearths in the ballroom, but Red was Valleydan, and gooseflesh on her arms still felt like summer. Sweat dried in her hair, now hopelessly straight, careful curls loosened by heat and hands.

Breathe in, breathe out, steady her shaking shoulders, blink away the burn in her eyes. She could count the number of people who loved her on one hand, and they all kept begging for the only thing she couldn't give them.

The night air froze the tears into her lashes before they could fall. She'd been damned from the moment she was born—a Second Daughter, meant for the Wolf and the Wilderwood, as etched into the bark in the Shrine—but still, sometimes, she wondered. Wondered if the damning was her own fault for what she'd done four years ago.

Reckless courage got the best of them after that disastrous ball, reckless courage and too much wine. They stole horses, rode north, two girls against a monster and an endless forest with nothing but rocks and matches and a fierce love for each other.

That love burned so brightly, it almost seemed like the power that took root in Red was a deliberate mockery. The Wilderwood, proving that it was stronger. That her ties to the forest and its waiting Wolf would always be stronger.

Red swallowed against a tight throat. Biting irony, that if it hadn't been for that night and what it wrought, she might've done what Neve wanted. She might've run.

She looked to the north, squinting against cold wind. Somewhere, beyond the mist and the hazy lights of the capital, was the Wilderwood. The Wolf. Their long wait was almost ended.

"I'm coming," she murmured. "Damn you, I'm coming."

She turned in a sweep of crimson skirts and went back inside.

Chapter Two

Sleep came only in fragments. By the time sunrise bled into the sky, Red stood by the window, tangling her fingers together and staring out at the Shrine.

Her room faced the interior gardens, an expanse of carefully maintained trees and flowers, specially bred for their hardiness against the cold. The Shrine was tucked into the back corner, barely visible beneath a blooming arbor. Sunrise caught the edge of the arched stone and painted it muted gold.

The Order stood scattered among the greenery, crowding the flowers, a sea of white robes and piety. Every priestess that called Valleyda home, plus all who had traveled, from the Rylt across the sea and Karsecka at the southern tip of the continent and everywhere in between. Each Temple had a white tree shard, a small splinter of the Wilderwood to pray to, but it was a special honor to trek to the Valleydan Temple, where they had a veritable grove of them. A privilege, to pray among the bone-white branches that made the prison of the Kings and beseech their return.

But this morning, none of the priestesses stepped inside the Shrine. The only person permitted to pray among the white branches today was Red.

The glass fogged with her breath. Absently, Red drew a finger through the cloud. Their nursemaids had done that long ago, illustrating stories on the windowpane. Stories of the Wilderwood as it was before the creation of the Shadowlands, when all the magic of the world was locked within it to make a prison for the god-like creatures that had reigned in terror.

Before, the forest had been a place of eternal summer, a spot of solace in a world ruled by violence. According to the nursemaids, it'd even been capable of granting boons to those who left sacrifices within its borders—bundled hair, lost teeth, paper dotted with blood. Magic had run freely in that world, available to anyone who could learn to use it.

But once the Five Kings bargained with the forest to bind away the monstrous gods—to create the Shadowlands as their prison—all that magic was gone, pulled into the Wilderwood to accomplish its monumental task.

But the forest could still bargain, even then—it bargained with Ciaran and Gaya, the original Wolf and Second Daughter. In Year One of the Binding, the same year the monsters were locked away, they'd asked the Wilderwood for shelter from Gaya's father, Valchior, and her betrothed, Solmir—two of the fabled Five Kings. The Wilderwood granted Gaya and Ciaran's request, giving them a place to hide, a place to be together forever. It bound them into its borders and made them something more than human.

That's where the nursemaids stopped. They didn't talk about how the Kings entered the Wilderwood again, fifty years after the Binding, and never returned. They didn't talk about Ciaran bringing Gaya's dead body to the edge of the woods, a century and a half after the Kings disappeared.

Red still knew the tale. She'd read it hundreds of times, both in books counted as holy and in those of lesser import. Every version of it she could find. Though some of the details differed, the broad strokes remained. Ciaran, bringing Gaya to the Wilderwood's border. Her body, half rotted, wound through with vines and tree roots as if she'd been tangled in the very foundations of the forest. His words to those who saw him, a few unimportant northern villagers who suddenly found themselves part of religious history.

Send the next.

And so, a love story turned to horror, as surely as eternal summer faded to withered fall.

Red drew her hand away as the edges of her foggy canvas faded. The trails her fingers left looked like claw marks.

A knock at the door, nearly tentative. Red leaned her forehead against the window. "A moment."

One breath, deep and cold, then Red stood up. Her nightgown stuck to the chilled sweat on her shoulder blades as she tugged it off. Almost unconsciously, her eyes strayed to the skin above her elbow. Still unmarked, and she had to fight to keep hope from sinking teeth into her chest.

There was no account of what the Marks were supposed to look like, only that they appeared on the Second Daughter's arm sometime in her nineteenth year, exerting an inexorable pull toward the north, toward the Wilderwood. Every morning since the year turned, she'd carefully inspected her skin, peering at each mole and freckle.

Another knock. Red glared at the closed door like the force of her ire could penetrate the wood. "Unless you want me to pray naked, you'll *give me a moment.*"

No more knocking.

A wrinkled gown puddled by her feet. Red pulled it on and opened the door, not bothering to comb her hair.

Three priestesses stood silently in the corridor. All were vaguely recognizable, so they must be from the Valleydan Temple, not visitors. Maybe that was meant to be comforting.

If her disheveled appearance took the priestesses aback, they didn't show it. They only inclined their heads, hands hidden in wide white sleeves, and led her down the hall, out into the cold, bright air.

The holy throng in the gardens stood stone-still, heads bowed, flanking the flower-decked entrance to the Shrine. Each priestess she passed made Red's heart ratchet higher in her throat. She didn't look at any of them, kept her gaze straight ahead as she ducked into the shadows beneath the arch, alone.

The first room of the Shrine was plain and square. A small table stocked with prayer candles stood by the door, the statue of Gaya tall and proud in the center of the room. At the statue's feet, the white bark with its inscribed sentencing, a piece of the tree where Gaya and Ciaran had made their bargain. Gaya's sister, Tiernan, had helped the two of them escape, and she brought the bark back as proof that Solmir's claim on Gaya was void.

Red frowned up at her predecessor. It was a deft bit of work, what made Gaya revered and the Wolf reviled, a delicate filling-in of unknown history. The Five Kings had disappeared in the Wolf's territory, therefore he was to blame. No one quite knew what he was supposed to be accomplishing by trapping the Kings—more power, maybe. Perhaps he was just doing as monsters do, having become one himself as the forest he was tied to twisted and darkened. The Order said that Gaya had been killed trying to rescue the Kings from wherever Ciaran had hidden them, but there was really no way to know, was there? All they knew was that the Kings were gone, and Gaya was dead.

Stuttering scarlet prayer candles—*scarlet for a sacrifice; I guess prayer counts*—provided the only light, and it wasn't enough to read by. But Red knew the words by heart.

The First Daughter is for the throne. The Second Daughter is for the Wolf. And the Wolves are for the Wilderwood.

The candlelight flickered over the carvings on the wall. Five figures to her right, vaguely masculine—the Five Kings. Valchior, Byriand, Malchrosite, Calryes, and Solmir. Three figures on the left-hand wall, carved with a more delicate hand. The Second Daughters—Kaldenore, Sayetha, Merra.

Red brushed her fingers over the blank space next to Merra's rough outline. Someday, when she was nothing but bones in the forest, they'd carve her here.

A breeze filtered through the open stone door, ruffling the gauzy black veil behind Gaya's statue. The second room of the Shrine. Red had been there only once before—a year ago, her nineteenth birthday, kneeling as the Order priestesses prayed that her Mark would appear quickly. She found little reason to linger in places of worship.

Still, a year hadn't been enough to dim the memory of the white branches lining the walls, cuttings from Wilderwood trees cast in stone to stand upright. The pale, dead limbs never moved, but Red remembered the strange sense of them *reaching* for her, like ferns and growing things did when she couldn't keep her splintered magic lashed down and tightly controlled. She'd tasted dirt the whole time the priestesses were praying.

Her fingers picked nervously at the wrinkled fabric of her skirt. She was supposed to enter the second room, supposed to spend this time readying herself to enter the Wilderwood, but the thought of being among those branches again made her blood run winter-cold.

"Red?"

A familiar figure stood in the doorway to the garden, outlined in morning glow against the Shrine's gloom. Neve hurried toward her, a newly lit prayer candle guttering in her hand.

Confusion bloomed in Red's chest, though it was chased with no small amount of relief. "How did you get in here?" She looked over Neve's shoulder. "The priestesses—"

"I told them I wouldn't enter the second room. They didn't seem happy about it, but they let me through." A tear broke from Neve's lashes. She swiped it roughly away. "Red, you can't do this. There's no reason for it beyond words on shadow-damned *bark*."

Red thought of riding headlong through the night, hair whipping, her sister at her side. She thought of thrown rocks and a fierceness that made her chest ache.

And then she thought of blood. Of violence. Of what coiled beneath her skin, a seed waiting to grow.

That was her reason. Not monsters, not words on bark. The only way to keep her sister safe was to leave her.

There were no words of comfort. Instead she pulled her twin forward, Neve's forehead notching into her collarbone. Neither of them sobbed, but the silence was almost worse, broken only by hitched breathing.

"You have to trust me." Red murmured it into her sister's hair. "I know what I'm doing. This is how it has to be."

"No." Neve shook her head, black hair matting against Red's cheek. "Red, I know... I know you blame yourself for what happened that night. But you couldn't have known we were being followed—"

"Don't." Red squeezed her eyes shut. "Please don't."

Neve's shoulders stiffened beneath Red's arms, but she went quiet. Finally, she pulled back. "You'll *die*. If you go to the Wolf, you'll die."

"You don't know that." Red swallowed, trying unsuccessfully to level the knot in her throat. "We don't know what happened to the others."

"We know what happened to Gaya."

Red had no response for that.

"Clearly, you're determined to go." Neve tried to raise her chin, but it trembled too much. "And clearly, I can't stop you."

She turned on her heel toward the door, swept past the carved Five Kings and Second Daughters, past the guttering candles of useless prayers. More than one blew out in her wake.

Numbly, Red picked up a candle and a match from the small table. It took a few curses before the wick finally caught, singeing her fingers. The pain was nearly welcome, a bare thread of feeling weaving past the shell she'd built.

Red slammed her candle into the base of Gaya's statue. Wax puddled, dripped down the edge of the inscribed bark.

"Shadows damn you," she whispered, the only prayer she'd make here. "Shadows damn us all."

Hours later, bathed and perfumed and veiled in crimson, Red was officially blessed as a sacrifice to the Wolf in the Wilderwood.

Courtiers lined the cavernous hall, all dressed in black. More people crowded outside, the citizens of the capital rubbing shoulders with villagers who'd traveled from far and wide for the chance to see a Second Daughter consecrated by the Order.

From Red's vantage point on the dais at the front of the room, the audience looked like one shapeless mass, something made only of still limbs and eyes for staring.

The dais was circular, and Red sat cross-legged on a black stone altar in its center, surrounded by a ring of priestesses specially chosen for the honor from Temples all over the continent. All wore their traditional white robes with the addition of a white cloak, a deep hood pulled up to shadow their faces. They stood with their backs to Red. The priestesses who hadn't been chosen as attendants wore cloaks, too, a solemn row of them sitting directly in front of the dais.

In contrast, Red's gown was as scarlet as the one she'd worn to the ball, but shapeless this time—in any other circumstances, it would be comfortable. Her hair was unbound beneath a matching blood-colored veil, large enough to cover her whole body and spill over the edges of the altar.

White, for piety. Black, for absence. Scarlet, for sacrifice.

In the row behind the priestesses, Neve sat between Arick and Raffe, poised at the edge of her seat. Red's veil made all of them look bloody.

The Valleydan High Priestess, the highest religious authority on the continent, stood directly in front of Red. Her cloak had a longer train than any of the other priestesses', and to Red, it almost looked a brighter white. She faced the altar, back to the court, the train of her cloak dripping over the edge of the dais to gather in a puddle of white fabric.

Overflowing piety. A high, skittering laugh wanted to lodge in Red's throat; she swallowed it back.

Eyes hidden in the deep shadows of her hood, the High Priestess stepped forward. Zophia had held the position for as long as Red could remember, her hair long devoid of whatever color it'd once been, her face grizzled with an age that could be determined only as *old*. She held a white branch in her hands with all the gentleness of a mother cradling a newborn, and passed it off to the priestess at her right with the same care.

Though stoic, most of the other priestesses at least had some sort of emotion on their face—joy, for most, kept subtle but still there. Not so for the priestess now holding the branch shard. Cold blue eyes beneath a sweep of flame-colored hair watched Red with an expression reminiscent of someone observing an insect. Her gaze didn't waver as Zophia reached forward and lifted Red's veil, gathering the yards of fabric in her hands.

The fear she'd steeled herself against rushed in when the veil lifted, like it had been a sort of armor. Red's fingers clutched at the edge of the altar, nails close to breaking against the stone.

"We honor your sacrifice, Second Daughter," Zophia whispered. She stepped back and raised her arms toward the ceiling. All around, the Order mirrored her in a wave, starting at the front of the dais and cresting around to the back in a sea of raised hands.

For a brief, shining moment, Red thought of running, of forgetting about the splinter of magic that lived in her heart and trying to save herself instead of everyone else. How far could she get if she launched herself from this altar, tangled in crimson gauze? Would they wrestle her back? Knock her out? Would the Wolf care if she arrived bruised?

She dug her nails into the stone again. She felt one split.

"Kaldenore, of House Andraline," the High Priestess announced to the ceiling, beginning the litany of Second Daughters. "Sent in Year Two Hundred and Ten of the Binding."

Kaldenore, no blood relation, born of the same House as Gaya. She'd been a child when the Wolf brought Gaya's body to the edge of the forest, when the monsters burst from the Wilderwood a year later—a storm of shadowy things, by eyewitness accounts, shape-shifting bits of darkness that could take whatever form they chose. By the time Kaldenore's Mark appeared, the monsters had been haunting the northern villages for nearly ten years, with reports of them sometimes getting as far as Floriane and Meducia.

No one knew what the Mark meant, not at first. But one night, Kaldenore was found sleepwalking barefoot toward the Wilderwood, as if compelled.

After that, things had fallen together, the words on the bark in the Shrine and the meaning of Gaya's death becoming clear. They'd sent Kaldenore to the Wilderwood. And the monsters disappeared, faded away like shadows.

"Sayetha, of House Thoriden. Sent in Year Two Hundred and Forty of the Binding."

Another name, another tragedy. Sayetha's family was new to power and mistakenly believed the tithe of the Second Daughter applied to only Gaya's line. They were wrong. Valleyda was locked into its trade no matter who sat on the throne.

"Merra, of House Valedren. Sent in Year Three Hundred of the Binding."

She, at least, was a blood ancestor. The Valedrens took over after the last Thoriden Queen produced no heir. Merra was born forty years after Sayetha was sent to the Wilderwood, while Sayetha's birth was only ten years after Kaldenore left.

"Redarys, of House Valedren. Sent in year Four Hundred of the Binding." The High Priestess seemed to raise her hands higher, the branch clutched in her fist casting jagged shadows. Her eyes dropped from her reaching fingers, met Red's. "Four hundred years since our gods bound the monsters away. Three hundred and fifty since they disappeared, bound away themselves through the Wolf's treachery. Tomorrow, when the sacrifice has reached twenty years, the same age Gaya was when first bound to the Wolf and Wood, we send her consecrated, clad in white and black and scarlet. We pray it is enough for the return of our gods. We pray it is enough to keep darkness from our doorsteps."

Red's heartbeat was a staccato pounding in her ears. She sat still as the stone altar, still as the statue in the Shrine. The effigy they wanted her to be.

"May you not flinch from your duty." Zophia's clear voice was a clarion call, sweetly resonant. "May you meet your fate with dignity."

Red tried to swallow, but her mouth was too dry.

Zophia's eyes were cold. "May your sacrifice be deemed enough."

Silence in the chamber.

The High Priestess dropped her arms, taking the white branch back from the red-haired priestess. Another priestess came forward, holding a small bowl of dark ashes. Gently, Zophia dipped one of the tines of the branch into the bowl, then drew it across Red's forehead, leaving a black mark from temple to temple.

The bark was warm. Red tensed every muscle in her body to keep from shuddering.

"We mark you bound," she said quietly. "The Wolf and the Wilderwood will have their due."

Chapter Three

The court set out at sunrise, packed into lacquered carriages for the short trip to the Wilderwood. Red's led the way. Other than the driver, she rode alone.

One scuffed leather bag sat at her feet, packed to the brim with books. Red wasn't sure why she'd brought them, but they sat against her like an anchor, keeping her tethered to her aching muscles and still-beating heart. Other than the clothes on her back, the bag was the only thing she was taking into the Wilderwood. At least she'd be prepared on the off chance she survived long enough to read.

She'd slipped into the library to pack as the sun rose, pulling her favorite novels and poetry books from the shelf. As she worked, her nightgown's sleeve fell back from her arm.

The Mark was small. A thread of root beneath the skin, delicately tendriled, circling just below her elbow. When she touched it, the veins in her fingers ran green, and the hedges outside the library window stretched toward the glass.

The pull was subtle, beginning just as her eyes registered the Mark snaking over her arm. Gentle, but inexorable—like a hook was dug into the back of her chest, tugging her gently northward. Reeling her into the trees.

Red squeezed her eyes shut and put her hands to fists, pulling in breath after aching breath. Each one tasted like grave dirt, and that's what finally made her cry. Wrung out, lying on the floor with books piled around her like a fortress, Red sobbed until the dirt taste turned instead to salt.

Now her face was scrubbed clear, the Mark hidden by the sleeve of the white gown she wore beneath her cloak.

White gown, black sash, red cloak. They'd been delivered to her door last night by a cadre of silent priestesses. She'd thrown the pile into the corner, but when Red woke up this morning, Neve was there, laying them out one by one on the window seat. Smoothing the wrinkles with her palm.

Silently, Neve helped her dress—handing her the white gown to tug over her head, tying the black sash around her waist. The cloak came last, heavy and warm and colored like blood. When every piece was in place, they'd stood still and quiet, staring at their reflections in Red's mirror.

Neve left without a word.

In the carriage, Red pulled the edges of the cloak tighter around herself. She couldn't keep her sister close, but she could keep this.

The world rolled past her window. Northern Valleyda was hills and valleys and open vistas, as if the Wilderwood allowed no trees but its own. When she and Neve stole the horses and fled north the night of their sixteenth birthday, she remembered being awed by the emptiness. She'd felt like a falling star on a clear night, pelting through the dark and the cold.

There were villagers by the road sometimes, quietly watching the procession pass. She was probably supposed to wave, but Red stared straight ahead, the world cut to the edges of her scarlet hood. The Mark thrummed on her arm, the tug of it making all her insides feel unstable and shaky.

The road stopped well before the Wilderwood—none but the Second Daughter could enter, and no one else would want to try, so there was no reason to make the way easy. A bump as the carriage wheels rolled into frosted grass, crossing into some borderland belonging to neither Red nor the Wolf.

Red's limbs moved nearly of their own accord. She gathered her skirts, slung her bag of books over her shoulder. She stepped down carefully. She didn't cry.

The driver turned the horses around as soon as Red was free of the carriage, without a second glance. A strange hum emanated from the edge of the forest, repellent and beckoning at once. Pulling her forward, warning everyone else to stay back.

The array of carriages behind her ringed the road like beads on a necklace, the line of them almost reaching the village. Everyone who'd traveled to see the tithe paid, waiting silently for the job to be done.

Ahead, the Wilderwood towered, casting shadows on the frost-limned ground. Bare branches stretched into fog, so tall she couldn't see their endings. Trunks bent and twisted like frozen dancers, and the bits of sky caught between them seemed darker than they should, already shaded twilight. The trees grew in a straight, exact line of demarcation from side to side as far as the eye could see, a firm boundary between *there* and *here*.

She'd been given no instruction on what to do next, but it seemed simple enough. Slip between the trees. Disappear.

Red took a step before she had the conscious thought, the forest drawing her like a leaf on a current. A sharp breath as she planted her feet. The Wilderwood would have her in moments, but shadows *damn* her, she'd set the terms of her own surrender.

"Red!"

Neve's voice cracked the quiet. She climbed from her carriage, almost stumbling on the hem of her black gown. Sunlight caught the edge of the silver circlet in her hair as she marched over the field, determination blazing on her face.

For the first time she could remember, Red prayed, prayed to

Gaya or the Five Kings or whoever might be listening. "Help her," she muttered through numb lips. "Help her to move on."

Whatever remained of Red's life waited beyond the trees, but Neve's was here. The thought was sharp and strange-shaped, that for the first time since their conception, she and her twin would both be alone.

Another figure emerged from the carriage behind Neve. Red's stomach dropped, thinking it'd be Arick or Raffe, the three of them launching one last effort to change the unchangeable. But when the figure made its slow way around the carriage, head held high, it wasn't Arick.

Mother.

Red favored her mother in appearance. The same honey-gold hair, the same sharp cheekbones, a breadth to their hips and breasts that twig-slender Neve didn't share. Watching her mother cross the frost-covered field was almost like looking in a mirror, watching her own sacrifice.

The thought felt like it should mean something.

Neve reached her before their mother did, her breath the rattle of a sob tenuously caged. She pulled Red close, thin hands gripping her shoulders.

"I'll see you again," she whispered. "I'll find a way. I promise."

Her tone waited for an answer. But Red didn't want to lie.

Their mother's shadow fell over them, darker than the shadows of the trees. "Neverah. Return to the carriage, please."

Neve didn't turn to look at Isla. "No."

A pause. Then Isla inclined her head, as if in concession. "Then we'll say our goodbyes together."

This should be a *moment*, Red knew. Merra's mother had been so distraught when they sent her daughter to the Wilderwood, she'd nearly abdicated. Sayetha's mother had to be sedated for days after. Kaldenore's had to be sedated *before*, going half mad when the Mark appeared on her child's arm, when it was finally discovered that all Second Daughters born to Valleydan queens were bound by Gaya's bargain with the forest.

But goodbyes were reserved for people who knew each other, and Isla had never bothered to know Red.

The Queen's arms twitched beneath her cloak. "I know you think me cruel." The whisper plumed from her mouth like a ghost. "Both of you."

Neve said nothing. Her eyes flickered to Red.

Years of silence dammed in Red's throat, years of wanting emotion she could never quite hold. "I would've preferred cruel," she said, knowing the words meant she owned the cruelty now. "At least cruel would've been something."

Isla stood corpse-still. "You never belonged to me, Redarys." A tendril of gold escaped the black net holding the Queen's hair, long enough to nearly brush Red's cheek. "From the moment you were born, you belonged *here*. And they never let me forget."

The Queen turned, striding toward her carriage. She didn't look back.

Slowly, Red faced the trees, following the gentle, insistent tug of her Mark. Leaves rustled, dim on the edge of her hearing, though she should be too far away for the sound to carry. Deep in her chest, her splinter of magic, the Wilderwood's twisted gift, opened like a flower to the sun.

Neve turned with her, peering into the forest with fear and unveiled hatred. "It's not fair."

Red didn't respond. She squeezed Neve's hand. Then she started toward the Wilderwood.

"I promise, Red," Neve called as she walked away. "I'll see you again."

Red looked back over her shoulder. She wouldn't stoke the embers of things that couldn't happen, but she could speak a truth uncolored by them. "I love you."

The answer, the end. The tears in Neve's eyes spilled over. "Love you."

With one last look at her sister, Red tugged up her scarlet hood, muffling every sound but the beat of blood in her ears. She stepped forward, and the trees swallowed her up.

It was colder in the Wilderwood.

The temperature dropped instantly, cool enough to make her glad of her cloak. As Red crossed the tree line, pressing into that infernal hum, bruising pressure built against her skin. It was almost enough to make her stumble onto the forest floor, almost enough to make her cry out—

But the pressure and the hum were gone as soon as she settled both feet beyond the forest's border, leaving her in leaves and deep, undisturbed silence. The only thing that moved was the fog, a sinuous crawl over the ground.

Beneath the sleeve of her gown and the heavy crimson of her cloak, the Mark gave one more twinge. Then the feeling of that subtle pull was gone. Red rubbed at it absently.

The trees were strange. Some were short and gnarled, but others grew tall and straight, their bark unnaturally white until it met the forest floor. There it bent and twisted, dark rot standing out in ropes like corroded veins. Some of the trees had the rot only around the roots, but on others, the corrosion stretched up taller than Red.

The white trees had limbs only at the crown, swoops of graceful bone-like bark. Just like the branch shards in the Shrine.

One white tree stood just inside the forest's border. Black rot grew over halfway up its trunk. Even the ground around it seemed dark, and smelled somehow cold. The nearby trees, brown-barked and thatched with irregular branches, had no rot on them at all.

Other than the trees, Red was alone.

With deep, shaky breaths, she willed her heart out of her throat. Her unwanted magic curled through her ribs, a languid unfurling, a subtle hint of green etching her veins. She expected it to riot, to race for release, and she clenched her teeth in anticipation of every tree in the damn forest reaching for her.

But her power stayed docile. Almost like it was waiting for something.

Still, there was an awareness here. Red was *seen*, Red was *marked*. The trees knew her, they remembered—her blood on the forest floor, a terrible rushing, a gift of power she didn't want and couldn't control.

For a brief, blinding second, Red wished for a match, even though it'd do her no good. Sayetha's mother tried to burn down the Wilderwood, and so had Neve. It did nothing.

The back of her wrist pressed against her teeth, a hissing breath pulled through her nose. She didn't want the Wilderwood to see her cry.

When the threat of tears passed, Red tightened her grip on her bag of books and peered into the gloom. No use prolonging the inevitable.

"I'm here!" It reverberated, echoing and distorting, tuned to minor keys by space and silence. Then the mad specter of a laugh in her throat: "Am I *acceptable*?"

Nothing happened. Fog drifted silently, tangling and curling through branches, dead leaves.

Frustration drove her teeth together, the despair of seconds ago transmuting into fierce anger. She felt roots arching toward her under her feet, felt bone-colored boughs stretching over her head. Instinct told her to fight the magic down, but this was the Wilderwood, where it belonged. Where it'd been *born*. "I'm here, shadows damn you!" she screamed into the gloom. "Come collect your *sacrifice*, Wolf!"

The Wilderwood seemed to bend toward her. Anticipating. Like she had something it wanted.

The recklessness was gone as soon as it came. Spots spun in Red's eyes as she gasped, fists closing, or trying to—her fingers were held straight by the forest floor beneath them.

Her brow furrowed at the sight of her hands against the ground. She didn't remember kneeling, didn't remember pressing them to the dirt.

Before she had a chance to stand, her hands began to sink.

In an instant soil covered her arms to the wrist, her fingers dropping deep to tangle in thready roots. They brushed against her hands like sentient things, searchingly prodding at her knuckles, the creases of her palms. A sharp prick at her nailbed, the slithering feeling of a root trying to work its way into her skin.

Red's heart ratcheted, panic closing her throat as she desperately tried to work free, wrenching her hands in the dirt to escape that probing root. Branches brushed against her scalp, tangled in her hair. Laying claim.

The magic in her center reached forward, slow but implacable, a vine growing through a summer that counted days in her quickened heartbeat. It felt like it would reach right out of her skin to meet the forest that made it.

No.

Her teeth cracked together. Red forced her magic down, swallowing that dirt-taste, pressing until she thought she might collapse from the effort of folding a part of herself up and hiding it away. Sweat stood out on her brow when her magic was finally contained, coiled back into the places she'd made for it. Her wrists burned green with power she wouldn't let loose.

Red yanked her hands from the forest floor. Broken root tendrils slithered away as she wiped her palms on her knees, like snakes going back to burrow.

Three white trees bent toward her, all seeming closer than they had a moment ago. Their graceful, swooping branches dipped low, a hand frozen right before it reached to caress.

A soft sound boiled and spilled over—for a moment, it almost sounded like a voice, like a *word*. But it broke apart before Red could make sense of it, fading into nothing but breeze and rustling leaves.

In the following silence, three blossoms dropped from the same bough of a flowering bush, one of many dotting the forest floor. The small white blooms were brown and withered before they hit the ground.

It gave Red the unsettling impression of a price being paid.

Swallowing hard, she stood, hitching her bag over her shoulder. "I suppose I'll have to find you, then."

She set off into the woods.

Red didn't know how long she'd been walking when the thicket rose before her, grown up around one of the white trees. Short, scrubby bushes wrapped the trunk, thorns pointed outward at wicked angles. Through the close growth, Red could barely see the black rot spreading up the tree, crawling toward the clustered branches at the top.

A thorn caught in her hood as she tried to skirt around the thicket, one she'd swear hadn't been there before. The crimson fabric pulled back from her face. Another dagger-sharp thorn drew a bloody line down her cheekbone.

Red clapped her hand to the wound, but the damage was done. A bead of blood rolled slowly down the thorn, coming to its end and dropping to another, ever closer to the dark-ravaged trunk of the white tree.

If she tried to reach through the tangle and smear it away, she'd only catch more thorns, spill more blood. So Red stood, and watched, and waited, dread roiling beneath her ribs.

Her blood touched the white trunk, hesitated. Then the tree *absorbed* it, took it in like water to parched soil.

Tripping over leaves, Red backed away from the tree until she collided with another, this one also thin and pale, also twisted with black rot. Underbrush tangled in her skirts, and Red tore herself away, the rip unnaturally loud in the silent forest.

That sound again, reverberating up from the forest floor, rustling leaves and stretching vines and clattering twigs cobbling themselves into something like a voice, something she didn't so much hear as *feel*. It boiled up from her center, from the shard of magic she kept lashed down through white-knuckle effort.

Finally.

It's been only one for so long.

A tree limb broke from a trunk, fell to the forest floor. It shriveled at once, years of decay packed into seconds, leaving nothing but a desiccated husk.

Red's teeth hummed, the hairs on her arms standing on end. Branches arched toward her, roots slithered beneath her feet, and she stood frozen as a deer in the path of an arrow.

This was what she'd prepared for, in the deepest parts of her mind, the places she didn't have to look at too closely. She'd denied it to Neve, saying they didn't know what happened to the Second Daughters who crossed the border. But she'd known there could be nothing here but death, and she thought she'd prepared for it.

Now that it waited, shaped like clawed branches and twisted roots, she realized that preparation wasn't acceptance. All the quiet acquiescence she'd swallowed over twenty years erupted, spilled over, drove her teeth together not in fear but in rage. She wanted to *live*, and damn the things that said she shouldn't.

So Red ran.

Vines swung for her, the leaf-strewn ground buckling to trip her feet. The white trees bent and arched as if fighting against invisible bonds, screaming for release.

Like the forest was an animal desperate for her blood, and something held it back.

Finally, Red reached a clearing. White trees ringed it, quivering, but she ran to the center, where the ground was only moss and dirt. Her knees hit the soil, her breath rasped, skirt in tatters and twigs in her hair.

The moment of calm shattered with a sound of splintering wood. One of the white trunks, slowly splitting, like a smile cutting from one side of a mouth to the other.

The trunk opened wider, gleaming with sap-dripping fangs. One by one, smiles cut across the other trunks, smiles full of teeth, smiles that wanted blood.

Red lurched up on shaky legs, started running again. Her feet were numb, a stitch pulled at her side, but she ran on and on.

Eventually, her knees gave out, vision narrowed to a pinprick. Red collapsed in a pile of leaves, forehead pressed to the ground.

Maybe this was the fulfilling of the bargain. The stories of Gaya's body, riddled with root and rot—maybe the Wolf wouldn't decide whether or not she was an acceptable sacrifice until after his Wilderwood consumed her like it'd consumed Gaya in the end, waiting to see if it spat out the Kings in return. Maybe he'd been the one holding it back as she ran, whetting its appetite with the chase to unleash it when she was spent.

Red's eyes closed against the expectation of teeth in her neck.

A minute. Two. Nothing happened. Sweat sticking her hair to her face, she looked up.

An iron gate rose from the ground. Double her height, it stretched from side to side, curving around before disappearing into the gloom. Pieces of a castle showed through gaps in the metal—a tower, a turret. A ruin, half consumed by the forest around it, but it was *something.*

Red stood on shaky legs. Slowly, she pressed her hands to the gate.

Chapter Four

It didn't open.

Red's eyes flickered over the iron as she nervously wiped her hands on her torn skirt. If there was a latch, it was too small to see. No hinges, either—the gate was one unbroken piece of iron. It rose to two swirling points, as if to mark an entrance, but the bar down the center was as solid as the rest of it.

"Kings on shitting *horses.*" Teeth bared, Red slammed her hands against the metal. She'd made it through a fanged forest, she could find a way to open a damn gate.

A rustle. Red glanced over her shoulder. Only two of the white trees were visible in the gloom, but both of them looked closer than they had before.

Red tried to lift her hands to pound on the gate again, but they wouldn't obey. Her palms refused to move, like they'd somehow grafted onto the iron. Sliding in the leaves, Red tried to wrench free, but the gate held her fast, the rasp of her breath loud in the silent fog.

She felt the trees' regard, heavy on her shoulders, lifting the hair on the back of her neck. Watching. Waiting. Still hungry.

Something shifted under her hand, breaking the cycle of shapeless panic, crystallizing it into sharpened, focused fear.

The surface of the gate was *moving*, slithering like she'd cupped her hand over an anthill. Rough metal rippled against her skin, tracing the lines in her palms, her fingerprints.

As suddenly as it started, the crawling feeling stopped. The solid bar of iron split slowly down the middle, bottom to top, like a sapling growing from the ground. With a quiet hitch, the gate fell open.

A moment's pause, then Red stumbled forward. As soon as she was through, the gate closed behind her. She didn't have to look to know it was solid again. When she peered at her palm, it was unblemished but for a few spots of rust.

The ruined castle rose from fog and shadow, reaching almost as tall as the surrounding trees. Once, it might've been grand, but now the walls looked to be more moss than stone. A long corridor stretched to her left, ending in a jumble of broken rock. Directly ahead, a tower speared the sky, a weathered wooden door in its center. What looked like a large room was built onto its right side, in considerably better repair than the corridor. Crumbling piles of stone dotted the landscape—remnants of collapsed battlements, fallen turrets.

No white trees grew past the gate.

The tremble in her legs steadied. Red wasn't sure what safety looked like here, but for now being away from the trees was enough.

The slice on her cheekbone still stung. Hissing, Red gingerly touched the cut. Her fingertips came away stained with watery blood. Ahead of her, the weathered door loomed.

He was somewhere in there. She could feel it, almost, an awareness that pricked at the back of her neck, plucked at the Mark on her arm. The Wolf, the keeper of the Wilderwood and alleged jailer of gods. She had no idea what he'd do with her now that she was here. Maybe she'd escaped his forest only to be thrown back in, the Wolf making sure the bloodthirsty trees finished whatever they'd started.

But the only other option was to stay out here, in a chilled, unnatural twilight, waiting to see if the iron gate would be enough to hold the Wilderwood back.

Well, damn the myths. She was just as much a part of those stories as he was, and if her destruction was imminent, she'd rather be the architect than a bystander. Hitching her bag on her shoulder, Red strode forward and shoved the door open.

She expected darkness and rot, for the inside of the castle to look as uninhabited as the outside. And it would have, were it not for the sconces.

No, not quite sconces—what she'd thought was a sconce was actually a woody vine, snaking around the nearly circular walls. Flames burned at equidistant points along its length, but the vine itself wasn't consumed, and the flames didn't spread farther. She couldn't even see char marks, as if the flames were simply being held there, anchored to the wood through some invisible bond.

However strange the light was, it illuminated her surroundings. She stood in a cavernous foyer under a high, domed ceiling. A cracked solarium window filtered twilight over her feet. Emerald moss carpeted the floor, clustered with toadstools. Before her, a staircase, moss covering the first few steps, leading up to a balcony ringing the top of the tower. She could barely make out the impression of vines through the shadows, twining over the railing, dripping toward the floor. The corridor she'd seen from outside stretched to the left of the staircase, and the sunken room to the right, its arched entrance broken at the top.

All of it was empty.

Red's boots made soft shushing noises against the moss as she stepped forward. When she looked more closely, there were signs of occupancy—a dark cloak hung on the knob of the staircase, three pairs of scuffed boots sat by the broken archway into the other room. But nothing moved in the ruin, and everything was unnaturally silent. Red frowned.

Behind her, a light blinked out. Slowly, Red looked over her shoulder.

Another flame along the strange vine extinguished.

She almost tripped in her haste toward the staircase, noting as she put her foot on the bottom step that there was no light up there at all. Red backpedaled, changed direction, wheeling around the stairs. Light glimmered ahead of her, flames lining another staircase, this one leading down instead of up. Red ran toward it, the room around her plunging rapidly into twilight.

The last flame blinked out as she reached the stairs. She paused, breathing hard, waiting to see if the lights before her would do the same. But the flames remained upright and glowing, lit along another strange, unburnt vine.

The carpet of moss covered the first few steps here, too, but soon it gave way to thin roots, crisscrossing over the stone like veins. Red kept her eyes on her feet to keep from tripping, counting her steps as a mainstay against panic.

The stairs ended on a small landing, housing a wooden door and nothing else. Red pushed it open before she could talk herself out of it.

It didn't creak. Warm, friendly light flooded the edges of the door, seeped onto the landing like a rising sun. Red stepped in as silently as she could. She froze, familiarity first a blade, then a balm.

A library.

Back—she stopped herself before she thought the word *home*; it would hurt too badly and didn't feel wholly accurate, anyway—back in Valleyda, the library had been one of the places she spent the majority of her time. Neve had lessons most days, things beyond the simple writing and arithmetic Red had been taught, so Red was left largely to herself. She'd read most everything in the palace library, some things twice. It was one of the few ways to soothe her mind when it started churning and spilling over itself, connecting fears in spiderwebs she couldn't disentangle. The scent of paper, the orderliness of printed words, the sensation of page edges beneath her fingers smoothed the waves of her thoughts to placidity.

Most of the time, anyway.

The presence of books was really the only similarity between the palace library and this one. Overstuffed shelves stood in straight rows. Books cluttered small tables, and a pile of them stood precariously by the door, topped with a half-full mug of what smelled like coffee. Candles with strangely unwavering flames gave the room a golden glow—wait, not candles. Shards of wood, curiously unburnt, same as the vine above.

Her bag fell to the floor with a muffled *thunk*. Red held her breath for half a second, but nothing stirred in the stacks. The sound she made might have been a laugh had there been more force and less fear behind it. A library, in the depths of the Wilderwood?

Cautiously, she stepped forward, trailing her hands over book spines. The scent of dust and old paper tickled her nose, but there was no trace of mildew, and all the books seemed cared for, even the ones that looked impossibly old. Someone was minding this library, then. Much better than they seemed to be minding the rest of the castle.

Most of the titles she recognized. The palace library carried a renowned collection, second only to the Great Library in Karsecka at the southernmost tip of the continent. *Monuments of the Lost Age of Magic, A History of Ryltish Trade Routes, Treatises on Meducian Democracy.*

Up and down the rows she wandered, letting the familiar sights and smells of a library seep the broken-glass feeling from her eyes. She was almost calm when she reached the end of the fifth row.

Then she saw him.

Red's breath came in a quick, sharp gasp, ripping the quiet in two. She pushed her hand against her mouth, like she could force the sound back in.

The figure at the table didn't seem to notice. His head bent over an open book, hand moving as a pen scratched over paper. The lines of his shoulders spoke of strength, but that of only a man rather than a monster; the fingers holding the pen were long and elegant, not clawed. Still, there was something otherworldly in the shape of him, something that hinted at humanity but didn't quite arrive there.

"I don't have horns, if that's what you're wondering."

He'd turned while she was staring at his hands. The Wolf narrowed his eyes. "You must be the Second Daughter."

Chapter Five

He didn't stand, peering at her down a hawkish nose that had been broken and haphazardly mended, probably more than once. His hand, large and thatched with thin scars against white skin, dropped his pen and ran through his hair, black and overlong, waving messily against his collarbones. He'd half turned in his chair to look at her, carving out the line of his profile in lamplight—the cut of his jaw was severe, and there were tired lines around his eyes, but he didn't look much older than her. Past his twentieth year, but not his thirtieth.

There was nothing in his form that carried monstrousness, but still that intangible sense of... of *other*, of a human frame that didn't house a wholly human thing. His proportions were just out of the realm of normal—too tall, too solid, shadows around him darker than they should be. He could pass as a human on first glance, but it was a mistake you'd make only once. The Mark on her arm thrummed when his gaze met hers.

Red swallowed against a bone-dry throat. Her mouth worked, but no sound came out.

The Wolf raised an eyebrow. Dark circles bruised the skin beneath narrow, amber-colored eyes. "I'll take your silence as a yes." The scarred hand on his knee tremored slightly as he turned away from her, picked up his pen, and resumed his scribbling.

Red didn't realize her mouth hung open until she snapped it shut, teeth clicking together. The tale of the Wolf bringing Gaya's body to the edge of the forest detailed only how *she* looked, making no mention of his own appearance. Everyone knew the Wilderwood had made him different, something not quite human, though no one knew the specifics. But the Wolf's story was one of mythic beasts, and as it was told through the centuries, he became one, too.

These scarred hands, this overlong hair, this face too hard-edged to be handsome—she'd thought she was prepared for anything, but she wasn't prepared for this. The Wolf was a man before he was a monster, and the figure before her didn't fit neatly into either category.

"You're welcome to stay in the library," the Wolf said, turning back around in his chair with welcome nowhere to be found in his tone, "but I'd prefer it if you didn't lurk behind me while I'm working."

The dream-like unreality of seeing the Wolf and the Wolf looking mostly like a man made her tongue loose, made her latch onto the only part of this that might still align with what she'd been told. "Will you let the Kings go now?"

That made him face her. His eyes flickered over her leaf-tangled hair, her shredded skirts. They paused a moment on the slice across her cheekbone, briefly widened.

Red had nearly forgotten it. She reached up, touched the cut. Her fingertips slicked—still bleeding, then.

His assessment ended, the Wolf turned back to his work. "The Kings aren't here."

It was the answer she'd expected, faithless as she was. Still, it landed like a punch, and the sigh she pulled in shook a little.

His shoulders stiffened. He'd heard. The Wolf eyed her over his shoulder, angular face shadowed. "They're still on about that, then? The…the Order, was it?"

"The Order of the Five Kings." The answer came mechanically. Red felt like a child's toy, wound up and set spinning with no clear direction. "And yes."

"Subtle." One scarred hand ran over his face. "Sorry to disappoint you, Second Daughter, but the Kings are gone. They aren't something you'd want returned, anyway."

"Oh." She couldn't summon anything more.

The Wolf sighed. "Well. You came. Your part in this is fulfilled." He gestured toward the door. "I'll count us even. I'll get someone to lead you out, and you can go back the way you—"

"No, I can't." She could've laughed at the ridiculousness of it, if her throat hadn't felt like she'd swallowed a forest's worth of splinters. "I came to you, and we can't leave after we come to you. This is it. I have to stay."

His hand froze, surprise on his rough-featured face. "You don't," he said quietly, with a vehemence that would've startled her had she still felt capable of being startled. "You truly don't."

"Those are the rules." Her mouth felt like it was moving of its own accord, her head clamorous though her words came matter-of-fact. "Once we come to you, we can't leave. The forest won't let us."

The Wolf's fingers gripped the back of his chair, hard enough that Red absently thought it might snap. "The forest will let you leave if I make it." Nearly a growl.

Red clutched the ragged edges of her torn cloak. "I'm staying."

Something almost fearful flashed in his eyes. "Fine, then." He faced away from her again, muttering a curse. "Shadows *damn* me."

"This doesn't make sense." Another swallow, like working her throat might free up words from the maelstrom in her head. "If you don't want me here, if you were just going to send me back, why did you demand we come in the first—"

"I'll stop you right there." The Wolf stood, unfolding from his chair with his pen held like a dagger. He loomed a head and a half taller than her, broad-shouldered and knife-eyed. "I didn't *demand* anything."

"Yes, you *did*. You brought Gaya to the edge of the forest, you told them to send the next one, you—"

"None of that was me." He advanced a step, voice matching hers in intensity. "Whatever you think you know is clearly *wrong*."

He spat the word as he stalked toward her, and the dark shadow of the Wolf and the flash of his teeth were enough to finally send fear spearing through the numb fugue her mind had become. Red crossed her arms over her chest, hunched into them like she could make herself smaller.

The Wolf paused, stepping back with his hand half raised in something like surrender. Anger bled out of his face, another emotion flickering there. Guilt.

"I..." He looked away, ran a tired hand over his face. Sighed. "I had no more part in this arrangement than you did, Second Daughter."

Confusion made a snare of her thoughts, tangled as roots in dirt. Again, she found herself latching onto the simplest pieces, the things she could understand and fix in the face of all she couldn't. "My name isn't *Second Daughter*. It's Redarys."

"Redarys." It sounded strange in his mouth. Soft, somehow fragile.

"And you're Ci—"

"Eammon." He turned, dropping back into his chair.

Red's brow creased. "Eammon?"

Scarred fingers picked up his pen, his tone now clipped and business-like, all that vulnerability gone in an instant. "Ciaran and Gaya were my parents."

Silence. Red shook her head, mouth forming words that broke apart before they became sentences. "So you... you didn't..."

"No." Expressionless, though tension carved the curve of his shoulders beneath his plain, dark shirt. "No, I didn't bring my mother's body to the edge of the Wilderwood. No, I didn't tell anyone to send the next Second Daughter." A long, deep breath, rattling in and out of his lungs. "Neither one of us really had a choice here. Other than you choosing, *vehemently*, to stay."

His tone wanted an explanation for that, but Red didn't know how to give him one. She said nothing.

The Wolf shifted, sitting with his legs stretched out beneath the desk and his back slumped against the chair back, arms crossed and face still turned away. "They sent you off with the usual fanfare, I see," he said, deftly changing the subject. "With that damn red cloak."

She twitched at the fabric, now muddy and torn. "Scarlet for a sacrifice."

The reminder made the air feel weighted. A beat, then the Wolf waved a hand. "Leave it in the hallway, and one of us will burn—"

"*No.*" It came out sharp, a word made a weapon.

He glanced at her over his shoulder, a line drawn between dark, heavy brows.

Red pulled the edges of the cloak closer, like she could still feel Neve in it somewhere. Neve helping her dress, Neve finally letting her go. "I want to keep it."

The line between his brows deepened, but the Wolf nodded. When he spoke again, it was careful, quiet. "How long has it been since the last... the last one came?"

"A century." She crossed her arms against a sudden shiver. "A century since Merra."

A muscle in his back jumped. He looked down at his hands, the scars standing out against his skin, and slowly closed them to fists. "Damn."

Red wanted to respond, but nothing came. The fire had bled from them both. Now there was only this strange, mutual exhaustion.

The Wolf—*Eammon*—gave his head one firm shake. "If you insist on staying, don't go outside the gate. The forest isn't safe for you." Then he turned back to his work, ignoring her completely, and Red knew she'd been dismissed.

With no idea what else to do, Red drifted back into the library stacks.

Her thoughts were too scattered to organize. In all her darkest imaginings about what might happen when she entered the Wilderwood, she never expected...*this.* A Wolf who wasn't the figure from the legends, but his son. A Wolf who didn't want his sacrifice, who tried to send her back. What bitter irony, that he and Neve seemed to be in accord.

But Red belonged here. The magic that made her taste dirt and turned her veins green made it clear, the magic that could wreak such destruction if she didn't keep it contained, and she was so tired of being afraid.

It wasn't your fault. Neve had said it the night of the ball, said it countless times before. But it had been Red's half-drunk and half-mad idea to steal the horses and run for the Wilderwood, to scream at the trees and see if they screamed back. And when the thieves came with their knives and their bladed smiles, when her hands were still bloody and the shard of the Wilderwood's power was newly curled around her bones, Red had—

She clenched her fists tight, scoring half-moons into her palms until the pain covered the memories, faded them to specters. She was dangerous. Even if Neve didn't remember.

And if she wanted to keep her sister safe, Red had to stay here. Whether the Wolf wanted her or not.

The warm familiarity of the bookshelves kept her together, knit her back into herself as she wandered between them. She hoped there might be novels, something other than the dry tomes she'd seen earlier. One volume looked promising, *Legends* gilt-inscribed on the spine. Red didn't think of the still-bleeding slice on her cheek when she reached to pull it down, and her bloodied fingers smudged the canvas. "Oh, *Kings*."

Eammon rounded the corner, books stacked in his arms. He glanced at the blood-smeared cover before his eyes darted back to the cut across her cheekbone. A moment of that same close scrutiny he'd given it before, then he placed his stack of books on the ground. "What happened there?" Something wary lurked in his tone, like the question had a right and a wrong answer.

"A thorn," she said. "It's not *deep*, I just…they were around one of those white trees…"

He still crouched from where he'd set his books down, and now his hands curled almost like claws. It would've frightened her were it not for that glint of alarm in his eyes. "The white trees?" His voice was quiet, but there was an urgency to it. "Did you bleed on it?"

"Kind of, but it wasn't on purpose and there wasn't much—"

"I need you to tell me exactly what happened, Redarys."

"It's just a scratch." She wiped her bloody fingers on her cloak, discomfited by his worry and his sternness. "A thorn got my cheek, and the white tree…absorbed it, somehow…"

Every line in his body tensed.

"And it chased me here. The Wilderwood did, I mean." To say it aloud sounded ridiculous. Red's cheeks heated, making the cut seep anew.

The Wolf stood then, slowly reaching his full height and covering her in his shadow. When he spoke, his tone was measured, belying all that worry in his gaze. "Is that all?"

"Yes. All it did was chase me." Incredulity sharpened her answer. "If that wasn't supposed to happen, perhaps you should keep better control of your damn trees."

Eammon's brow arched, but relief was in his suddenly slackened shoulders. "My apologies." He held out his hand, tentatively gesturing to her cheek. "Allow me to make it up to you."

Red eyed his hand, lip between her teeth. Something about it looked…familiar, almost. It pricked at the back of her mind but wouldn't commit to the solid form of a memory.

She nodded.

His skin was warm. The crosshatched scars on his fingers were rough against her cheek as the Wolf laid his forefinger carefully along the cut. His eyes closed.

Something stirred in the air between them, a gust of warmth, scented with leaves and loam. Red's vision bloomed golden, the Mark on her arm thrumming again. In her center, the splinter of her magic teased open, a flower feeling spring on winter's sharpened edge.

A fraction of a second, then the sting of the cut was gone. Red didn't realize she'd closed her eyes until she opened them again.

There, on the Wolf's cheekbone, a wound the mirror image of hers. She lifted her fingers disbelievingly to her face. Still tacky with blood, but the skin was whole.

The Wolf knelt quickly, ducking his head to gather his books again, but not quite fast enough to hide his eyes. The whites of them were threaded with green, a verdant corona blooming around the amber-brown irises.

"The benefits of being bound to the Wilderwood are few." Books in hand, Eammon rose, turning to stride back into the stacks. He seemed taller than before, quite the feat when his previous height was already considerable. There was a strange quality to his voice, too—a slight echo, a resonance that reminded her of leaves caught in the wind. "That's one of them."

For a moment Red stood still, fingers resting against her unmarked skin. Then she started after him. *Thank you* hovered in the back of her throat, but something about the set of his shoulders said he neither needed nor wanted it.

"The rules here are simple." Eammon shoved a book into its place on the shelf. "The first: Don't go beyond the gate."

The odd, echoing quality was gone from his voice now—the Wolf sounded only gruff and tired, with no echo of falling leaves.

"Easily done," Red muttered. "Your forest is less than hospitable."

His frown deepened at that. "Second rule." Another book slammed home. "The Wilderwood wants blood, especially yours. Don't bleed where the trees can taste it, or they'll come for you."

Her fingers curled, still copper-scented with blood. "Is that what happened to Gaya and the other Second Daughters?"

The Wolf froze, another book halfway pushed into place, expression stricken. It took Red a moment for her mind to catch up with what she'd said, and when it did, she wanted to sink into the floor. Reminding him of his mother's death. What a wonderful way to start their cohabitation.

But Eammon recovered without comment, though he pushed the book the rest of the way onto the shelf with perhaps more force than necessary. "More or less, yes."

Arms now emptied, Eammon stalked to the library door. When he reached it, he turned, peering at her down his crooked nose. "Third rule." The new cut on his face leaked too-dark blood, deep crimson with a thread of green that looked almost like a root tendril, but his eyes were normal again, no longer haloed emerald. "Stay out of my way."

Red tightened her crossed arms over her chest like they could be a shield. "Understood."

"There's a room you can use in the corridor." Eammon pushed open the door and gestured her out. "Welcome to the Black Keep, Redarys."

The door shut behind her, and Red was alone.

It wasn't until she sank onto the bottom step that she realized where she'd seen his hands, why their shape and scarring looked so familiar.

The night of her sixteenth birthday, when Red had cut her hand on a rock and accidentally bled in the forest—when the Wilderwood splintered its damning magic into her bloodstream by way of her cut palm—she'd seen something, painted on the canvas of her closed eyes. A vision. Hands that weren't her own, large and scarred and thrust into the dirt, just as hers were. A sense of rushing, blinding fear that mirrored hers but *wasn't* hers.

It was only a panicked flash, vague and unclear, shrouded in branch-shaped shadows. Up until this moment, she'd almost thought she'd imagined it. But now…

Now she'd seen them in the flesh. Now she knew whom those hands belonged to, and knew no part of that night had been imagined.

The hands she'd seen were the Wolf's.

Chapter Six

Red gripped at the roots of her hair until her fingers felt numb, forehead pressed against the heels of her hands. That night still etched in her mind with crystal clarity, at least up to a point. Once the thieves who'd followed them attacked and the bloodshed began, she'd blocked parts of it out.

But the flash behind her eyelids of something happening *elsewhere*, of scarred hands and immediate panic...she remembered that, now, remembered it with such detail she couldn't believe she'd once thought it imagined. A moment of connection to someone other than herself, and that someone had been the Wolf.

He'd *been* there, somehow—been there when magic rioted out of the Wilderwood, when it climbed through the wound in her palm and made its home in her chest. Was it his fault, then? Had the forest shattered magic into her at his direction?

Gently, she laid her fingertips against her cheek, still blood-smeared from the wound he'd taken. If the Wolf had given her this damn power on purpose, surely he wouldn't have tried to send her back? Wouldn't have given her rules that were supposed to keep her safe from his forest?

Red groaned against her palms.

She was tempted to stay seated on the staircase until Eammon deigned to emerge from his library, to see if she could wrench more answers out of him. But Red was weary, and the floor was cold, and the idea of waiting for someone who explicitly wanted to avoid her was exhausting.

He'd told her not to leave the Keep, so logically, the Keep was safe. And it was her new home. As unwieldy as that thought felt, she might as well explore it.

Wearily, Red stood and started back up the long, root-threaded staircase.

There was light at the top of the stairs, as if someone had come along and reignited the fires jeweling the unburning vine in the foyer. Red paused on the landing, peering at the strange, makeshift sconce.

The flames were anchored on the vine. It *should* be burning. But through the bright, yellow-white hearts of the flames, she could see that the vine itself appeared wholly unharmed.

She thought of the wood shards in the library she'd first assumed were candles, how they also carried flame but stayed unburnt. Wood and vine, both growing things, locked in some strange symbiotic relationship. The splintered power in her chest felt restless.

Red backed away, venturing into the center of the ruined foyer. Above her, lavender sky shone through the cracked solarium glass, neither any brighter nor any darker than before she'd fled down the stairs. No moon, no stars, nothing to give any indication of time passed. Just endless twilight.

Though somewhat dim, the light from the burning vine and the solarium window was steady, and Red could see the remains of carpet on the mossy floor, shreds of something that had once been grand. The threads of nearly rotted tapestries hung on the walls, tangled with vines and thin roots. Too muddied to tell what the pictures might've been, for the most part, though she could pick out the vague shape of faces in one of them.

She frowned at it, eyes narrowed to put together the patterns. A man and a woman, it looked like. Holding hands, maybe. Her hair was long. His eyes were dark.

Gaya and Ciaran. Eammon's parents. If she needed further proof that he was who he said, this would be it. Even though the tapestry was worn nearly to ruin, she could tell the man depicted here was not the man she'd just met in the library. His face was softer, more classically handsome. His chin canted upward at an angle that dared the viewer to try him, an expression she knew just by looking at it wouldn't be worn naturally on Eammon's face.

And Gaya... she was more muddied than Ciaran, the shape of her harder to make out. Beautiful, aloof in a way that the smudged tapestry highlighted rather than obscured.

That frustrated Red on some deep level, a knotted emotion she couldn't quite parse out to its composite parts. All the Second Daughters, more icon than individual. Defined by *what* they were instead of *who*.

She frowned a moment longer at the tapestry before walking over to the broken archway at the other side of the stairs.

The arch led into what looked like a sunken dining room, one chipped stone step at the edge of the threshold. A large window framed the courtyard on the right side, the glass choked with climbing greenery and thin, spiderwebbed cracks. A scuffed wooden table sat in the center of the room, with three chairs clustered haphazardly at one end. On the back wall, another, smaller door on rusted hinges led to what she assumed was the kitchen. Other than that, the room was empty.

Three chairs. Her brows drew together. The tales told of no one here but the Wolf, but then again, the tales also hadn't said there was more than one Wolf, and the current one was a tall young man with scarred hands and a sour disposition. It seemed the tales weren't exactly reliable. Really, she had no idea who else—*what* else—might be lurking in the Keep.

One of us will burn it, the Wolf had said when he saw her torn cloak. Implying there was more than one inhabitant of this ruin.

As if in answer, there was a sudden clatter, like a dropped armful of pots and pans. Red heard a brief, muttered curse from behind that smaller door at the back of the room, and then a laugh from another voice, light and musical.

Her courage wasn't quite steeled enough to investigate. Red's mind crowded with thoughts of twisted poppets made of sticks and thorns, crafted from the Wilderwood and set to servitude by the same strange magic that kept the vine unburning. After the fanged trees, nothing seemed out of the realm of awful possibility.

She backed away from the broken arch, not stopping until the small of her back hit the staircase rail in the main foyer. Her shoulder jostled the dark coat hanging on the knob of the newel post, sending up a faint whiff of fallen leaves and coffee grounds.

Red turned, peering upward. The landing at the top of the staircase was still hidden in shadow, a darkness that had scared her away before. Now that she felt somewhat less skittish, the upstairs seemed more intriguing than foreboding.

Despite being partially covered in moss, the stairs looked sturdy enough. She placed her mud-caked boot on the first step.

The moss moved under her feet like she'd stepped on a snake, seeping farther up the stairs, collecting toadstools and thin roots in its wake. The greenery gathered together, an army amassing, and became a solid wall of growing things, blocking her path.

Red stumbled backward, shaking off the weed tendrils knotting around her ankles. "Five *Kings*," she cursed quietly. "Point taken."

Dirt streaked the hand that reached up to push sweaty, leaf-matted hair from her eyes. She needed a bath, and badly, though she'd have to put her dirty clothes back on afterward. She hadn't brought more. Hadn't expected to need them.

The thought sank into her mind with serrated teeth. The fierceness with which she'd run for her life in the Wilderwood had been gut instinct, primal force. Now the consequences: a life. Already she was hours older than she ever expected to be.

She had no idea how to start coming to terms with that.

Red pressed her fingers to her eyes until the sharp feeling behind them dissipated. Once she was calmer, she shook her head, straightened. The Wolf said her room was in the corridor, and there was only one she could see, though it ended in a riot of ruin.

The oddly lit vine provided the light here, too, though the flames were smaller and more sporadic. Moss covered the floor and grew halfway up the walls. Blooming things she couldn't name threaded through the ruined jumble at the hall's end, a tangle of leaves and flowers and broken rock.

It looked like the Wilderwood had broken into the Black Keep more than once, leaving most of it a ruin. Not exactly a comforting thought.

Doors lined the hallway, but only one looked like it'd been disturbed recently. A jagged line of dirt and a green stain on the wood marked where growth had been cleared away, leaving a semicircle of bare wooden floor ringing the threshold. Already moss crept over it, taking back the space it had ceded.

Gingerly stepping over the moss, Red pushed the door open.

The room beyond was small and sparsely furnished. Dusty, still, but at least cleared of greenery. The walls were bare. A large window with vines crawling up the outside looked out on another courtyard, where a stone wall ran from the back of the hallway and down a gently sloping hill to meet the iron gate. Another tower sat directly behind the one she'd entered, short enough to be hidden from the front. Small trees grew around its base, and her heart stuttered for the half second it took to realize they weren't bone-colored. Between the trees twisting around the structure and the flowering vines threading through them, the tower looked more grown than built.

A fully made bed stood in the corner by the window, linens faded but clean, with a fireplace set into the wall by its foot, neatly stacked with wood. To the left of the door, a small alcove housed a chamber pot and wide iron tub, already filled with water. A wardrobe was pushed into another corner, an age-spotted mirror hanging next to it on the wall. Large handprints marked the dust on the wardrobe's side. The size of them matched Eammon's.

He'd told her she could leave, but prepared for her to stay. It made her wonder how much of his insistence that she could return home was planned, and how much of it had been impulse, a knee-jerk reaction born from some emotion she wasn't sure of.

Cautiously, Red walked over to the bed. With a quick breath, she ducked and peered beneath it, not sure what she was looking for, but sure she wouldn't relax until she checked.

Nothing but remnants of moss. Her lips thinned as she straightened, headed next for the wardrobe.

She opened the doors quickly, prepared to snarl at anything that might rear up from the depths, but the snarl melted slowly to bewilderment.

Dresses. A row of them. Simple cuts in muted colors, jewel tones that would blend into a forest. Red pulled one out, deep green, careful not to let it brush against her dirt-smeared cloak. It looked like it would fit.

Red laid the gown out on the bed and closed the wardrobe. Then she stepped back, pressed her knuckles against her teeth, and let out one slightly panicked, slightly relieved, wholly confused sob.

This was what she wanted, wasn't it? To lock herself and her sharp magic away in the Wilderwood. To ensure that she could never bring harm to Neve or anyone else she cared about ever again; that the destruction she'd wrought with her power the first time was the only time.

This was exactly what she wanted.

The satisfaction was hollow at best.

She gulped in a deep breath, held it until the burn in her lungs canceled out the one in her eyes. Carefully, Red shrugged out of her cloak. Her flight through the Wilderwood had left it worse for wear, pockmarked with rips and dirt, but Red handled it like it was priceless finery.

It was ridiculous. She was clearheaded enough to know that. Ridiculous that she'd want to keep the thing that marked her as a sacrifice. But the memory it carried was the one of Neve, helping her get dressed, smoothing out the wrinkles as she'd done so many times before. Other than Red's, her hands had been the last to touch the scarlet fabric.

There were other, fiercer reasons, too. Reasons that came from that same deep place that was ferally pleased with the cruel coincidence of her childhood name. The part of her that would smile as she grabbed a bladed legacy and felt it make her bleed.

Red held the cloak in her hands for a moment, working the weave of it between her fingers. Then, with the same care she'd used to take it off, she folded it so the worst of the rips didn't show and placed it in the wardrobe.

Valleydan Interlude I

There were no priestesses in the gardens as Neve walked to the Shrine. She'd expected to fight her way through a throng of them, white-robed and mealymouthed, waiting to see if their sacrifice finally brought back their gods. Official vigils for the Five Kings' return started at midnight, she knew, so she had some time, but she was still surprised at the garden's emptiness.

Her fingers arched like claws, her teeth clamping so hard into her lip she nearly broke the skin. It was probably good none of them were here. She might do something unbecoming of a First Daughter.

Her feet barely made a sound over the cobblestones, the moonlight soaked up by the dark fabric of her gown. It was different from the one she'd worn for the procession, less ornate, but still the black of absence. She didn't know when she might bring herself to wear a different color.

Truly, Neve didn't know why she'd bothered coming here. She'd never been one to take solace in prayer, though there'd been a time when she tried. Right at sixteen, after... after what happened with Red, she'd tried religion on for size for a week or two, to see if it smoothed the rough edges of her thoughts, made them harder to cut herself on. Her sister was a pawn, a piece to be moved—send her to the Wilderwood, and maybe this time, the Five Kings would come back. At the very least, she'd keep the fabled monsters away. There was nothing either of them could do to change it, and maybe there was comfort to be had there, if she could feign piety. A balm for the ache of it.

There wasn't. The Shrine was nothing but a stone room full of candles and branches. No comfort. No absolution.

And the way Red *looked* at her, those two weeks she'd tried religion. Like she was watching the digging of her own grave.

So now, as she stalked toward the Shrine in her mourning black, she knew it was pointless. Any words she could say, any candles she could light, would do nothing to fill the gnawing empty place her twin had left. But grief was like gravel in her slipper, and she felt it more when she was standing still.

The Shrine would at least give her a private place to cry.

Neve walked beneath the flowered arbor into the shadows of the stone room beyond. Then she stopped, eyes wide and glassy, the sobs she'd wanted to let free frozen in her throat.

Not empty. Three priestesses stood around the statue of Gaya, red prayer candles guttering in their hands. Still in their customary white robes, but no cloaks. Those were only for the ceremony that blessed Red as a sacrifice.

The priestess closest to the wall carved in Second Daughters saw her first. Some muted emotion flickered across her face—pity, but a faint kind, like one might have for a child who'd lost a pet.

Neve's fingers balled into fists at her sides.

Gently, the priestess placed her candle by Gaya's feet, anchoring it in the already-puddled wax of other prayers. She clasped her hands before her as she approached. "First Daughter."

A gentle accent, her *r*'s touched with a burr. Ryltish, probably, one who'd trekked across the sea for the privilege of praying here, of seeing the historic sacrifice of a Second Daughter. Neve said nothing, her nails pressing crescents into her palms.

The other two priestesses exchanged glances before turning back to their prayer candles. Smart. They could read the wish on Neve's face, the hope that one of them would say something to stoke the fire in her chest to a blaze.

If the Ryltish priestess realized the error she'd made in approaching, she didn't show it. The faint pity on her face deepened, pulling down her lips. "It's a great honor, Highness," she said quietly. An ember of fervor shone in her green eyes. "For your sister to go to the sacred wood, to appease the Wolf and bring us safety from his monsters. We have great hopes she'll be the one to make him release the Kings. And an honor for you, too, to one day rule over a land that shares the sacred wood's border. The Queen of Valleyda is the Queen most loved by our gods."

Neve couldn't stop her snort, loud and undignified in this place of stone and quiet flames. "An *honor*," she repeated, her brow arching incredulously. "Yes, what a great honor, that my sister was murdered for the possible return of the Kings you've decided are gods." The snort became a laugh, half-mad and sharp, bursting from between her teeth and making her breath come short. "How *blessed* I am, to hold sway over a barren, frozen land on the edge of a haunted forest."

The Ryltish priestess seemed to finally recognize her mistake. Her eyes were wide, pretty face frozen and pale. Behind her, the other two priestesses stood still as the statue they prayed to, wax dripping over motionless hands.

She didn't realize she'd advanced a step until the priestess lurched backward, trying to keep distance between them. Neve's lips curled back from her teeth. "You have it so easy," she murmured. "All you Order priestesses from far away. Safe behind your borders, miles from your *sacred wood*."

The Ryltish priestess almost lost her balance when her calf bumped against Gaya's stone feet. Crimson wax marred her hem. Still, her eyes didn't leave Neve's, and her cheeks were nearly the same color as her robe.

"It's almost pathetic." Neve cocked her head, the barest curve of an acidic smile touching her mouth but not her eyes. "Your religion asks nothing of you. You throw a girl in white and black and red into the Wilderwood every few centuries, when a Second Daughter comes around, but nothing *you* do is enough to bring back the Kings. Maybe they don't want to come back to such cowardly penitents, who never do anything but send pointless sacrifices and light pointless candles."

All three priestesses watched her silently, three pairs of wide eyes fixed on her face. The wax dripping down their fingers had to be scalding, but it wasn't enough to make them move, wasn't enough to break them from the terrible spell of her sadness and how it made her cruel.

Neve forced her fingers straight, uncurling them from fists. "Get out."

They obliged without a word, taking their prayer candles with them.

Finally alone, Neve slumped, like her anger had been the only thing holding her up. She caught herself right before she leaned on Gaya's statue. She refused to look for any kind of comfort there.

Instead, Neve walked through the dark gauzy curtain behind the stone effigy into the second room of the Shrine.

She'd been here only once before. When she was officially named as the heir to the throne on her tenth birthday, they'd wrapped her in the coronation cloak, embroidered with the names of the former Valleydan queens, and brought her here to be prayed over. To her child's eyes, the white branches had seemed tall as trees themselves, casting needle-edged shadows on the stone walls.

That's what she expected when she walked through the curtain—a forest like the one that had devoured her sister. But it was only a room. A room filled with branches cast in marble bases, most no higher than her shoulders. A Wilderwood in miniature. Nothing like what she'd seen when she and Red raced toward its border four years ago. Nothing like what Red had just disappeared into.

Neve's chest burned, too heavy and hollow all at once. She couldn't hurt *that* Wilderwood.

But she could hurt this one.

The limb of a branch was in her hand before she had the conscious thought, before her mind caught up with her body. She wrenched her fist to the side, and it came off the main bough with the crack of rending bone.

Neve paused for only a moment. Then, with a fierce snarl and teeth bared, she wrenched off another, relishing the *snap* it made as it came away, the feel of the wood giving beneath her hands.

She didn't know how many branches she tore into before she felt a presence behind her. Neve turned with splintered wood held in her two fists like daggers, her dark hair waving against her face with the force of her breath.

A red-haired, white-skinned priestess stood in the doorway, face implacable. She looked vaguely familiar—from the Valleydan Temple, then. Neve wondered if that would matter. The vagaries of heresy weren't something she was familiar with, but wrecking the Shrine would probably make an easy case for it. What would that punishment be for a First Daughter, the one meant for the throne? Neve tried to care, but couldn't quite find the energy.

And yet, the priestess did nothing. She stood there, silently, cool blue eyes surveying the damage before rising to Neve.

Slowly, Neve's breathing returned to normal. She released her fists, the two branch shards she'd held clattering down to the stone floor.

Neve and the red-haired priestess stared at each other. There was something like a dare in each gaze, a measuring of mettle, though Neve didn't know what she was measuring for.

Finally, the priestess stepped farther into the room, picking deftly over white wooden splinters. "Come," she said, in a voice that was brusque though not unpleasant. "If we clean up, no one will ever notice."

It took Neve a moment to understand what she was saying, so far was it from what she expected. But the priestess bent down, gathering white splinters in her hands, and after a moment, Neve joined her.

A small pendant swung from the priestess's neck, circling like a pendulum. It looked like a shard of wood, like the leavings of Neve's rampage scattering the floor. The only difference was the color; where the branches were the pure, shining white of bleached bone, the priestess's pendant was threaded through with black.

Neve frowned at it. Strange, for a priestess to wear jewelry—it wasn't exactly forbidden, but none of them did it, going about clad only in their white robes with no further adornment.

The priestess saw her looking. A small smile tugged up her mouth as she caught the pendant, rolled it between her fingers. "Another piece of the Wilderwood," she said, by way of explanation. "It breaks more easily than you'd think, with the right pressure. The right tools."

Neve's brows drew together. The priestess watched her as if she saw the shape of her questions and wanted to draw them out. Neve shut them behind her teeth.

For all her destruction, the mess she'd made fit easily in their four fists. The priestess made a bowl of her full white skirt, gathering all the shards before bundling the fabric in her hand like a pocket. "I'll dispose of this."

"You mean make more jewelry out of it?" Neve couldn't keep the bite from her voice. She was *tired*, so tired of keeping her composure. Of pretending all of this didn't bore beneath her skin and scour her out.

"Oh, no." Despite the flippancy of the response, those blue, implacable eyes watched her carefully. "These aren't right for that. Not yet."

Disquiet thrummed under Neve's ribs.

The red-haired priestess stood still, managing to look regal despite the awkward way she held her robe to contain the wood shards. "You're here because of your sister?"

"Why else would I be here?" Neve wanted it to come out fierce, but it was quiet and thin. She'd spent all her fierceness. "I have no interest in praying."

The priestess nodded, taking Neve's blasphemy in stride. "Would you like to know what happened to her, when she crossed into the Wilderwood?"

It struck Neve silent for a moment, such a heavy question asked in such a casual manner. "You...you *know*?"

"So do you." The priestess shrugged like they were discussing something as benign as the weather. "Your sister is tangled in the forest. Like Gaya was, like all the others. She went to the Wolf, and he bound her to it, just as he is bound."

Neve knew the story. The Wolf bringing Gaya's forest-riddled corpse to the edge of the wood, a macabre token of the tithe he then demanded. It made sense, that the other Second Daughters would be bound similarly. That the Wolf somehow wove the Wilderwood into their bones, knit them into its foundations, ensuring they couldn't escape.

"But she's alive." A bare rasp of sound in the quiet, and Neve didn't inhale as she waited for the answer.

The priestess nodded, turning toward the door. "But she's alive."

On legs that felt numb, Neve followed the red-haired priestess back through the Shrine out into the dark gardens. She took a few steps forward, passing the other woman to inhale cold, bracing air.

Midnight was close. Soon all the priestesses who'd come to see Red sacrificed would gather here, to pray throughout the night that she would be deemed acceptable by the Wolf, that he would finally free the Five Kings from their unjust imprisonment.

When Neve closed her eyes, she could still see that scarlet cloak disappearing into the gloom between the trees.

She's alive.

"You'll keep this quiet." Neve meant it as an order, but it came out more like a question.

"Of course." A pause, heavy. "You have the right idea, First Daughter."

It was enough to make her eyes open, to make her gaze snap over her shoulder. The priestess stood still and placid behind her, face revealing nothing.

"The Wilderwood won't let her go." Her red hair fell over her shoulder as she tipped her head, as if in deference to Neve's grief. "It has weakened, this past century, but not enough. She couldn't escape even if she tried." Moonlight caught her eyes, made them glitter. "At least, not right now."

Something toothed and hopeful leapt in Neve's chest. "What do you mean?"

The priestess lightly touched her odd wood-shard necklace. "The forest is only as strong as we let it be."

Neve's brow knit. The night air chilled them into a frozen tableau.

"Your secrets are safe with me, Neverah." The priestess gave a small bow then glided away, her pale robe disappearing into the dark garden.

Cool breeze on her arms, the scent of early-summer flowers heady in her nose. Neve concentrated on these things, grounded herself with them. In her head, a scarlet cloak flickered in and out of a dark, dark forest.

Chapter Seven

The water in the tub was cold enough to make her teeth chatter when she dipped in her hand, but Red was too filthy to care. She pulled off her tattered white dress and black sash, kicking them into a pile on the floor—those, someone could burn. Shivering, she sank quickly into the tub before the cold could change her mind, and scrubbed at her hair until her nailbeds turned blue, extracting twigs one by one and letting them clatter to the floor.

Leaves matted her hair, too. As she pulled them out, Red noticed they were each blushed with green along the veins.

She frowned at one of them, tracing the lines with a fingertip. Addled by fear and confusion, her memories of the Wilderwood were probably less than reliable. But she'd swear that every leaf she saw outside the protection of the Wolf's gate was gray and withered, the colors of autumn leaching rapidly into winter.

Red flicked the leaf from her wet fingers with more force than necessary.

When her nails were free of dirt and her hair free of forest, Red stepped from the tub, teeth clenched against the cold. Naked, she skulked across the room, feeling strangely exposed to the vines on the window, and grabbed the dark-green gown off the bed. She pulled it on without bothering to dry off, fabric sticking to her wet skin.

As she stood in front of the age-spotted mirror and attempted to untangle her hair, her stomach rumbled.

There'd been breakfast, before the procession left the Valleydan capital, but Red hadn't managed to eat much, and couldn't even remember what it was. Since then: a bloodthirsty forest, a surly Wolf, miles run on adrenaline alone.

Red set her teeth. This room was clean and safe and isolated; the last thing she wanted was to go wandering through the ruined Keep on the off chance she might find some toast. But her stomach twisted again, its growl more insistent.

During her earlier exploration, there'd been that small door with rusty hinges at the back of the dining room. The one behind which she'd heard the curse and the laugh. Red still didn't feel quite brave enough to face who- or whatever made those noises, but she was pretty sure that room was a kitchen. And maybe the things she'd heard in it were elsewhere by now.

Thief-furtive, Red crept from her room. It was too cold to forgo shoes, really, a pervasive chill in the air that the half-forest walls didn't cut, but her boots were still caked in enough mud to make her clumsy. She wanted to be able to run if she needed to.

The sky through the cracked, domed window above the foyer was mostly unchanged. Maybe slightly darker, if she squinted, but still twilight. The Wilderwood seemed caught in a perpetual gloaming, trapped between day and dusk.

A murmur came through the broken arch across the hall, too muffled to make out, but the cadence and low, graveled tone were familiar. The Wolf.

Red kept her back against the wall as she inched closer to the arch. Feeling the stone behind her was somehow reassuring, even moss-furred as it was, a solid thing to hold on to.

"She's here?" A different voice, answering Eammon's indistinct mutter. It at least sounded human, touched with a melodious accent that reminded her of Raffe's. The laugher from before? "So that's why the Wilderwood seemed so restless."

"*Restless* is one way to put it," Eammon grumbled.

"I would've gone with *desperate*." This from a new voice, masculine and deep, but not as rough as Eammon's. The voice she'd heard from behind the door, cursing after the clatter. "The Wilderwood needs two, and it knows she's here now. You've held it alone for too long."

A pause. "We've had this discussion," Eammon said, clipped and stern.

No answer, though Red thought she heard a sigh. A moment, then the musical voice spoke again. "Well, did she find you?"

"In the library," Eammon answered. "How'd she know to go to the damn library?"

"It's not like there's anywhere else to go, really. You can't *hide* from her, Eammon, no more than you could from the others. What'd you expect?"

In response, Eammon grumbled a long and mostly unintelligible curse, something about the Five Kings and what they could do with certain appendages.

"Where is she now?" the second, masculine voice asked. "Do you know? Or did you just turn her out of the library and hope for the best?"

"I told her to stay in the gate and away from the trees," Eammon answered. He neglected to mention the third rule, Red noticed, the one about staying out of his way. The omission seemed deliberate.

The masculine voice, admonishing: "Do you think that will change anything?"

Silence, tense as a bowstring. Red found herself holding her breath.

"There's a breach to the east." The other, melodic voice gently changed the subject. "Nothing's come through from the Shadowlands yet, but I'm sure it won't be long. The sentinel tree was half covered in rot when I saw it earlier, and sinking fast. I threw some blood on it, but it didn't make much difference." A light sigh. "There's been more breaches than usual lately."

Shadowlands. Here was another fairy tale suddenly made concrete. The Shadowlands were the prison the Wilderwood created, a place to trap monsters. Dread prickled at the back of Red's neck.

"Far more breaches," the deep voice agreed. "I haven't found a sentinel tree free of shadow-rot in days. Some of them aren't very far gone, but it won't take long before they show up here. That's a lot of potential holes for something to come through."

The forest had been empty of monsters when Red entered. At least, empty of the kind that had supposedly come from the Wilderwood before Kaldenore went to the Wolf—shape-shifting things made of shadow, formed from scraps of forest and bone. Red hadn't thought much of it, preoccupied with running from fanged trees that wanted her blood. But this mention of the Shadowlands, of a breach, of something coming *through*...

"The Wilderwood is weak." Eammon, tired. "But I can fix it."

"Not without a knife." The musical voice, shaded dark. "Not without a knife, or without becoming—"

"It doesn't matter how I do it, so long as it's done."

"If she's here, it's because she's needed, Eammon." The second, deeper voice, brusque. "Whether you want that or not."

"Getting one more person tangled in this mess has never helped before. Not in a way that lasts." The sound of a chair scraping across the floor. "You know that, Fife. It never has, and it never will."

Red's heartbeat thudded in the hollow of her throat.

The Wolf rounded the edge of the archway with fire sparking in amber eyes, his jaw clenched tight. Red pushed off the wall to meet him, hands balled into fists at her sides. Behind Eammon, she saw fleeting glimpses of two other people—a small, delicately featured woman with golden-brown skin, and a pale, lanky figure with a shock of reddish-gold hair—but all her attention was commanded by the Wolf, by the terrible possibilities of what she'd overheard and what it could mean. "What's breached?"

He backpedaled when he saw her, his hands once again rising like she was something to be warded off. The Wolf's eyebrows slashed downward. "Eavesdropping is rude."

"You're one to talk about *rude*." She matched his narrowed eyes. "I repeat, what's breached?"

His hands, still held defensively between them, slowly fell. Eammon stared at her for a minute, some internal debate weighing his gaze. Then he tried to shoulder past. "None of your concern."

Red turned with him. "I beg to differ."

"I'm sure you do."

"Is it the monsters?"

He froze, hand half outstretched for the coat hanging on the knob of the moss-covered stair railing. "What do you know about the monsters?"

"I know they came from the forest before Kaldenore went in, and they disappeared afterward." To say she *knew* that seemed strange, after so many years of thinking it little more than a tale to frighten children. But in the past day she'd spent here, old doubts had been scrubbed away with the same speed as new ones had surfaced. "I know that you supposedly would've unleashed them on the world again if I hadn't arrived."

He'd blanched at the mention of Kaldenore's name, those long, scarred fingers falling back to his thigh as he turned to face her. "I didn't send the monsters." He swallowed, a visible tic in his throat. "They weren't... they weren't on purpose."

One more thing she didn't know how to make sense of—this hulking, scarred man who seemed just as horrified by his forest as she was. "So that story is true?"

"That story is true." He turned away, ran a hand through his long, dark hair. "But rest assured, it won't happen again. Regardless of whether you'd come or not, I'll never purposefully unleash *anything* from this damn forest, and in fact work quite hard to keep it all contained."

Cold comfort, especially hedged by *purposefully*. "So where are you going, then?"

"To do Wolf-things." Eammon grabbed the coat and swung it over his shoulders in one motion, turning toward the door.

The decision was split-second and out of her mouth before she could give it too much thought. "I'm coming with you."

The Wolf rounded on her, teeth glinting in the light of the flames along the unburnt vine. "You most *certainly* are not."

"Then give me a better answer than *Wolf-things*."

Eammon's hands tensed into knots by his sides. His mouth worked as if looking for that better answer; he swallowed whatever he found. "It's not safe for you," he said finally. "You know that."

"*Safe* around here seems a relative concept at best. And I'd like to see for myself that you're holding up your end of the bargain. That no monsters will be leaving the confines of your forest."

The dim light caught his eyes, emphasized both their color and the depth of the shadows beneath. "You could just trust me."

Her chin tipped up. "Give me a reason to."

They stared at each other, Red and the Wolf. It could've been a contest of wills, if it felt like something either of them could win.

"I promise not to bleed," Red said softly. "That's the only way it will come for me, right? If I bleed?"

He didn't answer. Eammon's gaze pinned her in place, unreadable. Then he jerked his chin toward the corridor. "Go get boots. You can't traipse through the Wilderwood barefoot."

Her mud-caked boots were right inside her room's door. Red knocked off the worst of the muck and laced them quickly, half convinced the Wolf would change his mind if she dallied too long. She thought of grabbing her scarlet cloak from the wardrobe, but it had suffered enough indignities today.

When she came back into the main hall, Eammon had shrugged off his coat. He held it out like an offering but didn't meet her eyes. "It's cold."

After a moment's hesitation, she took the proffered coat, swung it over her shoulders. It hung to her knees, smelled of old books and coffee and the cinnamon-bite of fallen leaves, still warm from where he'd worn it.

Brows drawn down, Eammon opened the door and stalked into the fog.

Chapter Eight

The sky dimmed toward violet, casting the Wilderwood around them in shades of black and deep blue. The yellow light from within the Keep extended only inches into the gloom before being swallowed by shadow, like the forest wouldn't permit too much illumination.

"Keep up." Eammon's stride was one to two of hers, and he didn't seem inclined to slow. The violet light caught the edge of a dagger at his waist.

Red walked quickly, staying close to his back. The sleeves of his coat were long enough to completely hide her hands, and she balled the worn fabric into her fists as she pulled it tighter. It was damn cold in whatever passed for *night* around here, but if Eammon felt the chill, he didn't show it. She supposed he was used to it by now.

"Don't touch anything." Fog swirled over the gate ahead of them, deepened the shadows around Eammon's shoulders. "Stay within reach of me at all times." He turned just enough for her to see a fierce one-eyed glare. "And remember, no bleeding."

"Not planning on it."

"Good."

Eammon touched the gate. As it had when Red entered, the split in the metal bloomed from the ground, traveling up the iron until the door swung open. The Wolf stepped into the thicker fog beyond, sending it eddying around his feet.

The trees seemed to press closer as she followed him into the forest. White branches swooped through the gloom above their heads, scythes waiting for the word. Red eyed them as she inched closer behind Eammon, near enough to feel wafts of his warmth and see the work of muscle under his shirt. "We're looking for a Shadowlands breach, correct?"

An affirmative grunt.

"And what does a breach look like, exactly?"

"Darkness." Eammon pushed aside a tree branch; from the corner of Red's eye, it looked like the twigs curled inward, fingers toward a fist. "Like a pool of black mud, either on its own or around a white tree, if we get to it quick enough. A place where the Wilderwood didn't hold strong enough and the Shadowlands pushed through."

"I think I may have seen one." The ring of darkness around the rotting white tree she'd seen when she crossed the border, the one at the very edge of the Wilderwood—that matched Eammon's description. "When I first…first arrived."

"Probably." It was terse. "They aren't exactly uncommon anymore."

Red carefully stepped over knotting roots, around strange flowers and reaching thorns as she followed the Wolf through the shadows of the Wilderwood. She could almost hear the forest *breathe*, hear it in the rustle of branches and the slither of vines, and her skin prickled with the sense of being watched. This forest was alive, alive and sentient.

She stepped closer to Eammon's back again.

His outstretched arm was next to invisible in the gloom, and Red ran right into it, a line of solid warmth across her chest. Her feet skidded on leaves, and she grabbed his hand to steady herself. His scars were rough under her fingers before he pulled away, shooting her a dark, unfathomable look.

A white tree stretched into the deep-violet sky before them, wide enough that three people couldn't hold hands around it, crowned with bone-white branches. Its roots cut through the earth, threaded with black, shadowy rot, the infection climbing the trunk like rising floodwater. In a perfect circle around the roots, the earth was dark and soft, spongy, like long-dead flesh.

"Far gone," Eammon said under his breath, "but at least we got to it before the sentinel ended up at the Keep." He stepped up to the ring of infected ground, fingers twitching toward the dagger at his belt, as if checking to make sure it was still there. "Stay back," he ordered as he crouched at the dark edge of the rot. "Do *not* move."

Red nodded. She might not trust him, not quite yet, but that wasn't enough to make her venture into the Wilderwood alone.

The Wolf reached for the dagger again, but his fingers faltered this time. "Too much blood today already," he muttered to himself, drawing his hand away from the blade with a sigh. His head tipped forward, eyes closing. "Magic it is, then. Dammit."

Eammon pushed up his sleeves, and in the dim, Red thought she saw an etching of green along the veins of his forearm, deepening as he took a breath, fading as he let it out. Slowly, some of the tightness in his shoulders bled away.

She hadn't noticed just how tense he looked until she saw him relaxed—like he'd carried a heavy burden, and now laid it down.

Nothing moved, but Red felt as if the Wilderwood leaned closer. She crossed her arms, warily eyeing the trees. Earlier, when she'd pelted through them fear-blind and bloody, she'd had the sense of the forest as something shackled, held back.

Now she had the sense of shackles loosening.

Eammon placed his hands right at the edge of the breach, fingertips a hairbreadth away from the spongy, rotten ground. His head bowed forward, all his concentration diverted to the task at hand. Another flaring of green in his veins, this time in his neck as well as his forearms. Something dark edged through the skin of his wrists, right above the bone. It looked almost like bark.

So distracted was she by the changes, Red didn't notice the root snaking out of the underbrush until it hooked around her ankle.

Her startled cry was quick and strangled as she hit the ground, shins barking against rocks and raised roots. Vines studded in thorns wrapped her viper-quick, tying her to the forest floor. Deep in Red's chest, the shard of magic the forest had left in her bloomed steadily, inexorably outward.

The Wilderwood hesitated a moment, all those white trees poised and waiting. Then they dove.

The thorns lashing Red down bit deep, bringing up blood. White roots burst from the ground around her, arched toward the ragged wounds the thorns opened in her skin. She screamed, pain and fear ripping through the silent forest.

"Redarys!"

Eammon stumbled up from the ground, legs unsteady, like whatever he'd been doing at the edge of the shadow-pit had left him a husk. Panic shone in his eyes, the whites of them once again tinted green, the veins in his fingers blazing emerald as he fumbled for the dagger at his belt. "Hold on, I—"

The Wilderwood drowned him out, shrilling triumphantly in a voice of cracking branches. The vines shackling Red opened new blooms, wide and pale in the unnatural twilight; the leaves beneath her blushed from faded autumn to summer-bright as her veins ran green and her mouth filled with the taste of earth. The splinter of magic in her middle grew up and out, stretching greedily toward the hungry white trees.

She thought of Gaya, root-riddled, consumed. Kaldenore, Sayetha, Merra, three more this forest had drained. It'd take what it needed and damn what was left, unless she found a way to stop it, to contain it, to cut it off—

With an inner strength born of distilled panic, Red took hold of the magic rushing out of her and *snapped*.

The forest exploded outward with a bone-rattling *boom*. Roots and branches and thorns skittered as Red shoved her magic down. It was painful, this denying, making herself a cage for a wild thing, but still she pushed it away, hiding it deep. Bound, banished, slashed off like her will was a knife.

The dirt-taste faded from her tongue; the veins in her wrist ran from verdant green to blue. The Wilderwood screamed, one more keening sound, then was silent.

She expected desolation when her eyes opened, but there was none, no torn limbs or felled trees. The Wilderwood stood still as a stunned animal. Red pushed up on shaky legs, dirt falling from her torn skirt, from her borrowed coat.

Eammon's eyes were wide, the dagger held loose and forgotten in his hand. "What was *that*?"

"Don't act like you don't know, not when I just saw you try to use it." The way his veins greened was near a mirror to hers. "*Power.* Power from this *fucking* forest. You were there when I got it. You were there when…when it took hold of me, that night. I saw you."

The panic in Eammon's eyes bloomed slowly into horror. "No," he whispered, shaking his head. "I…I tried to stop it, I thought I stopped it from—"

A deep rumble cut him off, coming from the white roots cutting through rotten ground. It struck them both into silence, eyes locking to the tree.

"Shit." Eammon flipped the dagger around in his fist, shoving her behind him with the other hand. "*Shit.*"

He didn't go to the edge of the breach again, didn't try to call up whatever arcane forest magic he'd used before. Instead he sliced into his palm, a moment of such nonchalant and unexpected violence that Red flinched.

But he wasn't fast enough.

The edges of the shadow-pit receded with unnatural quickness, like water draining from the bottom of a pierced bowl. Rot drained into the tree roots, turning them pitch-dark, climbing up the white trunk and covering it almost completely in churning corruption.

Eammon lunged toward the tree, bleeding fist outstretched. But before he could reach it, the last bit of darkness drained from the dirt into the roots, and the ground around them erupted. Sharp twigs and leaves shot into the air, all tinged with shadowy black, throwing Eammon backward and away from the trunk as rot surged up almost to the branches.

Red crouched, arms thrown protectively over her head. The tree, now fully rotted, slowly began to sink into the ground.

Around them, the rest of the Wilderwood watched, still and silent and somehow mournful.

With the same terrible, unnatural quickness, the shadow-touched forest detritus cobbled itself together, knitting a body out of ruin. Old bones tugged free of the forest floor, some animal, some human, some too strange-shaped to be either, all corrupted with threads of shadow that seeped up from the roots of the sinking tree.

This was it, Red knew, in the quiet part of her mind that seemed to float above her fear. Here was the shadowed monster from the fairy tale, facing off against a man changed by a forest. It was real, all of it was real.

When the chaotic roiling of bones and darkness and growing things stopped, a woman stood in its place.

Her hair was long and dark, her eyes an acidic emerald. She smiled, and mushrooms sprouted between her teeth. "You think this time will be any different?" The voice sounded nothing like a human. It was deep and somehow creeping, oscillating in the air, the lowest string plucked on an untuned harp. "This story has played out over and over again. It's such fun watching from below, but it always comes to the same conclusion. You aren't strong enough, Wolf-pup. Just like your father."

Eammon bent half double, his seeping hand pressed against his battered ribs, the other brandishing the still-bloody dagger toward the creature. His breath rattled in and out of his lungs, his teeth glinting in the unchanging twilight.

The forest-and-shadow woman moved the blade aside with an almost-gentle finger, careful not to touch his blood. Lichen grew from her nailbeds. "It gets harder and harder to hold on to yourself, doesn't it? The magic crowds you out, so you open a vein instead. But you can't bleed enough to hold it off forever. Can't bleed enough to keep the Shadowlands closed, can't bleed enough to keep everything trapped." The thing turned its eyes toward Red, soil dripping like tears down moss-scabbed cheeks. "This ends in roots and bones. For all of you. It always ends in roots and bones."

Suddenly the specter of the girl changed. In an instant, she was prostrate on the ground, the terrible pieces that made her hidden away. Instead she looked like a corpse, the regular corpse of a young woman.

Red recognized her, though it took a moment. She'd seen the portrait in one of the books in the library.

Merra.

A blink, and Merra's stomach ripped, the sound visceral enough to make Red's gorge rise. Tree roots spilled from the hole, flowing out of the bloody cavity in a mess of gore.

Merra's corpse stayed still a moment. Then it let loose a sound that could've been a cackle or a scream, standing again, hands outstretched toward Eammon in a posture of near-surrender. Skin decayed into forest; moss ate at fingers formed of wrong bones.

It shook Eammon loose from whatever horror had held him frozen. Mouth twisted, he lurched forward, swiping at the creature not with the dagger but with his bleeding hand. The girl-shaped thing laughed again, a thin, reedy sound this time, and crumbled apart at his blow. Eammon turned and rushed toward the tree, running over raised roots like stones in a river, dagger slicing into his palm anew.

But the creature wasn't gone, not yet—like as long as the breach remained open, it could regenerate itself. It melted out of Merra's shape, churning its bones and leaves to make amalgamations of more faces, half forming and falling away. One feminine, heart-shaped, sweetness turned to terrible. Another narrow-chinned and full-lipped. A woman with Eammon's amber eyes, a man with his angular jaw.

"Why even try?" The thing turned to watch Eammon, making sure he saw every facet of its changing face. "A forest in your bones, a graveyard beneath your feet. There are no heroes here."

Eammon snarled, teeth bared as his palm wept the same too-dark, green-threaded blood Red had seen when he took her wound in the library. He slapped his hand against the tree trunk, pressed until blood seeped between his fingers, dripped down his knuckles. The tree was half sunken now, the branches nearly scraping the top of his head.

Slowly, the rot receded, fading down the tree and back into its roots, like Eammon's blood was something it had to escape, then out of the roots and back into the ground. The sinking reversed as the rot disappeared, the tree righting itself by incremental degrees. Eammon bled and bled, his eyes closing, knees beginning to buckle.

The creature twitched, melting as the tree regrew, features running back into forest and shadow. "You know what happens to heroes, Wolf-pup?" The thing reared back, no longer trying at human shapes, just a lick of darkness studded in bones and twigs. "They *die*."

Eammon's eyes opened as the creature surged forward. He turned and slammed into it with his bleeding palm.

The thing pooled into the spongy, rotten dirt. Eammon kept his hand pressed against it as it shrank down, jaw clenched like holding it there took monumental effort, the rot on the ground disappearing at the same rate as the white tree behind him grew. Finally, the creature disappeared into the earth, and Eammon's hand touched only the forest floor. The cuts on his palms didn't drip when he lifted them away from the now-healed breach.

Still kneeling, Eammon looked up, met Red's eyes. For a moment that felt like years, they stared across the gulf between them, and neither had the words to fill it.

Eammon stood on shaking legs. He edged past her, careful not to touch, and stalked into the Wilderwood.

Red stood gape-mouthed, staring at the now-healed tree. The rot was gone, chased out by Eammon's blood. But when she looked down at the roots cutting through the ground, she thought she could see minuscule threads of darkness already creeping back up the pale bark. The Shadowlands, pressing through again.

She whirled, following the Wolf into the gloom.

He didn't speak, their silence growing colder the longer it lingered. Red pulled his coat around her again, wafting the scent of books and coffee and leaves. "Who was that?"

"A shadow-creature. The breach got big enough for it to slip through. Ten minutes, and that sentinel tree would've shown up as a sapling at the Keep, and it would've needed far more blood to send it back to where it's supposed to be. Healing them before they move is far easier, if you can catch them."

He was rambling, trying to change the nature of her question by overwhelming it with other answers. "You know what I mean." Red picked at the hem of his coat. "I recognized Merra. Who were the others?"

A long moment of silence, long enough to make her wonder if he'd answer her true question at all. When he did, his voice was clarion-clear and stripped of emotion. "Kaldenore," he said, finally. "Then Sayetha. Then Gaya. Then Ciaran."

A parade of death. Red bit her lip. "The Second Daughters, and... and Gaya... the Wilderwood drained them."

He nodded, one jerk of his chin.

"What about Ciaran?" She kept it to names, not titles. If Eammon avoided saying *mother* and *father*, she assumed it best if she did, too.

The Wolf pushed aside a branch from the path, harshly enough that it nearly cracked. "Wilderwood drained him, too."

The gate rose out of the fog; Eammon laced his fingers through the bars, nearly leaning against them as the opening bloomed. He paused for a moment when the iron swung inward, as if he had to gather the energy to step forward. *Too much blood*, he'd said before, and he moved like it.

When the gate was safely sealed behind them, Eammon turned, eyes glinting. "Back there," he said carefully. "When the Wilderwood... came for you. How did you make it stop?"

"The same way I've been doing for four years." She wanted it to come out accusing, but it was thin and hollow in the cold air. Red avoided his eyes, staring instead at a hole one of the thorns had torn in the sleeve of his coat.

"The Wilderwood had you. I didn't get to you in time." She couldn't tell if he meant it as a confession or an accusation. "It's desperate enough that it should've drained you in moments, but it didn't, because *you* stopped it. You're going to have to give me specifics, Redarys."

"I don't *know* specifics! Ever since my sixteenth birthday, when I came here and cut my hand and bled in the forest, I've had this... this *thing*, inside, like a piece of power I'm not supposed to have, something that makes plants and growing things act strange around me. Sometimes I can hold it back, but sometimes I can't, and when I can't, bad things happen!"

"Plants and growing things. Things with roots, under the Wilderwood's influence." Eammon's face was drawn into pale, tight lines, his voice canted low, as if he was working through some difficult equation aloud. A thoughtful hand rubbed over his jaw; he looked up, addressing her again. "When you first entered the forest today," he said, words strung as deftly as beads on a bracelet, "you said a thorn cut your cheek. Did you mean—"

"When I crossed the border, I ended up with my hands in the dirt. I don't know how, I don't remember doing it, but it clearly had something to do with this power." Even saying it now made Red shiver, thinking of movements she didn't choose to make. "But I stopped whatever it was trying to do. I didn't let the magic out, I kept it contained, and it stopped. That's all I did this time, too. Keep it contained."

A strange grief shone in Eammon's eyes, a regret she couldn't quite make sense of. "I don't understand," he murmured. "I thought—"

"You don't *understand*? I saw you the night it happened! You're *part* of it! I saw your hands when it all rushed in, right before it stopped!"

That changed him, altered the harsh line of his jaw and the wounded light in his eyes. "It stopped." As if the words had been the scaffolding that held him fast, his shoulders dropped, relief in their shape. "I stopped it from happening."

"Stopped *what* from happening?"

Eammon didn't answer, gaze on the ground as he pulled in a deep breath. "I couldn't keep it from you entirely. But I stopped what mattered. I kept it from..." He trailed off into silence, hand passing over his face, leaving a streak of green-and-scarlet blood across one cheekbone. "It could be different this time."

Red gritted her teeth. "What do you mean?"

"Your power. It's a piece of the Wilderwood. Part of it making a home in you."

"I gathered."

"I understand wanting to hold it back, to push it away. But if you learned to use it, maybe the Wilderwood wouldn't have to...to take anything else." Hope was a barb in his voice, something that could cut. "Maybe it would be enough, just for you to use what you have already."

"I don't understand. The Wilderwood wants to *take* something?" She swallowed past the lump in her throat. "It hasn't taken enough already?"

"You don't need to worry about that." His voice was the steadiest it'd been since fighting the monster at the tree. It was almost enough to make her believe him. "All you should concern yourself with now is learning to use the magic the Wilderwood has already given you."

"I can't use it." Red barked a laugh, another plume of smoke into the twilight air. "Maybe *you* can, but I can't."

"If you can control the power enough to keep it contained, you can control it enough to turn it to your will." The Wolf rubbed at his jaw again, thinking. "I'll have to figure out the particulars—"

"*Figure out the particulars*? You don't even know how it *works*? But you just—"

"This is different. *You're* different. The others... they were connected to the Wilderwood, too, but not like this." Again, that knifepoint hope, so raw it nearly hurt to hear. "This could fix it."

It should've been comforting, that she was different from the Second Daughters who came before. Different from the three women the Wilderwood had consumed. But all Red could think of was blood and branches and the slumped body of her sister, a four-year-old memory still fresh as the day it happened.

The taste of dirt was still in her mouth, no matter how much she swallowed. Red shook her head. "It's dangerous," she murmured. "It's not something that can be *used*."

"We don't have much of a choice." Eammon finally stopped fidgeting, peering at her sternly down his twice-broken nose. "I will do my best to keep you safe from the Wilderwood, Redarys, but you're going to have to help. I can't do it alone. I've tried."

That awful, echoing voice thrumming through the fog. *You can't bleed enough to hold it off forever.*

He watched her, in that quiet courtyard under a starless sky, and Red had to drop her eyes from his. The ache there was too sharp, pain and weight she couldn't put words to. She thought he probably couldn't, either.

After a moment, the Wolf turned toward the Keep. Wordlessly, Red followed.

Eammon stopped just inside the door. His face was carefully neutral, but his eyes still sparked. "Are you satisfied, then?" A twitch of scarred hands. "Did I give you reason enough to trust me?"

Red nodded.

The Wolf stalked up the stone staircase. Behind him, the moss and twigs rose, blocking the way, closing him in.

Valleydan Interlude II

The book wasn't where it was supposed to be.

Neve frowned at the paper in her hand, a reference with author name and shelf number. It was a book of poetry she was after, one written by a trader who had a rhyming system for navigating Ciani rivers. Not exactly a popular item. It was forbidden to take things completely out of the library, anyway, though Red did it all the time—

She stopped, pressed a hand against her stomach at the sudden ache. *Kings*, she had to stop doing that. Thinking of Red as if she were still here. It'd been only a day, but every hour felt like a dagger.

Tears burned behind her eyes, too sharp to fall.

"What if we *didn't* visit with the venerable Master Matheus today?" Behind her, Raffe twisted her vacated chair, straddling the seat and folding muscular arms over the ornately carved back. "What if, instead, we did... literally anything else?"

Had it been anyone other than Raffe, Neve would've snapped at them to leave her be. As it was, the grin she cracked was half genuine, though exhaustion made the edges pull down. After her ill-fated trip to the Shrine, she hadn't slept much. "I assume by *not visiting*, you mean we should skip his lecture on southern weather patterns and their effects on imports?"

Valleyda was at the very top of the continent, landlocked, with the Wilderwood to the north, the Alperan Wastes to the east, and Floriane blocking the way to the western coast. It made trading a nightmare, but that was why Valleyda was the best place to learn about it—they'd thought through to the bottom of any commerce issues one might encounter, because they'd encountered all of them.

Valleyda's only power was in religion, in sharing a border with the Wilderwood and being locked into the Second Daughter tithe that protected the world from monsters, but it at least led to most countries being willing to offer fair prices. No one wanted to anger the Kings by cheating the kingdom that might one day provide the sacrifice to set them free, or sour the prayers they paid for from the Temple.

Still, crop scarcity would always be a fear, especially when the passes blocking Valleyda from Meducia and Alpera froze so early in the year. Neve's marriage to Arick was mostly to lock in a sea route, making Floriane a province and providing Valleyda with unfettered access to its coastline.

The tired grin on Neve's face became slightly harder to hold.

"Precisely what I mean," Raffe answered. "I find I can't summon a shred of enthusiasm for the subject of commerce at present." The late-afternoon light through the window teased muted gold highlights along his long, elegant fingers.

Neve pressed her lips together. She spent far too much time watching Raffe's hands.

"It's summer," he continued, "or as close to it as it gets around here. Forgoing one droning diatribe won't kill my father's business. And if it does... well." A shrug. "I'm not terribly worried about it."

Neve dropped into the chair across from him. "What if you didn't have to worry about it at all?" She picked at the wrinkled reference paper, tearing it into a tiny snowdrift. "If you didn't have a business to run, trade routes to learn. What if you could do anything?"

Raffe's playful smile fell a fraction, handsome features turning introspective. "Well, there's a question." His gaze strayed to her hands on the table.

Warmth rushed to Neve's cheeks. She couldn't deny an attraction to Raffe—she didn't think *anyone* could; the man was handsome as a fairy-tale prince and had the kindness and charm to go with it—but nothing could happen between them, not with her betrothal cemented. Still, that didn't stop the *want*, and it didn't stop the simple pleasure of knowing that her wanting was returned.

Raffe settled his chin on his arms, dark eyes curious as they flickered from her hands to her face. "What about you? If you could go anywhere, where would you go?"

Her answer came instantly, and it banished all the warmth his eyes had brought her, replaced it with an inexpressible ache. "I'd go find my sister."

A line drew between Raffe's brows. When he spoke, it was on the end of a sigh. "You did all you could for her, Neve."

She had, and it wasn't enough.

"It isn't your fault."

Then whose was it? Fate twisted one way, and Neve was born first. None of it was fair, and none of it was right, and she should've tried harder to change it. Should've done something other than beg Red to run, long after it became clear she wouldn't.

Raffe's hand stretched out. It hovered over hers, a moment's hesitation, before his fingers settled across her wrist. He was warm, so warm, almost enough to call her out of the cold place she retreated to inside herself, where she could grow numb and distant. She'd spent a lot of time there, recently. Numb and hollow was better than raw and hurting.

"You have to stop blaming yourself, Neve. She made a choice. The least we can do is honor it." He paused, swallowed. "Honor her memory."

Memory. The word slashed her open. "She isn't dead, Raffe."

She thought of what the red-haired priestess in the Shrine had told her, what had happened to Red when she crossed into the Wilderwood. Tangled in the forest, bound to it. It'd been at the back of Neve's mind all day—her sister threaded with vines, fodder for a ravenous wood.

But alive.

And hadn't part of her known that? She would've felt it if Red died. There would've been something, some sort of absence, and Neve still felt horribly whole.

Raffe didn't dispute her. Still, there was nothing like faith in his eyes, and the thought of trying to explain it to him, to put the thing into words, was exhausting.

So Neve pulled in a deep breath, measured it so it wouldn't shudder. "The gardens," she said, pasting on a smile. "Not exactly exciting, but it's somewhere to go."

"Better than lessons." Raffe stood, gallantly offered his arm. "Will Arick be joining us?"

He said it lightly, but there was worry in his tone. Neve's pasted smile fell. "No." She threaded her arm through his. "Honestly, I'm not sure where Arick is." She hadn't seen him since they returned from the Wilderwood, the three of them packed into one black carriage, lost in separate silences. Neve remembered thinking that was the only thing redeeming in the whole day, the whole *year.* If they had to lose Red, at least they could sit with the loss together, find a way to hold it together.

But then Arick slunk off to lick his wounds alone.

Raffe sighed. "Me either."

She squeezed his arm, unspoken comfort. Then the two of them drifted through the library doors out into a sun-filled hall.

Neve wasn't exactly sure why she'd suggested the gardens. She and the red-haired priestess had cleared the mess she'd made, and she'd assured Neve no one would notice. Still, it was probably wise for Neve to keep a wide berth of the Shrine, at least for a few days. But she felt drawn out there, like probing a bruise to see how badly she could make it hurt.

As they turned the corner, the glass double doors to the gardens opened, emitting a procession of white-robed Order priestesses.

Most of them had left by now. After the midnight vigils, when it became clear the Kings weren't returning, the priestesses who'd traveled to see Red's sacrifice departed, back to their own less revered Temples. Neve had seen them file out of the Shrine that morning, after she'd woken from scant hours of broken sleep, the remnants of scarlet candles in their hands as the sun blushed the sky.

The vigil stopped at sunrise and it was now well past noon, but this group of priestesses had the dark-circled eyes of people just released from prayer. There weren't many of them, fewer than twenty arranged in double lines. At their front, a tall, thin woman with ember-colored hair.

The priestess from last night. Her odd branch-shard necklace was nowhere to be seen.

Neve didn't recognize all the faces with her—some of them didn't hail from Valleyda, must've stayed behind when the rest of their sisters departed. The fact made a vague, unformed disquiet coil in her chest.

The red-haired priestess's eyes flickered over her, but she showed no sign of recognition. Instead she turned and spoke with one of the other sisters behind her, too low for Neve to hear, before walking away down a different branching corridor.

Relief made her stomach swoop, though she wasn't quite sure why. Still, Neve frowned after the redhead. The only thing down that hallway was another door into the gardens, and hadn't she just come from there?

The rest of the priestesses walked slowly past them, and Neve moved on instinct. She grabbed the closest one's arm in a grip tight enough to bruise.

"*Neve*," Raffe whispered.

To her credit, the priestess showed no emotion other than a widening of her eyes. "Highness?"

"What were you doing out there?" Neve had no patience for pleasantries, not today. "The vigils are over. Clearly, the Kings aren't returning."

Halfway to blasphemy, but again, all she got was a slight widening of eyes. "The official vigils are over, yes," the priestess conceded. "But a small number of us have kept up our prayers."

"Why?" It was nearly a snarl. "Why keep praying to something that doesn't hear you? Your gods aren't coming back."

Oh, she was fully heretical now, but Neve couldn't bring herself to care. Beside her, Raffe stood rock-still.

The priestess smiled mildly, as if the First Daughter of Valleyda wasn't seconds from clapping hands around her throat. "Perhaps not. The Wilderwood holds them fast." A pause. "Help may be required for it to let them go."

Words from last night slithered in Neve's mind, like pieces of a dream. *The Wilderwood is only as strong as we let it be.*

Confusion cooled her anger, made her clenching fingers fall open. Unfazed, the priestess inclined her head, a movement echoed by the others behind her. Then they glided away.

"Well, *that* will end poorly." Raffe ran a nervous hand over his mouth. "She's going to tell the High Priestess—"

"She won't." Neve knew it. The same way she knew the redheaded priestess wouldn't tell anyone she'd wrecked the Shrine. Something about that branch-shard necklace, the way they spoke of the Wilderwood almost as an enemy rather than a holy site, told her that nothing about this would ever reach Zophia's ears.

Raffe looked at her through narrowed eyes but remained silent.

Gently, Neve pulled her arm from his and walked to the double glass doors of the garden. She didn't look to see if Raffe followed, but she heard the clip of his boots across the floor, heard him shut the doors behind her.

When they were outside, Raffe took a deep breath, rubbing a hand over his close-shorn hair. "Listen. I know you're upset—"

"They sacrificed her." Neve turned, chin tilted. Raffe was closer than she'd thought, his full lips only inches away. Her breath felt like a razor. "They sacrificed her for *nothing*."

"Maybe it wasn't for nothing, even without the Kings returning." He said it carefully, a blade to carve a silver lining. "The tale of the monsters, before Kaldenore—"

"It's horseshit, Raffe. If the monsters were real, we would've seen them that night."

No need to clarify *which* night. The night of rocks and matches and a Wilderwood impervious to both. The night of the men that followed them, that were horribly slain by... by something.

Neve didn't actually remember most of it, after the thieves arrived. She'd passed out when one of them hit her in the temple with a dagger hilt, and hadn't woken up until they were back in the capital and under heavy guard.

But Red remembered. And Red thought it was her fault.

Guilt iced her spine, guilt and cold certainty. Whatever had happened, whatever Neve couldn't remember, was part of what drove her sister into the Wilderwood.

"It was for nothing," she repeated softly.

This time, Raffe had no response.

Neve walked down the path, trailing her fingers over the blooming hedges, letting the points of sharp leaves catch her skin. One pricked hard enough to bring a bead of blood to her fingertip.

Behind her, a sigh. Raffe's footsteps echoed on the stone as he walked away.

She closed her eyes against early-summer sun, the light illuminating veins and capillaries, making her vision look veiled in blood.

"What about a bargain?" The voice was hushed and hoarse, like the speaker hadn't had a decent night's sleep in a week. There was something familiar in it, but it was too quiet to be sure.

The voice came from beside her, hidden in a bower of wide pink blooms—clearly, this conversation wasn't meant to be overheard.

But Neve didn't move.

"Impossible." This second voice was brusque, vowels clipped and precise. Also familiar. "The Wilderwood has twisted, its power has grown weak. It will no longer accept paltry things like teeth and nail clippings. Not even blood, if it's not from a fresh wound."

There was something leading in the tone. As if meaning hid behind the words, things implied rather than spoken.

That tone locked the familiarity into place. The red-haired priestess.

"No," the priestess continued. "A dead sacrifice will no longer do. It would require more, if it could be accomplished at all, a heavier price both in the bargaining and in the aftermath. Our prayers have told us so." A pause, then, cadenced like a litany: "Blood that has been used in bargains with things beneath is blood that can open doors."

Neve's brow furrowed, but the other voice sounded too distraught to try to puzzle out the cryptic nonsense. "There *has* to be a way."

"If there is, dear boy," the priestess murmured, "you must be prepared to give, and keep giving." A pause. "The Kings take much, but they give much in return. Serving them brings opportunity to your door. I know."

A rustle as someone stood from the bench hidden in the blooms. Cursing silently, Neve spun away, tried to make it seem like she'd been absorbed in examining a flower bed on the other side of the path.

From the corner of her eye, a flash of white. "Do come to me with any further questions," the priestess said. "Our prayers this morning, after our less dedicated sisters left, proved most... insightful."

A disheveled-looking boy stepped out from behind her. "I will. Thank you, Kiri."

Neve froze, fingers on a wide yellow bloom.

Arick.

The priestess—Kiri, she finally knew her name now—looked once at Neve. Her smile was cold as she dipped a nod and glided back toward the castle.

If he was surprised by her presence, he didn't show it. Arick ran a hand through hair that looked like it hadn't been combed in a week. "Neve."

"Arick." A stone-heavy second of quiet. "We've been worried about you."

The worry was well earned, it seemed. His face was pale and drawn, hollows carved beneath his green eyes. He jerked his head toward the flowering trees and disappeared.

Neve cast a look around before ducking beneath the boughs, though it was ridiculous to fear being caught—he would be her Consort, after all. Cementing that sea route for Valleydan trade through Floriane.

A dull ache started in her temples.

Neve pushed aside pink blooms, revealing Arick already sitting on the bench beneath the arbor. The wan look of him, waxen skin and shadowed eyes, was incongruous against the backdrop of flowers.

He said nothing as she settled beside him, the bench so small she couldn't help the press of their legs. They'd been easy friends before sixteen and betrothal, and even after, when Red was still here, a buffer between them and the inevitable future. Now she didn't know how to act.

She shifted on the bench. "How are you?"

"Not well."

"Me either."

Silence bloomed around them. No words felt right. All she and Arick had in common was grief, and how could you build a conversation on that, much less a life?

"I tried." Arick leaned forward, running both hands through his already-wild hair. "The night of the ball, I tried to get her to run."

"We all tried. She wouldn't listen."

"There has to be a way to get her back."

Neve chewed her lip, thinking back over the conversation she'd overheard. Thinking of who he'd been having it with, and of ruined shrines and bark shards. "Arick," she said carefully, "I don't want you to do anything foolish."

"More foolish than running to the Wilderwood to throw rocks at the trees?" There was a ghost of levity in his voice.

She smiled to hear it, though it was a tired, faded thing. "I suppose I'm not one to talk." In more ways than he knew.

Arick's shoulders slumped, the momentary lightness gone as soon as it had come. "I'm going to find a way to bring her home."

Neve glanced at him sidelong. She knew he loved Red. But she also knew Red didn't love him and never had. She'd certainly cared for him, but her sister hadn't wanted to shatter any more lives than she had to when she crossed into the trees. And though Arick's feelings went deeper, he'd seemed to understand. Neve had expected his mourning, but she'd expected it to pass quickly. Arick was resilient.

"I know you thought I'd get over it," Arick said, as if her thoughts were something he could see in the air above her head.

"That makes me sound cruel," she murmured.

"I don't mean it that way. I just mean..." A sigh. "Things have gone easily for me, Neve. Mostly because I've let them. I've never fought for anything, never taken a path that offered any great resistance, because I wanted things to be *easy*." His teeth gnashed on the word. "But I can't just let this go. If there's anything worth fighting for, it's her. And not even because I love her. Just because... because it isn't right. She deserves a life, too."

The sliver of hope in Neve's chest was a splinter, small and mean and terribly *bright*, sharpening her grief to a razor-edge. She didn't know how to articulate it, not with all the added complications of her and Arick and Raffe and the tangled threads connecting them, priestesses with strange necklaces and ruined white trees in a stone room.

"Good," she replied, because it was the closest thing she could shape that barbed hope into.

He looked at her, nearly surprised, then relief softened the tendons in his neck. Like he'd been waiting for her benediction. "I'll be gone for a while," Arick said. "Didn't want you to worry."

"Back to Floriane?"

No answer. After a moment, Arick stood. He offered his hand.

Neve took it, let him help her up, though her brow stayed furrowed. Arick's green eyes searched hers, lips twisted. Then he pressed a quick kiss to her forehead.

"I'll be back soon," he whispered. "I'll find a way to save her, Neve." He slipped out of the flowered trees.

Neve stood beneath the boughs for a long time, skin tingling where his lips had brushed. A slow, vague guilt closed crushing hands around her throat, like she'd unknowingly passed down some kind of sentencing.

But Red was alive. And they had to find a way to save her.

Chapter Nine

The unchanging light made it impossible to know how much time had passed when Red woke, head fuzzy and aching. For a moment, she didn't remember where she was. When she did, it only made the aching worse.

She sat up, middle twisting. In the chaos of the night before, she'd completely forgotten to ask about food. Now her empty stomach gnawed at her spine.

Eammon's coat hung on the hook inside the door, thorn-slashed and muddy. Red peered at it with her lip between her teeth, then threw a wary glance at the vines pressing against the window. For now, at least, they were still.

The water in her tub was clean, but still freezing. She washed quickly, pulled on a gown—midnight blue this time—and stood in the center of her room, somewhat at a loss for what to do now.

Here was her new life, as vast and dark and featureless as the forest that held it.

No. Red shook her head. She couldn't fall into despondency now, not when she'd lived in spite of every expectation. This new life might be strange, but she *had* it, and that was a miracle in itself.

She hadn't run away, despite all of Neve's begging. But she'd lived anyway. And she owed it to her sister to make something of that.

Another rumble of her stomach pulled her mind away from the

shapeless stretch of a day she'd never expected to see. "Food," she declared. Brows set in determination, Red wrenched open the door.

A tray sat on the mossy floor past her threshold. The toast was burnt, slathered liberally with butter, next to a mug of black coffee. Both were hot, but whoever—or whatever—had brought them was long gone. Nothing moved in the main hall but drifting dust, and the leaves at the corridor's end didn't stir.

Red was too hungry to care about where breakfast came from. She sat with her back against the mossy wall and ate the toast in three bites. The almost-ash crust tasted better than anything she'd ever eaten in Valleyda.

The coffee was strong, and Red sipped it slowly, wondering if whoever brought the food would return. Probably one of the other voices she'd heard talking to Eammon last night. She had a hard time imagining the Wolf cooking.

The wreckage at the end of the corridor looked different. Yesterday there'd been only flowering bushes and moss, broken rocks and roots. Now one thin, pin-straight sapling rose from the tangle, reaching almost to the ceiling.

Coffee sloshed over the lip of Red's mug as she scrambled up, burning her fingers. The sapling stood tall and still, with no sign of shadowy corruption on its bark. Not like the tree last night, rotted and listing in a pool of spongy dark ground.

What was it Eammon said? Something about how if one of the white trees in the forest—*sentinel trees*, she remembered now, he'd called them sentinel trees—was infected badly enough with rot, it would leave its place, show up in the Keep?

The sentinel stood silent, thin and pale as a specter in the gloom. Not where it was supposed to be, but not an immediate threat, either. Still, the memory of them opening trunks to bare wood-shard teeth was fresh, and Red kept a wary eye on it as she rolled her now-empty mug between her hands and backed down the hall.

The foyer stood echoing and empty, dust motes dancing in seams of twilight beneath the cracked window. Other than the dust, Red was alone.

Then the door opened.

She crouched like she'd hide herself in the mossy remnants of carpet as the weathered wood swung wide, weak lavender light outlining a slight, feminine form with a cloud of curls and a curved blade in her hand. Something dripped off its sharpened edge, a mix of sap and what looked like blood.

The woman stopped, narrowing dark eyes in a brown-skinned, delicately featured face. "Redarys?"

The musical voice from last night, the one she'd heard speaking to Eammon. Apparently from a human throat. Sheepishly, Red straightened, cheeks coloring. "I...ah..." she stuttered, hands waving uselessly, halfway to a curtsy before she realized that was probably ludicrous. "Yes. That's me."

The other woman snorted, but she cracked the corner of a bright smile. "I figured the chances were good. I'm Lyra." She stepped farther into the foyer, pulling a cloth from a small leather bag at her waist and scrubbing it along the bloody edge of the blade as the door closed behind her. Without the glare, the blood on her clothing was obvious, her white shirt and dark leggings nearly covered with still-wet copper, tendrils of shadowy rot, and tar-like sap.

Red made an involuntary gulping sound. "Are you all right? Kings, how are you *walking*?"

Lyra looked confused for a moment, then followed Red's gaze. "Oh, that. Don't worry, Eammon is the only one who slices himself up on the spot—he's the Wolf, all tangled up in the Wilderwood, so it likes his blood straight from the vein. It isn't as picky about the rest of us." Lyra tugged a small vial from her pocket. Deep-scarlet liquid sloshed as she wiggled it in the air. "I used at least five of these," she said, like it was an explanation of some kind. "Lots of shadow-creatures out today. I needed to come back and replenish my supply." She grimaced, starting toward the broken archway and the sunken room beyond. "Probably change clothes, too."

Confusion replaced Red's alarm, drawing her brows together. She followed Lyra into the room. "That's *your* blood?"

"Of course." Lyra shrugged. "Might be Fife's, actually. We both have the Mark, so blood from either of us will work on a shadow-creature." She pushed open the small door at the back of the room, revealing a tiny kitchen. "Our blood can hold saplings steady for a day or so and slightly help with rotting sentinels, too, but it won't do shit for breaches."

Weathered-looking wooden cabinets lined the back wall, with a small woodstove in the corner and a scuffed table. Lyra went to the cabinet nearest the stove and pulled it open. Inside, rows upon rows of glass vials, all filled with blood. Deep crimson with no trace of green, not like Eammon's.

Red sank into one of the chairs at the table, her thoughts snaring, knotted as old thread. Last night, when Eammon fought the corpse-bone-forest-thing... *shadow-creature, monster of legend,* Kings, *it's all real*... his blood had been what finally brought it down. Apparently, Lyra—and Fife, whoever that was, presumably the other voice she'd heard—could use their blood to fight shadow-creatures, too.

But when Red bled in the Wilderwood, it attacked her. Those white trees became predators. Was it because she was a Second Daughter, something about her blood and the bargain it was tangled with making the forest treat her differently?

And who *were* Fife and Lyra, anyway? The myths didn't mention anyone else living in the Wilderwood.

"You said you have a Mark?" Her question interrupted the *clink* of vials as Lyra stuck handfuls of them in her bag.

"Anyone who's bargained with the Wilderwood has one." Lyra paused in her packing to push up her sleeve. There, in the same place as Red's—a tiny ring of root, just beneath the skin. It was smaller than Red's Mark, the tendrils not reaching quite so far, but unmistakably the same.

Lyra tugged her sleeve back down. "A tiny piece of the Wilderwood. That's why my blood and Fife's work against shadow-creatures—the power of the forest cancels out the power of the Shadowlands."

"And the Wolf's blood, too?"

"The Wolf's blood, certainly." A laugh, but rueful. Lyra grabbed one more vial, then closed the cabinet, clipping the bag to her belt as she moved toward the door. "Though his piece of the Wilderwood could never be called *tiny*."

As strange as the idea of bleeding into vials was, there was comfort in it, relief. Eammon wanted her to learn to use the magic the forest had saddled her with, seemed to think that would keep the sentinel trees in check. But surely it wasn't the only solution when magic and blood ran so congruently here. Her not bleeding where the trees could taste it was his first rule, but maybe it would be different if the blood came from a vial instead of a vein.

And Red would rather bleed goblets full than try to use that damn magic.

"So is there a knife around?" she asked. "Something I can use to bleed into—"

"No." Lyra spun away from the door, dark eyes narrowed. "I mean, I don't...I'm not..." Lyra stopped, sighed. "Ask Eammon. He'll know." She pulled her shirt out from her middle, made a face. "I've *really* got to go change. I'll see you around."

Red watched her go, still slumped over the scuffed table. Again, that sense of untetheredness, of unreality, of not being sure what to do or how to move.

Books. The thought was a beacon, something to cling to. *I brought books.*

Too bad she'd left them in the library. Red didn't know what hours Eammon kept—the unchanging twilight made night and day unclear—but it seemed safe to assume he'd be there.

Ask Eammon, Lyra had said. But Eammon would just talk about using magic again, turning that piece of the forest coiled around her bones toward her will.

A deep breath, squared shoulders. If he asked her about it, she'd tell him she hadn't decided yet. She would find her books and retreat to her room and try to numb her mind for a few hours before she had to think about any of this again.

The wood-shard candles in the library were all lit with their strange, flickerless flames, illuminating the stacks in strobing light and shadow. Red closed the door behind her as soundlessly as possible. The same mug perched on the same stack of books near the door, empty this time. She eyed it for a moment before purposefully untangling her hands from her skirt and striding between the shelves.

There was no sign of the Wolf himself, but his clutter remained. One book left open amid a sea of papers and pens, another stack piled by the desk, left in shadow by the wood-shard candle.

Red crept toward the desk cautiously. Eammon would be none too pleased to see her paging through his notes, but curiosity overrode her unease. She peered at the scribbled-over paper.

It looked like…a shopping list? Things like *bread* and *cheese* were scrawled in slanting, messy handwriting, some crossed out. *Ask Asheyla about boots* was written near the bottom, and, ink still gleaming, *new coat.*

She grimaced. Her attention turned from the list to the open book.

The visible page was a table of contents. No title, but she recognized some of the chapter names—"The Great Plague," "A Taxonomy of Lesser Beasts," "Rites of the Old Ones." It was tempting to sit and flip through, but Eammon's things looked as though he'd left in a hurry. He could be back any moment.

Red turned to resume her search, but the stack of books by the desk caught her eye. Something about them seemed strange, the proportions wrong. She took a step closer, then reared back.

Legends sat at the top of the stack, the book she'd smeared with her blood the day before. And the Wilderwood had half consumed it.

Thin, snaking roots wormed their way in through the cracks in the stone wall, slithering out to latch onto the spot of blood on the cover. They stretched through the canvas, through the pages, seeping down the rest of the stack like it was the soil they were planted in.

Cursing hoarsely, Red stumbled away. But the roots were still, as if momentarily satisfied, and her heart slowly migrated back behind her ribs.

Her books. That's why she was here. *Her* books, not the one she'd inadvertently marked with blood, another thing lost to this cursed, encroaching forest.

The leather bag was on the other side of the desk, hidden just outside the ring of unflickering candlelight. Red looped the strap over her shoulder, hurrying to the door.

She crouched before she pushed it open to riffle through the bag. After all that running on her twentieth birthday, she wasn't sure if all her books had made it. One, in particular, she wanted to make sure hadn't been lost.

A sigh of relief as her fingers closed over the familiar leather binding. Red pulled it from the bag, running her palm over the flaking gilt. A book of poems. The only gift she could ever remember receiving from her mother.

She'd been ten, already a voracious reader. It was days past her birthday when Isla entered her room, alone, no retinue to accompany her. "Here." It hadn't been wrapped, and Isla hadn't quite met her eye. "This seemed like something you would like."

It hadn't been. Not at first. But when Isla left, nearly as soon as Red closed her hands on the book, she'd sat down at her window and read the whole thing through twice.

The poems were childish, and she knew them by heart now. She hadn't opened the book to actually read it in years. But she liked to keep it close. Proof of one moment of warmth.

Red packed the books back in her bag and started up the stairs.

She stopped short at the sight of the figure in the hall.

A shock of reddish hair was his most identifying feature, and vaguely familiar. He knelt before the sapling she'd noticed that morning, peering at its roots. One white-skinned hand he kept tucked close to his middle, marked with violent lines of scar tissue.

This must be Fife, then.

He muttered a quiet curse, tugging something from his pocket—another vial of blood—and reached toward the tree.

"Careful!" The sight of flesh so near something she'd seen bare its teeth pulled the warning out of her before she could call it back. He lived in the Wilderwood, of course he knew he should be careful.

The figure froze before turning his head, arm still outstretched. A ginger brow raised.

Red shifted on her feet. "Sorry, I just...they bite, sometimes."

The brow climbed higher. "They only bite *you*, Second Daughter."

If that was meant to be comforting, it missed the mark by a mile.

Forest detritus had already grown up around the tree, vines and flowering bushes. Carefully, Fife peeled them back, peering at the base of the sapling beneath.

"Kings." He sat back on his heels. "This is the second one in as many days to come into the Keep." With a practiced motion, Fife uncorked his vial with one hand, the scarred and withered one still held close to his middle, and poured the blood over the roots of the sapling. Nothing changed, not that Red could see, but he took no further action. His eyes darted to her. "Did you do anything to it this morning?"

"To what? The tree?"

"Yes, the tree. Did Eammon tell you to do anything?"

"No." Incredulity made the word sharper than she meant it. "He told me to stay away from it. From all of them, I mean. All the white trees."

Fife's lips pressed together, regarding her for an unreadable second before turning back to the sapling. "Well, that should hold until Eammon can get to it." He pressed up from the floor. "Since he is apparently still determined to do this on his own."

Red's brows drew together, looking from Fife's retreating back to the sentinel sapling. A twist of her lips, and she turned to follow him down the corridor. "I'm Redarys. But you knew that."

"Correct."

"And you're Fife."

"Two for two."

"So your blood doesn't just kill shadow-creatures, then. It does something to the trees?" Lyra had mentioned that in the kitchen, something about holding saplings steady.

The question finally made him stop his march down the hall, giving Red a sidelong glance. "Keeps them stable," he answered after a laden moment. "Holds off the worst of the shadow-rot until Eammon can move them back where they're supposed to go." The march to the foyer resumed.

Red followed, though the quick look he gave her said he wished she wouldn't. "Thank you for breakfast," she ventured, dropping her bag of books at the corner.

"Best cook in the Keep." Fife headed for a door behind the once-grand staircase. "Not that it's saying much. Eammon thinks bread and cheese are acceptable for every meal, and Lyra's culinary skills begin and end at tea."

He reached up to push the door open. As he did, his sleeve fell back from his arm. Another Mark, the mirror image of Lyra's.

Fife saw her looking. "We all have one around here. Gaya and Ciaran weren't the only ones foolish enough to make bargains."

Red's hand drifted to her own Mark, hidden beneath her dark-blue sleeve. "I made no bargain."

"Neither did Eammon." He shoved open the door. "But the original Wolf and Second Daughter are gone, so the Wilderwood makes do with the next best thing."

The door spilled them into the back courtyard, with its crumbling stone wall and strange forest-wreathed tower. Fife went left, following the path of Red's broken corridor. Three more white saplings pushed up from the rubble at the end, stretching into the fog.

She hung back as Fife approached them. "I take it those aren't supposed to be here, either?"

"A quick study, aren't you?" Fife peered closely at the sapling's roots. Black rot boiled over them, though the surrounding earth still looked solid, not like the rotten sponginess she'd seen the night before. "He'll have to heal these first," he muttered, uncorking another vial of blood and pouring it over the ground. The rot receded incrementally, so small a difference Red wouldn't have noticed if she hadn't been watching. "They're already weakening. The one inside can wait, it isn't shadow-rotted yet."

"Shadow-rotted?"

Another arch look, like her questions irritated him. But Fife pointed through the fog, to the forest beyond the gate. "See that?"

Right at the edge of the tree line was a black spot on the forest floor—the same dark, damp ground that produced the creature from last night. Red nodded.

"That," said Fife, "is an empty place where one of these sentinels is supposed to be. It felt the Shadowlands pushing through, so it came loose and regrew here, closer to Eammon, so he could heal it. Only the stronger ones can do that. The others just rot where they stand, leaving breaches we have to find and close."

"Like the one last night. It was rotting when we found it, but he said it would've ended up at the Keep in ten more minutes."

Hazel eyes snapped to hers. "He let you go with him?"

Incredulity in his voice, thick enough that Red wondered if she shouldn't have said anything. She shrugged. "He wasn't *happy* about it, but yes."

"Hmm." Fife studied her a moment longer, brow furrowed, before facing the forest again. "He must've really wanted to convince you of his trustworthiness, then."

Red shifted on her feet.

Fife gestured to the lines of rot on the sapling's trunk. "The more the shadow-rot eats through the saplings once they're here, the harder they are to send back. Sentinels are like bricks in a wall, each placed strategically. Move one, and the whole thing gets weaker."

"The whole what?"

"The whole Wilderwood."

Red tightened her arms over her chest, peering nervously at the still, white trees. The *sentinels*. They looked like shards of bone thrust into the earth. "So they're...good."

"The sentinels aren't *good*." He said it like the notion was ridiculous. "But they aren't bad, either. The Wilderwood has a job to do, and it takes what it has to in order to do it."

"And what it has to take is blood."

A covert glance. "Right now," Fife said carefully, "yes."

"Why everyone's blood? It seems like the Wolf's is the only thing that does much."

Another pause, another unreadable look. "Eammon has the strongest connection to the forest," he said after a moment, weighing out his words. "Only his blood can heal the breaches, his blood or his magic. Whichever he feels safest using at the time."

She thought of last night, how Eammon had put his hands to the ground before resorting to his dagger, the bark edging through his skin, his veins running green. Magic, and it changed him, tipped the balance of his body more toward forest than man.

Dread spiked in her stomach, though she wasn't sure exactly why.

"Lyra and I have connections to the forest, by virtue of this damn thing"—Fife pointed his chin at his Mark—"but it's weak. We can slow shadow-creatures down, kill them if they're weak enough, stabilize the sentinels until Eammon can get to them. But he's the only one who can really fix anything." A quick flicker of his eyes. "Him, and you."

Red swallowed. Tension weighed in the air, as palpable as the fog around their feet.

She turned away, facing the tower and the Keep. "Where *is* Eammon?" She'd expected to run into him at some point; it wasn't like there were many places to hide in the crumbling ruin. The fact that she hadn't made something almost like worry itch at her, especially after what she'd seen last night.

"He went out to heal another breach Lyra found this morning. He'll be back."

If Eammon was already healing more breaches, he must be in fine enough shape. The faint itch of worry faded, though not completely.

They reached the Keep door at the top of the sloping hill. It creaked when Fife pushed it open. "I'm going to find some food." Almost begrudgingly, he added: "Do you want to come?"

A split-second decision, and Red shook her head.

He looked at her a moment, brows drawn down. "Stay within the gate," he finally cautioned before pulling the door shut with a snap.

She probably should've followed. But now that she was outside, the idea of being within those ruined walls again was suffocating. Red turned away, wandered farther into the courtyard.

The air of the Wilderwood was chilly, and fog coiled low over the ground, crawling up her skirt. The sky was a wide expanse of lavender, clear of moon and star and cloud. Pretty, in a strange, uncanny way. Giving the saplings at the bottom of the hill another wary glance, Red walked in the opposite direction, vaulting over the short stone wall to go around the Keep's side. Piles of stone rose out of the fog, sleeping giants.

Something caught her eye beyond the gate. A shape, rising from the mist, falling back into fog before she could quite make sense of it. Red stopped, narrowing her eyes.

The shape bobbed up again, like someone who'd stumbled forcing themselves back to their feet. Cautiously, Red stepped forward, her feet silent on the mossy ground.

The figure rose once more, close enough now for her to make out a face. High cheekbones, aquiline nose. Eyes green as summer.

Her breath went icy in her lungs, her heart paused in her chest. Surely not. None but the Second Daughter could pass into the Wilderwood, none but her could cross over. Impossible, but—

The fog eddied around a form she knew.

Red was in control of herself enough not to run, but only just. She wound through the mist and the broken stones of the fallen Keep like someone in a trance, scarcely daring to breathe until she was an arm's length away, looking down on a familiar dark head, familiar shoulders, familiar green eyes in a scratched and bleeding face. He looked spent and bloody, eyes ringed in shadows, clothes torn by his flight through a hostile forest.

"Red," Arick gasped.

Chapter Ten

Arick?" Emotion raked her voice over coals, made it raw and shaking. "How did you... *why* are..."

"Open the gate." Tear tracks ran through the dirt on his face. "Let me in, and I'll tell you everything."

"You shouldn't be here. Arick, I don't know how you got past the border, but—"

His groan cut her off, low and animal sounding. Arick pressed a hand to his side, blood blooming through his shirt. "I came to save you." He looked up, green eyes strangely cunning, voice stronger. "Let me in, Redarys Valedren."

"I don't know *how*. There's some kind of enchantment on the gate, I don't think it will open—"

"I know how." Arick still crouched, but was motionless, like his body were a fragile thing he might jar apart if he moved. "Come to us, Second Daughter, and we'll show you." A smile, bright and sharp, as Arick held out his hand. There was something *off* about it, darkness running along the lines in his palm. "If you must be part of one of them, the shadows will give you a cleaner end."

Red froze, prey in the endless moment before the trap closed. This was wrong. Something was terribly wrong.

With a frustrated gnash of his teeth, Arick threw himself against the gate.

His hands turned to claws as he raked them against the metal, nails elongating, darkening. The veins in his neck were black where they should've been blue, and black filled the whites of his eyes, building up, spilling over. "Don't you want it?" he snarled in a voice that wasn't his, a voice that sounded like screams down forgotten corridors, layered and latched together. "One way or another, there will be an end. It's just a matter of which side you want to tangle with, Second Daughter."

Panic tugged at the magic shard in Red's center. Her mouth filled with the taste of earth, her wrists blazing green as she tried to clamp her power down and scramble backward at the same time.

The thing wearing Arick's face lunged forward again. A black claw reached through the gate and wrapped around her ankle. "The Wilderwood is weak and desperate, the gods it holds grow stronger. The forest won't stop looking for a way in, Redarys Valedren, and when it finds one, it'll drain you like a wineskin, leave all those pretty bones."

Terror finally shattered her tenuous control. Red screamed as the green veins in her wrists climbed her forearms, reaching toward her heart. Splintered magic erupted, spinning vines from the earth to wrap the creature's clawed hand.

It howled, lurching away from the gate, but the cry of pain became a bray of laughter. "The magic is weak," it taunted. "Stings, but it won't do much, Second Daughter, not unless you open your skin and let it take you, root and branch and bone and blood."

"You'll have your blood," came a rasping voice from behind.

The Wolf's hand landed on Red's shoulder, pulling her backward from the gate even as he ran forward and opened it with a touch. There were new slashes on his palms, bloodless, like they'd lost everything they had to give already. Still, Eammon reached for his dagger as he ran, mouth a rictus of expectant pain.

The shadow-thing reared up, not playing at human shapes anymore. Now it looked exactly like the thing that had emerged from the breach last night, nothing but darkness and pieces of dead things.

"Do you have any left to give, Wolf-pup?" A cackle that felt like needles in Red's ears. "What happens once you bleed yourself dry? When you lose yourself to the forest, and it takes you just like it did your father?"

The last word arrested the Wolf's movement, like it was a net thrown over him. A thudding heartbeat where Eammon stood frozen, dagger held steady. Then, teeth bared, he flipped his palm over and sliced into the back of his hand.

A hiss of pain as he pushed down, pushed until finally green-threaded blood seeped around the blade. To Red, still dazed, the tendrils at the edge of the cut looked studded with tiny leaves.

Eammon tugged the dagger out of his skin, blood tracing the dips of his knuckles, painting his scars. With a growl, he backhanded the shadow-creature.

The thing broke apart, scattering bones; the shards feathered into smoke before they hit the forest floor. Still, that laugh reverberated, making the very trees shudder, and it spoke again in a hissing, fading voice as the pieces dissolved. "Only a matter of time."

Then the shadow-creature was gone, the only sign of it a burn mark scored into the earth.

The Wolf stood there a moment, staring down at the ground. Sweaty strands of black hair had escaped their queue, sticking to the side of his neck. The cuts on his hands looked inflamed, and he held them gingerly by his side as he staggered toward the gate, an opening blooming for him as soon as he touched the metal.

"Is bleeding the only way to kill them?" The question came out shaky, to match the tremor in Red's limbs. "Because Lyra said—*What* are you doing?"

He'd dropped to his knees and grabbed her ankle, twisting it this way and that as if looking for wounds. "I could ask you the same thing." Apparently satisfied, he released her, like touching her skin was as welcome as slicing his hand had been, a necessary unpleasantness. "What about last night made you think approaching *anything* beyond the gate would be a good idea?"

"I thought it was different. I didn't hear the breach—"

"You wouldn't have, unless you were there when it opened." Eammon jerked a thumb over his shoulder, toward the gate. Blood dripped sluggishly down his wrist. "Nothing in this forest is safe, especially not for you. I assumed that was *abundantly* clear."

Red rubbed her ankle, banishing the ghost of his touch. "It looked…" Now it seemed ridiculous, but damn if she was going to tell him that. "It looked like someone I knew."

"You thought *someone you knew* came traipsing through the Wilderwood and made it all the way to my gate? Really, it's remarkable you—"

"It looked *human*. More human than the thing last night." Red stood, glaring up at him. His dark hair had come fully unbound, falling messily over his shoulders, shadowing his burning eyes. "I know it was foolish to think it was. But it looked like *him*."

"Him." Quiet, stern.

Red swallowed. "Him."

Silence. Finally, Eammon sighed, hands hung on his hips, head angled toward the ground. "It was convincing," he conceded. "That shadow-creature had time to make a decent mask before it reached the Keep. I don't… I don't fault you for being fooled."

Well. That was unexpected. Red crossed her arms and worried at a loose thread in her sleeve. "Would it have gone away if I bled on it? Like you and Lyra and Fife?"

"I thought I was clear about you bleeding."

"Answer the question."

His jaw worked before he swiped a hand over his mouth and looked away. "No."

Not the truth. Not the whole of it, anyway, between what Fife asked in the corridor and the shift of Eammon's eyes. She'd known him for only two days, but the Wolf was bad at lying.

"The Wilderwood can't last much longer like this." Eammon reached up, began retying his hair. "Sentinels are uprooting and coming to the Keep in droves, too quickly for me to heal before the rot sets in. Breaches stay open for days. I used to be able to keep them in check, but I can't anymore." A tense pause, a thread set to snap. "Not alone."

Red's stomach twisted in on itself.

Hair now bound, Eammon's hands dropped. He kept his gaze turned away, toward the gate. "If you use your magic—"

"I *can't* use it." Every time she entertained the thought, the memories crashed up on the shore of her mind. Branches, blood, Neve. Violence that nearly killed her sister, and all of it her fault. "I'd rather bleed. There has to be a way—"

"There *isn't*." Warmth and library scent as Eammon stepped forward, his voice strangely apologetic, eyes raised to hers through clear effort. "Believe me, Redarys. The magic is the easiest way."

Her eyes pressed closed. Red shook her head.

"Why are you so determined to think yourself helpless?" His voice cracked over the word, like it was something he could punish. "You can't afford that luxury—"

"*Luxury*? You think this is a *luxury*?"

"It's a luxury to ignore it," he snapped. "To decide you'd rather pretend it doesn't exist, and damn everyone else."

"It seems to me like we're all damned anyway!"

His expression shifted, tangled, too many emotions for her to make sense of. Red's pulse ticked in her throat. They stayed like that, bent like bowstrings, neither willing to be the first to look away.

Eammon finally broke, eyes closing as his face turned away. "So it does." He started toward the gate, silent and stoic. "I have to go close the breach before that thing cobbles itself together again." A press of his hand, the bloom of an opening in the iron. The gate swung out, stirring fog, and the Wolf stalked into the Wilderwood.

Red frowned after him as Eammon disappeared into the trees. Her limbs felt locked, paralyzed by fear and regret.

What Eammon wanted was impossible. Even if her power was something she could use, her mind was too shackled by fear to let her. Every time it surged, all she could see were her memories of carnage, and it froze her, choked her, focused everything in her only on lashing it down.

But the Wilderwood was darkening. Deteriorating. She'd seen the barest hint of the things it held back, and it was enough to fill her with a bone-deep terror of what else might be waiting.

If it failed—if the Shadowlands broke through completely, if monsters stalked the world like they had before—what would happen to them?

What would happen to Neve?

"Kings and shadows, I missed it."

Lyra emerged from the fog. She frowned at the burn mark the shadow-creature left on the ground, fiddling with a vial of blood in her hand. "There's a breach southward, right at the Valleydan border. I stayed far enough back to be safe but still managed to bloody it up. I could tell something had already escaped, but I thought I'd beat it here."

"Eammon took care of it." Red's ankle tingled with the memory of his touch, incongruously gentle against his sharp anger, as she pointed beyond the gate. "He went that way, to close the breach."

"Hmm." A shrug of narrow shoulders as she turned into the eddying fog, headed toward the Keep. "Well. He doesn't need me to navigate, then."

The curved sword on Lyra's back shone like a sickle moon. Earlier, Red had been too addled to take much notice of it, but now its shape looked somehow familiar. She studied it as she followed Lyra back to the castle, mostly to keep from thinking of Arick's face on wrong bones, of Eammon stalking into the forest with a hand sliced to shit and barely bleeding.

Another moment of scrutiny, and the word she was searching for came to her. "Is that a *tor*?" Raffe had a *tor*, worn on his back for state functions. According to tradition, Meducian Councilors' oldest children trained with them for a year after their parents were voted in, symbolizing that Councilors' duty was to serve their country with all they had.

"Sure is." She sounded almost amused.

"I thought they were ceremonial."

"Technically." Lyra didn't draw the weapon, but her fingers closed gently around the hilt like a worry stone. "But they're just as sharp as any back-alley dagger."

They rounded the side of the Keep, approaching the ruined corridor that held Red's room. Lyra walked down the sloping hill toward the white saplings in the rubble. Red hung back.

Roots and vines wound through the rocks at the end of the hall, clusters of moon-colored flowers twisting toward the fathomless twilight sky. There was a tilted beauty to it, the way the Keep and the forest tangled together, like one fed the other. A kind of beauty that made Red shiver, wild and feral and frightening.

Those *had* been leaves in Eammon's wound, studding the edges of the cut. Tiny leaves in his green-threaded blood. She thought of the changes she'd seen in him when he worked his strange magic, bark on his forearms and shifting branches in his voice. The Wolf and the Wilderwood, tied together in ways she couldn't quite fathom, the line between them constantly blurring.

Down by the saplings, Lyra shook her head. "Fife was right," she called as she trudged back up the hill. "There's more of them. *Kings.*" The weight of her sigh tossed one corkscrew curl up from her forehead. "Eammon will be bleeding for days."

Red pressed her lips together.

Behind them, the door to the Keep banged open, Fife's hair shining like the sun they couldn't see. He looked to Lyra, mouth quirked, the first trace of pleasantry Red had seen on his face. "You're back early."

"Got hungry." Both of their manners seemed to relax, like seeing the other calmed their nerves. "Did Eammon get more supplies? He said he was headed that way after healing the first breach this morning."

"Yes, though his taste in cheese is still suspect. Next time, I'll go, since he seems incapable of following a list." Fife frowned down the hill at the saplings. "I told him those should be taken care of first. Before he moves the other."

Lyra's brow lifted. "Other?"

"There's one in the corridor," Fife answered grimly. "Turned up this morning."

A pause. Lyra's eyes flickered to Red, something unreadable in the anxious twist of her lips. "Did you see it?"

Her tone wasn't accusing, exactly, but there was a strange surprise in it, like if Red had seen the sapling, she should've done something about it. The same assumption Fife had this morning.

"I saw it," Red said carefully. "Should I have gone looking for Eammon, to let him know?"

Puzzlement creased Lyra's brow. "I suppose you could, but why wouldn't you just—"

"He told her to stay away from it," Fife interrupted.

Lyra looked at him, mouth twisted in an expression that was pity and resignation at once. Fife gave a tiny shake of his head, an entire conversation happening between them without words.

Red shifted uncomfortably on her feet.

A moment, then Lyra forced a smile, eyes flickering to Red. "Eammon has a plan, I'm sure." Her dark gaze went back to Fife, almost like she was trying to reassure him. "Always does."

"Always does," Fife repeated quietly.

Red tried to return Lyra's tentative smile, but her mind was a riot—the Wilderwood coming for her, fangs in the trees, pits of shadow, and Eammon's bleeding hands.

She shut her eyes, gave her head a tiny shake. Fife and Lyra talked quietly to each other up ahead, an ease between them that was somehow soothing even as her thoughts snared. Focusing on the cadence of their voices rather than the forest and the fog, Red followed them into the Keep.

Valleydan Interlude III

The empty chair across the table yawned like a chasm.

It had been easier to ignore when Arick ate with them, the few times it happened before Red left. Awkward as dinners with only Arick and Queen Isla were, he'd acted as a buffer when he played the dutiful Consort Elect, a retaining wall between her land and her mother's cold sea. But now he was gone, fled with his grief and his sudden desire for heroism, and the dining room was a tomb with only two occupants.

No dinner with the Queen had ever been comfortable, really. Neve and Red hadn't dined with their mother often, but when they did, they sat across from each other, Isla in the middle. Though those dinners had been nearly silent, at least Neve hadn't been completely adrift. Red had been her anchor.

Now Neve stared into her empty plate, knowing every bite of dinner would go down like lead, knowing an hour here would feel like a day. Since Red left—since Red was *sacrificed*—time with her mother felt like a penance. Especially since Isla appeared wholly unaffected. If she carried the same ache Neve did, the Queen kept it hidden too deep to show.

The door opened and servants appeared, rolling in a single cart stacked with dishes. Even the smell of food made Neve's nose wrinkle.

Reverently, one of the servants lit the three tapers in the center of the table—one white, one red, and one black. Isla bowed her head. After a moment, Neve begrudgingly followed.

The Queen's eyes flickered expectantly to her daughter. Neve's lips tightened over her teeth.

With a sigh, Isla closed her eyes. "To the Five Kings we give thanks," she intoned, "for our safety and our sustenance. In piety and sacrifice and absence."

The candles were snuffed. The servants filled their plates, topped their wine, then left, quick and silent. Neve didn't touch her fork, but grabbed her wineglass and took a hearty swallow.

"The Rite of Thanks is two sentences, Neverah." Isla took a dainty bite. "Surely it wouldn't hurt you to make a show of faithfulness now and then."

"I'd rather not, thank you." Neve drained her glass. In the corner of her eye, her mother's hand tensed on the table.

Isla took a swallow of wine. When she put the glass down, more forcefully than necessary, it made a small, crystalline *pop*. "I let the two of you grow too close," she said, so quietly her mouth barely moved. "Back when you were children, I should've put a stop to it. I should've protected you—"

"I'm not the one who needed protecting."

The Queen flinched.

The part of Neve that wanted to be a dutiful daughter felt a twist of pain at that. The same part that wished for something to cling to, for stable ground in this sea of guilt and uncertainty. That was what a mother should be, wasn't it? Stable ground, even once you were grown? But Isla's role in this was indelible, her complicity shaped as a missing daughter in a red cloak and violence she quietly accepted as collateral damage.

Neve loved her mother, but her mother deserved to flinch.

Her throat was a knife-ache, her fingers arched like claws on her knees beneath the table. Silence stretched, and she wished soundlessly for her mother to fill it with something. Anything.

When Isla finally moved, it was minuscule, a slump in her shoulders as she sighed. For one moment, the mask slipped, the icy Queen suddenly tired and hollow. But then her eyes rose to Neve's, her composure reassembling itself. "This reminds me," she said, as if they were having a normal conversation. "We should begin wedding preparations."

Neve's mouth hung partially open, the change in topic so abrupt her mind had to catch up. When it did, it was a white-hot riot, and her reply was truth stripped free of politeness or preamble. "I don't want to marry Arick. You know that."

"And you know it doesn't matter." Isla straightened, eyes reflecting candle-flames. "You think I wanted to marry your father? A man twice my age who only remained in court long enough to make an heir, and died before he knew he'd made *two*? The First Daughter's marriage is always political. There are precedents. You are not the exception." Isla drained the rest of her wine. "Neither of you could be the exception."

"Arick is in love with Red." Neve wanted to throw it down like a gauntlet, but it came out too brittle to be a weapon.

Still, some chord seemed to strike in her mother, drumming beneath her veneer of indifference. Isla's eyes closed, her hands slackened on the tablecloth. The breath she pulled in was shallow.

Then her eyes opened, trained on empty air. "He's more foolish than I thought, then." She stood, slowly, like every movement was an effort. "That could be good for you, Neverah. Foolish men are easy to rule."

The Queen left, gliding out the door with her ice-blue skirts trailing over the marble floor. She moved stiffly, but no one other than Neve would notice. She'd been trained in that same glide, the one that spoke of graceful power, and she could see the fault lines where it cracked.

A full wine bottle sat in the center of the table, uncorked and ready for pouring. Neve didn't bother, drinking straight from the neck.

When nothing was left but lees, she stood on unsteady legs. The room pitched and spun, but no one offered an elbow for her to genteelly clasp—the dining hall was empty, and no servants waited just outside to attend to any royal needs. She must've scared them off with her unqueenly manners, her uncouth conversation.

In her inebriated state, it was almost funny.

Neve walked slowly out into the hall, hand tensed to steady herself on a wall if the need arose. She didn't know the hour, other than it was late; the paned windows were velvet-dark, scattered with stars.

The windows faced north, toward the Wilderwood. With a motion made sloppy by too much wine, Neve spit on the floor in front of the glass.

Something caught her eye, disappearing around a corner. A flash of red and white, familiar in a way that would probably be obvious if she weren't drunk. Brows knit, Neve walked forward, around the corner where whatever it was had disappeared.

Priestesses. Maybe two dozen, a few more than she'd seen when she argued with Raffe yesterday. Each of them held a candle, which wasn't odd in itself—Order priestesses often carried scarlet prayer candles. At first, Neve thought the candles in their hands were black, like she'd stumbled on some late-night funerary procession or leave-taking rite.

Her eyes narrowed. No, not black. These candles were colored light charcoal. The same gray as a shadow.

The group glided silently down the hall, headed toward the gardens. Leading them, the red-haired priestess. Kiri.

Of course.

"You!"

Neve barely recognized the voice as hers at first. Even the single exclamation was somehow slurred, which probably should've been embarrassing, if she could muster the feeling.

The priestesses' shoulders went rigid, each one, like children caught stealing sugar cubes. They looked to Kiri for instruction, but she seemed unbothered. Slowly, she turned around, the movement made syrupy in Neve's wine-addled perception. Her small branch-shard pendant swung from her neck, the strands of darkness on the white bark nearly invisible in the gloom.

They stared at each other a moment. Then Kiri glanced at one of the others, nodded. A small, sharp smile turned up the corner of her lip.

Cool blue eyes flicked to Neve as the rest of the priestesses continued soundlessly down the corridor. "Can I help you, Your Highness?"

Her momentary ire had cooled, smothered by the strangeness of the priestesses in the dark, their silence and shadow-colored candles. "I saw you yesterday," Neve murmured, more curious now than angry. "You were talking to Arick."

"I was." The flickering light twisted the lines of Kiri's face.

"What did he want?"

The priestess's face remained implacable, the flame from her shadow-gray candle dancing in her eyes. "The same thing you did, that night in the Shrine."

A shiver rolled through Neve's shoulders. "You told him how to save her."

No answer. Just silence, just jittering shadows on the wall from Kiri's gray candle.

"But how do you know?" Her voice sounded so small in the dark. "How do you know what happened to Red, how do you know how to get her back?" A shaky swallow. "Why didn't you tell me first?"

Kiri's hand reverently closed around her branch-shard pendant. "Since I was a child," she said quietly, "long before I joined the Order, I have served the Kings. I have been guided by them to seek clarity, to know the true ways of things. It is not everyone who can be trusted with truth, Highness. It is a volatile thing, a fearful thing." Her grip on her pendant tightened. "Caution is key, and moving in secrecy to make way for moving in light."

"I can be trusted." Neve nodded, only once, though the movement was sure to knock loose the start of a headache. "I want the truth, Kiri."

Silence and wavering candlelight, cold blue eyes watching her, taking her measure. Kiri's hand twitched on her pendant again. A dark, copper-scented smear marred the pad of one finger, and her eyes fluttered closed as she pressed it to the wood, almost as if she were listening to something.

Her eyes opened as she released her pendant. "Come." Kiri resumed her slow glide down the corridor, taking the only light source in the hall and leaving Neve in darkness. How late was it? Why were none of the sconces lit?

Neve stared after her. "Where are you going?" It wasn't accusing. It was genuinely curious.

The flame's flicker caught the edge of a small, secretive smile as Kiri glanced over her shoulder. "Come," she repeated, then turned toward the door to the gardens.

To the Shrine.

The priestesses filtered outside, hands cupped around the flames of their candles to guard them from the night breeze. Neve shifted back and forth on her feet. "Kings on shitting *horses*." Soundlessly, she followed after them, out into the dark.

None of them looked at her as they walked silently down the garden paths, gliding like a sea of ghosts. The moon was new, and the deep night turned the shapes of the hedges beastly, made every arch a waiting monster.

Into the mouth of the Shrine, back toward the gauzy dark curtain. Kiri ducked in first but didn't hold it open, making every priestess enter separately so no glimpse could be caught of the room beyond.

She knew what was back there, but gooseflesh still prickled over Neve's skin.

The last priestess disappeared through the curtain. Neve took a deep breath. Then she ducked through, too.

The miniature Wilderwood. The priestesses, ringed around it with their odd gray candles. But something was different. The branch shards were marked, smeared with darkness. Blood? But no, the color was wrong, the scarlet of it marked through with threads of black. *Kings*, her head hurt.

"Neve?"

She whirled around. Arick stood behind her. A bandage wrapped around his hand, streaked crimson. In the center of his palm, a dark spot radiated on the white fabric like a miniature sun.

His weary face broke into a genuine smile. "I found a way."

Chapter Eleven

It took her nearly four days, as best she could count in the perpetual twilight of the Wilderwood, to work out a plan. Red spent the time mostly in her room, surrounded by her books, letting the familiar passages be an escape. She was good at escaping.

Strange and nebulous though her days felt, there was at least somewhat of a rhythm to them. Three meals in the tiny kitchen behind the seldom-used dining room, sometimes with Fife or Lyra, sometimes alone. The cupboard was well stocked with simple fare, and though her culinary skills were next to nonexistent, she was in no danger of starving. Fife was mostly silent, and Lyra was cordial but distant.

And when the sky darkened toward violet, if she was anywhere near the foyer, she'd see Eammon.

The first time was an accident, the day after he saved her from the shadow-creature that looked like Arick. Having read through most of the books she brought, Red went down to the library to look for more. The venture was successful—a shelf in the back corner was stacked with novels and poetry books, all with the scuffed covers and dog-eared pages that spoke of frequent use.

She was carefully climbing the stairs with her hoard when she saw him.

He stood just inside the still-open door, limned in darkening light. The Wolf's head bowed forward, exhaustion in the slump of his shoulders, hair unbound and shadowing his eyes. One hand held his dagger, the other covered in cuts that wept some slow blood but mostly a thin, greenish sap. Bark covered the skin right above his wristbone. Though bent, she could still tell he was taller. Magic twined around him like a wreath.

Red stayed silent, but still his eyes snapped to her, like the atmosphere changed with her presence. Eammon straightened, his sliced-up hand pressing to his middle, lips lifting back from his teeth in a grimace of pain as he sheathed his dagger. His eyes glittered, rung by dark circles, the whites shaded emerald. It looked like he might collapse where he stood, like refusal to look weak in front of Red was the only thing keeping him standing.

Maybe she should've said something, but Red had no idea what words would be right. What was she supposed to do, ask him how his evening was going?

Connected gazes, unreadable emotions flickering across two faces. Then Eammon jerked his chin, a truncated greeting and dismissal in one, and slowly climbed the stairs up to the second floor of the Keep.

The next morning, there'd been three new sentinel saplings in the corridor. The sign of three new breaches opening in the Wilderwood, three new opportunities for monsters to escape. Three new places for Eammon to bleed as he tried to hold all the tattered edges of the forest closed.

That'd been the moment her plan started to form.

Now, in what passed for very early morning, she stood at the door to the back courtyard, her hand against the wood but not quite pushing it open. She'd briefly considered attempting this experiment with one of the saplings inside the Keep, but then she might be seen.

And Eammon had been so insistent about her not bleeding.

Her stomach churned as she finally strode out into the swirling fog, toward the crumbled end of the corridor where saplings stretched bony branches into the pale-lavender sky. The glass vial she'd nicked from the storage closet in the kitchen was slick in her hand. At the bottom, scarlet as the cloak in her closet, three drops of blood.

It wasn't much. There'd been no weapons in her room, so Red just worked at a hangnail until she'd torn it off, squeezing her finger to drip the scant blood into the vial.

Just enough to see if it made a difference. Just enough to see if there was any other recourse than trying to use the magic that had almost killed her sister.

The memory of the Wilderwood chasing her after the thorn cut her cheek still made her pulse thunder. But, she rationalized, that blood had been straight from the vein—the only way the Wilderwood would accept blood from the Wolf, according to Lyra. And Eammon was part of the forest, tangled up in it...maybe giving blood the same way he did was what made the Wilderwood come for her, what made it try to worm its way beneath her skin. If she bled first into the vial, there'd be no wound for the forest to try to invade.

And she had to do *something*. Eammon was clearly at the end of a fraying rope; the thought of shadow-creatures breaking free of the forest was unconscionable.

Her magic wasn't something that could be used, of that she was convinced. Fear drowned her, fear had its claws deep in her heart. Magic was a dead end, but surely there was something else she could do. There had to be.

Red stopped in front of the sentinel farthest from the gate. Mossy rock shored around its roots, mist tangled like ribbon in the thin beginnings of its branches. She didn't touch it, but she drew closer than she had to any of the other sentinels she'd seen, and something about being close made the atmosphere change. The air seemed to hum against her skin, strange but not unpleasant, and when she blinked, she saw golden light behind her eyelids.

A deep breath. A straightened spine. It took her a couple of tries to uncork the vial, and when she did, the coppery scent of blood seemed stronger than it had right to. With a steady hand, Red held it over the roots of the sapling.

"What are you doing?"

His voice was soft. She looked over her shoulder.

Eammon stood just behind her, fog eddying around his boots and in the tendrils of his loose, too-long hair. His face betrayed nothing, eyes dark and inscrutable, full lips slightly parted.

The vial stayed steady in her hand, but she didn't pour it out. "I think you were lying to me before," Red said. "I think my blood *can* kill shadow-creatures and heal the sentinels. If Fife's and Lyra's and yours can because of the Mark, then so can mine, no matter how… how *different* I am from the other Second Daughters."

She expected him to refute her again, to stick by his lie. But Eammon didn't move, other than the tic of his throat as he swallowed. "It's not quite that simple, but you're right. Your blood can do those things." Still soft-voiced, still calm and stoic as the trees around them. "But the price is more than I'm willing to let you pay, Redarys. If you give the Wilderwood blood, it won't stop there. It can't."

The shadow-creature forming itself into Merra's corpse, roots spilling from her ripped stomach. Gaya, dead and forest-tangled. The other Second Daughters, disappearing into the trees, called into the darkness. Tied to the Wilderwood, but in a different way than Red was. A difference Eammon wouldn't fully explain, other than it had to do with the awful, destructive power growing in her bloodstream like a vine.

This ends in roots and bones.

Red glared at him, the hand holding the vial beginning, slightly, to tremor. "Maybe *I'm* willing to pay it. Maybe I'd rather bleed on your trees and face whatever the consequences are than try to use this damn magic."

Incredulity in his tone now, but also a sadness that plucked at a chord in her middle and made her hand shake more. "You fear yourself that much?"

"You were there." It was nearly a whisper. "You saw how terrible it made me."

"I only saw part. I was concentrated on... on other things. But I know this power is volatile, especially at first. Whatever happened, I'm sure it's not as terrible as you remember it." A tentative step forward, a scarred hand stretching toward her. "*You* aren't terrible."

Their eyes locked across the moss-and-fog-covered ground. Finally, slowly, Red let the hand holding the vial drop to her side. Then she reached out, placed it in his outstretched palm. Her eyes stung, her breath came with a sharp sound, but the Wolf was kind enough to pretend not to notice.

His fingers brushed hers as he took the vial, scars rough against her skin. "Is that why you were so insistent on staying here? Because of that night, what happened?"

She nodded, not trusting herself to fit words into the space between them.

Eammon sighed, pocketing the vial of her blood and running a hand through his hair. "I've been trying to think of alternatives. Something else we could do, something that would—"

Bound.

A quiet rustle of underbrush, a clatter of branches shaping a word. On one of the rocks near Red's foot, moss browned, withered.

Must be bound. Must be two. Like before.

More moss dying, curling into brittle tangles. The Wilderwood's price for speech.

Two. Gaya and Ciaran. A Wolf and a Second Daughter, bound together.

Magic is stronger when there are two.

This came quieter, like the forest was tired. Grass died beneath

Red's feet, went brittle. Quickly, she backed away, and almost knocked into Eammon.

His hand landed on her shoulder, steadying and warm, scored by cuts that weren't quite healed yet. Red's feet felt clumsy as she stepped back, crossing her arms to stave off a chill.

He looked at her, eyes made dark by the shadow of his hair, mouth pressed to a line. His hand hung in the air for an abbreviated moment, still where her shoulder had been, before falling, making the mist eddy around them. The Wolf's eyes tracked thoughtfully over her face, like an answer to some silent riddle was written on her skin.

Then he turned, striding away into the mist, leaving her alone.

Night was so judged by tiredness and the sky somewhat darkening from lavender to plum, though it seemed Red was the only one in the Keep trying to structure time by an absent sun. Lyra was patrolling again, *tor* on her back and vials of blood in her pockets. Fife was in the kitchen, having taken on cleanup duty after dinner.

She didn't know where Eammon was. But she'd be going to find him soon. As soon as she worked up the nerve.

Red paced before her fireplace, thumbnail between her teeth. She still wore the dress she'd changed into before eating with Fife and Lyra, burgundy and thus far free of dirt or blood. Fife remained standoffish, but Lyra tied them together, folding them into a fragile but pleasant camaraderie. Clearly, she and Fife had known each other for untold years, and time and circumstance had born a strong connection. Red felt out of place next to them, an interloper, and found herself wondering if the other Second Daughters before her had felt the same.

Not that either of them mentioned the other Second Daughters, or sentinels, or magic threaded in blood. They never did. Still, such things gnawed at the back of Red's mind even as Fife and Lyra talked lightly of other things.

You fear yourself that much?

She did. Four years now of constant, low-level anxiety, churning at the very base of her mind, replaying that night in snatches when she slipped enough to allow it. How her magic, freshly splintered from the Wilderwood, had ripped people into pieces, left a sea of blood on the leaves. How she hadn't been able to control it.

How it almost killed Neve.

But maybe...maybe it didn't have to be like that. Eammon had said the power was volatile at first, so maybe now that it'd coiled in her for years, it would be easier to harness. To direct. She'd have him there to help, as close to an expert in Wilderwood magic as she could get.

And that image of him entering the Keep, bent and bloodied, forest edging through him—that stuck with her. He kept spilling himself into the Wilderwood and letting the Wilderwood spill into *him*, doing everything he could to hold it on his own. Not pushing her. Giving her time, even when the waiting ran him into the ground. A week she'd been here, and her presence hadn't helped Eammon or the forest at all.

She owed it to him to try. She owed it to Neve. In the end, wasn't this just one more step in keeping her sister safe? Making sure the monsters she now knew for certain were real didn't escape the Shadowlands? The horse was bought, no sense letting it founder now.

Pacing halted, deep breath taken. Then she turned from the hearth and strode purposefully toward the door.

A knock stopped her short. Red froze.

A muttered curse precluded another knock, this one sharper.

Red fetched up her voice from the back of her throat. "Yes?"

"May I come in?" He'd shaped his low rumble to try to sound accommodating, but it didn't quite fit.

"It's your Keep."

"It's your room."

A moment of hesitation, laced with surprise. Then Red opened the door.

The Wolf had to slump to look under the lintel. He'd tied up his hair since this morning, made a messy knot of it at the back of his neck, though black strands still waved against his collarbones. Ink-stained fingers pulled nervously at his sleeves, but there was no trace of nervousness in his face, sharp-jawed and hard-planed as always. White bandages wrapped both his hands.

Red motioned him in. Eammon ducked past, stopping just inside the threshold. Her room looked smaller with him in it.

Silence, growing heavier the longer it was left. Red gestured to his hands. "Will they heal?"

His brow furrowed, like he didn't know what she meant, then he looked down. A rueful noise in the back of his throat. "As much as they ever do."

"I'm glad you're here, actually." Red swallowed. "I was just coming to..."

But then his bandaged hand turned, and the firelight caught on something shining silver in his grip. *Dagger.*

Red lurched backward, eyes wide and mind tangling. Maybe he was finally tired of her hedging, maybe he'd decided draining her himself would help him more than her magic would, how many vials would every drop of blood in her body fill—

Eammon looked at her like she'd gone mad before following her gaze to the blade. He held up his hands in surrender. "I'm not going to *stab* you."

"Are there other uses for daggers?"

High flags of color on his cheekbones. "That's what I wanted to talk to you about."

Tension prepared for violence ebbed away. Red's pulse regulated to a proper rhythm, though something in his eyes made each beat hit like a hammer.

Eammon ran one of his bandaged hands through his hair, looking at the fire in the grate instead of at her. "I…" He stopped, sighed, spoke again in a rush that ran the words together. "Have you heard of a thread bond?"

It took her a moment to organize the words into meanings, the question was so unexpected. "I think so. It's a binding ceremony, right? A folk marriage. Where you don't need a witness or a blessing."

"Yes." It was clipped, and his eyes didn't leave the fire. "You each give a part of yourself—hair is customary—and bind it around a piece of your new, shared home." The hand that didn't hold the dagger fished in his pocket and pulled out a shard of wood, bone-pale. Sentinel bark.

Bound, the Wilderwood had said. *Must be bound. Must be two.*

Understanding was a slow bloom of heat in her chest. "Is this a proposal?"

Eammon didn't answer, pushing back his hair again. The tips of his ears burned scarlet. "The Wilderwood is trying to re-create what it had before, with Gaya and Ciaran. We can't give it that, not exactly, but we can get as close as possible." He flipped the dagger nervously between his fingers. "A marriage like they had would be a good step. And I think it might make your magic…easier to manage."

Red's mouth worked, but she wasn't sure how to shape the knot in her middle into language. "Oh" was all she could muster.

Another, heavier silence hung, and in those few seconds, Red's life up to this point crashed lightning-quick through her head. When Neve first bled, and their mother began speaking of betrothals and alliances. When Red did, a few weeks later, and none of the same conversations happened—she was spoken for, had been since she first drew breath, and no suitors would be coming for her. Those first few desperate times with Arick, thinking it was as close to cherished as she could get. Her life had been a house of cards, pieces stacked delicately on top of one another more by ease of construct than by a choice truly made, because weren't things hard enough without her making them any harder?

But here was Eammon. Far from the monster she'd been told to expect, far from anything she'd managed to imagine. Eammon, offering her a choice.

He needed her. She doubted she'd ever hear the words from his mouth, but it was clear in everything that had happened since she crossed the border of his forest, in the words of the Wilderwood earlier as they faced each other in the fog. There had to be two, but he wouldn't force her to stand with him. Wouldn't make her do anything she didn't wholeheartedly choose to do.

Her pulse thrummed in her throat.

Eammon watched her face, the play of incomprehensible emotion across it, and shook his head. "Forget it. I'm not even sure if—"

"It's a good idea."

His teeth clicked together.

"Worth a try, anyway." Red took a tentative step forward, pulling her tangled braid over her shoulder, untying the bit of twine that kept it bound. Her hair was still damp, wavy from where she'd braided it wet. She shook it loose, lifting her chin to meet the Wolf's gaze.

"If this is a proposal," Red said quietly, "my answer is yes."

He swallowed, a click in his throat, that unreadable light flickering in his eyes. Then he nodded.

The space between them felt cavernous. Eammon moved first, cautiously. He held the dagger out by the hilt. "You first." The corner of his mouth twitched. "Call it an exercise in trust."

"You'll have to sit somewhere." Red waved her hand at his head. Truly, the man's height was ridiculous. "I can't reach."

A pause—the only place to sit was the bed, and both of them seemed to realize it at the same time, if the sudden widening of eyes was any indication—then Eammon knelt. "Better?"

She nodded, once. Something about his posture, kneeling like a penitent, made her insides unsteady.

His hair was softer than she expected, smelled like coffee and old books. "Did you do this with the others?" Red forced a laugh, but it sounded as nervous as she felt, and her stomach flipped end over end. "How many wives have you had now?"

He was still beneath her hand, his voice low. "Just you."

So he hadn't married the other Second Daughters. The fact, inexplicably, made her stomach feel tangled with her spine. "Why not, if the Wilderwood is trying to re-create what it had?"

"Didn't need to." He shifted on his knees. "The Wilderwood re-created it in other ways."

It did nothing to untangle her stomach from her spinal cord, but it did make her cheeks heat, a flare of irrational embarrassment she was glad he couldn't see. "Lucky us."

A low grunt.

Red picked up a lock of hair behind his ear and managed to cut it without bloodshed. "Done."

Eammon stood gracelessly. His unbound hair fell over his forehead as he held out his hand for the blade.

Red turned, breath shallow as the Wolf's scarred fingers lightly touched her neck, warm and rough. He plucked up a lock of hair from the same place she had, brushed the rest of it over her opposite shoulder. A soft *snick*, and a length of dark gold shone in his hand.

"Does it matter how we tie it?"

"We have to do it together, but that's it, far as I know." His eyes flickered to hers, a tentative curve to his lips. "This is my first marriage, remember?"

Further stomach tangling.

After a moment of hesitation, Eammon pulled the white bark from his pocket. Messily, they wound the strands around the shard of the sentinel tree. Their hands kept bumping together.

Something else happened as they wound their hair around the bark. Red...*loosened.* If her chest was a knot, her rib cage made of tangled rope, it felt like that knot unraveled, an inverse reaction to what she and Eammon did with their hair. The splinter of magic coiled in her center felt lighter somehow. Less like something lying in wait to wreak havoc, more like a tool she could take hold of if needed.

Eammon had said that a marriage might make her power more manageable. It seemed he'd been right. Binding herself to him—to the Wilderwood he ruled—made the shard of it she carried feel more like an integrated part of her, rather than something she had to cage.

When it was done, the pale bark was almost completely hidden in gold and black. Red looked toward the window and the forest outside, not sure what she expected to see. "So this will make the Wilderwood better?"

"It should." Eammon pocketed the wood shard. He flexed his hands, once, as if searching the atmosphere for a change. "The sentinels want you...closer."

"Marrying you certainly brings me *closer.*"

A flash of color across his cheekbone again. "That's the idea."

"And that's what holds back the shadow-creatures," Red said, choosing not to comment on the blush. "The sentinels."

"Been studying, have we?"

"Fife explained. Reluctantly."

More expectant silence. Red couldn't quite cobble together what she wanted to say, how to say it. An apologetic overture didn't seem right anymore, not with her hair in his fingers. Not when he was her *husband.*

So when she spoke, it was blunt. "Do you still want me to try to use the magic?"

His eyes snapped to hers.

"Because I will." Shadows flickered over the walls. She watched them instead of Eammon. "It scares me, and nothing good has ever come from it. But I think us…what we just did will make it easier. And if it will help you—help the forest—I'll try."

Eammon said nothing, but his hand arched toward the wooden shard in his pocket, the token of their binding. "You don't have to," he murmured. "I don't want to make you do something you don't want to do. *Anything* you don't want to do. This is entirely your choice."

"And I've made it." Too far in to back out now. "If you can teach me to use the Wilderwood's magic, I want to learn."

Firelight carved hollows into his angular face, flickered in his eyes and made them honey-colored. No green in them, which relieved her more than she quite understood. "Meet me in the tower in the courtyard when you wake." A pause, and his next words were quiet. "I'll make sure it doesn't hurt you. Or anyone else. I promise, you have nothing to be afraid of."

She nodded. The air between them felt like something solid, something that could be shoved out of the way.

Eammon opened the door into the twilight-painted corridor. As he stepped over the threshold, he pointed at the fire. "No need to worry about dousing that before you sleep. The wood won't burn out or let the flames move to anything else."

"How did you manage *that*?"

He gave her a wry grin. "Perhaps that will be our lesson tomorrow." Her new husband turned and walked into the darkness of the hall, leaving her alone in her room. "Good night, Redarys."

Chapter Twelve

Red's breath was one more cloud in the fog-covered courtyard, spiraling from her lips in the chill air. She craned her neck upward as she followed the wall to the tower. From this angle, the windows at its top lined up perfectly, forming gaps of sky in the stone.

The moss-covered door creaked slightly as she pushed it open, startlingly loud in the silence of the Wilderwood. Beyond it, a staircase climbed up into darkness. Overgrowth lined the walls, leaves and pale blooms papering the gray rock in shades of white and green. Unlike the Keep, it didn't seem sinister here—part of the structure, rather than an invader. Still, she took care not to touch it.

The staircase spiraled upward far enough to make her winded before finally ending right in the center of a circular room. No greenery here, but four equidistant windows set into the curved wall with flowers and vines carved into their sills, a wooden imitation. A merrily crackling hearth stood between two of them, filled with wood that didn't char, and a small wooden table flanked with two chairs sat near enough to feel its warmth. The midnight-blue ceiling rose to a point over the central stairs, where a paper sun hung, crafted in layered gold and yellow.

Painted silver constellations spangled out from the paper sun, exquisitely detailed—the Sisters, hands stretching from north to south to meet in the center; the Leviathan, cutting through the western sky; the Plague Stars, clustered together above the rough outline of a ship. According to legend, the Plague Stars had appeared to guide the vessel carrying traders infected with the Great Plague back to the mainland. The stars had snuffed out the moment those afflicted were suddenly, miraculously cured.

"This is beautiful," Red murmured, turning in a circle with her eyes still on the ceiling.

A brief snort snapped her attention away. Eammon leaned against the windowsill behind her, one hand in his pocket, the other clutching a steaming mug. His hair was tied back, the short tuft where she'd cut it for their thread bond sticking out awkwardly behind his ear. "The handiwork of the Wilderwood. The tower and the Keep sprang up when Gaya and Ciaran made their bargain, fully furnished." He sipped from his cup. "A housewarming present. Ciaran built the rest of the Keep around it."

Ciaran. Gaya. He never referred to them as his parents, only by their names or titles. Turning them into distant people who didn't require warmth.

She knew the feeling.

Red went to the hearth and chafed her hands. The windows had no panes, and the room was as cold as the forest outside. "So the Wilderwood made these?" She gestured to the paintings on the ceiling.

"No." Eammon walked to the table in the center of the room and poured more coffee from a waiting kettle. Another mug sat next to it; he looked to Red, eyes a question. At her nod, he filled the second mug, too. "Gaya painted them."

Her eyes turned to the constellations again, an odd, weighty feeling in her chest.

"Any particular reason to meet here?" She picked up the mug he'd poured her, wrapping her hands around its warmth. "Pardon the observation, but you don't seem to like it much."

He made a gruff noise that might've been a laugh. Eammon sank into one of the chairs, tipping it back on two legs. "Because this place was made by the Wilderwood, so its magic is stronger here."

The knot of her magic still felt looser this morning, teased apart, untangled. The result of their quick thread-bond marriage, she knew, but now that she turned her thoughts to it, some of the ease might come from the tower, too. Blooming along with the flowers on the walls as she moved up the stairwell.

Still, the thought of using it hollowed a pit in her stomach.

The coffee was strong, and bitter enough to make Red pull a face. "Could the Wilderwood's magic manage to conjure up some cream?"

"Afraid not. I'll add it to the supply list." Eammon took a long drink of his own. "For all its force, the Wilderwood's power is rather limited. It can affect growing things, or anything else connected to the forest, but that's about it."

"It can heal wounds, too."

"Only if the wounded person is connected to the Wilderwood."

She tightened her grip on her cup to keep from touching her face, the place along her cheekbone where the thorn had scored her a week ago. "You didn't really *heal* it, though," she said. "You just... took it. It showed up on you."

"Pain has to go somewhere." The chair legs creaked as Eammon leaned back. "It's a balance. The vine that lights the Keep will hold the flames without burning, but it won't grow. Neither will the branches the firewood was cut from. Wounds can't just go away—they're transferred."

They didn't look at each other, but the awareness was solid as a stare. Red took another sip of her bitter coffee.

"Your power must work similarly to mine," Eammon said to the ceiling. "Since they're the same thing. Mostly."

Her brow furrowed. "But when I can't keep it contained, I don't... like how you..." She trailed off, not sure how to phrase it delicately.

"You don't change like I do." Quiet but matter-of-fact.

"No," she murmured. "I don't."

A visible swallow down the column of his throat. "My ties to the Wilderwood are stronger than yours," Eammon said. "And when

I use its power, it...takes part of me away. The changes fade, usually, but it's still unpleasant. And some things linger." He shrugged, stilted. "That's why I use blood, sometimes. It works the same way the magic does, without opening me up to quite as much *alteration*."

The last word came out bitter. Still looking at the ceiling, Eammon rubbed at the spot above his wristbone where she'd seen bark edge through his skin.

Red nodded, sliding her gaze from his silhouette to the wavering reflection in her coffee mug. "So I won't change, because my magic isn't as strong as yours."

"Exactly. Not as strong, and more chaotic."

"To put it mildly."

"We should focus on control, then. Channeling only a small amount at a time, directed to a specific task."

Nerves sparked, sending her floundering for some distraction to stall the inevitable. Red sank into the chair across from him, mug clenched tightly between her palms. "Why does the magic affect growing things?"

"When Ciaran and Gaya made their bargain, the sentinels rooted in them. Became part of them." The belabored chair legs squeaked as Eammon leaned back, reciting history to the paper sun. Willing to let her put this off, if having every question answered would make her more comfortable. "So the Wolf and the Second Daughter can control the things of the earth, the things with roots. They're under the sentinels' influence, and thus under ours."

Her mind riffled through all the times she'd had to steel herself against her seed of magic, miles and miles from the Wilderwood. "For having such a limited purview, the sentinels' *influence* seems to stretch rather far."

"I wouldn't know. It's been centuries since I could leave this damn forest." The four chair legs clattered to the ground. "It traps Wardens better than it does shadow-creatures."

"Wardens?"

"The words for 'Warden' and 'Wolf' are remarkably similar in most of the continent's ancient languages."

"There has to be more to it than *that*."

"Ciaran was a huntsman." Eammon stood and strode across the room to one of the vine-carved windows. A small ceramic planter sat there, green ivy curling over the edge. He picked it up and brought it to the table, bracing his hands on either side. "Before he ran off with Gaya, his proudest achievement was slaying a giant, monstrous wolf that prowled at the edges of his village—a child of one of the things trapped in the Shadowlands, before they all died off. They called him the Wolf long before he came here, and the word for 'Warden' wasn't different enough for them to stop." He flashed her a sharp smile and slid the ivy in her direction. "To be honest, I prefer Wolf."

"Maybe people wouldn't think you a monster if you were called the Warden instead."

"Maybe I don't mind them thinking I'm a monster."

It was meant to sound fierce, and on the surface it did. But there was something about the depth of belief in it that plucked a chord in her chest. Red lightly twisted one of the ivy tendrils around her finger.

Eammon sat properly in his chair this time, no precarious tipping backward. "We'll keep it simple." He gestured to the ivy. "You're going to make that grow."

Red slid her half-drunk mug to the side, hoping he couldn't see the tremor in her hands as she settled them on either side of the pot. "How exactly do I do this without calamity, then? We made the magic easier to manage, but I'm still not exactly confident."

The mention of their marriage, oblique as it was, made their eyes dart away from each other.

"Focus your intention," Eammon said after a laden moment. "Once you have it clearly in your mind, open up to the forest's power. It's... intuitive." He looked up from his scarred knuckles to her face. "It's part of you."

Part of you. She thought of the changes magic wrought in him, the bark and the green eyes, the height and layered voice. A scale tipping back and forth, man to forest, bone to branch.

The bloom of magic in her middle stretched upward. Something she could wield, if she was brave enough. If she could swallow down the memories of the times before—

Red closed her eyes and gave a slight shake of her head, like those thoughts were something she could physically dispel. "I'm ready."

"I'm here."

The quiet reassurance soothed some of the anxious tension in her limbs. Letting out a long, slow breath, she tried to quiet her racing thoughts, to focus her intention. Growth, roots digging deeper into the soil as ivy leaves spread wide.

When it was clear in her mind, she reached for her power. Tentative, the barest touch, but it opened like a flower.

And for a brief, gleaming moment, Red thought she could do it.

But memory was a current, and the deliberate touch of power pulled her under, drowned her in panic. All of it ran behind her eyes like it was happening over again: an eruption of branch and root and thorn, blood spraying, rib cages shattered by sharp trunks, Neve slumping to the ground—

"*Red!*" She heard it through a haze, distant as shouting into a cyclone. All she could see was black forest, black sky, all she could taste was soil and blood. Distantly, she felt her spine locking up, her throat working for air that wouldn't come, her body shutting itself down in a final attempt to keep her magic shackled.

A strong grip on her shoulders, turning her to wide amber eyes. The Wolf's warm, scarred hands against her cheeks. "Red, let *go*!"

His voice, his eyes wrenched her from memory's grip. Red gasped, pulling air into lungs that suddenly worked again.

Eammon released her almost immediately, like her skin burned. "What in all the *shadows* was that?"

The table's edge dug into her back, a counterpoint to her thundering pulse. "I can't do it. I thought I could, after the thread bond, but I can't."

"You have before. You did *a week* ago."

"That wasn't control! That was barely containment!" Red slashed her hand toward the window. "Want to try throwing me to the Wilderwood again? See if that sparks some *control*?"

Eammon stepped back, hands raised in surrender. Firelight flickered across the scars on his palm.

The door below clattered open and shattered the fraught silence, footsteps rushing up the stairs. Fife's reddish hair topped the landing, sweaty strands stuck to his forehead.

"Word from the Edge," he panted. "Breach to the west, but there's a complication."

"What kind of complication?" Eammon's eyes were still on Red, somewhere between angry and wounded.

Fife's jaw tightened. "They were looking for a break in the border again. Found a full breach instead. And someone... fell."

That was enough to pull Eammon's attention away. He nodded, one jerk of his head. "Lock the Keep, then come back here. It's more secure."

"I should come with you."

"Too dangerous. If someone has already fallen into a full-fledged breach, they'll be looking to pull in others. You'll be more helpful here." Eammon's gaze flickered nearly imperceptibly to Red, then back to Fife.

The other man's brows drew together. He nodded.

As Fife disappeared down the stairs, Eammon crossed to the fireplace. A long knife gleamed on the mantel, as well as the short dagger he'd worn before. The one he sliced his hand with. Eammon took both. "Stay here." He glanced at her over his shoulder, eyes stern. "Do *not* leave the tower."

Questions and admonishments rioted through her head. But when Red opened her mouth, what came out was "Be careful."

Chapter Thirteen

Red sat next to the window with her thumbnail between her teeth. Fife had brought a basket of slightly wrinkled apples for lunch, but worry gnawed her middle in place of hunger. Ridiculous. Worrying over the Wolf, going to do Wolf-things, was ridiculous.

And yet.

She wouldn't necessarily call Eammon a friend. She wasn't sure if she even *liked* Eammon, despite the strange kinship they'd forged in mutual entrapment. But he'd saved her, twice now, and even if it was more because he needed her than for any personal reason, it still counted for something. He hadn't quite gained her friendship, but he'd gained her trust, and the fact it was their only tether made it stronger.

And if something happened to Eammon, what would that mean for the Wilderwood? Would the burden of it all, the weakened sentinels and the shadow-rot and the monsters clamoring for release, fall wholly to her? Red didn't think she could keep it up alone, not for long. Eammon hadn't been able to. What would happen to Neve, to the whole world beyond the Wilderwood, when she inevitably failed?

And so, worry. Stomach-churning, palm-tingling worry, and her eyes fixed to the forest so she didn't miss his return.

Fife watched her from the chair Eammon had vacated, turned around backward so his good hand could rest on its back. He'd been silent since he returned to the tower. While the awkward quiet might've bothered Red in any other situation, right now she was too full of nerves to notice until it was broken.

"He'll be fine, you know." Fife tapped a knuckle against the back of the chair. "This is business as usual around here. Well, other than someone falling in the breach, but even that, Eammon can take care of more easily than the rest of us. The villagers push at the border all the time."

His voice startled her, but it wasn't unwelcome. Red's brow knit. "What does that mean, *push at the border*? And what villagers?"

"At the Edge, beyond the Wilderwood's northern boundary line. Descendants of the explorers who tried to see what was behind it, long ago—when the borders of the forest closed while they were still back there, they were trapped. The Wilderwood won't let them through, but that doesn't stop them from looking for weak spots, thinking they can find a place that will let them out." Fife shrugged. "It's pointless. If you're stuck here, you're stuck here for good."

Red had never heard of the Edge, or anything beyond the Wilderwood, but it didn't seem like Fife would be the one to ask for more information. Not when the resentment in his tone was nearly palpable.

She was too consumed with anxiety to muster much curiosity, anyway.

"He just looks..." She trailed off, unsure how to frame the bruises around Eammon's eyes, the tightness of his jaw. "Tired."

"We're all tired." Fife grabbed an apple with his uninjured hand, and again Red's eyes caught on the thin band of root around his arm. The skin under her sleeve itched—she'd kept her Mark covered ever since it appeared, other than showing it to Eammon that first day in the library.

"Did he take some vials with him, do you think?" she asked, thinking of the wounds in his hands and how they seemed to leak more sap than blood. How the bleeding was to stave off the forest from changing him. "In case he... runs out, needs more?"

"He won't. My and Lyra's blood is next to useless compared with his."

"Why do you two keep bleeding, then?"

"Terms of the bargain." He tapped his Mark. "When you bargain for a life, your end of the deal isn't fulfilled until you've spent a certain amount of blood in the Wilderwood's service. Apparently, I haven't bled enough yet."

Again, resentment, simmering under the surface of his voice like a killing current. Red reached for an apple, mostly for something to do with her hands. "What did you bargain for, Fife?"

The hitch in the air between them made her think he wouldn't answer. Then his eyes flicked to hers, guarded. "How much do you know about treating with the Wilderwood?"

"Not as much as I probably should, considering."

Fife arched an incredulous brow, then shrugged. "Every bargain bore a price. You know the smaller ones, the lost teeth and the bundled hair. But bargaining to save a life was different. The Wilderwood marked you, and the Wilderwood could call you in. No one knew what for. I made my bargain, got my Mark, and didn't know what it would do to me until the forest called me back, reeled me in like a damn fish and bled me like one, too." He tossed his spent apple core into the hearth. The uncharring wood hissed. "Lyra and I were the only two who ever tried bargaining for a life. Foolish of us."

"Or brave," Red offered quietly.

"Her, maybe. Not me." Fife sat back, withered hand held tight against his middle, and fell silent. Red didn't pick at the quiet.

"There was a girl," he said after a moment, almost to himself. "She was in an accident. Leg smashed in a stone mill. The wound suppurated, she grew fevered. Death was inevitable. So I bargained. My life for hers." Reddish hair feathered across his freckled brow as he shifted in his seat. "She married someone else, but it was probably for the best. The Wilderwood closed up only two years after that, and it called Lyra and me in before it did, fools with Bargainer's Marks and a debt to a forest. I would've left her a widow."

Red twisted at the stem of her mostly uneaten apple. "Is that what happened to your hand, too? Part of your bargain?"

His face shuttered, and his hand twitched like he might try to hide it. But then Fife sighed, looking down at the mass of scar tissue. Lurid lines marked him from knuckle to wristbone, most heavily concentrated around the veins of his wrist. "No. This happened when I tried to meet the terms all at once—spill all the damn blood the forest wanted. Didn't work, obviously. All I did was sever a few tendons and pass out for three days." He shrugged. "I've never seen Lyra so angry. Or Eammon so quiet. Took a bit for things to go back to normal after that."

That thick scarring, concentrated over his wrist... pity contracted her heart, but Red kept it from her face, knowing it was the last thing he'd want. "I'm so sorry, Fife."

"Don't be." Gruff, but not angry. "If I hadn't bargained, I wouldn't have met Lyra."

The stem of Red's apple broke off. "Are you two..."

"No," he answered quickly. "Well. Not like *that*, not really. It's complicated." Fife tapped his unwounded fingers against the back of his chair, searching for words. "Lyra isn't one for romance. Never has been. But she's the most important person in my life, and has been for centuries now. That's enough."

Red nodded, sensing she shouldn't pry further. He'd already spoken more to her in the past five minutes than he had in her whole time at the Keep. "What did Lyra bargain for?"

"Not my story to tell." Fife reached for another apple. "It's longer and more noble than mine."

They lapsed into silence, still somewhat chilly, but more comfortable than before. Red lifted her apple to take a bite, but before it reached her mouth, something... *faltered* in her vision. A flash of green shadows, shaped like leaves and branches.

It reminded her of that night. When the Wilderwood rushed her, as if her sliced palm was something it could seep into. When she first saw Eammon's hands, the connection between them forged in branch and blood.

Her brow furrowed as she shook her head. She hadn't had a vision like that in four years; no reason to think she'd have another now. Across the table, Fife was oblivious, crunching an apple and staring into space, lost in thought.

She pressed her lips to a white line.

When the strange faltering came again, it was nothing so subtle as forest-shadows. This was a lightning strike behind her eyes, completely washing out the tower to show her something else entirely. The potted ivy on the table stretched green fingers toward her, the withered apples plumped and blushed scarlet.

Fife cursed, jumping from his seat, but Red didn't hear him. Red didn't see the tower anymore, nor anything in it. Instead, like the night of her sixteenth birthday, she saw hands.

Scarred hands, holding a dagger, palms running with green-threaded blood.

And beyond them—a creature, a monster. Vaguely man-shaped, but as if a man had been taken and twisted in ropes of shadow, the form bent to wrong angles and painted in dripping black. Milky eyes, a howling mouth. Behind it, fog shifted around a white tree with dark rot climbing its trunk.

The creature gave a low laugh, tripping up a discordant scale, and raised its clawed fingers before slashing down.

Another shadowed rush of leaves and branches. Her eyes saw only the tower again. Red's mouth opened and closed on a choked sound as she clutched her stomach, sure she'd feel viscera spilling warm and slippery.

But it wasn't her facing a monster. It was Eammon. Eammon, the vision of him even stronger than it'd been before.

The thread bond made her magic easier to wield—at least in theory, when she wasn't utterly frozen by bloody memories. Apparently, it gave them other abilities, too. Tied them so tightly together that she could see through his eyes.

See that something was terribly, horribly wrong.

"Are you all right?" Fife arched a brow.

"I..." She didn't know how to articulate what she'd seen. Past or present? Future? The parameters of this new bond between them were entirely alien. "I saw Eammon. Eammon getting hurt, hurt by something...something *dark*..."

Fife's eyes went wide and worried. "You *saw* him?"

"It's happened before." She didn't know quite how to explain it, so she didn't try. Red stood quickly, her chair toppling behind her. "I have to go."

"Absolutely not." Fife's head shook so vehemently, his hair stuck up. "Eammon said—"

"I can't just *leave* him." Shadowed forest-shapes still edged in at the corners of her eyes, sharp twigs and climbing vines. In her chest, power swirled, growing up and out, making the already-overgrown ivy on the table quiver. "It was real, Fife, just like last time. I have to do *something*."

His brow furrowed with an emotion she couldn't quite identify. Finally, Fife sighed, standing. "Fine." He turned to jog down the stairs. "But when Eammon wants to know whose idea it was, don't expect me to save your ass."

The Wilderwood was eerily still as Red and Fife made their way between the trees, its attention drawn elsewhere. Fog stretched sinuous fingers into the lavender sky, threading between mostly bare branches.

"Northwest, since they came from the Edge," Fife murmured, following a compass in his head. "And probably close by." His teeth flashed. "Kings-shitting *stupid* Valdrek."

Red barely heard him. She pushed through the undergrowth,

weaving around thorns and catches of leaves, her focus singular—*Find Eammon.*

As far as what she could do once she found him... that, she wasn't quite sure of yet.

Sentinel trees scattered along their path, tall and pale. Black rot climbed them all, sometimes only at the roots, sometimes past Red's knees. She could smell it when they came close—empty and cold, ozonic. The ground around them was solid, for now, but she couldn't keep from wondering how long that would hold. When they'd come loose from whatever magic moored them in place and show up at the Keep, a silent sign for Eammon to either spill more blood or risk tipping his internal scale further into forest.

A sound ripped through the quiet. A roar.

Fife met her eyes. Simultaneously, they broke into a run.

Branches whipped past, Red barely avoiding their sharp ends, still remembering Eammon's rule, the only one he seemed intent on her keeping—*don't bleed where the trees can taste it.* Labored breath a harsh bellows in her throat, the thrash of Fife's feet through the underbrush making a metronome. *Don't bleed don't bleed don't bleed.*

Voices up ahead, curses made ethereal by layers of fog. Possibilities flickered through her mind and lent her speed—Eammon wounded, Eammon gored, Eammon dying in puddles of leaf-flecked blood.

But when she reached him, Eammon was whole. Whole and snarling.

He stood with his back to them, arms outstretched, precisely cut slashes in both palms leaking green-chased scarlet down his wrists. Before him, a sentinel listed to the side, covered in black rot, on the verge of collapse. Roots slashed through rotten dirt, the slow-spreading ring of darkness like a seeping wound. Bloody handprints marked the ground, and there the edge of infection receded, barely. Already, the small amount of forest floor Eammon had managed to clear was rotting again.

Instinctively, Red took a step back, colliding with a warm figure.

At first, she thought it was Fife. But the arm attached to the hand clapping over her mouth was clad to the wrist in gray leather vambraces.

"Quiet," an unfamiliar voice hissed in her ear.

Red didn't need the directive. The creature stalking back and forth across the rotting sentinel's roots, as if guarding it, stole any speech from her throat.

"Wolf-snarls, small snarls, snarled in the trees." The thing might've been a man, once, and that made it worse. The way he moved was wrong, low and lurching, on legs with knees bent backward. His shirt hung open at the arm, a long, dark slash marking his swollen bicep. Shadow crawled from the wound, inched over his skin, rotting it as surely as it rotted the ground. "Saw the shadows," he singsonged, pacing back and forth. "Saw the shadows and the things in the shadows, and the things in the shadows have *teeth*."

Eammon's bloody fingers twitched, trying to call forth branch and thorn. The whites of his eyes shaded greener, veins in his neck turning verdant, but other than a bare twitch of the underbrush, the Wilderwood didn't answer.

Blood and magic, both running thin.

A fractioned moment where the look on his face was close to helpless. Then, with a snarl, Eammon sliced into his palm again.

"Why aren't you helping him?" Red tried to lunge forward, her whisper slashing through the air, but whoever held her had an iron grip. "*Help* him!"

"What do you want us to do, girl?" the voice behind her hissed. "Our blood won't do shit for the Wilderwood, and we don't need someone else getting shadow-infected."

Her eyes darted, searching for Fife. He stood slightly behind her, among others clad in green and gray, blending into the colors of the dying forest. These must be the villagers he spoke of.

She caught his eye, wildly jerking her chin toward the falling sentinel in its spreading pool of rot. But Fife shook his head, fear in his eyes, and Red remembered what Eammon said in the tower—that Fife coming with him was too dangerous.

That someone already fallen would be looking to pull others in.

"How long can you last?" The thing advanced toward Eammon on twisted legs. One snapped, made weak by calcifying shadow. He dropped to his knees and kept coming, crawling through the rotten earth. "Not long, not long alone. Especially not now, now that the Wilderwood smells something *fresh*."

Dark circles stood out around Eammon's eyes as he knelt, pressed his bleeding palm to the earth again. This time, the shadow-rot didn't recede at all. It inched unceasingly forward, and the leaves it touched on the forest floor crumpled, withered.

He couldn't stop it alone.

Her body made the decision before her mind could make her stop. Red lurched, throwing herself out of the grip of whoever held her. They were surprised enough to let her go, and she slipped on the leaves, backpedaling away from the advancing tide of rotten ground.

Eammon's gaze snapped to her, the frustration in his eyes blazing to fear. He shook his head, sharp, but Red ignored him. She moved quietly along the edge of the shadow-pit, hands opening and closing along with the bloom of forest magic in her middle. It pulled her toward the Wolf, the bond between them making it easier to grasp, easier to direct. The specter of dark memories tried to rear up from the corners of her mind, but her fear for Eammon eclipsed it, gave it no room. Power sang down her veins, washed them green.

The Wilderwood still seemed wrung out, exhausted and pushed to its limits. But when Red twitched her fingers, the branches quivered.

Eammon bared his teeth. He cut the air with his hand—*go back*—but Red shook her head. Another step closer, power coalescing—

And she stepped on a twig.

The crack could've been a spine, for how loud it sounded. Red froze, hand outstretched toward Eammon. For the first time since she'd known him, the Wolf looked terrified.

The creature raised his nose to the wind. Sniffing. "And oh, here it is." The shadow-bloated head swiveled to face Red. "Fresh *blood*."

The word was a lunge, and the seconds stretched too long, her heartbeats coming in measured ticks. *Beat* and the creature launched in her direction, *beat* and its dark-rotting hand raised, *beat* and the once-human nails elongated to claws.

Beat and Eammon sprang in front of her. The claws raked him instead, slicing through fabric and flesh.

Magic rioted in her middle, the sight of Eammon's blood finally giving space to memories of all the ways it could go wrong. It shivered in her grip, the ease their marriage had bought slipping away as Eammon crumpled before her. Magic wasn't the only way to heal the breach, though, and the glint of the knife as it fell from his hand to the ground was a sharp, clear reminder even as her magic slipped toward chaos.

Damn his rules. Red grabbed the dagger and slit her palm.

Her hand slammed to the dirt, blood seeping into the forest floor. Her intention was a scream in her throat, reverberating through every part of her, too focused to be ignored. "*Stop!*"

The shadow-pit obeyed.

It wasn't slow, not this time. The edges of the rotted ground shifted backward, surging toward the roots of the sentinel, disappearing beneath them. The tree righted itself with a *boom*, shock waves skittering over the forest floor. Distantly, Red was aware of those people at the fringes falling backward, unable to keep their balance on unsteady ground.

A moment of silence, of stillness. The creature watched her with wide eyes, still swimming in shadow. Eammon looked from the bloody dagger to Red's hands subsumed in dirt, horror on his face.

And something in Red...*shifted*. The tide of her magic turned, no longer rushing out but rushing *in*.

Rushing in, and bringing the Wilderwood with it.

Something slithered against her hand in the dirt. A tendril of root, working its way into the cut in her skin. The forest laying claim. It had a taste of her, and wanted more.

If you give the Wilderwood blood, it won't stop there.

Pain brought a snarl to her mouth, but the sound that ripped through the clearing didn't come from her. It came from Eammon.

He lurched from the ground, his scarred and leaking hands closing around her shoulders, wrenching her out of the dirt. The slithering feeling of roots against the cut sharpened, then let go as her hands came free of the ground.

Eammon crouched, slamming his hand to the forest floor, still churned with Red's blood. No new cuts in his skin. Instead, changes, like that day in the library when he healed her cheek: Bark closed around his forearms like vambraces, the veins in his neck and beneath his eyes going green. Emerald ringed his amber irises, until no white was left.

"*Leave her*," Eammon growled at the now-healed sentinel, at the surrounding Wilderwood. His voice was layered, resonant, like it echoed through leaves. "This one isn't yours."

The Wilderwood shivered. It gave a sound almost like a sigh.

Eammon's breath came in pants as he collapsed on his knees next to Red. His chest bloomed crimson and green in three stripes, more blood coming as he ripped a strip of fabric from the bottom of his shirt and tied it messily around her hand.

Then he sat still, eyes searching hers as green slowly leached away, wide and terrified and so tired.

A groan split the moment in two. Eammon flinched.

The creature on the sentinel's roots twitched. Parts of it shrank—the claws that had rent Eammon's middle contracted back into the shape of a human hand, the milky eyes that had been wide as saucers grew smaller, grew blue. His monstrous height halved, his legs righted themselves, broken bones snapping back together and ripping a scream from his throat. Shadow hissed out of the cut on his arm.

The half-man, half-monster creature collapsed on the roots, twitching, crying. She'd healed the breach, but not him, not completely.

Red turned away.

"We can take it from here." The man who'd caught her when she and Fife first careened into the clearing stepped from the cover of trees. His hair was snowy blond, braided elaborately over his shoulder and into his long beard, paler than his white skin. Silver rings glinted in its length, a style Red had seen only in history books. The others stepped from the shadows, all dressed in the same greens and grays.

The man looked to Red, face inscrutable. "Thank you."

Red managed a nod. Without the distraction of rushing forest and saving Eammon, the sight of other humans in the Wilderwood was enough to shock her to silence.

Now that the breach was safely closed, Fife joined the rest as they gathered sticks from between the trees, lashing them together to make a rough sling. One of them pulled a roll of bandages from his pack. "Careful not to touch the cut," Fife cautioned. "It needs to be bound."

Eammon stood on unsteady feet. "I'll do it."

His brow arched at Eammon's wounds, but Fife offered him the bandages. Slowly, like every step was pained, Eammon approached the man on the roots. He swallowed hard before kneeling to wrap his shadow-infected arm.

Sling made, Fife stepped back to Red, still seated on the ground. Blood seeped through the scrap of Eammon's shirt wrapped around her palm. *I keep ruining his clothes*, she thought distantly.

"These are the villagers?" Her voice was hoarse as she pushed up, standing on numb legs. "From the Edge?"

Fife nodded, arms crossed and eyes narrowed.

"And they're the descendants of the explorers who went beyond the Wilderwood. Before it closed up and wouldn't let anyone but a Second Daughter pass." She shook her head. "The official records say the explorers all died. None ever sent word."

"They couldn't." Fife shrugged. "Once the Wilderwood closed up, they were stuck behind it, with no way to return or contact the outside world. They grew old, had children, who in turn grew old and had children. Now there's a whole country of them back there, providing entirely for themselves."

She eyed the people ringed around the clearing, all watching Eammon with anxious faces, all dressed like they'd stepped out of the past. "And you said they were looking for a weak spot? What does that mean?"

"A place the Wilderwood would let them pass through."

Red snorted weakly. "It would appear they found one."

"They usually do," Fife said. "The Wilderwood is more relaxed about the northern border. Has less to guard from, I guess. Eammon, Lyra, and I can even leave the forest from that side, though we can't go far, and it's not exactly pleasant." His jaw clenched. "But the Valleydan side is locked tight, and that's the one that matters."

The villagers loaded the wounded man into the sling. He moaned softly, still caught between human and monster. Eammon gave him one long look before turning to the man with the rings in his hair, presumably the leader. "Send word when you can." Despite the wounds in Eammon's middle, his voice was steady. "Do you have somewhere to keep him?"

"Tavern basement has worked in the past. It's built strong." The man shook his head, silver rings clinking. "Bormain helped build it. Damn, Bormain was *drinking* in it two days ago."

"Was this a planned expedition?" Eammon's question was cold.

The man rubbed a hand over his mouth, looking away from the Wolf. With a sigh, he nodded, once.

"It's pointless, Valdrek." There was anger in Eammon's tone, but it was thin, like he didn't have the energy for it. "Even if it lets you in on the northern side, you can't get all the way through."

"Why exactly is the forest still so weak? It should be strengthening, beginning to open its borders again, not closing them up in case the monsters rattle their cage." Valdrek jerked his head at Red. "Isn't that the point of you getting your new blood?"

"It's Lady Wolf." Eammon's eyes could cut. "Not *new blood*."

Pin-drop quiet. "I see." Valdrek's gaze darted from Eammon to Red. "Well. That's new. Congratulations, Wolf."

Next to her, Fife's brow furrowed, then rose. "*Oh*."

Red's cheeks burned. She didn't realize a title came along with her new marriage.

Eammon walked toward them, tall and straight, but Red saw the white line of effort his mouth became, the way his hand kept twitching to his side.

"That doesn't look good," Fife observed.

"It looks worse than it feels." It was almost certainly a lie, but Eammon's tone didn't invite argument. When Red looked to Fife, he gave a slight shake of his head. Prying would be pointless.

"I'll go on ahead, then. Tell Lyra everything is taken care of." Fife jogged toward the tree line, muttering unintelligibly, but Red caught the phrase *self-martyring bastard* in there somewhere.

Pain laced Eammon's features. The ragged hem of his shirt showed a stripe of blood-muddied skin. He opened his mouth, closed it again, throat working an empty swallow. Red, with nothing to feed into the waiting silence, just pressed her lips together.

Behind them, the shadow-infected man muttered nonsense under his breath. Red looked back over her shoulder, and his blind, milky eyes stared right at them.

"Solmir says hello, Wolf," Bormain murmured.

Chapter Fourteen

Eammon stood frozen, staring wide-eyed across the churn of dirt and forest debris the clearing had become with a look halfway between terror and rage. Then his hand locked around Red's elbow, vise-like, and he led her into the trees, so fast she almost stumbled.

Solmir. It took Red a moment to place the name, to find its meaning among the mental images it conjured of candles and stone. When she did, her steps stuttered.

Valchior, Byriand, Malchrosite, Calryes, Solmir. The Five Kings.

Her mouth opened to ask Eammon why in all the shadows Bormain would've mentioned one of the Five Kings, but her muffled sound of pain eclipsed the question. Her hand felt like it was on fire beneath the makeshift wrapping they'd made of his shirt, and Red's knees buckled as she clutched it to her chest.

Soft shushing noises, warm hands unwrapping her palm. The cut she'd made was a line of livid scarlet, as if a month of infection had sped through in moments. Pain thrummed with her pulse, an echo of it hammering just below her elbow, around the ring of her Bargainer's Mark.

One thought, fleeting but clear: *The Wilderwood isn't pleased with me.* She'd stopped something from happening, something it wanted. The same thing it'd wanted four years ago, the first time her blood met the forest floor.

Eammon had stopped it then, and he'd stopped it again now, and the Wilderwood was growing more and more impatient with them both.

Those warm hands covered hers. A breath, and the stabbing pain was gone, both in her hand and in her Mark. Another slice opened Eammon's lacerated palm, a twin to the one she'd cut on her own, turning heart and lifelines into messy crossroads. A curse gnashed through his teeth, his uncut hand pressing against his forearm, where his Bargainer's Mark was hidden beneath a torn and bloody sleeve.

Taking her pain, again. Hurting for her, again.

"You didn't have to do that," Red murmured, suddenly embarrassed. She pushed herself to stand, though her legs wobbled, and turned over her palm to see whole, unbroken skin. Rusty streaks of blood crusted on her wrists.

"I was going to say the same thing." Eammon paced away from her, the rush of pain he'd taken apparently manageable now, one hand on the jut of his hip and the other running shakily through his hair. It had all come unbound and hung down his back like an ink spill. "What in all the *shadows* did you not understand about staying in the tower, Redarys?"

Red crossed her arms, the skin he'd healed smooth and somehow tender. "I saw you."

"You *saw* me?"

"I had a... a vision, I guess."

His brow arched incredulously. "A vision."

"It was like that first time. The night I cut my hand, bled in the forest, but stronger. More vivid. Like our connection is..." She trailed off and turned her head, cheeks suddenly burning. Her fingers picked at the fabric of her sleeve covering her Mark. "Like it's deeper now, after the thread bond."

Calling it a *thread bond* rather than a marriage was supposed to feel less awkward, even though they meant the same thing. Still, her tongue nearly stumbled over it, this fragile thing she was never supposed to have.

Silence hung heavy in the cold air. Finally, Eammon sighed, rubbing a hand over his face. "Well," he murmured, "that's something."

Red's lips twisted.

"So this"—his hand waved between them—"makes it so we can see each other." A snort. "In times of *distress*."

"Apparently."

"Wonderful." Eammon rubbed at his eyes again. "What did you see, exactly?"

"Your hands." Red untangled a leaf from her hair, grateful for something to look at other than the Wolf. "Like last time. But also Bormain, and the sentinel." She paused. "That's why I knew you needed help. I saw you cut yourself, and saw that it wasn't working."

The leaf Red freed from her hair twisted to the ground, brittle brown brushed with green. When it touched the forest floor, the color slowly leached away.

"I suppose we should try to keep the distress to a minimum, then," Eammon said, eyes on the leaf.

"Rather difficult around here."

"It's the best I can do at the moment." Eammon turned, the movement twisting the wounds in his middle. A curse gritted through his teeth, blood and sap seeping into the fabric of his shirt. He leaned back against a tree, like he suddenly couldn't keep himself upright.

"That looks *bad*, Eammon."

His eyes darted up at the sound of his name—cheeks coloring, she realized it was the first time she'd addressed him directly with it, in over a week of knowing each other.

Well, he was her husband now. She couldn't call him *Wolf* forever.

"Can you heal it?" she asked hurriedly, chasing the echo of his name away. "Like you did my hand?"

"Can't heal yourself." His eyes closed, head tilting back against the tree trunk. "Balance, remember? Pain going somewhere?"

Her step forward was tentative, her reach more so. "I could..."

"No." His eyes snapped open. "You could *not*. You've done quite enough for one day, Redarys. Let's not add further mangling of my insides to the list."

That stung more than she cared to admit. Red snatched back her hand. "You'd rather I'd left you to be mangled alone, then?"

"Has it occurred to you that I wouldn't have *been* mangled if I hadn't had to protect you?"

"You *needed* me."

It hung heavy as an executioner's ax. The Wolf looked away. "I suppose I did."

Red arched a sardonic brow, though the tick of her pulse seemed to land a fraction harder. "Now, that wasn't so hard, was it?"

His rueful laugh turned to a grimace, hand pressing harder against his abdomen. Red peered worriedly at the blood outlining his fingers. "Are you—"

"It's *fine*."

Lips pressed to a tight line, Red directed her attention to the site of her own injury, since he seemed determined to ignore his. "It didn't hurt when I first cut it," she mused, flexing her fingers. "Just after." She paused. "That's happened before, too."

The night she'd tried to defy the Wilderwood, the night of Neve and blood and a vision she didn't understand. After they'd been collected from the carnage, her hand had felt bathed in flame, a sharp and stabbing pain that couldn't have come from the thin slice across her palm. The physicians were baffled and didn't know what to do other than give her watered wine until the pain subsided. It did, eventually, but it took two days.

Eammon shifted, still leaning against the tree. "It's the Wilderwood," he said finally. "Something about connecting with it through blood." The answer seemed truncated, like there should be more tacked onto the end, but the Wolf didn't offer anything else, face turned slightly away so she could see only the line of his profile.

Red frowned, scrubbing a spot of dried blood off her wrist. "Probably something about it being upset, too." Meant to be leading, but the only sign that Eammon might take the bait was the bob of his throat as he swallowed. "The Wilderwood doesn't seem pleased that we haven't let it do... whatever it is it wants to do."

The Wolf still didn't look at her. "That, too."

Hands mostly clean, Red crossed her arms, arched a brow. "Does it hurt *you* that badly? Every time?"

"It used to." With a grimace, Eammon pushed away from the tree trunk, took a lurching step forward. "Come on."

Red fell into step behind him, and for a minute, the only sound in the Wilderwood was the unsteady tromp of their boots. "He mentioned the name of one of the Five Kings," she said finally, because she couldn't think of a way to finesse her confusion into delicate questions. "Solmir. The one who was supposed to marry Gaya. Why?"

Ahead of her, Eammon half turned to fix her with one amber eye. A long sigh, then he pivoted to weave through the underbrush again. "How much do you know about what's in the Shadowlands?"

"Nothing. Much like every-damn-thing else, I know nothing other than the myths, and thus far, it seems like those are mostly horseshit."

"They get the broad strokes, but yes, mostly horseshit. The Shadowlands imprison shadow-creatures and mythic beasts and the Old Ones—those are the things that were more like gods than monsters." He discussed monsters so mildly, did the Wolf, pushing aside branches to clear their path through the dark wood. "But the Five Kings are in there, too."

Her steps faltered, stopped. Red's mouth hung open. "But I thought you said the Kings weren't here?"

"They aren't *here*. They're in the Shadowlands. And contrary to current religious belief, I have no way to let them out. Not unless you want everything imprisoned in the Shadowlands to come with them and the whole Wilderwood to fall, which I assure you, you don't." Eammon pushed up a branch, holding it out of the way so they could pass. "The Wilderwood and I might not see eye-to-eye on methods, but we're in agreement on principle."

She thought of the shard of the forest in her, the larger one in him, the push-and-pull of fighting against something that was part of you and separate at the same time. "How did they end up there?"

"They bargained. You know that part. Bargained to make the Shadowlands, to make a place to hold the monsters. The Wilderwood accepted, but in order to accomplish such a thing, it needed an immense amount of power." All of this in a voice only slightly strained, though Eammon's shoulders were rigid lines and his hand pressed against his middle as he walked, like something might fall out if he didn't hold himself together. "Before, magic was part of the world. Just... *there*, to be used by anyone who could learn. To make the Shadowlands, the Wilderwood pulled all that magic inward, trapped it. Created the sentinels, created the Shadowlands beneath."

"And the Wardens."

"Them, too. The Wilderwood needed help to sustain its new prison. Ciaran and Gaya had truly awful timing." The hand that wasn't pressed against his bloody stomach curled into a fist. "Fifty years after they'd made their bargain, the Kings decided they wanted magic back. Tried to unravel the whole thing by cutting down the sentinel where they'd made their deal. Instead, it opened up a hole into the Shadowlands and bound them there, with the monsters they'd banished. The Wilderwood takes its bargains very seriously. That's when it closed up the borders, too—didn't want anyone else trying to go back on a bargain, or make a new one." A shrug, stilted and pained. "There's a moral lesson in there somewhere. People with power resent losing it, and too much power for too long a time can make a villain of anyone."

The beginnings of a headache pricked at Red's temples. "That still doesn't explain why Bormain mentioned Solmir, if all the Kings are there. Why him, specifically?"

The name tensed the muscles in his back, but Eammon's voice stayed even. "Who knows. Bormain fell through a breach and into the Shadowlands. There's no way to know what terrible things he saw." Up ahead, the iron gate to the Keep loomed out of the fog. "Don't think too much of it. Shadow-infection affects your mind as much as it does your body."

Red's eyes narrowed, but she said nothing.

Eammon touched the gate. "Stay within the walls of the Keep for the rest of the day," he said as it swung inward. He gave her a stern look over his shoulder. "I mean it, Red. The Wilderwood has been... restless since you arrived, and every time it tastes your blood, it seems to get worse." The flicker of a tired grin. "I've saved you, you've saved me, let's call it even. Don't get yourself into another situation you'll need rescuing from, at least not for a day or two."

"Same goes for you."

"I'll do my best." Eammon staggered past the gate, foot catching on a loose rock; he stumbled slightly, clutching his middle. "Kings on shitting *horses*."

"Are you sure you don't want me to—"

"Quite sure."

The door to the Keep banged open, silhouetting Lyra's curling hair and slender figure. "And *when* were you planning on telling us you got married?"

Red stopped in the center of the courtyard. "I..."

"Delightful," Eammon muttered, staggering up the hill with his bloody shirt sticking to his skin. "I'm going to kill Fife."

Valleydan Interlude IV

"No amount of money is going to make that caravan move."

Belvedere, the Advisor of Trade, was a prim, ascetic man, with close-cropped dark hair just touched with gray at the temples and a strong, prominent nose, a handsomeness noted by men and women both. His looks were only part of his appeal, though—he had a wonderfully smooth, rich voice, the kind that was easy to listen to even when delivering terrible news.

As the Advisor of Trade, he did that often.

"The Alperan Pass is far snowier for this time of year than usual," he continued. "Still navigable, but it probably won't be for long. The caravan doesn't want to risk getting caught in it with no way out."

"Unacceptable." The word was sharp, but Isla's voice wasn't—from Neve's vantage point at the other end of the long table, her mother was pale as the shaft of sunlight through the window. Golden flyaways haloed her head and dark rings surrounded her eyes. She hadn't looked well for four days now, since the night she and Neve dined together, and though no one commented on it outright, others were starting to notice.

It made Neve nervous.

Next to Neve, Kiri sat silently with the High Priestess, face revealing nothing. Tealia, another Order priestess, sat on the other side, her ostentatious show of listening a contrast with Kiri's calm.

According to Kiri, she desperately wanted to be named Zophia's heir, and knew that the best way to do that was by making herself seem like an attractive option to Isla. There might be a ceremony of votes, but the position of heir was decided almost solely by the sitting High Priestess and the Queen, and everyone knew it.

As if she could hear her thoughts, Kiri's cold blue eyes slid to Neve, then away.

"The Alperan grain shipment is the largest we receive all year. It feeds more people than every other import combined." Isla shook her head, but slightly, like movement made her feel ill. "You think we can pass out loads of olive oil and tea to the masses come autumn? There will be a revolt."

Belvedere raised his hands. "I've told them as much. We've offered a massive sum to the Dukes—the Second was going to take it and force the caravan to move on, but the First and Third outvoted him. I proposed crossing into Meducia and shipping from there, but the Cevelden Range is apparently in rockslide season, necessitating sea travel, so that was met with resistance, as well."

Neve could've told him that. Meducia shipped north by sea during every season but spring, when the growth of trees on the Cevelden Range anchored the ground enough to keep rockslides to a minimum. The range was the only path by land from Meducia into Valleyda, so now, in summer, shipping by sea would be a requirement—a huge cost in both time and money. Valleyda was landlocked, and the grain would have to travel from Alpera all the way across Meducia to the sea, then to the Florish coast, and then across Floriane to finally reach Valleyda. And with the current unrest in Floriane, it was unlikely the shipment would make it all the way to Valleyda, anyway.

Apparently, Belvedere needed a lesson or two with Master Matheus.

"The Florish coast, then." This from Zophia, and everyone sat up straighter as she spoke—even Neve, though she slightly hated herself for it. "It appears to be our only option, whether the Dukes like it or not. Take whatever impressive price you've dangled in front of them and tell them to use it to ship the grain across Meducia to the sea, then it can go from there to Floriane Harbor."

"Insurrectionists, Your Holiness." To his credit, Belvedere didn't let that smooth voice *sound* irritated, though it sparked in his eyes. Maybe Neve should give him more credit. "Anything we ship to Floriane Harbor will be seized by those who oppose our annexation."

"Kill them, then." Tealia nodded at her own suggestion, that wide-eyed look of feigned interest still on her face. "It's a holy crime to steal from Valleyda. They should know better, especially since we just sent a Second Daughter. No one would fault us for teaching a lesson."

Terrible, and made more terrible because it was true. All of Valleyda's power lay in religion. The Valleydan priestesses, by virtue of their closeness to the Wilderwood, had greater power of prayer than any other country. People traveled from all over to beseech in the Valleydan Shrine, and the other kingdoms sent boggling wealth in prayer-taxes for everything from good weather to the birth of heirs. That was enough to make the rest of the continent fall in line, and when one added in the recent tithe of a Second Daughter, it only increased piety. The stories of the monsters who burst from the Wilderwood a year after Gaya's death and didn't disappear until after Kaldenore entered the forest were well remembered. Red's sacrifice hadn't brought the return of the Kings, but the monsters hadn't returned, either. Even for those who didn't fully believe the old tales, one young woman was a small price to pay for complete assurance they wouldn't repeat. As far as political power went, Valleyda's was currently at a height.

Neve's teeth clicked together, her fists pressing nails against her palms beneath the table. "I won't allow force to be used against the Florish."

Five pairs of eyes snapped to her, surprise in every gaze but Kiri's. Isla, across that long table, stared wide-eyed at her remaining daughter.

Belvedere cleared his throat, recovering before anyone else. "The First Daughter is correct," he said. "We want the Florish to work with us. If not happy to be part of Valleyda, at least *willing.* Killing civilians will only turn public opinion even more sour than it is."

Tealia looked cowed, but Zophia only waved a hand, as if the murder of Florish insurrectionists was of little importance to her either way. "Then we marry Neverah off to Arick. Make Floriane's provincial status official, so the harbor becomes ours. The people loved his parents before they passed, so it's possible him marrying into the Valedren line might change minds, or at least distract them with a spectacle." Rheumy eyes turned to Neve. "Within the week."

Her mouth was too dry to say anything, consent or denial or otherwise. Neve's marriage was something she'd been able to push off for four years, far longer than she should've been allowed to, but with the encroaching sacrifice of her sister to the Wilderwood, no one had paid the preparations much mind. It seemed an abstract and distant thing, something to be dealt with later, always later.

Later was now, and Neve wanted to do nothing so much as bolt from the room and keep running.

"Let's not be hasty."

Kiri's voice was quiet, but it echoed against the walls. She sat with her hands folded in her wide white sleeves, her head deferentially tilted toward the High Priestess. "I understand your reasoning, Holiness, and in any other circumstances, I'd agree. But Tealia is correct, at least on one thing."

The other priestess's cheeks colored.

"Piety is higher now than ever before," Kiri continued. "After the birth of a Second Daughter, after sending her to the Wilderwood as intended. And look!" She spread her pale hands. "No monsters.

Once again, we've kept the continent safe." Her hands folded again, eyes glittering. "Perhaps the sacrifice didn't bring back the Kings..."

Neve thought of the Shrine, of branches and blood, and the bark-shard pendant hidden in the drawer of her desk.

"...but still, her birth was a sign that they are listening. That they long for freedom, that they send us sacrifices in the hope that one will be enough to placate the Wolf. And they trust Valleyda—trust *us*—with that holy mission." Fervent words, but delivered evenly. Kiri's cold eyes slid once more to Neve. "If we remind them of that, effectively, Alpera should do anything we ask. And so should everyone else."

Silence as they all weighed Kiri's words. The High Priestess shifted in her seat. "True enough, Kiri," she conceded. "But how do you propose we remind them?"

For a stretching, awful minute, Neve imagined the possibilities, the things she knew could be done with the strange yielding of their time in the Shrine. *Magic.* Magic Kiri claimed they pulled from the Shadowlands itself.

It was still hard for Neve to swallow—even with proof staring her in the face, years of quiet agnosticism were hard to overcome—but there really wasn't any other explanation, and the results were undeniable. The small experiments she'd seen were convincing enough. With that power, trees could be withered, fields stricken dead, fertile farmland turned dark and cold.

Kiri's lip rose in a smirk. "Prayer, of course."

The tightness in Neve's chest eased, but only slightly.

"Since his return, Arick has been far more pious," Kiri continued. "He spends many nights in prayer in the Shrine, meditating on how best to help our countries. I believe he would be glad to help us, even before his marriage to Neverah."

Tightness, coiling again.

"I propose that Arick accompany me and a selection of others to the Florish coast," Kiri continued. "We will hold a prayer to clear the harbor."

Widened eyes all around the room. Floriane's harbor was in a picturesque bay, and the mouth of it often became choked with seaweed in the summer, sometimes so much that it blocked traffic. When that happened, workers had to dive in and clear the mess by hand. The Order prayed for it to remain clear at the beginning of every summer, for the Kings to somehow prevent the seaweed from overgrowing and blocking the ships. Some summers the growth was a problem, and some it wasn't. Neve thought the prayers had very little to do with it one way or another.

Zophia raised a grizzled brow. "Prayers are most effective in Shrines, Kiri, not harbors. And the prayers for a clear sailing season were already made weeks ago, when Floriane sent their tax."

Kiri dipped her head. "True. But I believe that the Kings will see the need for a miracle in this tumultuous time, and grant one. Mark me, when we make our prayers at the harbor, the mouth of the bay will be entirely cleared, and there will be no question that it was our beseeching that made it so."

Another, longer pause. Zophia's mouth drew to a pucker, her face inscrutable. "Such faith," she murmured.

"A pretty idea, but unrealistic." Tealia didn't stick her tongue out and wag it, but her tone was the same as if she had. Her eyes darted from the High Priestess to Kiri. "Even if the Kings grant your request, who's to say the Florish insurrectionists won't kill you before you're able to make your prayers? You're putting quite a lot of faith in their piety."

"To the contrary." Kiri's smile could cut glass. "I'm putting quite a lot of faith in the Five Kings. Or do you not think them capable of keeping us safe from a few unhappy rebels, Tealia?"

The other priestess shut her mouth, cheeks burning. Zophia looked between them, frowning, then to the Queen.

At the end of the table, Isla sat still and quiet, her eyes far away. The fist of fear closed tighter around Neve's heart.

"Your faith is admirable," the High Priestess said finally, when it became clear Isla wasn't going to respond. She turned to Kiri. "And I think it's worth a try, though I'm sure the Queen and I are in agreement that guards should accompany you as well."

"One or two, perhaps." The cut-glass smile didn't quite meet Kiri's eyes. "Truly, I don't think more will be needed."

Zophia made an unconvinced sound but didn't press further. "I'll approve it, but we must move quickly. Sending the shipment through Floriane will add days to its arrival. If after your vigil things still seem unstable, we can always go back to marriage."

"I don't see why we don't anyway." Belvedere, cutting back into the conversation after minutes of silent listening. "Surely it can't hurt."

His eyes were on Neve, expecting her to answer, but Kiri did first. "Of course not," she said primly. "But a royal marriage is a joyous affair. If at all possible, Neverah should have time to plan it as she sees fit."

Relief wanted to flood her chest, but worry chased it. Neve watched the priestess with a clenched jaw. Something about all this felt transactional. Whatever help Kiri offered would come with the expectation of being repaid.

The only question was how.

Details were arranged, dates set, and guards appointed. Kiri, Arick, and her priestesses—chosen by Kiri herself, to save the High Priestess the strain—would depart in two days, after an announcement had been sent to Floriane's capital. The Three Dukes of Alpera were still visiting, having not yet returned home after seeing Red off, so Belvedere could bring the proposal to them before nightfall.

Neve hung back as Belvedere and the priestesses left the room, each of them bowing to Isla and then to her before exiting. Kiri held her gaze as she bent forward, still with that slight, cold smile. "Perhaps I will see you this afternoon, First Daughter. I plan to pray." Then she glided from the room.

Slowly, Neve stood, walking from her end of the long table to where her mother sat. Up close, she could see a sheen of sweat on Isla's brow, the way her hands kept twitching on the folds of her gown.

"Mother?" Her voice came tentative. "Do you need me to help you to your room?"

A moment, like she didn't hear her at first. Then Isla shook her head, standing on unsteady legs. "No. I might be ill, but I'm not an invalid."

"Perhaps you should get some rest."

She half expected another caustic answer, but instead her mother just sighed. "Yes. Rest." She pushed the door open, walking slowly enough down the hallway that it looked like a leisurely stroll instead of a way to keep from stumbling.

Neve watched her go, chewing her lip so hard she almost broke the skin. Then, brows drawn down, she strode toward the gardens.

Despite the pleasant weather—by Valleydan standards—there weren't many people lingering among the hedges. The few who were didn't acknowledge Neve other than with dips of their heads as she walked with single-minded determination toward the Shrine.

Kiri waited, hands tucked into her sleeves. Something jutted against the underside of the fabric covering her collarbone. The wood-shard pendant, worn but hidden.

That same sharp smile lifted her mouth as the priestess watched Neve approach. "Fancy meeting you here."

"Stop with the games." Neve pitched her voice low, made a concentrated effort to unclench her hands from fists for the benefit of anyone who might observe them. "Your plan for Floriane is foolish. The Alperans are probably just holding out for a better price. If Belvedere keeps at them—"

"Your first mistake is to think this is only about grain," Kiri cut in. "Yes, the Alperans are just greedy. Yes, Belvedere, with all his cunning, could probably make a deal with them in a day or so. But this is a golden opportunity, Neverah. One we would be foolish to pass up."

There was a subtle heft to that *we*. Neve crossed her arms. Her heartbeat marked time against her rib cage.

"Zophia is old," Kiri continued. "Her time draws near. Tealia"—her lips pulled into a grimace—"is currently slated as her successor. It's not an exaggeration to say her appointment would be disastrous for our... experiments."

Inside the Shrine, mere feet away, the bloodied branch shards of the Wilderwood waited. Neve shifted on her feet.

"Arick and I going to Floriane serves three purposes, all of them necessary for us to continue weakening the Wilderwood's hold on your sister." Her hands resurfaced from her wide sleeves, ticking points off on her fingers. "It reinforces our religious power, serving as a reminder to Floriane and everyone else that we are favored, that word from the Valleydan Temple is law. It gets us our grain. And once we're successful, it might make the Queen reconsider Zophia's heir."

There was the crux of it, the repayment Kiri would expect for momentarily weaseling Neve out of her marriage. "The Queen? Why not Zophia herself?"

"She's set in her ways." Kiri waved a dismissive hand. "And between the two of us, more concerned with wine than with her devotions, most evenings. She's made a decision, and nothing but word from the Queen will make her change it, simply because doing so would be an inconvenience."

"So I try to get my mother to appoint you as the heir," Neve said, breaking it down to its most blunt terms, "while you and Arick reinforce our religious power by clearing the harbor." Her eyes narrowed. "Which you seem very convinced you can do."

"Of course I can." Kiri lifted her hand and lightly touched one of the leaves on the hedge next to the Shrine. The veins on her wrist went dark, as if shadows ran there instead of blood. An iced, ozonic scent peppered the air—the atmosphere right before a lightning storm, but somehow cold. What emptiness might smell like.

The leaf Kiri touched browned, withered. Fell.

This was what the twisting of the trees in the Shrine bought, the second piece of the dual reward for weakening the Wilderwood. The possibility they could debilitate it enough to let Red go, and this power of... of death, of decay.

Seeing that magic at work would be enough to make anyone cooperate.

Neve chewed her lip, not quite ready to give in just yet. "Becoming High Priestess is quite the repayment for nothing more than the delay of a marriage neither party wants."

"Why just a delay, Neverah? Once I am High Priestess, I will hold quite a lot of sway with your mother. Perhaps enough to get you out of marrying Arick entirely." Kiri paused. "Perhaps enough to push her toward someone else as your betrothed."

Something like hope lapped at the bottom of her heart. Neve swallowed. "That would be a pleasant outcome."

"Quite." Kiri reached out, touched the hedge again, almost absently this time. Again, the shadowed veins; again, a cold scent and a dead leaf.

A slight breeze nudged the desiccated leaf toward Neve's foot; she sidestepped it, unwilling to let it touch her.

"Come now, First Daughter." Kiri tucked her hands back into her sleeves, veins now undarkened. "Don't be skittish. You could do it, too, if you wanted. All who give blood can."

"No, thank you." Her voice was prim, but the metronome of her pulse sped up. "The power doesn't matter to me. Only weakening the Wilderwood's hold on Red so she can escape."

The priestess's eyes flickered, as if in any other circumstance she might've rolled them. "Yes. Well. Rest assured, the Wilderwood is weakening, which should loosen its ties to your sister. We're both getting what we want."

On the cobblestones, the dead leaf fluttered. The breeze picked up, pushed it farther away.

"In any case," Kiri said, "this will be convincing enough to get us our grain." A flash of teeth in the weak sunlight. "I wouldn't be surprised if we can raise prayer-taxes after word gets around. Yes, we'll all get what we want, just like I was told."

A shiver pricked down Neve's spine. Their religion was one of contrasts, of material proof and nebulous belief—the Wilderwood and the Second Daughters, forest and flesh, paired with the fear of shadowed monsters and the conviction the Kings were trapped and needed to be freed. Why else would they be absent? What other reason could they have for returning to the Wilderwood fifty years after the Binding, other than through some treachery that kept them from the world they'd saved? People created stories to fill the gaps they didn't understand, and religion grew up around it like rot on a fallen tree.

Four hundred years was long enough for there to be facets of both fact and faith, concrete evidence and myths that became holy truths. But this power...this twisting of one concrete pillar of belief, wringing out its magic to prove something...it took those two opposing forces and melted them together in a way that both terrified and exhilarated her.

Strange, that she'd find faith in blasphemy.

Neve nodded, a sharp dip of her chin. "It seems we have a plan, then." She turned on her heel and strode away, back toward the palace.

Behind her, the wind finally caught the dead leaf from the hedge, twisting it into the air.

Chapter Fifteen

The noise at the door didn't sound like a knock.

Red looked up from her book, frowning. It was late into the night—as best she could tell, anyway. She'd eaten hours ago with Fife and Lyra, apples and hunks of hard cheese and coarse bread. After they'd returned to the Keep, Eammon had disappeared up the stairs, presumably to his room, and she hadn't seen him since.

She'd told Lyra about his wounds, but the other woman didn't seem overly concerned. "Eammon is used to bleeding," she'd said, slicing an apple. "He knows how to take care of himself."

"Could you heal him? If he needed it?"

"Not in the way you're thinking. Fife and I aren't connected enough to the forest for that." A delicate brow arched. "Healing is only between you two."

That'd sent Red into silence for the remainder of the meal. She hadn't eaten much, and as she drifted back to her room, she kept reaching up to touch the place on her cheek the Wolf had healed.

Now, hours past dinner, there was another sound at the door. Still not a knock—more like something sliding against the wood, the slow scratch of a nail.

When she and Neve were small, they'd play at trying to frighten each other. Red would hide in the curtains to jump out at her unsuspecting twin, but Neve preferred more subtlety. Once, she'd scratched against the foot of her bed for an hour, frightening Red so much she called for the nursemaid. That's what this noise sounded like—someone scratching.

Thinking of Neve made her heart contract. She slipped a finger between the pages of her book. "Hello?"

No answer. Briefly, Red thought of Eammon, slumped against her doorway in a blood-caked shirt, finally willing to accept her healing.

Improbable. But still, she cursed, rising to wrench open the door.

The hall was empty, the light through the distant solarium window illuminating only the curls of leaves, the edges of thorns. Even when the sky was lavender, the corridor was unsettling; in the deep violet of a forest-muddled night, it nearly seethed unease.

Red swallowed, stepping back toward her threshold, reaching behind her to retreat to her room. But instead of the open space of her doorway, her hand brushed along a smooth, unfamiliar surface next to it. Slowly, Red looked back over her shoulder.

White bark, stretching spindly fingers up into the gloom. A sentinel.

More scattered through the ruined hallway, easy to spot now that she'd seen the first, tall and pale as picked-clean bones. They hadn't been there when she came back from dinner. These were new saplings, the harbingers of new breaches into the Shadowlands. How many had opened, in the mere hours between then and now?

Not evil, she'd been reassured, not dangerous on their own, but wanting her blood with consequences Eammon was determined to keep her from. Inhuman and wild, not good or bad, existing outside of the binaries she understood. His warning from earlier rang in her head—*the Wilderwood is restless, and every time it tastes your blood, it seems to get worse.*

It'd tasted her blood today, drunk it long and deep. Tried to do more before the Wolf stopped it. What she'd told him after, about the forest being upset with them, seemed to ring even more true under the heavy regard of the saplings in the corridor.

Red backed away from the white tree like it was a wild animal, deft and cautious. But the sentinels weren't the only new growth in the Keep—two steps, and her heel caught on a tangle of new-sprouted thorns. Slicing pain drove her teeth together as one drew a bloody line over her ankle.

Half a second of stillness, of expectant silence. "Oh, *Kings*."

The forest erupted.

The window in her room spiderwebbed, cracked like a starburst, vines slithering through the broken pane. They wrapped the walls in seconds, crushing the posters of the bed, curling vise-like around the wardrobe. Thorns sprang sharp and reaching from the ground, leaves stretching like straining fingers. The sounds of rush and ruin collected, became a bellow, and the Wilderwood *lunged*.

Moss lumped up to trip her, vines lashed for her feet. A thicket burst from the floor, filled with sharp branches; one slashed across her arm, and where her blood splattered, the forest soaked it up like water to parched ground.

Her first instinct was to careen down the hall, but then Red remembered her cloak, still in the wardrobe now wrapped in vines in her room. Her tattered, threadbare cloak, the one Neve had draped over her shoulders. A symbol of a sacrifice she'd somehow outlived.

Damn if the Wilderwood was taking that from her.

Teeth bared, Red ran through her open door, dodging reaching branches and curling leaves. She tore at the vines with her bare hands, ripping them away—the Wilderwood made a thin, screeching sound, terribly like a scream. Wrenching open the warped and broken wardrobe, Red tugged out the still-dirty crimson fabric of the cloak, balling it against her chest and jumping the threshold just before the lintel cracked, collapsing the room behind her.

The Wilderwood howled as Red pelted around the corner. She felt it in her bones as much as heard it in her ears, caught and amplified by the piece of its magic coiled in her middle.

You begin and begin, yet never see it finished!

One of the bushes by the corner withered instantly, leaves dropping all at once as the twigs curled inward in a death throe. The Wilderwood paying its price for speech.

Stone rained from the ceiling of the corridor, littered the floor as vines and roots rioted through and broke it apart. Red clasped her arms over her head and leapt to huddle under the solarium light, cloak falling next to her on the floor.

"Red!"

The stairs shuddered as Eammon thundered down them, barechested, hair unbound. He glared at the advancing forest with a snarl on his lips, hands arched into claws and tendons tight on his neck.

The Wilderwood's shriek was deafening, a cascade of sapling and thorn reaching for her on the floor. Eammon jumped down the rest of the stairs, almost lost his balance, landed before her in a wild-haired crouch. He came up on one knee, hands outstretched, every muscle in his body strained.

Fear brought a strange sort of clarity, and Red's eyes went straight to Eammon's bare arm, to what she knew would be there. A Bargainer's Mark, larger and more intricate than hers. Tendrils twisted off the band of roots, spiraling beneath his skin in delicate patterns, stretching down to the center of his forearm, up past his elbow.

Already he called up magic, and the changes it wrought came swiftly—the veins in his hands ran green, not just his wrists, but his neck, too, running down the curvature of his shoulders. Bands of bark edged through the skin of his forearms, from wristbone to where the tendrils of his Mark began. He grew taller, his hair longer, a glimpse of ivy leaves when it shifted over his back.

The Wolf and the Wilderwood, tangling, blurring, fighting for dominance. Stopping the forest's advance was a battle too intimate to be won with blood.

Eammon lifted his green-veined hands toward the corridor. Then his fingers curled to fists, as if taking hold of something, and he jerked them back.

A *boom*, a compression of air. It reminded her of that first night, when she'd clamped down on all her own power and sliced it off, just on a larger scale. He'd pulled the Wilderwood in, let his internal balance tip, then lashed all that power down. The forest had no choice but to obey.

The Wilderwood gave one more howl that faded slowly into normal forest sounds—twigs snapping, branches stretching, then silence. Eammon shuddered, dropping to brace on knees and elbows. Slowly, slowly, his veins ran from bright green to blue. The bark on his forearms slipped under his skin, though a rough band remained right around his wrist, like a bracelet. The heave of his bare back perfectly matched the slow sway of settling leaves.

When he finally looked back at her, hair stuck to his forehead by sweat, the whites of his eyes were spiderwebbed with green, a halo of it around his irises.

The encroaching forest sliced off right where the hallway branched, as if by some giant scythe. Cut roots twitched feebly on the moss like dying beetles, their movements synced to the rhythms of Eammon's breath. Five sentinels stood just inside the edge of the corridor, a wall of bone-white trees.

Red and the Wolf crouched on the ground for a moment, two pairs of shoulders shaking, two pairs of wild eyes surveying a hall lost to a forest. Eammon's gaze dropped to the cloak puddled by her knees, puzzlement creasing his brow when his eyes rose back to her face.

Fife skidded out from the dining room, still fully dressed. His eyes widened, mouth working a string of curses. "Kings. Shadows *damn* us."

Lyra ran from beneath the broken arch, stopping short and clapping a hand over her mouth. Behind her palm, her jaw worked, but all that came out was "Oh."

Eammon regained composure before Red did, standing on

shaking legs. She noticed he hadn't lost all the height magic gave him, not this time, though the rest of the changes were slowly leaking away. The green leached out of his eyes, and the last of the bark-vambraces slipped beneath his skin as he pushed his hair back from his forehead.

"What happened?" Fife looked from the forest to Eammon, taking in his slightly increased height with nothing more than a worried swallow and the flicker of a gaze at Lyra. "I checked the one in the corridor this morning. No shadow-rot."

"I don't think it had anything to do with shadow-rot." A slight echo in Eammon's voice, but it faded before he'd finished speaking. Bandages covered the wounds on his stomach, and new green-threaded blood seeped slowly through the fabric. He looked to Red, then away, rubbing between his now-only-amber eyes with thumb and forefinger. "It's getting worse," he murmured. "It's *never* been like this."

Lyra glanced at Fife, worry in the line of her mouth. Neither of them spoke.

Red let herself be helped up by Fife's good hand. "Are you hurt?" he asked brusquely.

She shook her head.

Concern twisted the elfin angles of Lyra's face, lips pursed as her eyes flickered over Eammon. Containing the Wilderwood's magic had given him only about an inch more in height, but it still hadn't gone away, a fact that seemed to unnerve her. "There's a linen closet somewhere," she said finally, turning to Red. "We can make a pallet in my room—"

"Neither of you is sleeping on the floor." Eammon still looked at the corridor, at the ruin the forest had made it. A tremor went through his hand; he closed it to a fist.

"There are four of us and three beds. *Someone* will have to."

"And it will be me." Eammon didn't meet anyone's eyes as he turned toward the stairs. "She can have my bed. I'll sleep in the hall."

His tone brooked no argument. Lyra's lips quirked, gaze flicking from Eammon's retreating back to Fife's face in an unspoken conversation. "Well. Pleasant dreams, I guess."

"That seems awfully optimistic," Fife muttered, but he was abruptly silenced by Lyra's elbow in his ribs.

Eammon was halfway up the stairs and hadn't looked back once. With a deep breath, Red placed her foot on the bottom step. The moss that had grown into a wall to keep her away now smoothed out in welcome.

Mouth set in a determined line, Red balled her cloak in her arms and followed the Wolf.

Chapter Sixteen

The forest growth petered out at the top landing, scraps of green fading to bare stone beneath her feet. It felt strange, after more than a week of moss, and cold enough to numb her toes.

When they reached the balcony, Eammon turned to the right and pushed open a wooden door, revealing another, smaller set of stairs. Warm light from above flickered over his back as he climbed, slightly hunched over the slashes in his middle. His Bargainer's Mark seemed darker than before, its deep-green color stark as ink against his skin.

The Wolf's room was the very top of the tower, circular beneath a vaulted ceiling crisscrossed with wooden beams. An open wardrobe stood next to the staircase, but clothes were scattered across the floor in messy piles. Eammon kicked them under the wardrobe. "Kings," he swore, pressing a hand to his stomach.

Opposite the stairs, a stone fireplace cut into the wall, the source of the warmth and flickering light. Next to it, a bed was shoved between two large, glassless windows, the sheets tangled and the coverlet half on the floor. Books and empty mugs were piled around the bed, and the desk against the wall by the wardrobe overflowed with marked-up papers, an open inkwell, a leaking pen.

Eammon stumbled to the desk, one hand on his middle while the other tried to straighten the piles.

"You don't have to do that."

No response, but Eammon stopped his fruitless organizing, turning to face her with an unreadable expression. His eyes flickered to the cloak, still balled in her hands. "You went back for that?"

She nodded.

A line drew between his brows. "I can't say I understand why."

"It..." But she wasn't sure how to finish, how to put it into words. "It's mine."

He didn't press her for further explanation. They stood frozen, gazes locked, neither knowing quite how to move.

Eammon broke away first, looking instead at his still-cluttered room. With a sigh, he bent to gather the fallen coverlet. "I'll sleep at the base of the stairs. If you need—*shit*."

He dropped the blanket, hand pressing hard against his stomach. Blood welled through the bandage, more green than crimson, dripping down the plane of pale, scarred skin.

Red strode forward, put her hands on his shoulders, pushed him to sit against the wall. "You've reopened the wound."

"I'm aware."

"Do you have more bandages?"

"Top drawer."

She crossed the room to the desk and rummaged through the noted drawer, past shredded bits of paper and broken pens. "Bandages are more effective when they're kept *clean*."

"They've worked fine thus far." Eammon shifted, cursed. "If you haven't noticed, I get sliced up rather often."

It reminded her of what Lyra said before. *Eammon is used to bleeding.* Her mouth firmed, and she dug through the mess with renewed determination.

Finally, she found them, buried beneath a scribble-covered notebook and a layer of pencil shavings. Fist full of gauze, Red came back over and crouched next to him, peeled away the sodden bandage as another curse hissed through Eammon's teeth. Three deep strikes scored his skin, bisecting chest and stomach. Tiny green tendrils curled from the ragged edges, almost too fine to see, flecked with fragile leaves.

Her eyes flicked from the carnage to Eammon's face, stricken with sudden worry. "It's not shadow-rotted, is it?"

"Can't be." Eammon's jaw clenched tight. "Too much Wilderwood in me to let in anything else."

Too much Wilderwood, indeed. His height still hadn't lessened from the magic he'd harnessed as the corridor collapsed. Barely an inch, but it felt portentous to Red, made nerves spark along the back of her neck.

There was a tiny scar on his cheek. One she hadn't noticed before, too faint to see from afar. A thin white line across his cheekbone, the same place where he'd taken her cut that first day in the library.

A scar he'd gained for her.

Their closeness sparked her power, like it had before in the clearing, making Red sharply, painfully aware of every growing thing in the Keep below them, in the courtyard outside. Magic bloomed, arched toward her fingertips, as if the sight of his wound and the bond between them pulled it forward. "You have to let me try to fix it."

Eammon leaned his head back against the wall. "Not a good idea." His words were scaled back and stilted; he could force only so many up his throat. "Too much."

Too much pain, and it had to go somewhere. Her bent hands hovered over his skin, conviction sharpening the edges of her voice. "I can do it."

"Why?" Dark hair shadowed Eammon's eyes, where she read everything he didn't say. Why was she so determined to try healing him, when before the idea of using her power was met with such resistance?

Red wasn't sure how to answer. The only thing she was sure of, when it came to Eammon, was that she wanted him safe. She *cared*. The caring was a complicated, layered thing, but that was the only kind of caring she knew.

"Because I have a vested interest in you not dying." Then, somewhat softer, "And I owe you."

Eammon's eyes searched hers. Finally, he nodded, grimacing as he shifted against the wall, spelling out clipped instructions. "Focus your intention. Connect to the forest's power in you. Touch the wound. Draw it in." His mouth went suddenly fierce, brows drawn low, and when he spoke it was sure and strong. "Not all of it, Redarys. Promise me."

She swallowed against a dry throat. Nodded. Then, fighting to keep her hands steady, she placed them against his skin.

Eammon was always warm, but this heat was fevered, sickly. His green-and-scarlet blood lined her fingers, pricked with leaves, and Red had to close her eyes to concentrate, to guard against the fear that mounted in her head at the sight of him hurt so badly.

But even the fear had its purpose. Something about it—something about it being for *Eammon*—made her power easier to wield, easier to shape. Her caring, magnified by their shared splinter of magic and the marriage they'd made, fashioned the chaotic power into something she could use.

It still scared her, how unexplainable it was. The connection between them forged in forest. Earlier, when she tried to grow the ivy, she'd been thinking of Neve and violence, of carnage she couldn't control. But then there'd been the vision, proof that the way she and Eammon had tied themselves together made her stronger. And now, when the task before her was meaningful—when she wanted him safe, both because of that strange caring and because she feared what might happen to all of them if he wasn't—she could treat her magic like a tool to be used rather than something to contain.

Intention clear, Red took hold of her power, opened herself to it. And she didn't drown.

It flowed, rich and heady, deep green. A thin tendril, winding through muscle and bone like a root snaking toward the sun, waiting for her will.

The wounds burned under her hands. Slowly, carefully, Red let them in.

If there was pain, she didn't feel it. The beat of power was steady, sure, a flow that matched her pulse. For the first time, this felt *right*, and the feeling was intoxicating. She took a little, then a little more, pushing herself—

"Red, stop!"

Her hands were empty. Red's eyes opened, face sweaty and breath labored.

Eammon's hand hovered above her cheek. He pulled back as her eyes opened, cold air replacing his warmth.

"You took too much." His eyes were clearer than they'd been since the breach. "*Dammit*, Red."

She looked down. Crimson bloomed across her abdomen, barely visible through the thin fabric of her nightgown. A wound, but not nearly as awful as his had been—she'd taken only part, not the whole. Still, as if the sight sparked her nerves to working, pain seared across the cuts, brought a hiss to her teeth. "Shit." She sat back, hand pressed against her stomach. "You've lived with this all day? *More* than this?"

Eammon pushed off the wall, brow furrowed, legs shaky. "That was too much," he said again, almost to himself.

"But it worked." After the initial burn, the wounds weren't so bad. Pain had to go somewhere, yes, but it seemed to come in a quick flare, all of it at once. Gingerly, Red lifted her hand from her middle, noticing as she did that her veins were traced in brilliant emerald, not just her wrists, but all the way up her arm. They faded almost immediately, ran blue again. "You're...well, not good as new. But better. No more *mangled insides*."

Eammon hung his hands on his hips, glowering down at her. Triple stripes of faint red with white-scarred lines in their centers marked his chest and stomach. "*Less* mangled." Then, lower: "Thank you."

Silence fell, their fragile camaraderie overshadowed by awkwardness. Eammon unhooked a poker from over the hearth and halfheartedly stirred up the embers, banishing the chill from the open windows. "You can put your cloak in the wardrobe," he said to the fire. "If you want."

The tattered fabric lay on the floor where she'd dropped it, distracted by Eammon's bleeding. She picked it up, padded across the room. There was plenty of space in the wardrobe, since most of Eammon's clothes seemed to live on the floor. The clothes that had made it inside were darkly colored and scented like leaves. Red tucked her scarlet cloak next to a stack of Eammon's shirts.

She crossed back to the fireplace and sat on the floor, wrapped her arms around her knees. "It made you taller," she said after a moment, quietly. "I mean, it made you taller, and then it didn't go away."

Eammon stiffened, pausing a moment in his stirring of the fire. His eyes flickered down, as if taking stock of himself, before closing. "So it did."

"Has that happened before?" She kept her arms around her knees and her voice lightly conversational, but worry gnawed at her stomach. "A change from the magic staying permanently?"

One more stir of the embers, a spiral of sparks in the cold air. "No," he said curtly, replacing the poker on the mantel.

The worry grew sharper teeth, bit deeper.

"It was a lot of power." Quiet, meant as much for himself as for her. "More even than I've used healing a sentinel before. That's probably why. I just harnessed more than normal. Let more in." He rubbed at his eyes. "Should've at least tried blood, though it wouldn't have been enough."

"No pleasant options available, I guess."

An affirmative grunt.

Red watched him from the corner of her eye, how his tense shoulders tapered to his hips, how his midnight hair fell across his brow.

The scar on his stomach was a mirror image of hers, just like the Bargainer's Mark. There was a strange intimacy in it, one that sharpened the alchemy of worry and guilt clawing up her insides.

Her husband, the Wolf. Scarred for her, scarred for everyone else, locked in a constant fight with a forest that was part of him.

"Downstairs," she ventured, turning her gaze to the flames so he wouldn't catch her staring. "You said it's never been this bad before."

Nothing from Eammon. After a moment, he sighed. "It hasn't."

"Is it my fault?"

"No, Red." For all his clear reticence to discuss this, the rebuttal was immediate. "None of this is your fault."

"But if it's only gotten worse since I came—"

"Your situation is unique. Your connection to the Wilderwood—I've never seen anything like it before." His shadow moved over the floor as he came to stand beside her. Eammon's mouth worked, eyes unreadable, like he could call up the exact words he wanted from the flames if he stared at them hard enough. "The others were bound to the forest, but not like this."

Red curled further into her knees. "They were bound in ways that killed them."

It was hard to tell in the dim, but she thought his face blanched. "Yes," he said quietly. "But you aren't. You *won't* be. And yes, because it's so different, everything has been... difficult to navigate. But I promise you, we will figure it out."

Together. It went unspoken, but the ghost of it hovered in the air. *We'll figure it out together.*

Eammon turned, bending with a minor grimace to gather the coverlet. "I'll sleep downstairs. If you need—"

"It's *freezing* down there."

"Thus, the blanket."

"You're being ridiculous."

He shrugged, walking toward the stairs.

"You know, sharing a room is not an unheard-of thing for married people to do."

He froze, glanced back at her. Red closed her mouth, biting her lip to keep more foolish words from escaping. Her pulse thrummed in the wounds they shared.

She stood, crossed her arms, suddenly vulnerable in his amber-eyed scrutiny. "Do you snore?"

"Used to." Eammon turned his attention to the blanket in his hands. "It's been a while since someone was in a position to tell me if the issue persists."

"Well," Red said, shoring up false confidence, "I'll let you know."

The corner of his mouth flicked up, dropped again. After a moment, Eammon walked to the other end of the room and spread his blanket next to the wall. He stretched out on his back, hissing as his shoulder jostled against the floor.

Red sat gingerly on the bed, setting the sheets to rights. They smelled like him, paper and coffee. Exhaustion weighed her eyelids when she slid between them, but the awareness of Eammon across the room chased sleep out of reach.

She hadn't shared a room since she and Neve were small. They'd stay up too late, telling stories, arguing, playing dress-up with clothes in the wardrobe. Her chest felt iron-banded. "Who told you that you snore?"

His small movements paused, just for a moment. "Someone I used to share a room with," he answered finally.

Before today, before she'd felt his blood under her hands, she might've left it at that. As it stood… "*Really?*"

In the dim light, Red couldn't see him, but she could imagine him—the bandage on his middle a square of white, hands behind his rumpled head. "Her name was Thera," he said finally. Softly.

Thera. "Not another Second Daughter?"

"No." A quick cut of an answer. "The Second Daughters and I… there was nothing like that, not with any of them."

Red's hands tightened over her stomach, lacing over new wounds. "Who was she, then?"

"A girl from one of the villages beyond the border," Eammon murmured. "From before the Kings wounded the Wilderwood. Before it closed in on itself. Gaya and Ciaran were still alive. I wasn't the Wolf yet. Young and stupid."

"You still look rather young, to be honest, though I won't comment on the *stupid* part."

"Another Wilderwood benefit. I guess I age like a tree."

"Better-looking than a tree. Slightly."

A huff of hoarse laughter. Red quirked a tiny grin in the dark.

"All told," Eammon continued, "my life was fairly normal before I was the Wolf. Other than having fairy-tale characters for parents. I could leave."

Once, he could leave. That made it almost worse. "What happened?"

"I'd been staying with Thera, in the village. We fought—she wanted to get married, I didn't—"

Her stomach flipped.

"—so I came back here for the night." She heard him shift against the floorboards. "And that night, the Kings wounded the Wilderwood, tried to cut down the sentinel where they'd made their bargain and were pulled into the Shadowlands. The borders closed. I couldn't go out. She couldn't get in." A pause. "I inherited my father's horrific timing, I suppose."

"That's terrible," Red murmured.

"It was centuries ago." But there was still a ghost of grief in his voice, an old wound healed but well remembered. "Haven't been with anyone since."

"Why not?"

"Other than the obvious issue of being stuck in a forest?" A weak snort, another shift against the ground. "The Wilderwood is difficult to hold together. It takes near-constant concentration, especially when I have to keep it from...from doing things I don't want it to do." He paused, next words quieter. "There's not much of me left to give to another person."

Red worked her thumbnail against the weave of his sheet.

"And you?" Hushed, but with genuine curiosity. "Surely there was someone, in the twenty years before you came here."

When she closed her eyes and tried to remember Arick's face, all she could see was the twisted thing from the gate, built of darkness and malice. "One."

Silence, shatter-ready. "If you didn't have to be here," Eammon began, barely above a whisper. "If you could do anything you wanted, what would you do?"

The question felt more complicated than it should've. Red's whole life was under the shadow of the Wilderwood. Considering anything else hurt too much, so she just...didn't. Now that there were options, now that a life stretched before her tied to the man across the room, she wasn't exactly sure what *wanting* looked like.

"If I could do anything I wanted," she answered, "I would let my sister know I'm safe."

Eammon's sigh was shaky. "I'm sorry, Red."

She sat up on her elbow, peered through the ember glow to where Eammon lay, one hand pushing back his hair and the other on his chest. Dim light revealed only his edges—broad shoulders, crooked nose. He turned, and their gazes locked.

"I'm sorry, too," she breathed.

The permanent line between Eammon's brows softened. Wordlessly, he nodded.

Red lay back, rolled on her side. After a moment, she heard Eammon do the same, and his breathing slowed, evened out.

Eventually, so did hers.

Valleydan Interlude V

Order funerals were morbid affairs. And since this one was for the High Priestess, it seemed even more somber than usual.

Neve's black veil blanketed everything in shadow, made the pyre and the priestesses and the gathered courtiers look like they moved through thick fog. Nerves twisted in her stomach. This had happened too fast, too quickly for her plans to be fully woven. It felt like holding tight to the reins of a runaway horse.

Zophia's body lay prostrate on the pyre, wrapped to her chin in the black cloak corpses wore for burning. The dark cloth was covered in tokens from all over the continent to signify the Order's unity—each country with its own Temple, each Temple with its own High Priestess.

The value of the tokens the other Temples had sent for this burning was staggering. Olive oil from Karsecka, pounds of fragrant blooms from Cian, bottles of dark liquor brewed with gold flecks shipped over from the Rylt. There was far too much to actually include on the pyre, most of it packed away in the Temple's stores with the prayer-taxes. A happy coincidence, really—the sum Belvedere had ended up paying Alpera to reroute the grain was truly astronomical, and some of the riches brought for the funeral could offset the costs.

Though the expense was vast, the grain had arrived safely. The story of Kiri and Arick's prayers clearing the mouth of the bay were nothing but rumbles, whispered rumors in hushed tones. At first, that had puzzled Neve, but it was apparently how Kiri preferred it. A folktale of a miracle, she said, would prove more useful to them than something proclaimed by the Temple. Support from the bottom up would be more useful than from the top down. She'd clutched her wood-shard pendant as she said it, face carefully blank, like she was reciting something she'd heard rather than explaining thoughts of her own. It'd made Neve's insides feel twitchy, and made her glad she'd never actually worn the pendant Kiri had given her. But she nodded along.

From her place behind the pyre with the other candidates for the High Priestess's replacement, Kiri glanced over, blue eyes glinting ice. The slightest bend of a cold smile, then she looked away.

A torch passed. Neve's part of the plan began now.

Zophia's possible successors walked in a circle around the pyre, their seventh and final lap ending in a line behind it. As one, they turned to Neve and Isla. The Queen and the First Daughter had the front row to themselves.

Isla looked worse. She'd been on a steady decline in the week since the trade meeting. Today cosmetics made her cheeks less pale and her eyes less listless, but there was no mistaking her thinness, the slump of her shoulders. Her health had been one of the things delaying Neve in trying to change her mind on the High Priestess's heir. She'd gone to visit her mother nearly every day, but the silence of her sickroom was oppressive, and Isla had usually been asleep, anyway.

Then Zophia died, with Tealia still selected to replace her. But there was a loophole. One Neve would be exploiting as soon as the call went out for the useless, ceremonial vote.

A tiny prayer, murmured in her mind, the scrap of faith she'd unexpectedly found in all her heresy. *Make her listen.*

A warm hand landed on Neve's shoulder, there and then gone,

and she almost jumped out of her skin. A quick glance back—just Raffe. He gave her a fleeting smile, squeezed her shoulder once.

It should've been comforting. Instead, Neve's heartbeat sped.

The red rose petal in her hand was limp and crumpled, creased with sweat. The other courtiers in the room made great shows of looking from their petals to the gathered priestesses, as if this vote actually counted for something.

Next to Raffe, Arick's brows drew low, his petal turning between his fingers. Dark circles marked the skin under his eyes. The meeting in the Shrine last night had run late. He had a new bandage on his hand, unbloodied, though a speck of black still marked the center of his palm. She'd been concerned the first time she saw him bleed from it, but no one else seemed to be, so she kept quiet.

According to Kiri, it was working. The Wilderwood was weakening, loosening its hold on Red. That was what mattered. Everything else, they could figure out later.

She darted another glance at Raffe. The sunlight through the windows made his eyes glow honey-colored, reflected gold along the edge of his mouth. She hadn't told Raffe anything. Not because she didn't want to—it was a constant struggle not to let the whole thing spill over—but because he wouldn't understand. The strange, dark ideas of Kiri and her followers might scare him off.

They even scared Neve a bit, though she was sure most of them were nonsense. Skirting the line between heresy and piety, practicality and fanaticism. An interpretation of the Five Kings that made them both more and less human.

Here they all were, partners in half-measure blasphemy, and Neve was about to lay the final brick in the wall.

Isla rose, and the court followed. The priestesses stood behind the pyre with ramrod spines, hands tucked into wide white sleeves, eyes fixed forward. Kiri's hair shone almost the same color as the bright-red petal in Neve's hand.

"One passes, and another takes her place." Isla's words were calm, solemn. She held her petal aloft. "Tealia, in the names of our lost Kings and the magic of bygone eras, I ask that you take up this task."

Tealia didn't have the guile to look surprised. Mouth a pleased grin, she inclined her head. "As you ask."

According to ceremony, other nominations should be heard here. Neve pulled in a deep breath, waiting.

But Isla turned to the assembly, the matter seemingly concluded. "By our—"

"I have a nomination."

Neve expected her voice to sound quiet and thin, a match for her quaking fingers. Instead it rang clear as she held her petal aloft. She stepped forward, eyes on Kiri, not looking at her mother. "Kiri, I ask that you take up this task."

Kiri didn't feign surprise. She nodded, eyes straight ahead, stone-solemn. "As you ask."

Isla's face blanched, but she didn't let her petal drop. "What is the meaning of this, Neverah?"

An accusation, not a question. She'd expected as much, and it had kept her awake once she realized this was the course she'd have to take. An answer her mother would deem acceptable, something weighty enough to give her pause.

Red would've known what to say. Red always knew how to spar with their mother, how to shape words into daggers and let them fly, or use silence as a blade in itself.

All Neve had was her grief, artless and aching and hopefully shared.

"Things can change." Neve kept her voice from breaking, there at the end, though it was a close thing. "Just because something has always been one way doesn't mean it has to be that way forever. Red can—"

"That's quite enough." But Isla's voice rang hollow, her eyes distant from more than illness. Grief, finally, dredging up from whatever deep well the Queen of Valleyda kept it in.

So Neve pressed on. "Mother, we can bring her *home*."

Pin-drop silence. Raffe looked at her with his mouth agape. Arick gave a slight, sad smile. Kiri did nothing.

The petal between Isla's fingers trembled. Her dark eyes closed; her chest swelled with a deep breath.

Neve didn't take one.

Glass-fragile silence, then the Queen turned away. "By our lost—"

"*No*." Neve's petal fell to the ground, her sharp retort ricocheting through the hall. According to tradition, the appointment had to be unanimous. If it wasn't, the assembly was cloistered for hearings until they reached a decision. "If there's more than one—"

"*Neverah*." Isla's voice sliced hers off, strong despite how frail she looked. "This has been decided."

Shock painted Raffe's face, petal hanging limp in his hand. Neve gave him a pleading look, though she had no idea what she was pleading for. Her hands opened and closed on her skirts, helpless. Isla was so married to tradition, so set on doing things the way they'd always been done...it hadn't occurred to Neve that her mother wouldn't follow Order strictures. That the Order would *let* her.

Perhaps Kiri wasn't so far off after all. Perhaps it'd always been about power, the definitions of what passed as holy kept purposefully mutable.

Raffe inched forward, but Arick's hand on his shoulder stopped him. Neve couldn't read the look in either man's eyes.

The priestesses, ever the picture of calm, stared straight ahead. Even Tealia, though visibly shaken, schooled her face to placidity. A flutter of white sleeves as the candidates put their black candles to the pyre, all those gifted riches going up in flames.

Some indecipherable emotion lived in Kiri's pale face. Her eyes flickered to Neve and Arick for one lingering, laden moment, and then away.

When Isla spoke the confirmation, she didn't look at Neve. "By our lost kings and the magic of bygone eras..."

The petals rose high, the pyre caught, and Neve's plans ground away to dust.

The knock at her door was quick and brusque, almost furtive. Neve paused in her pacing, brows knit. Her picked-over dinner tray was already cleared, and she'd told the maid not to bother coming to help her undress.

Another furtive knock. "Neve, open the door."

Raffe.

She pulled him inside, cheeks flushing. She and Arick alone in her room would be gossip; she and Raffe would be a scandal. "Do you have any idea how much trouble you'd be in for coming without a chaperone?"

"Probably as much as you're in for that stunt at the confirmation." His brow arched. "What were you *doing* today?"

Neve sank into the chair at her desk. She didn't have the energy for pretense. "You know what I'm doing."

Not the whole of it, no. But Raffe knew her enough to know that all of this had to be about Red.

Raffe swore, rubbing a hand over his closely shorn hair. "You have to let it *go*, Neverah. It's eating you up, and I..." He trailed off, sighed. In one fluid motion, Raffe sank to a crouch before her, pulled her hands into his. Neve knew she should remind him of impropriety, of whispers. But his hands were so warm.

"Neve." He said her name like a touchstone, a still point he could come back to. "Red is gone."

"She's alive," Neve whispered to their tangled hands.

"Even if she is, she's bound to the Wilderwood. She's lost to us."

So close to the truth, myth and fact a nimble dance.

Raffe's grip tightened. "You have to stop trying to lose yourself, too."

Neve was already lost. Her mind was a forest, full of deep shadows and tripping vines, a labyrinth of regret. And now that their plan had failed, that *she'd* been the one to fail...She didn't realize a tear had fallen until she tasted salt.

He caught her tear on his thumb, his palm cradling her cheek. "What would you want her to do? If she'd been born first, if you'd been for the Wolf, what would you want her to do?"

"If I'd been for the Wolf," Neve whispered fiercely, "I would've fought. I would've *run*. If I'm going to give myself over to some magic woods, it's not going to be for something *useless*."

"But *she* didn't run." Raffe tucked a lock of hair behind her ear. "Her choice was to go. And you have to find a way to live with that."

Neve's mouth pressed to a bloodless line, her eyes closing as her forehead tipped against his.

"Cozy in here," said a voice from the doorway.

Her eyes snapped open; Raffe dropped her hands and stood, straightening his coat.

Eyebrow cocked, Arick lounged against the doorframe, wine bottle in hand. He swaggered into the room and offered it to Raffe, tripping slightly on the rug's edge. With a tight smile, Raffe waved it away, but the look he shot Neve was edged in apprehension.

"Didn't mean to interrupt." Arick slumped into the chair across from Neve. His hair was a scattered mess of black across his forehead, his eyes bloodshot and bruised. He held his bandaged hand close to his chest. "Things took an interesting turn this afternoon, didn't they?"

"Maybe you can get through to her," Raffe said, crossing his arms. "Tell her she has to let this go."

"Perhaps I can." Arick took a long drink. "I'm her betrothed, after all."

Raffe's jaw clenched.

"Or perhaps," Arick said, swirling his remaining wine, "I can support whatever decision Neve makes."

The flash of Raffe's teeth was too sharp to be a smile. "Even when those decisions are dangerous?"

"What's life without a little danger, Raffe?"

"You're *drunk*."

"I imagine you two would have a better time if you followed suit."

"I'd have a better time if you stopped talking about me like I'm not here." Neve pressed her fingers to her temples, trying to ease the pounding in her head. She'd thought Arick might come to discuss an alternate plan. Instead, he seemed focused on nothing but drinking to forget, and it made rage stoke deep in her chest, the quiet kind that could be dangerous.

The kind that made her think about shadowed veins and called-up power, and how using it would be so easy.

Raffe sighed. "Neve..."

"Leave me, please." She took a deep breath, raised her face. "I'm tired."

Raffe's mouth twisted like he might speak. But his eyes darted to Arick, and he stayed silent.

Legs unsteady, Arick stood, clapped Raffe chummily on the shoulder. "You heard the lady."

Stiffly, Raffe turned to the door. Arick followed. But when he reached the threshold, he looked back at her, jerked his chin toward the bottle he'd left on her desk.

"Might help you sleep." The bandage on his hand stood out stark against the shadows. "It's helped me."

Neve frowned. "Have you had trouble sleeping?"

He didn't smile, though his mouth spasmed like he might've

tried. "You could say that." Arick stumbled out. "Don't worry, Neve," he murmured, slurred but earnest. "All isn't lost yet."

She frowned, watching him lurch into the hall, leaving the door ajar behind him.

Neve grabbed the bottle by the neck and took a long drink. The wine was strong enough that her head felt light after one swallow, but it was preferable to the crushing weight of failure. She took another drink and wiped her mouth with the back of her hand.

In minutes, she'd drained the bottle, leaving her thoughts pleasantly fuzzy and filtering the edges of the day to a warm, blunted glow.

A flash of white in the hallway, seen through the still-open door. Neve stood on legs like a fawn's, rolling her eyes. If some maid was trysting with a courtier, she didn't want to hear it. She went to the door, taking a few tries to make her hand actually connect with the knob, and peered down the corridor.

A familiar white robe disappeared around the corner, a familiar flash of ember-red hair. *Kiri?*

Whoever it was, they were gone by the time she reached the hall. Neve pulled the door closed and fumbled out of her gown, finally falling into sleep.

Chapter Seventeen

The closet smelled like dust. Not an uncommon scent in the Keep, where the forest was as close as your next breath, but usually it was chased by other smells—greenery, dirt. This smell was, simply, dust. The smell of something left so long all other features had bled out.

Red waved her hand to keep drifting grit from her eyes. "It seems like it's been longer than a hundred years since this closet was opened."

"Take it up with Fife," came Lyra's reply. "Though in his defense, the Keep became much harder to clean once the forest started breaking in."

Eammon's stolen belt slipped toward Red's hips; grumbling, she pulled it back up. "Anything will be an improvement, I guess."

When the corridor collapsed, it took all Red's clothes with it. In the weeks since, she'd made do with the nightgown she'd been wearing, and Eammon's shirts in a pinch—they reached almost to her knees, and if she stole a belt, too, they were serviceable. Fife barely noticed, but the first time Eammon saw her in the makeshift gown, the tips of his ears turned scarlet.

Sharing a room was the only facet of their convenient marriage they adhered to, and even that was by technicality. Red slept alone, woke alone. The only sign Eammon had been there was his crumpled bedding in the corner, and his habit of leaving the wardrobe doors open. Red always closed them.

Some days, she didn't see him at all. He was in the library, or off in the Wilderwood. He didn't keep her same hours—no one did—and sometimes she'd wake to his nest of blankets completely undisturbed.

Every once in a while, there'd be a note on the desk in that messy, slanting handwriting, directing her to the tower. The magic she worked with his help was small, nothing so perilous as taking a wound—she'd grown the ivy in the pot and made the buds on a branch open into leaves with middling success. It wasn't as easy to direct as it had been the night she healed him, but it could be controlled, if she kept her memories in check and thought of Eammon, letting their bond of marriage and forest smooth her magic into something easy to grasp. Physical proximity seemed to help, too, but the thought of mentioning that to him felt vulnerable in a way she didn't want to examine too closely, so she kept it to herself.

Red shivered, the bare skin of her calves rising in goose bumps. In addition to being scandalous, Eammon's shirts did little to cut the constant chill of the Wilderwood. It had been Lyra's idea to go ranging for old clothes, and they'd checked every storage closet still standing in the Keep before finding them.

"I could lend you something," Lyra said, leaning against the wall. She cleaned her nails with a dagger, feigning nonchalance. "If you want."

Since she'd been at the Keep, Lyra had been quicker to friendliness than Fife, but still standoffish in her own way. In the past week or so, though, she'd made more overtures of friendship—telling Red about the shadow-creatures she saw in the forest, stories about her and Fife and Eammon's strange existence in the Wilderwood. Red's favorite so far was the time Eammon decided he was going to learn to cook and sent Fife to the Edge with a list as long as his arm of ingredients. Apparently, he'd nearly caught the kitchen on fire. Fife managed the food after that.

It made Red wonder about the other Second Daughters, how their time here had looked before the Wilderwood killed them, drained them. She supposed it was a vote of confidence that Lyra would try to reach out. It meant she thought Red would be around awhile.

Red leaned around the closet's open door, raising a deliberate eyebrow at Lyra's frame, much thinner than her own. "Trying to wear your clothes might end up more scandalous than wearing Eammon's."

Lyra shrugged. "Suit yourself."

The gowns were folded on the bottom shelf. Red sifted through the smooth silk and sumptuous brocade carefully, half afraid they might crumble in her fingers. They came in all different sizes, in styles she'd seen only in history books, and the weight of centuries packed into the fabric made them seem heavier than they should.

Lyra's head poked around the door, brows raised. The closet was behind the staircase, and pale light from the solarium window above turned her tightly coiled curls to a copper-threaded halo. "Well?"

The dress Red held was forest green, embroidered with golden vines along the sleeves and hem. "This looks promising."

Fife and Eammon were nowhere to be seen, so Red changed behind the staircase. The dress was tight in the chest and hips, but mostly fit. She held her hands out to her sides. "Suitable?"

"Suitable." There was a strange, half-uneasy light in Lyra's eyes that her smile couldn't shake.

Red picked at the embroidery. "Do you know whose it was?"

"Merra, I think."

Merra. The Second Daughter before Red. The fabric felt strange on her skin.

Lyra hitched at the strap that held her *tor*, checked the small bag at her waist to make sure it was stocked with blood. "I'm off to patrol. Wish me no monsters." She slipped through the door into the twilight.

Merra's green skirts slid over Red's bare legs, the sleeves itching her arms. She turned, headed for the staircase down to the library. If the day was hers, she planned to spend it reading.

Her eyes flicked over the corridor, a quick surveillance that had become part of her routine. The sentinels hadn't moved since the night the Wilderwood came for her—on the days they practiced using its magic, Eammon diligently checked her hands for wounds before she touched anything, and once made her bandage a papercut—but Red kept a wary eye out, just in case.

Her gaze carefully combed through the churn of roots and vines. Still, it took her a moment to realize what was wrong, the hole in the haunted tableau she'd grown so used to.

The sentinels were gone.

Panic iced her limbs; Red whirled, searching the shadows, sure the white trees had moved farther into the Keep, maybe preparing to come for her again. Nothing stirred but dust.

Slowly, Red crept to the precise line where Eammon had cut off the forest. Husks of leaves and thin roots littered the floor, still and silent.

A smear of blood marked one of the dead leaves. Crimson, green-threaded. Once she'd seen it, more bloodstains were easy to spot—on the moss, on the branches.

Fife checked the sentinels daily, stabilizing them with his own blood as much as he could. Thus far, they'd stayed clear of shadow-rot, fine to be left until Eammon had the strength to move them. But if he'd felt the need to bleed for them *now*, all at once…

Then it was getting worse. Still getting worse, despite her using the forest's magic, despite their thread bond. Still taking pieces of Eammon, whether let from a vein or a change in his body.

Red chewed her lip, made a split-second decision, and headed for the door.

In the courtyard, fog eddied over the ground. It cleared over an out-of-place shape in the landscape before hiding it again. Something tall and straight beyond the tower, by the gate.

Another sentinel.

And next to it, on his knees—Eammon. The sharp edge of the dagger in his hand caught the dim lavender light.

"Wait!" Red gathered Merra's skirts and rushed barefoot over the moss, the beat of her pulse a reminder of the blood on the floor. "Eammon, wait!"

His head shot up, shoulders straightening like she'd caught him at some forbidden thing. The blade angled toward his palm for a second longer before he pulled it back. When he stood, it was slow, as if his bones were too heavy for his muscles to lift.

Red stopped when she reached him, chest heaving. The sentinel sapling stood just inside the iron gate, stretching half again as tall as Eammon, the knobby beginnings of branches at its pale crown. "I saw the corridor," she said between breaths. "Why did you move them all at once?"

"I had to." Eammon's fingers curled inward, as if to cover the slashes on his palm, leaking sap. "Fife checked them this morning. Shadow-rotted, halfway up the trunks." He ran a tired hand over his face, left a streak of scarlet and green on his brow. "If I didn't move them back to their places now, I wouldn't have been able to at all. They would've rotted away where they stood. And I can't…the Wilderwood can't manage having that many weak spots."

The shadow-infected sentinel stood thin and pale in the unnatural twilight, stretching toward the starless sky like it could escape the ground.

"I don't understand. I'm using the magic. We got *married*." Her fingers curled to a fist, like she'd strike the bone-white bark. "Why isn't that enough?"

Eammon's eyes traced her face, something sorrowful in them. He didn't answer.

Red set her teeth. She took a tentative step forward, closing the fog-covered distance between them, and reached for the dagger in his hand.

Eammon snatched it back. "*No.*"

"What else am I supposed to do? My blood is the only thing that's made any damn difference so far!"

His eyes flashed, grip tightening on the dagger. "No," he repeated, the word like a shield.

"There has to be something else we can try, then. Something without blood." Her lip worked between her teeth, eyes flickering up to his. "What about the magic?"

Eammon looked away, almost a flinch. A hunch in his shoulders, as if he was suddenly hyperaware of that extra inch of height that had never gone away.

The changes scared him. And he was ashamed. Of the alterations the Wilderwood made, or of his fear of them, she wasn't sure.

"Maybe the changes won't linger," Red murmured.

"They did last time." Kings, he sounded so tired.

"You were doing it alone, then. You won't be anymore."

It took him aback, made a swallow work down his throat. A dart of amber eyes, from the sentinel to her, like he was cataloging the distance between. "I don't like you being close to them, Red," he said quietly. "Even when there's no cut for them to get into, no blood. I know what they want to do."

"And I know you won't let them." She crossed her arms, fingering the embroidery on her sleeves. "We got married, and it made magic come easier, but me growing ivy in pots clearly isn't helping you. So let's try this."

He didn't like it. Every line of his face said so, the full lips pulled flat, the heavy brows lowered.

"I trust you." She tried to say it lightly, but the words wouldn't come out flippant. "You should trust yourself."

Silence. Then Eammon sighed. Another swipe of his hand over his face, and when he looked at her this time, he finally noticed the dress, eyes going wide. "Where did you get that?"

"Lyra and I found it. I was tired of wearing your clothes."

Color flared across his cheekbones. "Fair enough."

Hairline fractures of shadow-rot crawled the sentinel sapling's trunk, stretching farther than they had moments ago. Red turned to it like it was an oncoming army. "Tell me what to do."

A heartbeat, then Eammon finally sheathed his dagger. "Show me your hands."

She held out her upturned palms. Eammon took them in his, scars rough against her skin, peering closely for any trace of a wound. Satisfied, he dropped them, and cold air rushed in where his warmth had been. "The placement of every sentinel is deliberate."

"Like bricks in a wall."

"Right. Like bricks in a wall." Eammon reached out, settled his hand on the white trunk. "In order to keep the Shadowlands from leaking through—in order to keep the wall strong—we have to put the sentinels back where they're supposed to be. When we heal them, they return to their place."

"So how do we heal them?"

"Directing magic to drive back the rot."

"Through touch, I assume." She didn't know why it came out so low, so hoarse.

Eammon's shoulders went rigid, his own answer graveled. "Yes."

The old scars on his hands were white, a match for the sentinel's bark beneath them. Instinctually, Red reached out, covered his hand with her own.

"The tree, Red," Eammon murmured.

She lifted her hand, cheeks flushed. After a moment's hesitation, she gently touched the sentinel.

It was like a current, as soon as her hand met the trunk, running through every limb and drawing up her spine. The power in her middle unfurled, blooming outward to press against her palm, a compass needle with the sentinel as north star. For a moment, her skin felt like an unwelcome barrier, holding back the union of something long torn apart. Red hissed between her teeth.

"What?" Eammon's voice crackled with anxiety, his frame all coiled tension.

"It feels different than I thought it would." She gave him a tiny smile. "What now?"

It seemed he might call the whole thing off, in the space between her question and his answer. Eammon's jaw worked, gaze flickering from her hand to her face. Red firmed her lips.

Finally, he sighed. "If sentinels are bricks in the wall, we're the mortar." Eammon's eyes shifted from her to the white tree. "Our magic is a piece of the Wilderwood. So is a sentinel. To heal it, we pour our power into it, channel it back to the source. The Wilderwood strengthens, and strengthens us in turn. Rain feeding a river that evaporates to become the rain again."

"A cycle." There was a synchronicity to it. Cycles of Wolves, cycles of Second Daughters, cycles of grief.

"Exactly," Eammon said softly. "You just let the magic move through you. Let it go."

The sentinel buzzed under her hand. Something gathered behind the bark, an energy drawn to her, pushing forward. Apprehension danced with anticipation in her middle.

It must've shown on her face. Eammon shook his head. "You don't—"

"No, I can do it." Red concentrated on the rush in her veins, the warmth of the bark under her palm. She made her breath slow, counted her metronome heartbeats until they were an even rhythm. Eammon next to her, Eammon needing help, smoothed the chaotic ocean of her power to placid water as she closed her eyes.

Deep green spilled through her mind, changing the shade of the darkness behind her eyelids. It painted her thoughts in shades of sea-foam and emerald, lit in the very center by a soft, golden glow.

The more she concentrated, the clearer it grew. The glow was the sapling, a shining shape in a sea of shining shapes. A golden network of tall, straight trees with deep roots, bright lights casting enough shadow to hold a world.

Some sentinels were dimmer than others—those weakened were candle-flames, while the sentinels holding strong flared bonfire-bright. Their roots were a knotted riot, jagged lines of gold. But all of them led to a familiar shape, their vast network collecting in a frame she knew.

Eammon. As part of the Wilderwood as any sentinel, roots winding through him like he was their soil. Man tangled inextricably with forest, equal parts branch and bone. Half subsumed in the Wilderwood, but not drained, not like his mother or father or the other Second Daughters. Holding it all with a strength she couldn't quite fathom, a determination that awed and frightened her at once.

He wasn't human. She'd known that, seen it proven over and over. He was something different, as mysterious as the forest he inhabited. The forest that inhabited *him*.

This was the first time the reminder made her chest ache.

"Red?" He sounded so tentative.

She pressed her fingers into the trunk like he might be able to feel it, a reassuring pressure. "I'm fine." A pause stretched long as her mind's eye surveyed him, the seed from which all the Wilderwood bloomed. "It's beautiful."

Silence. The forest seemed to hold its breath.

"Follow my lead," Eammon said finally. Then his golden form in her thoughts flashed bright. Liquid light seeped out of him, along the shining network he was tied to, going instead to the sentinel.

Gently, like a flower opening to the sun, Red let her power grow. It flowed up through her center and spilled out her palms, calmed and given purpose by Eammon's closeness. The light she let go wasn't as bright as Eammon's, but it was no less welcome.

The sentinel before them slowly brightened, its flickering candle-flame gaining strength as their light drowned out the shadow.

Red stood with her hands pressed against the white tree and let the magic cycle, the rain feeding the river. As the dim figure of the sentinel brightened in her mind's eye, she felt golden power flowing into her, too—at first, it made her start, spiked fear along her shoulder blades. But the Wilderwood, for now, wasn't interested in conquest. She was just a part of the cycle, a rung on the wheel. The bright, thin filament of magic it'd left in her glowed, winding languidly around her bones.

It felt...good. Good, and this was the first time she really believed it, despite the insistence from Eammon and Fife that the sentinels weren't malicious for all their want of her. It felt too simple a concept for such a complicated thing, but they were in accord, she and the Wilderwood, at least on the most basic level. They wanted the same things. It was bent on its own survival, its own need.

She thought of running through the forest on her birthday, the fierce desire deep in her gut to *live*. That's what she felt from the sentinel, from the Wilderwood it was attached to. A deep, reckless determination to live.

When the sentinel was gone and her palm touched Eammon's instead of bark, she had no idea how much time had passed.

Her eyes opened, banishing the shining network of the Wilderwood to see the man instead. He watched her with his brows slashed low, full mouth slightly parted, black hair falling over his forehead. The whites of his eyes were traced faintly in emerald, his shadow longer on the ground than it had been before, the edges feathered like leaves. He'd rolled up his long sleeves, and bark sheathed his forearms again.

Eammon didn't try to hide the changes magic wrought in him. He stood there, still, and let her see.

Her wrists pressed close to his, the network of her veins outlined in green. The urge to cover them was instinctual, but Red kept her hands steady. If he wasn't hiding, she wasn't, either. What they'd just done—healed the Wilderwood, if only a small part of it, together and unbloodied—wrought honesty from them both.

Slowly, the green in his eyes faded. Bark disappeared, revealing only scarred skin; his height lessened, the edges of his shadow on the ground grew more solid. No permanent changes, not this time, though that previous extra height lingered. Just another scar, another mark made for the forest.

He watched her a moment longer, the severe lines of his face unreadable as the veins winding up her arms faded back to blue. Then Eammon dropped his hand from hers and turned away.

Red pressed her palm against her thigh, banishing the lingering warmth of his touch. At their feet, where the sentinel had been, there was only unbroken moss. "Looks like it worked."

Eammon made a low sound of affirmation. Red followed his gaze—right beyond the gate, within the line of the other trees, the sapling grew.

Only it wasn't a sapling now. It was full-grown, thick-trunked. Leaves bloomed from the white branches clustered around its crown, vibrant and green.

"Looks like it did." There was something like wonder in his face, and it transformed the harsh lines of it, backlit by forest and mist.

Hidden beneath Red's sleeve, the Bargainer's Mark twinged. She pressed her hand against it, fleetingly, and forced her gaze back to the sentinel, away from him.

Already the green leaves had dulled, muted. One let loose from a branch, drifted to the forest floor.

Eammon hissed in a breath. She'd seen the forest woven into him, rooted between his bones—its failing hurt him.

"You aren't bleeding for it anymore," she said, the words fiercer for their softness. "This damn forest gets no more pieces of you while I'm here."

His eyes held a denying light, but when he looked at her, something tenuous and unreadable replaced it.

Her palm still buzzed where it'd pressed against the trunk, and Red shook it, trying to dispel the itch. "Are there any others? We can—"

"We aren't doing anything until you put some shoes on." Eammon gave her bare feet a pointed look.

She curled her toes into the moss. "The Wilderwood ate my boots, remember?" Barefoot had served her fine thus far—if she was only running through the courtyard to get to the tower or staying in the Keep, it wasn't so bad, and she'd stolen Eammon's socks when she needed them. "None of the Second Daughters left a spare."

His arm moved, and for a moment, Red thought he might pick her up to keep her feet from the cold ground.

But the moment passed, and Eammon turned toward the tower. "I dug through the storerooms and found an old pair you can have. I left them by the fireplace." He glanced over his shoulder, brow quirked, then faced the tower again. "They won't fit, but that didn't stop you with my shirt."

"It was too cold to be naked."

He didn't turn, but his hand spasmed by his side, and he made a choked noise. Behind him, Red grinned.

There was a slight tremor in Eammon's shoulders when he pushed the tower door open, though his stride up the stairs remained steady. He'd never been able to completely hide his exhaustion from her, and after seeing just how deeply the Wilderwood tangled in his frame, Red had a new understanding.

Even now, he tried to hide it. Like it was something shameful, something he was determined to bear on his own. It made Red want to slam magic into every tree in this Kings-shitting forest, to strengthen and punish them in equal measure.

"I have something to show you up here, anyway." Firelight glimmered over the silver constellations on the ceiling as he glanced at her over his shoulder. "Well. Two somethings."

He crossed to the lone table, nervously pushing back his hair. "They're not quite as good as new," he hedged. "But they're at least readable again."

Slowly, Red walked to his side. Books scattered the table, next to a familiar leather bag.

Her books.

She gave a little breathless laugh, reaching out to run her finger along their dusty edges. Lines of dirt crawled over the covers, green smudges where growing things had obscured the ink. "I thought I lost them when the corridor collapsed."

"Nearly. I had a shadows-damned time pulling them out of the moss."

Her vision blurred. "Thank you." The book of poems from her mother sat at the top of the pile. Burial had rubbed all the gilt off the cover. Red picked it up, cradled it to her chest. "Thank you, Eammon."

"You're welcome." He shifted, like he wasn't quite sure how to hold himself. His hand flexed by his side.

After a moment, Eammon stepped away, pointing to the fireplace. "Boots are there," he said unnecessarily. "Then, one more thing."

Red shoved her feet in the boots—far too big, but warm—and clomped over to join Eammon at one of the vine-carved windows. Something leaned against the wall next to it, swathed in gray fabric.

"This might not work." The look he gave her was stern, all the nervousness of before carefully tucked away. "But I didn't feel right keeping it from you."

"Ominous."

Eammon tugged off the cloth. Beneath, a mirror, or something shaped like one. The glass wasn't reflective—instead, a matte gray. The color within it shifted, like looking into a smoke-filled jar.

"What is it?"

"My mother made it with Wilderwood magic." Eammon glanced at her, eyes unreadable. "To see her sister, Tiernan."

Understanding was an undertow. Red's hands fell numb at her sides. She turned from Eammon to the mirror, wariness washed away by longing. She'd grown adept at pushing away thoughts of Neve, these past weeks in the forest, but just the mention of the word *sister* made her heart feel suddenly too big for her rib cage. "Oh."

"It's old," Eammon cautioned. "No one has tried to use it for centuries, and with the way the Wilderwood is now, it could be completely useless. But I..." He trailed off, took a breath. "You said, if you could do anything, you'd tell your sister you were safe. This won't let you speak with her, but hopefully, it will at least let you see her."

Gratitude seemed too small a term for the sudden lightness in her chest, like a weight she hadn't noticed she was carrying suddenly lifted. "Eammon..." She stopped, swallowed. "Eammon, this is..."

"I'm sorry," he said quietly. "I'm sorry this is all I have to give you."

"It's enough." Her answer came immediately, instinctually. In the firelight, his eyes looked like honey.

Red stepped forward, reaching for the mirror but not quite touching it. "How does it work?"

"Sacrifice." Eammon snorted. "Of course."

"Blood?"

"No." Quick, sharp. "I mean, it would work, but perhaps let's give the bleeding a rest."

Her rough braid fell over her shoulder; Red plucked out a split-ended strand and held it up. "This, then?"

Eammon nodded, arms crossed and jaw tense. "I'll be right here," he said, stern once again. "If something feels strange, in any way, I'm pulling you out."

Red made an absent noise of agreement, all her attention on the matte surface of the mirror. Carefully, she wound the long strand of her hair through the swirls of the frame. Then she stepped back, stared into its darkness, and waited.

Five heartbeats, six. Nothing. Disappointment tasted bitter in the back of Red's throat, and she was about to turn away, when something glimmered in the depths of the mirror.

The light of it caught her, reeled her in, a speck of silver in the gray. The longer she stared, the larger and more brilliant it grew, smoke billowing across its shine, growing and growing until it filled her vision entirely.

A blast of soundless light, like an exploding star, smoke whirling into dark cosmos.

And when the smoke cleared, there was Neve.

Chapter Eighteen

It was like looking through a window. No, not quite—like being *trapped* in a window, folded into the glass. She tried to move and couldn't, couldn't sense her limbs at all. Her awareness was stretched thin, diffused and refracted into mirror-light.

Neve stood in the Shrine, behind the statue of Gaya. Her figure was smudged, but still Red could see she was thinner than before, her cheeks gaunt. A bandage wrapped around her left hand.

Red tried to scream for her, forgetting it would be fruitless, that this mirror was one-way and only for seeing. Distantly, she felt the work of vocal cords, but there was no sound, nothing.

Still, her shout seemed to spark something, like her desire strengthened the magic that made the mirror. Gradually, Neve's image cleared, grew solid.

"We've been doing this for a month now, and she hasn't returned." Her sister was turned to the side, brows drawn down, dark eyes narrowed. Her lip disappeared between her teeth, an anxious tell she and Red shared. "Why hasn't she escaped?"

Red couldn't make out whomever Neve spoke to—they were blurred, shadowed. This mirror was built to show the First Daughter, and it did no more than that.

"It will take time." The voice came muffled, barely clear enough to hear. "Great things often do. Patience, Neverah."

"Is there no way to hurry things along?" Neve's arms crossed over her thin chest. When her head lifted, firelight caught on the silver circlet in her hair. More ornate than the one she usually wore. Familiar in a way that tugged at the back of Red's mind, that seemed somehow *off.*

"Perhaps."

"Tell me what we need, Kiri." Neve was no stranger to a commanding tone, but there was some new strength in it now. The voice of someone who knew beyond a doubt she'd be obeyed. "Tell me what we need, and I will make sure it happens."

The pause stretched uncomfortably long. The line of Neve's jaw tremored, once. She reached up and touched the circlet, adjusting it on her brow.

"I suppose you can do that with no restraint now, can't you?" There was something sly in the muffled voice. Something that pricked at the entire length of Red's spine. "Now that Isla is dead. Now that you are Queen."

Queen.

Even in her strange and suspended consciousness, Red felt the air leave her lungs, felt the breathy half-cry crawl its way up her throat.

In the mirror, Neve flinched, just barely.

Red felt Eammon's hands on her shoulders, knew he'd heard her, sensed something was wrong. His touch drew her from the vision, smoke and silver-bright eclipsing Neve's image, but not before she heard one last thing from that muffled voice.

"You could always offer more blood."

Then—the sharp bite of floor into her knees, the paper-and-coffee scent of Eammon bent over her. "Red?" His voice was calm but laced with barely leashed panic. "Red, what's wrong?"

"My mother is dead," she murmured, eyes wide. "My mother is dead."

Steam curled from the rapidly cooling mug of tea on the desk. Red couldn't quite summon the energy to reach for it. She sat on the bed, arms looped around her knees, and watched the steam twist silently into the air. The book of poems sat next to it. She hadn't realized she'd brought it with her from the tower until Eammon gently took it from her hands and laid it aside.

The murmurs at the bottom of the stairs were barely hidden by the pop of flames in the grate. "Are we sure it was real?" Lyra asked. "That mirror is ancient."

"She saw her sister." Eammon's voice. "That's what it was built for."

"But its power is from the Wilderwood." This from Fife, wary. "And things with the Wilderwood aren't going well lately. How can you be sure it showed the truth?"

"I just know, Fife." She could almost see Eammon rubbing at his dark-shrouded eyes. Then a sharp, brittle laugh. "Her mother is dead, and her sister is alone, and she's in this shadows-damned forest when she has no reason to be."

"No reason other than to help you," Fife said.

Silence from Eammon.

When Lyra spoke, it was hushed. "Eammon, you aren't thinking..."

"If she asked," Eammon said, "I wouldn't tell her no." Heavy silence, just for a moment. Then, quiet: "I should've made her go when she first arrived. The Wilderwood has no hold on her, not enough to keep her here. Not like the others."

There was no surprise in the resulting pause. Fife and Lyra had known something was different about Red, known it from that first day.

"So her being here doesn't do much, anyway," Fife murmured.

The low, rough sound of Eammon's sigh. "No."

Red squeezed her eyes shut.

Footsteps on the stairs. Eammon appeared, hair tangled around his shoulders. He frowned. "You're still awake."

"Can't sleep." Red reached over to the desk, took the now-lukewarm mug. The tea smelled pleasant, all spice and clove, and when she took a sip it warmed her chest.

Eammon held another glass in his hand, half filled with deep burgundy. He set it where the mug had been. "In case you need something stronger than tea." A brief smile flickered at the corner of his mouth. "Lyra told me to warn you it's not Meducian. Valdrek makes his own wine at the Edge, and I'm half convinced he waters it down before selling it to me."

She tried to answer his smile, but her lips barely lifted.

Gingerly, Eammon sat in the chair before the desk, hands clasped between his knees. The quiet hung thick in the air, broken only by the crackle of flame, but it was comfortable.

Red drained the tea, stared into the dregs. "Now we know the mirror works. I suppose that's a good thing."

"I'm so sorry, Red." He said it to the floor, like he didn't think eye contact would be welcome. "Did she look...was your sister..."

"She looked tired. Tired and...and sad." Red tried to shrug, but the movement was stilted. "I don't know if Neve is ready to be Queen. To take our mother's place."

"I don't think we're ever ready to take on what our parents leave us." Eammon studied his knotted hands. "The places left rarely fit."

White knuckles belied his nonchalance, translating his statement into a language they both knew. His parents' shadows, cast long and dark. The legacy of a Wolf and a Second Daughter neither of them had chosen.

"I'm more worried about Neve than I am sad about my mother." A confession, shame-scraped. "How awful is that?"

"Not awful. Grief is strange."

Red's relationship with Isla was a fraught and layered thing, not easily explained. But her absence, the gaping place left, made her want to try. The only absolution she could give her. "We…my mother and I…we were never close."

His knuckles blanched, hands still clasped between his knees. "Because of…" One hand came free, waved in the space between them.

"Not just that." Red shook her head. "She wasn't overly close with Neve, either, though I think she wanted to be." She studied the loose threads in the blanket, both of them keeping their eyes carefully from the other. "She needed an heir. She got two daughters in the bargain, and one she couldn't keep. It was easier for her to pretend I didn't exist. Especially after…" She trailed off, but she didn't really need an ending. The shard of the Wilderwood's magic in her center bloomed upward, the vague taste of earth on her tongue.

Eammon's shoulders sank, like guilt was something physical. Her fingers itched to settle on them, to smooth them back to straightness. To run them into his hair and make them both think of other things.

Red clenched her mug instead. She was well acquainted with guilt, and how it took more than warm hands or even warm mouths to banish it.

Guilt. It kept circling back to that.

"I know you didn't see everything that happened that night." She shifted on the bed. "But did you see me?"

"No more than your hands. I just…sensed you." A fall of dark hair hid his eyes; he pushed it back with a scarred knuckle. "I felt the Wilderwood rushing for something, though I didn't know what, not at first. But once it touched you, I felt your pain. Your panic. It drowned out everything else."

Her lips pressed bloodlessly together.

"I tried to stop it." He braced his forearms on his thighs. "Clearly, I wasn't as successful as I should've been. I couldn't keep all of it from you. But even though the Wilderwood gave you a piece of its power, I thought, maybe, I could keep you from being called. If I kept the forest strong, maybe your Mark would never show up. Maybe the cycle could break." He swallowed. "I wasn't successful at that, either."

Eammon had been trying to save her for years, pushing her away until he couldn't anymore. Until the Wilderwood decided it would have its due, no matter how much of himself the Wolf gave up.

A deep breath, and Red sat up straight, dropping her knees to sit cross-legged on the threadbare coverlet. She'd never recounted the whole of what happened that night she and Neve ran to the Wilderwood, not to anyone. Their attackers were dead; Neve had blocked it out. The memory was a wound, and she'd covered it up, never letting it breathe, never letting it heal.

It hadn't occurred to her before now that the memory wasn't only her own—parts of it belonged to Eammon, too. Another shared hurt, another mirrored mark. A burden that might lessen if they bore it together.

"It was our sixteenth birthday." Red spoke to the mattress, though she was painfully aware of Eammon's puzzled eyes on her. If she looked at him, it might break the spell, break the cadence that made this a story and therefore easier to speak. "There was a ball."

As if sensing what she needed, Eammon stayed silent. He sat still, waiting for her to go on, firelight playing over the angles of his face.

"It was... unpleasant. That was the first night I really noticed just how different Neve and I were. How different our lives would be." She paused. "My mother barely spoke to me."

Eammon's fists tightened between his knees.

"After, Neve found me crying. She asked me what she could do. I told her nothing, unless she knew a way to get rid of the Wilderwood. So that's what we tried." Red snorted. "Everyone was half drunk, so stealing horses was far easier than it should've been. We ran them all the way to the border."

The horses had lathered quickly, their breaths screaming in the cold night air. Red remembered thinking their northward flight hadn't taken enough time. She'd wanted to run under the star-strewn sky with her sister forever.

"The matches Neve brought didn't work," she continued quietly. "The Wilderwood can't be burned, we'd always heard that, but neither of us believed it until then. It scared her, I think, to see the proof of it—that the forest wasn't just a forest, that it was something more. Neve probably would've left after that, and that would've been the end. But I found a stone."

She'd picked up the rock, hurled it wildly between the trees. The sound it made wasn't loud enough for her, just a muffled *thud* in the underbrush. So she'd screamed, and once she started, she couldn't stop. Red had picked up rock after rock, throwing them blindly, getting closer and closer to the edge of the trees. She remembered how the hum pressed against her skin, vibrated in her bones. The forest allowing her closer when it wouldn't let anyone else.

Neve found her own stone, threw it at the Wilderwood, getting as near to it as she could. Her screams joined Red's, two lost girls on the edge of the world they knew, shrieking and throwing rocks because there was nothing else they could do, and they had to do *something*.

"One of the rocks sliced my palm," Red said, the memory playing on the back of her eyelids like a shadow show. "And I tripped as I threw it. I tried to stop the fall with my cut hand, landed just inside the border."

"And the Wilderwood came for you." Eammon's voice was rough and hushed, like he'd been silent for hours instead of minutes.

"And you stopped it," Red added smoothly. She didn't open her eyes; she knew it'd make her lose her nerve. But she felt Eammon look at her, felt his regard as heavy as an arm on her shoulder.

She paused for a moment before picking up the story again. "All that screaming attracted attention, and so had two girls on fine horses tearing down the road. I don't know how long they lay in wait, how long they watched us. But they got Neve, after she pulled me away from the forest by my leg. Held a knife to her throat. And I…" She squeezed her eyes shut tighter. "I let it go."

There'd been a moment of stillness, she remembered. A moment when the magic left splintered in her center had paused, nearly stunned, like vines stretched taut and sliced off. The veins in her wrists blazed verdant, traveling up her arms, through her chest, toward her heart. A bloom of golden light behind her eyes.

And her shard of splintered magic erupted.

A trunk had exploded through the ground and impaled one of the thieves, shooting out of his mouth covered in gore and viscera, spreading branches that broke bones. Vines slithered from the ground and ensnared another, pulling tight around his neck until his face bloated, turned purple, burst like a popped bubble.

The man holding Neve had stumbled backward, letting her fall to the ground in a dead faint. A root rose behind him, tripped him, and a thicket of thorns grew up in an instant. They'd ripped through his skin like paper, shooting out of his mouth, his eyes.

But the worst was Neve. She'd lain there, and thorns had sprouted from the ground around her, just one more body caught in the maelstrom Red had created. One more thing her chaotic forest magic might kill.

That was the first time Red cut off her power, a wrenching that felt like ripping her own spine from her skin. She'd cut it off, and fell to her knees, and screamed and screamed and screamed.

"I killed them." Her voice was a quick monotone now, tripping over words in the rush to get them out. "I killed them all. I nearly killed Neve, but I cut it off in time."

"That's why you said you had to stay here," Eammon said, fitting the pieces together. "When I tried to make you go."

Red nodded. She couldn't speak on that anymore, couldn't think of it too hard or the pain and guilt might close her throat. "After I made it stop, the forest…retracted. The vines and trees and thorns all sank back into the ground, and only the bodies were left." Bodies in pools of blood, so much dead meat, and her throat itched with a scream even now. A shudder started in her shoulders, and it didn't stop. "Neve fainted before she saw anything. She doesn't remember what I did. And when the guards finally arrived—hours later, it felt like—I told them the thieves had all turned on one another. But it was me. All of it was me."

Her voice dwindled, growing quieter and quieter, until the last words were a whisper. She didn't realize she was crying until she tasted salt, and she didn't realize Eammon had come to sit next to her until his rough palms cupped her face.

His thumbs brushed over her cheeks, obscuring tear tracks. Slowly, her shuddering faded, faded until she was still. When his hands dropped, she had to fight not to reach for them.

"You saved her." Eammon's voice was low, earnest. "None of it was your fault."

"I don't even think of it in terms of *fault* anymore." Red hunched over her crossed arms. "It happened. I have to live with it." Her eyes flickered toward him. "And before you taught me how to control this power, how to *use* it, I had to live with the fear that I might do it again."

Eammon's face was unreadable. "You'll go back now, then?" It was quiet, like he was afraid to give it too much sound. "Now that you know you can control it?"

"Of course not." Nearly sharp, incredulous he'd even ask. "You need me here."

His eyes widened, just by a fraction, and that slice of a second was enough for Red to wish the words were a physical thing she could stuff back in her mouth and swallow down.

But Eammon didn't refute her.

Red sighed, pushing her hair away from her face. "So I'm not sad about my mother's death, and I'm a murderer." She gave him the shaky edge of a smile, shattering before she could make it whole. "Two terrible confessions in one night."

"Nothing about you is terrible," Eammon murmured. "I've told you that before. You should believe it."

The moment seemed to stretch as they sat there, close and warm on one bed. Then Eammon stood gracelessly, running a hand through his hair. He picked up the glass of wine on the desk and took a sip before handing it to Red. "Fife is attempting soup. Do you want some?"

"I think I just want to sleep."

Eammon nodded, headed to the staircase. "Good night, then."

"You have to sleep, too."

He stopped, glanced over his shoulder with a raised brow.

Red took a swallow of wine. "No more all-nighters," she said firmly. "You're exhausted, Eammon."

"I promise I will sleep."

"Here. With at least a proper blanket. Not slumped over a table in the library."

The heavy brow climbed higher, the corner of his lip following. "Any other orders, Lady Wolf?"

Her cheeks flushed, but Red angled up her chin. "Not at present, Warden."

Eammon inclined his head in mock deference. Then he disappeared down the stairs.

Though not Meducian and certainly watered, she finished the wine all the same. Red settled into bed, movements stirring wafts of old books, fallen leaves.

But when she closed her eyes, she thought of Arick.

Arick, who was now the Consort Elect to the Queen, not just the First Daughter. Arick, passionate and brash, whose brain was the last organ he made decisions with.

No part of her was jealous, not anymore. Never truly had been—their relationship was one built of friendship and convenience and aching loneliness, and she knew it wouldn't last. The complicated feelings she'd had for him were stars in a noon-bright sky, memories drowned in new light.

But if her feelings for Arick were faded shadows, her feelings for Eammon were the pitch black of a room she hadn't had the courage to explore. The door was cracked, but if you didn't look too closely, you didn't have to think about what waited inside.

Slowly, the crackle of the fire lulled her to sleep, thinking of shadows and cracked-open doors.

Valleydan Interlude VI

The cloak was far too large, and Neve felt like a child in it, measuring her steps as she walked toward her silver throne. Her gown was silver, too, and so was the dagger strapped to her belt, all heavy pieces of ceremony. Behind her, two priestesses clutched the cloak's black velvet edge, angling it so the silver-stitched names of former queens along the hem caught the light. The threads of her own name were loose, embroidered in a hurry.

Everything about this was hurried.

The coronation was just a formality—by the laws of Valleydan matrilineal succession, Neve was effectively Queen the moment the life left Isla's body—but still, it seemed portentous, heavy. Her heart hammered like she'd run miles, even as her feet took small, precise steps, ever closer to the throne.

The morning after Tealia was confirmed as the High Priestess, Isla's condition markedly worsened. No amount of cosmetics could hide it, and she took to her bed, barely stirring other than to take a sip of broth now and then. A week, and she was gone.

A week, and Neve went from First Daughter to Queen.

The thought was a constant in the back of her mind, movements clicking along like clockwork. *My mother is dead.* It echoed as she ate, as she met with Kiri and Arick and the others in the Shrine. It reverberated between her ears even now, as Tealia watched her approach with wary eyes, flanked by white and scarlet candles. *My mother is dead, my mother is dead.*

And an extra layer of resonance, buried as deep as she could send it: *My mother is dead, and I'm not sad.*

Neve's emotions were an ocean of history and feeling, and sadness was just the foam. She thought for the thousandth time of that last dinner together, the tiny tells in the way her mother held her wine, how her eyes flickered—this had hurt Isla, too, hurt her in a way Neve couldn't begin to fathom. Had some small, indefinable thing gone differently, maybe they could've been united in ending the Second Daughter tithe and bringing Red home.

Neve couldn't think on that for long. It ached too much.

The strange, terrible synchronicity of it all still left her reeling. The High Priestess, then the Queen, sick then gone, making way for her plans even when she thought they'd gone awry. Neve was the eye in a storm of death; it swirled around her like a train on a gown.

Guilt climbed her throat as the silver crown descended to her brow, Tealia's fingers flitting away so as not to touch her skin. Even though the deaths were natural, they still felt like rocks around her neck, waiting for a sea. She made herself cold against them because it was all she could do, the only way to shoulder the weight.

She'd cried for Isla only once. That first night, alone in her room, clutching the darkened wood-shard pendant Kiri had given her until it cut into her already-sliced palm.

There'd been a strange moment of stillness then. An awareness, cold across her shoulders, like someone peering in at her through a fogged window. A breath of sound, but it seemed to be only in her head, like a word that wouldn't quite form.

She'd rubbed her blood off the branch shard, wrapped her hand in a bandage. Once the pendant was clean, the odd feelings passed. Still, she hadn't touched the thing since, and she regarded the drawer she'd shoved it in as one might look at a snake's cage.

Now, clad in heavy silver jewelry instead of wooden, she felt the heat of hundreds of candles making her cheeks flush. Half of them white, to symbolize the purity of her purpose, and half of them red, to signify the sacrifices she would have to make to rule.

None of them knew the half of it.

Neve rose and turned to face the court. Raffe stood on the front row, arms crossed and mouth tight. He tried to smile when he caught her eye, and Neve's cold heart lurched.

She'd stayed away from Raffe recently, both because of time and because of the bone-deep, logic-defying terror that somehow death had attached itself to her, clearing space where she needed it. It made no sense, and she knew it wasn't true. Neve hadn't killed anyone, by her order or her hand.

But she couldn't risk it. Not with Raffe.

They'd have time. When this was over, she and Raffe would have all the time in the world. Then she wouldn't have to worry about somehow endangering him, somehow marking him for death by her need.

"Neverah Keyoreth Valedren." Tealia's voice was high and breathy, a wash of sound in the vast hall. "Sixth Queen of her House."

Polite applause from the assembly. The room was barely full; only the few Valleydan nobles and a handful from Floriane and northern Meducia had traveled to be part of her hasty coronation. The other countries on the continent had done their duty by attending Red's send-off; they wouldn't be eager to venture into Valleyda's unpleasant chill again until prayer-taxes came due.

Arick stepped up to the dais, a thin silver circlet gracing his brow. A bandage still wrapped his palm, but it was clean, no trace of black or scarlet. With a reassuring smile, he offered his arm and walked her down the aisle. His muscles flexed beneath her palm, and his other hand came up to settle over top of hers.

Raffe watched them as they passed, and Neve kept her eyes trained straight ahead.

Things between her and Arick had shifted since his return. A strange, quick closeness born of keeping the same secrets about the Shrine, about what they did there. There was something different about him now, something she couldn't quite put her finger on. Arick, while a good friend, had always possessed a tendency toward self-absorption. It wasn't malicious, and didn't even seem purposeful—but Arick was looking out for himself, first and foremost, and things that didn't immediately concern him seemed to sail over his head.

Not so lately. He'd been attentive to her ever since Isla died. The morning after, he showed up at her door, bearing coffee and a platter full of pastries.

"I'm so sorry, Neverah." Odd occurrence number one: He'd never referred to her by her full name before. Usually Neve would balk at it, but coming from him, it sounded different than it did from courtiers. Used for its gravitas, to tell her he meant what he said.

Her lips had pressed together, a bloodless line. She nodded. Then, taking a breath, she'd said the thing that had bothered her the whole night through, the sharp part of a not-quite-grief. "It might make things easier."

The early-morning light in the window had washed out many of the details of his face, making him a sun-soaked blur with no shadow, but Neve still noticed his brow climb.

She'd swallowed. Squared her shoulders. "We do what we have to do."

A pause. Then a nod as Arick passed her the tray and cup. "We do what we have to do."

She knew what it looked like to everyone else, this new closeness between them. But Raffe knew she and Arick better than most, well enough to know neither of them could forget Red so easily. Still, there was sadness in the set of his mouth as he watched Arick lead Neve back down the aisle, and it made her stomach churn.

She wanted to tell him. She wanted to tell him so badly it felt like the words physically dammed in her throat. But Kiri and Arick insisted on complete secrecy. Kiri because the ideas of her second, smaller Order were technically sacrilege until she and Neve cemented them into religious truth with their political power. Arick because… well. She wasn't really sure.

The doors closed behind them. Neve dropped her hand from Arick's arm. "How long do we have?"

He glanced at the place on his arm where she'd touched him, a quick dart of his eyes with an emotion she couldn't read. "There's no rush. Give Tealia a few more moments to enjoy being High Priestess."

They were alone, but still Neve's spine went rigid. She whipped her head to look down the halls, to make sure they couldn't be overheard.

"Peace, Neverah," Arick murmured. "Everything will be fine."

She crossed her arms tightly over her chest, but his reassurance did somewhat loosen the knot in her middle.

"It will take Tealia at least ten minutes to get back to the Temple." Arick propped a foot on the wall behind him, mindless of the scuff marks his boots would leave. "Kiri should have the others already gathered inside."

Neve paced a tight line back and forth. "And you secured the position for her? At the Temple in the Rylt?"

"They expect her by the end of the week. Ryltish weather is even less agreeable than Valleydan, and they don't get many sisters willing to live there. They were happy to have her and anyone else who refuses to join the Order of the Five Shadows." Arick gritted his teeth. "I still find that name ridiculous."

Another slight loosening of that stomach-knot. The priestesses who didn't want to join them would be gone, out of Valleyda, across the sea. No need for her strange storm of death to touch anyone else.

Arick watched her pace with something apprehensive in his eyes, but he didn't speak, and nothing else about his stance spoke of nervousness. In fact, he looked nearly nonchalant, leaning against the wall with his arms crossed, an insouciant dark curl falling over his forehead.

The ten minutes passed. Arick's hand was gentle on her arm, halting her pacing. A small smile tugged at his mouth as he gestured her forward. "My Queen."

It stopped her cold, for a moment. But Neve recovered, returned a shaky half smile, and let him lead her to the Temple.

The Temple was built like an amphitheater, with only two corridors leading to the sunken main chamber—one from the palace gardens, and one, much longer and more guarded, from the city street. Both were completely empty. Whispers made a soft susurrus beyond the door as they approached, and Arick released her with a reassuring squeeze of her shoulder.

Neve closed her eyes, steadied her hands. Then she pushed the door open.

Tealia's face was calm, hands folded in her sleeves as she stood on the dais at the bottom of the room, but near-panic lit her eyes. Kiri and her followers from the Order of the Five Shadows fanned out behind her. The other priestesses sat silent in their graduating rows, dread hanging thick as candle-smoke.

The High Priestess ducked an abbreviated bow as Neve made her way down to the dais. "Your Majesty, to what do we owe the honor? Had I known you desired to meet, I could've set aside time for an audience." Fear made her brash, her eyes sparking anger even as her voice stayed solicitous. "There are protocols for such things. As I recall, none of them involve a priestess other than myself calling a gathering."

Behind Tealia, Kiri's face was expressionless, but malice lit her eyes. Neve said nothing, still gliding carefully down the stairs, channeling all that icy poise she'd learned from her mother. Behind her ribs, her heart beat like a hummingbird's.

The laugh Tealia summoned was shrill. "Surely, nothing we need to discuss involves every priestess in the capital?"

"It does," Neve replied.

Tealia's mouth clicked shut.

Neve reached the dais, finally. She had no script for this, and no energy to make it a long and drawn-out affair. She lifted one hand, placed it on Tealia's shoulder. "I thank you for your service. Now you are released from it."

Under Neve's palm, the High Priestess trembled. Neve had to fight the urge to wipe it on her skirt when she lifted it from the other woman's shoulder. "A position has been secured for you in the Rylt," she said, nearly running the words together in her desire to see this finished. "You depart in an hour. The Consort Elect will escort you."

Arick stepped inside the lip of the door at the top of the stairs, hands clasped behind his back. His face was stony.

Furious tears shone in Tealia's eyes, her mouth a cut of anger. "It's true, then," she rasped. "You've become a heretic. You think I didn't know what you were doing in the Shrine, that you and Kiri and the Florish whore you and your sister shared had some plan afoot?" She raised her voice, turning to the gathered priestesses. "You'll follow those who would profane the sacred forest? Queen or not, such sacrilege is fit only for a pyre—"

The dagger was ceremonial. In truth, Neve didn't even know if it was sharp—it'd been strapped to her waist as the servants dressed her in a hurry, just like everything in this damn coronation was a hurry, with pithy words about national strength. But she tugged it from her belt, without thinking, and held it to the former High Priestess's throat.

"The *sacred forest*," she said evenly, "is the reason the Kings haven't returned."

Silence. Kiri's mouth bent in a cold smile. At the top of the amphitheater, Arick's eyes glittered, something almost heated in them.

Tealia stared at Neve through righteous tears, pulse spasming against the blade's edge. "Blasphemer," she hissed. "These sins will only come back on you tenfold, Neverah Keyoreth. No one harms the Wilderwood and comes away unscathed."

Neve held the dagger steady and shrugged.

The deposed High Priestess took a shuddering breath, closed her eyes. When they opened, they were calm, and Neve dropped the dagger. She'd give Tealia this: When the priestess walked out, she did it with her head high, and she didn't try to hide her tears.

Neve looked out over the priestesses, a sea of white robes and shocked eyes. Her fingers felt numb around the dagger's hilt; when she sheathed it, the edge caught her thumb, drawing a stinging line.

Sharp, then. Her knees went watery, but Neve kept herself straight-spined. After all that had happened to bring her here, threatening someone with a sharp dagger shouldn't be shocking.

"There's room on the ship for any who would like to follow Tealia." Neve gestured to the door. "You heard her. You know what we believe. What we're doing."

Her voice rang with sincerity, though that thread of doubt still coiled around her heart. *It's for Red. It's all for Red.*

She turned to the priestesses behind her. "Kiri. By our lost Kings and the magic of bygone eras, I ask that you take up the task of leading your sisters."

The collective gasp had no sound, but it had presence. It was in the flicker of Kiri's eyes. It was in the way the air suddenly felt thicker.

Kiri inclined her head. "As you ask."

Neve held her breath as she faced the assembly. The other priestesses were wide-eyed, but none rose to dissent. Courage gathered in her middle.

"The sacrifice of the Second Daughter is a useless practice," she said, voice ringing in the silent hall. "Sending them to slake the Wolf's bloodlust does nothing. The monsters he held in thrall are long dead, if they ever existed as anything but myth. And he won't free the Kings, no matter the quality of sacrifice we send him." Her lips twisted around that. She had to relate to the priestesses in the same terms they'd use, but damn if they didn't taste bitter. "The Kings are trapped in the prison they helped create, held captive by the Wilderwood. There is power to be had in its weakening. When the Kings are freed, there will be even greater reward."

The Order listened silently, blurred to one creature in the pale wash of their robes. Arick stood behind them, having passed off Tealia to the guards. His jaw was tight, his eyes unreadable.

"The process has already begun. If we uproot enough of the Wilderwood, the Kings can come home." Neve swallowed. "Redarys can come home."

Kiri's head snapped to her, eyes crackling, but the new High Priestess said nothing.

"The ship for the Rylt leaves in half an hour." Neve started toward the stairs that would take her to the door. Her parting words were said over her shoulder, ricocheting off marble. "You can join us, or you can leave."

Chapter Nineteen

Rustling woke her, fabric rasping over wood. Red slit her eyes against the lavender light. At the other end of the room, Eammon sat up, rubbing his hand over his face. The muscles in his back flexed as he gathered his hair at the nape of his neck and tied it in a messy knot.

She'd seen him wake up every morning for nearly two weeks now, since she'd told him he had to start sleeping more. And every morning, her cheeks heated when the firelight caught his bare skin.

Eammon stood, rolled his neck and shook out his shoulders, tense from another night on the floor. She knew this routine. He'd stand by the fire a moment, waking himself up, before pulling a shirt from the pile that never quite made it inside the wardrobe. He'd glance at the bed, face unreadable, then pad quietly down the stairs in an attempt not to wake her.

But today was apparently different. Eammon shoved his feet in his boots on the way to the wardrobe, pulling out a black shirt and coat. The top drawer squeaked as he opened it, and he cursed softly under his breath, darting a look to the bed.

Red abandoned the ruse of sleep, though she stayed curled around her pillow. "Where are you going?"

He pulled the drawer the rest of the way out. "I didn't mean to wake you."

"Squeaky drawers will do that."

Eammon snorted, reaching into said squeaky drawer to withdraw a dagger in a sheath. He strapped it to his hip. "We need supplies. I'm going to the Edge."

Red hadn't left the Keep since Isla died, wandering between their room and the library and sometimes the tower, waiting for a summons from Eammon that never came. She'd felt lost and insubstantial, and now the opportunity to do something—anything—made *want* seize her by the throat. "Take me with you."

He paused. The intent to deny her was in his eyes, his head angling to shake.

She sat up, sheets puddling around her waist. "Please, Eammon."

Desperation must have hung in her voice. Eammon sighed, eyes on the ceiling. "Fine." He jerked his chin toward the wardrobe. "Get dressed. Meet me downstairs."

Red went to the wardrobe, grabbing one of Eammon's shirts and a pair of trousers she'd improbably found in the depths of the same closet that had held Merra's dress. Eammon had managed to salvage her boots from her old room since the ones he'd given her were far too large—the leather was hopelessly scuffed, but serviceable. She fished her cloak out of the drawer.

Eammon eyed it with his lips pressed together. "There's a seamstress in the Edge," he said carefully, like he expected her to stop him at every word. "If you... if you wanted that mended, she could do it."

She'd washed the thing, finally, rinsing away the dirt from her first flight through the Wilderwood. But the fabric was still thorn-ragged, the hem fringed with trailing threads. Red rubbed the rough weave of it between her fingers. "I'd like that."

He nodded. "Find a dagger that suits you," Eammon called as he started down the stairs. "And you'll want a sheath."

The sheath Red chose was meant to be worn on the thigh, strapped around the leg like a leather shackle. Choosing daggers and sheaths for them wasn't something she was well versed in, and it rubbed awkwardly as they made their way through the Wilderwood, boots over leaves the only sound disturbing the silence.

"You can move it to your arm, if you want." Eammon was a dark shape in the fog ahead of her. "Won't be as easy to draw, but it'll keep you from walking bowlegged."

"Will I *need* to draw it?"

"I doubt it, but it's best to be prepared."

Her hand closed around the unfamiliar shape of the hilt. "I'm surprised you let me carry one at all," she said. "What with the risk of bleeding."

Eammon stopped, glanced at her over his shoulder. "I'm trusting you to be careful," he said, and there was nothing playful in his tone.

Red released the hilt.

Their silence as they walked through the forest was mostly comfortable. An edge of tension remained, wrought by distance: Eammon had been scarce since her mother died, barely a presence at all. They'd exchanged a few words when they crossed paths, but nothing like the baring of truth they'd given each other the day they healed the sentinel, the day he showed her the mirror. The lay of the land between them had changed, mountains leveling to valleys, and his absence meant she hadn't had a chance to learn the navigation.

Maybe it shouldn't have hurt, but it did. And the careful way he held himself, like he'd measured the distance he wanted between them, was splinter-sharp and just as irritating.

"Is this why you've been gone every day?" she asked. "Going to the Edge?"

The way Eammon moved was a language to itself. The tension in his shoulders, worry. The way they bowed inward, resignation.

"I know you weren't close, but she was your mother." His softness was a rebuttal to her blade-edge. "I've complicated things enough for you there. I thought you needed time."

"Time alone?" It was quiet, but the silence of the Wilderwood made it carry.

His head dipped forward, breath clouding the air. "I didn't know if you'd want me around," he murmured. "Since I was the reason for . . . for the distance between you and her."

She'd caught his fingers before she had the conscious thought, and the contact startled him almost as much as it did her. Eammon looked from their linked hands to her face, surprise in his parted mouth.

"That," Red said, low and fierce, "is ridiculous. What was between my mother and I . . . it was messy, complicated. And yes, it had to do with the Wilderwood. But it wasn't your fault." Her gaze dropped, because his eyes were wide and wondering and his hands were easier to look at, their scars easier to read. "Don't go looking for guilt."

Eammon swallowed. "A character flaw of mine, I'm told."

She looked up, bent the corner of a smile. He returned it. And when he started back down the path, he let her keep holding his hand.

The talk of grief stirred it up in Red's chest, dust that never quite settled. Her grief for Isla was strange and distant. Death didn't gild her, it just fixed her in Red's memory, a line with a finite beginning and ending and no chance to be more than it had been.

"I don't think I can mourn her," Red murmured.

Eammon glanced at her, brow furrowed.

"I mourn the *idea* of her, maybe. The gap between what a mother is supposed to be and what she was." She blinked hard against the burn in her eyes, shook her head. "That probably doesn't make sense."

"It does. Sometimes you don't mourn people so much as you mourn who they could've been." His fingers tightened on hers. Red returned the pressure, grateful for a counterpoint. He pretended not to notice when she scrubbed the back of her wrist over her eyes.

A branch hung in their path, and Eammon let go of her hand to push it up, gesturing her past. His heat radiated like a beacon in the chill. A lock of hair had escaped his queue, fallen over his brow, and his head dipped almost low enough for it to brush Red's cheek.

She stood for longer than she had to, rooted there by the glint of his eyes, the library smell of him.

Then Eammon's arm came down, the low-hanging branch brushing the forest floor. He hurried forward, one stride to two of hers, and didn't take her hand again.

Heat burned in her cheeks.

The branch Eammon dropped twitched in the corner of Red's eye, spiny twigs curling toward her ankle. It eroded her pride enough for her to hurry until she pressed close behind him again.

Up ahead, a sentinel rose from the fog. Darkness shaded the roots, strands of shadow stretching up the white bark, nearly waist-high to Red.

Eammon stopped, eyes flickering between her and the tree. Tentatively, she took his hand, their conversation wordless.

He was rigid at first. But this was touch for a purpose, not just comfort, and his muscles relaxed into hers by slow fractions. Eammon stepped toward the tree like he had something to prove, and he nearly slammed his opposite hand to the bark, keeping the other in Red's grip.

The buzz of the bark beneath Red's palm was almost pleasant. She hadn't done this since the day the mirror showed her Neve, but her body remembered—the cycle of power, the golden network of the sentinels, the way it all coalesced in Eammon.

But something was different. Pockets of darkness marked the glow behind her eyes, holes where sentinels should be. Not weak candle-flames, not like they'd come loose from their moorings to turn up at the Keep—like they were *gone*.

Her fingers tensed, but Eammon slid his thumb over the flutter of her wrist, a wordless request to hold her questions.

When the glow of the sentinel before them no longer guttered and the shadow-rot was gone, Red opened her eyes. "What happened?" She could see the golden map like an afterimage, the holes where sentinels should be. "The sentinels that are missing, are they at the Keep somewhere?"

"No." Eammon's voice echoed in the quiet, with that strange, multilayered resonance born from working forest magic. He rubbed at his green-threaded eyes, the shadows beneath them deep. "No, they're not at the Keep."

"Then *where*?"

"I don't know." A grimace, but it was slight, like something he was trying to hide. "Only three are missing. As long as the others stay in place, it's manageable."

"When did this happen? *How?*"

"A few days ago. As for how…I'm not sure." The strangeness magic wrought in him bled out by slow degrees—eyes only amber, voice losing its echo. She watched carefully, making sure each one was gone, that the Wilderwood seeped back out of him as much as it could and left no more permanent marks. "Nothing like this has happened before."

"How do we fix it? How do we heal them if they aren't *here*?"

"*We* don't." Eammon let go of her hand, turning to stride between the trees. The emphasis was clear—whatever he planned to do, it didn't involve Red.

"But if—"

"We heal the ones we can. We send them back where they're supposed to be." His voice fell into the silence like the first brick in a wall. "That's all you can do, Red. You can't fix holes in the Wilderwood with hands on bark."

"Then tell me what else to do."

"Nothing." He turned on the word, coat flaring behind him, eyes burning down into hers. "*Kings*, woman, you can't do anything about this. Trust me."

It echoed that first night, when he'd asked for her trust, when she told him to give her a reason. He'd given them, over and over.

Still, this felt different. But the look on his face—fierce, halfway to fear—told her pushing him was pointless.

Red returned his glare. "Fine."

A beat, then a nod. "Fine." Twigs crunched under Eammon's boots as he turned back around, moved farther into the fog.

"You should've told me," she murmured. "Even if I can't do anything, you should've told me."

Eammon's shoulders tensed, but he didn't reply.

They passed no more sentinels. The fog thinned, the trees growing farther apart, bent and crooked. Up ahead, shards of light reached through the branches.

Sunlight. How long had it been since she'd seen the light of a full day, not couched in dusk?

Eammon glanced at her, like he could read the thought on her face. The corner of his mouth quirked to smile-shaped, but something sorrowful pulled down its edge. "The forest ends up ahead."

It was still strange to her that the Wilderwood was something with an *end*. It was a geographic anomaly. None could catalog where it stopped, so they assumed it simply *didn't*. Explorers had tried to map it—riding up the eastern border where Valleyda met the frozen expanse of the Alperan Wastes, and sailing along the western side, where it met the sea. None returned.

Now Red knew why. The Kings disappeared and the Wilderwood closed, and those who'd made their way behind it, through the sea or up the Wastes, were trapped there. She thought of Bormain and Valdrek, the people dressed in green and gray. The descendants of those lost adventurers, cut off from the world for generations.

"They have a sky," she said softly, looking up. "The regular sky, I mean. With the sun."

Another half smile, another darted glance with something slightly wounded in it. "They do." Eammon started forward, shafts of thin gold cutting the fog and burnishing his hair. Sunlight looked good on him. "Endless twilight, fortunately, only plagues the Wilderwood."

Red followed Eammon to the tree line, slipping between the trunks and out into the light beyond. She didn't realize she'd been holding her breath in expectation of pain until it didn't come. There was a slight *pop* of pressure, a soap bubble breaking against her skin, but nothing like the crushing vise she'd felt when she first crossed into the Wilderwood, the strange hum against her bones. It reminded her of what Fife told her, that day with Bormain—the borders on the northern side weren't closed up so tightly. The Wilderwood, it seemed, felt the need for such protection only from the rest of the continent.

Still, Eammon paused next to her, a muscle feathering in his jaw, a swallow working down his throat. Pain carved lines beside his mouth and made his shoulders stiff—the roots knotted around his spine tightening, pulling him back toward the gloom of his forest. It might let him go, on its northern border, but it wouldn't let him forget where he belonged.

Her lip worked between her teeth.

A few yards away, a large wooden wall rose up from the ground, carved with swirls and arabesques, set with massive double doors. From within, the faint sounds of a city—laughter and shouting, hawking merchants, livestock. Smoke twisted into a sky that faded from lavender to bright blue. Miles away to the west, a line of fog began on the horizon. It looked almost like an approaching storm, but as Red watched, it didn't move.

Eammon followed her gaze. "The sea is that way," he said. "The fog is so thick you can't see more than two inches from your eyes. Apparently, anyone who sails in it gets hopelessly lost, turned around in circles."

"Has anyone tried?"

"Not in ages." He jerked a finger over his shoulder in the opposite direction. "Same thing to the east, it's just too far away to see. Endless fog."

"And you can't pass through that, either?"

Eammon shook his head. "The Wilderwood was very thorough, after the Kings wounded it. Everyone unlucky enough to be stuck back here has no way to get out." His hand pressed against his side, mouth thinning as he turned to stride toward the city walls. "Come on. We need to make this quick."

Red watched him go with a line between her brows, the rigid way he moved at odds with his usual stalking grace. Bones wrapped in vines, a tether pulling him back. Another reminder—much as he might look human, he wasn't.

Still, her hand was warm where he'd held it.

Eammon rapped against the wooden doors. Red winced, used to the crushing quiet of the Wilderwood, but against the backdrop of village noises, Eammon's knock was barely heard.

The door creaked open, just a crack. A scrutinizing blue eye peered out. "Name?"

"Who do you think it is, Lear?" Eammon rolled his eyes, but it was with a grin. "I brought a guest."

The gatekeeper's eyes widened, as did the crack. Beyond, Red could see a bustling village, not unlike the Valleydan capital.

"My lady." The man had hair the dark auburn of autumn leaves and a handsome, clean-shaven face. She recognized him—he'd been in the forest the day she saw the vision and came after Eammon.

Lear pushed the door open wide. "Welcome, Wolves."

Chapter Twenty

The cacophony was deafening after weeks of near-silence in the Wilderwood. Children ran and shouted, donkeys brayed, sheep bleated. Dirt roads branched off the stone-paved main path, leading to earthen huts with grass roofs, the wooden lintels carved with the same graceful arabesques as the gates. They'd called it a village, but this was a city, almost as large as the Valleydan capital. Centuries of explorers' descendants, trying to make their own world since they couldn't get into the one beyond the Wilderwood.

Beyond the thoroughfare, Red could glimpse fields full of crops, distant grazing animals. It appeared the cold and barren soil that made Valleyda difficult to farm wasn't as much of a problem here. She wondered if it was some facet of magic, the Wilderwood making the land fruitful since it had them trapped here with no way to trade, relying only on what they could grow themselves.

No one seemed fazed by Eammon's presence, but Red drew their attention. Women whispered behind their hands as they passed; children stopped in their games to watch with wide eyes. All of them wore old-fashioned clothes, in shades of mist and forest and earth.

"They're looking at me like I have three heads," Red murmured.

"You're the first person from beyond the Wilderwood they've seen in a century," Eammon replied. "Something with three heads would be less conspicuous."

In a century, he said. Not *ever*. "So you brought the others here?"

He stiffened, just slightly. "Merra came once."

"Only once?"

"It was all she had time for." Eammon quickened his pace, and Red had to nearly run to keep up. Still, her eyes narrowed at his back.

The path opened into a wide market square, open-air stalls hemmed in by larger structures of wood and rock. Musicians gathered around a tree carved of stone in the square's center, so realistic that Red half expected the leaves to rustle. A pretty girl with silver-blond hair to her knees whirled in graceful circles to the drumbeat. She winked at Eammon, but when her eyes caught on Red, she faltered in her spinning. A quick recovery, then she tossed Red a wink, too.

The square was loud and crowded, sellers hawking everything from livestock and produce to jewelry and furniture. Red tried and failed to keep from staring. "Is the Edge their only city?"

Eammon caught her arm, pulling her out of the way of a laden cart. He kept his hold once the cart passed, and Red made no move to pull away.

"There are a few others, farther from the Wilderwood," he said. "Not many, though." His eyes tilted up for a moment, like he was calculating in his head. "The whole territory is about the size of Floriane, I think."

An entire country, hidden in fog and frozen in time. Red cocked a brow. "How do you know how big Floriane is?"

"I've seen *maps*, Redarys."

"Not any recent ones, I'd wager. Geography has changed in the past five hundred years, Wolf."

"Perhaps you can teach me, then."

"Perhaps. You seem studious."

"One of my many admirable qualities."

"Bold that you think I meant it as a compliment." But she grinned as she said it, and so did he as he lightly pinched her arm.

Eammon led them across the road, stopped before a stone building with a colorful stall set up in front. Bells hung from the corners, and swaths of fabric made the stall's roof. Clothes were folded on tables and hanging from beams, a fluttering army of gowns in forest colors, made in designs out of the past.

A woman with charcoal-silver hair braided elaborately around her head smiled when she saw Eammon. A younger woman sat beside her, hair strawberry gold, worn loose and threaded with flowers.

Eammon nodded to the older woman. "Asheyla."

"Wolf." The woman's blue eyes moved to Red, appraising and wondering at once. "And this must be the Lady. I'd heard you'd bestowed the title, finally." She dipped her head. "Congratulations and blessings on your marriage, Lady Wolf."

The title made Red's spine straighten. "You can just call me Red."

"I have one more thing to add to my tab," Eammon said, gesturing to Red's cloak. "Can you mend this?"

"I can mend anything, boy, even a cloak that looks like it's been shredded for thread." Asheyla looked Red up and down, scrutinizing. "It looks like everything else you ordered for her will fit. *Someone*"—her eyes flitted to Eammon—"didn't give me precise measurements." Gracefully, she turned toward the building, calling over her shoulder to the other girl. "I'll be back momentarily, Loreth."

The shop was empty, and the stone walls muffled the noises of the market outside. Wooden mannequins in the corners wore pinned-together gowns. Looms with half-completed bolts of fabric lined the back wall, and the counter held boot soles and strips of leather.

Inside, Asheyla gave Red's cloak another once-over, pale brows pulling together. "Are you sure you don't just want a new cloak?" she asked. "This one has enough holes that mending it will come to nearly the same amount of fabric."

"Mended," Eammon said from behind Red, close enough that

his breath stirred her hair. A brief pause. "I'll send Fife with more instructions."

Her brow quirked, but Asheyla didn't argue. Red shrugged out of the cloak, running the tattered length between her hands before handing it to the shopkeeper. Her reluctance to part with it must've shown on her face—the older woman's expression softened. When she folded the cloak in her arms, she did it with obvious care.

"It'll be good as new," Asheyla said softly.

Red swallowed. "Thank you."

A gentle nod. "The boots aren't quite done," Asheyla called over her shoulder as she crossed to the counter, where a stack of clothes sat tied with twine.

"Fife can pick them up," Eammon said.

Asheyla chuckled. "Tell him I'll find a bottle of wine Valdrek hasn't watered down. He's—"

A muffled roar cut her off, freezing the three of them in place. Caught between horror and madness and pain, the roar came again, this time with the sound of something scraping across stone. It reverberated from beneath their feet, somewhere under the floorboards. Red didn't realize she'd grabbed Eammon's arm until he made a small noise of protest when her grip tightened.

One more long scraping noise, one more roar. This one faded slowly, becoming almost a whimper at the end.

Eammon looked at Red like he thought she'd move away once silence fell. When she didn't, he put his hand over hers on his arm, large and rough with scars. "How bad is he?" Softly, as if he was afraid of being overheard.

"He lasted two weeks in the tavern." Asheyla used the same near-whisper as Eammon, slipping the clothes on the table into a rough-spun canvas bag with a drawstring top. "Bucked at the basement beams over and over until he finally snapped one. He's been here ever since, but..." She trailed off, blinking to keep the shine in her eyes from spilling over.

Bormain. They were talking about Bormain, shadow-infected and weeping the last time she saw him. Something worse now.

Red swallowed past a dry throat. Part of her still felt like it was her fault. She'd healed only the breach, not the man. She'd left the job half done.

You begin and begin, yet never see it finished. The Wilderwood had screamed it at her, that night the corridor collapsed. It was right.

Eammon sighed, taking his hand from Red's to rub at his temple. "Why has Valdrek not taken care of it?" It would've sounded callous were his voice not so pained. "If he still hasn't improved, Ash, it will only—"

"He's Valdrek's son-in-law." Asheyla's voice was stern. "He's family. Valdrek won't... won't *take care of it* unless there's absolutely no chance of recovery. Elia would never forgive him." The woman kept her eyes to her hands, busily tying packages in string, but all her awareness was on the Wolf, and her words came measured. "You've healed the shadow-infected before. Long ago." Her eyes flicked up. "You've lived long, Wolf, but our stories live longer still."

The line of Eammon's jaw tightened. "If I could do it, I would," he said softly. "But I can't. Not anymore."

Asheyla's eyes darted from Eammon to Red, lips a thin line, but she stayed silent.

Eammon turned to the door. "We should go. Fife gave me an extensive list." He walked past the threshold into the sunlight.

Asheyla's eyes followed him, still puzzled, but once she turned her face to Red she'd arranged it in a tired smile. She held out the canvas bag filled with new clothes. "Come back if something doesn't fit."

Red slung the bag over her shoulder. It was heavier than it looked. She shifted from foot to foot, a question on her tongue she couldn't quite shape.

"Before," she began haltingly, "when Eammon... healed people. How did he do it?"

"I wasn't born," the older woman hedged, picking at a roll of twine. "I heard the tale from my mother. According to her, he could do it with a touch." A sigh, a slight shake of her head. "But the Wilderwood wasn't quite so weak then."

Red thought of sentinels, of black rot and hands on trunks, sending light to conquer shadow. She nodded, gave Asheyla a smile, and followed the Wolf.

Outside, the sunlight made her blink, eyes still unused to brightness. Eammon leaned against a post on the porch, arms crossed, but when she emerged he pushed off. "Fife said we need—"

"We have to help Bormain."

He stopped, a soundless sigh raising his shoulders and letting them fall.

Red walked down the short steps of Asheyla's shop, stopping on the one below him. The stair gave him even more height on her, but she kept her spine straight. "I can help you heal him," she said firmly. "Like I did with the sentinel. It's the same concept, right?"

"It's far more complicated than that, Redarys." Eammon's eyes were stern. "Chasing the shadow-rot out of a person is dangerous. It takes more power than I have anymore—"

"But you aren't doing it alone." Red shook her head. "You don't have to do everything alone, Eammon."

His mouth was a tight line, hair shadowing his eyes. There was something waiting in the space between them, something vast and terrifying, but it narrowed down to this: the itch in her fingers to smooth along his jaw. The certainty that her palm would never feel right again unless it swept his hair off his forehead.

Red dropped her eyes; his were suddenly too much for her. "Let me help you, and we can help Bormain. We can at least speak with Valdrek about it."

He searched her face, lips slightly parted, as if looking for something he was both eager and terrified to find. Then he turned sharply, headed for the other side of the square. "Have it your way, Lady Wolf."

A wooden building stood directly across from the stone tree. Music and raucous laughter could be heard even before they mounted the stairs, and when the doors opened, they wafted scents of sweat and ale.

"Valdrek is usually here." Eammon shot her a warning look. "Stay close."

A bar stood across from the door, packed with people drinking and laughing and playing card games. The floor near the band was clear of tables and chairs, and dancers swirled in time to the music, some more gracefully than others. Eammon's broad figure cut through the crowd.

The back of the tavern was somewhat calmer, occupied by those more intent on drinks than dancing. Valdrek sat with his back to them, cards in his hand and a sizable pile of antiquated coins by his side. Red's eyes widened. She hadn't seen currency like that anywhere but a history book—it still featured the likeness of the last Krahl of Elkyrath, back before the country broke into city-states.

"Wolf," Valdrek said, selecting a card. Then, as if sensing her presence, he turned, raised a brow. "*Wolves.*"

She didn't recognize any of the other men at the table, faces ranging from interested to wary. Eammon jerked his head toward the corner, turning without looking to see if Valdrek would follow. Red hovered between them, lost in unfamiliar politics.

The older man heaved a sigh, setting down his cards. "Excuse me, gentlemen. I've a Wolf that needs attending to."

Eammon sat down in the back corner, running a tired hand over his face. Red moved to follow, Valdrek behind her.

"It appears you've worn him out, Lady." It could've been lascivious, but Valdrek sounded only curious. He gave her an assessing look as he brushed past, sinking into the chair across from Eammon. Brow furrowed, Red settled between them.

Valdrek had brought his tankard with him; he took a long swallow before setting it on the table. "Drinks, anyone?" He looked archly at Eammon. "Might improve your temper."

"Sorry to pull you away from your cards." Eammon sat forward, bracing his forearms on his knees. "I wasn't sure if your fellow players were aware of the... the situation."

He didn't have to clarify *what* situation. Immediately the bluster drained out of Valdrek, sinking his shoulders. "We've kept it fairly quiet." He shrugged, but the movement was pained. "The basement needed repairs after he got... agitated, but we passed the damage off as a wrestling match that got out of hand. Ash's shop is stone-built and should last longer." His mouth thinned, a spark of determination in his eye. "Until he gets better."

Eammon made no comment, but his clasped hands tightened between his knees.

"We're going to try to heal him." Red made her voice as confident as she could. "Eammon and I."

Valdrek didn't hide his surprise. He sat back in his seat, brow climbing. "Can you do such a thing now, Wolf?" Ragged hope in his voice. "I wasn't going to ask, with the Wilderwood so weak, but if you're strong enough with the Lady's help..."

"We can try," Eammon said shortly.

An assessing look darted between the two of them before Valdrek threw back the rest of his ale. "Differences abound." He snorted. "Marriage changes a man."

Eammon's jaw tensed. He stood in a rush, pushing his chair in behind him. "Let's get on with it, then."

Outside the shop, Valdrek told Asheyla the plan in a low voice. "I'd wait there," he told her, pointing toward the tavern. "Just in case. If you want wine, let Ari know, and tell him to skip the watered-down stuff."

Behind Red, Eammon stood still as the stone tree. He'd given Fife's list to Loreth, Asheyla's shopgirl, with instructions to have their supplies waiting with Lear at the gate.

"Healing someone shadow-infected is different from healing a sentinel." He used the same low, even tone he did at their lessons, though every line of his body was held bowstring-tight. "You have to direct power specifically to the affected places, rather than just letting it all go."

"Humans are somewhat more complex than trees," Red said. She held out her palm so he could check it for wounds, a now-familiar routine.

Eammon took the proffered hand but didn't inspect it, instead giving her a stern look from under lowered brows. "Don't touch him."

Red frowned. "Then how am I supposed to—"

"You touch me, I touch him." Scars brushed against her knuckles as he lightly squeezed her outstretched hand. "I told you, it's deft work, and it could be dangerous. You let your power go into me, I'll let it go into him."

Her lips twisted, but after a moment, she nodded. Eammon gave her hand one more squeeze, then dropped it, turning to follow Valdrek to the basement door.

It was thrice-locked, with a board nailed over it for good measure. Eammon and Valdrek hauled the board away, and Valdrek fished a key ring from his pocket.

"Restraints?" Eammon asked.

"All four limbs. Torso, too." Valdrek said it like it pained him, a visceral reminder they were speaking of his kin. Red thought of the name Asheyla mentioned—Elia, who must be Valdrek's daughter, Bormain's wife. Her eyes flicked to Eammon, still and stoic next to her, and sympathy speared through her chest.

The last lock fell away. Valdrek sighed. "It isn't pretty. Be prepared."

The room was dim. Tiny slats in the walls high above provided the only light, dust motes dancing in the glow. A harsh smell hit Red like a wall as she stepped over the threshold after Eammon and Valdrek, acidic and cold, intense enough to make her press her arm against her nose. The room was small, barely big enough for the three of them to stand shoulder-to-shoulder, and the short ceiling nearly brushed the top of Eammon's head.

In front of her, Eammon went rigid, stepping to the side as if trying to hide her in his shadow. Red pushed at his shoulder. After a moment of resistance, he moved enough for her to see.

They'd tried to make it as comfortable as possible, and that somehow made it worse. Bormain lay in a bed covered with thick blankets and surrounded by pillows, almost enough to hide the lengths of chain running from beneath the bedding to shackles set into the stone floor. One for each limb, and another that appeared to wrap around his middle, attached first to the bed frame and then to metal rings on the walls. Despite the restraints, there were gouges in the floor where he'd managed to scoot the bed from side to side. Red remembered the noises they'd heard above in Asheyla's shop, and shuddered.

Bormain didn't move. His eyes were closed, swollen black veins spidering from his eyelids to stretch down his face. The shadow-infected arm lay outside the blankets, at least twice its normal size and with skin fragile as a rotting fruit, staining the bedding dark and damp. The nails on his hands were hooked and overlong, the bones in his face too sharp.

The shadow-rot wasn't just making Bormain sick. It was… *remaking* him.

The grit of Valdrek's teeth was audible. "I haven't let Elia down here in a week, since he started…" He didn't finish.

Eammon's expression was unreadable. He put out his hand, gently maneuvered Red back behind his shoulder.

She let him this time. Red leaned close, standing with Eammon before her like a shield. "Is he asleep?"

"Not sleeping." The voice sounded like it came through a cut throat, thready and ragged. "The shadows stole my sleeping."

Slowly, Bormain lifted his head. The angle of it had to be painful, restrained as he was, but he showed no discomfort. His smile stretched too wide, nearly ear-to-ear, and he closed his milk-blind eyes to take a long, exaggerated inhale. "Smells so sweet. Barren soil, rootless soil." His eyes opened, snapped to Red, unnaturally quick. "There's blood on the wood, rootless Second Daughter. Blood to open and blood to close, old things awakened. Eons of patience rewarded."

Red fought the urge to press her face against Eammon's shoulder, to block out the whole scene in his warmth and library scent. Instead she fumbled for his hand. "We're here to help you," she said, and the words came out clear even if they were quiet.

"Help me?" Bormain threw his head back, braying at the ceiling. The dark, swollen veins in his throat pulsed. "Sweet Wolves, poor Wolves, *I'm* not the one who needs saving. *He's* waiting, *they're* waiting, everyone will get their chance." His head, still held at that unnatural angle, swung back and forth as he sang under his breath. "They wait and they spin, they spin nightmares new and old, remake the shadow and let the shadow remake *them*..."

Eammon glanced down at her, a question in his eyes, the expression easy to read. If she'd changed her mind, he'd take her out of here the moment she said so.

Red bit her lip, that sour guilt in her throat again. *You begin and begin and never see it finished.*

One nod, sharp.

With another burning look, Eammon started forward, moving almost soundlessly over the stone floor.

Bormain's singing dropped to a tuneless hum, his eyes closed and his head swinging gently back and forth like he'd lost interest. Red took a deep breath of the stinking air and tugged at the power curled in her middle. It spiked upward, blooming toward her fingers and Eammon holding them, veins greening and the taste of earth faint on her tongue. They stepped forward carefully, soundless as possible, Eammon's body drawn up like a spring set to snap.

Eyes still closed, Bormain stopped humming. "Your knotted string of death is fraying, Wolf-pup," he said, his voice ringing clear and precise. "They have help now. They're coming home, Solmir and all the rest."

The name stopped both of them cold, Eammon with his hand half outstretched. Bormain's laugh was broken and ugly. "So many endings, Wolf-pup, and you've seen them *all*—"

He was silenced by Eammon's hand slamming over one of the only places on his body left untouched by shadow—his mouth.

Tendons stood out on Eammon's neck as Bormain thrashed beneath his palm. "Do it," he gritted through his teeth. "Red, if you're going to do it, do it *now*."

Her teeth drove together, and Red let forest magic cycle out of her, flowing instead into Eammon.

Like before, when they worked together to heal the sentinel, her mind's eye beheld what her physical sight couldn't. Her own power was dim in comparison with Eammon's, only a thread running through her body, snaking in and out of her bones and organs. But Eammon—a riot of gold, light shaped like roots twisting through him, blooming, growing.

It almost made her stop, seeing how ingrained in him it was. Almost made her cut off the thin thread of her power when she remembered how it changed him, how it took him in pieces. Fear rioted, fear that somehow he'd be taken from her, and it would be her fault for making him do this and feeding power into the roots that grew beneath his skin. She opened her eyes with a gasp to see him looking at her, the shadow-sickened form of Bormain twisting on the bed beneath his green-veined hand.

"Don't." Clipped, focused, but with something in it that spoke of surprise, and a kind of longing. The whites of his eyes were wholly emerald. "Red, I'll be fine, don't stop."

A deep breath, his scent of falling leaves and coffee and paper drowning out the sickroom stench. Then she closed her eyes, and gripped his hand like a lifeline, and let the power blooming out of her keep feeding into him.

Behind her eyelids, Bormain looked like a void. A complete absence of anything, a vaguely man-shaped hole in all that golden glow. At first, the magic flowing from Eammon seemed almost eaten by it, swallowed. Each golden thread was deft and deliberate, like Eammon was sewing something up, mending a sock rather than a man. Eventually, the golden glow began to overtake the shadow, consuming it and canceling it out. She felt Eammon sway, heard Bormain's pained gasp as, slowly, light eclipsed the dark.

When Eammon finally let go of her hand, Red opened her eyes.

The man on the bed looked waxen as a corpse, but his skin was no longer threaded through with darkness. The nails on his hands were short and pale, not clawed, and the bones of his skull were the right proportions again. His chest rose and fell, shallow but steady.

Eammon hunched over the bedframe. Bark on his forearms, evident from where his sleeve had rucked up, height made greater by the magic he'd called. His veins were green, in his wrists and his neck and the bruised skin below his eyes, but darkness shot through them like heartbeats, flickering shadows.

"Eammon?" Alarm made her voice sharp.

He shook his head, once. Ground his teeth in his jaw. Slowly, slowly, the darkness stopped beating in his veins. They turned to green, then faded to blue, changes and shadow leaching out of him like blood from a wound. He shuddered, a grimace drawing his lips back from his teeth.

Pain has to be transferred. Eammon had taken the shadow-rot, let it cycle into him, and drowned it out in Wilderwood magic.

Her knees suddenly turned to water, exhaustion and relief coming like a fist to the temple. Red sagged sideways, and Eammon wrapped his arm around her, his veins now the color a man's should be, though the whites of his eyes still held a tracery of green. "I'm fine," he whispered into her hair. "I'm fine."

"You did it." Tears streamed down Valdrek's cheeks, and reverence lit his face. "By the Kings and all the *shadows*, you did it."

But Red didn't hear him, because she'd fainted dead away.

Chapter Twenty-One

She woke to the smell of a library, the rough weave of fabric pressed against her cheek. Red started, jerking in Eammon's arms, and the top of her head collided with his chin.

"*Kings*," the Wolf muttered. He put her down with one arm and raised the other, rubbing at his jaw. Most vestiges of magic were gone, other than that extra inch of height he'd gained the night the Wilderwood took the corridor. But the veins around his amber irises were still faintly green.

"Sorry." Red's cheeks blazed as she steadied herself, squinting against sunlight and the remaining haze in her head. They stood in the center of the Edge's main thoroughfare, the sky slanting dark overhead. "Where's Valdrek?"

"Still at Asheyla's with Bormain. They thought it best not to try moving him until he wakes."

Despite her aching head and still-watery legs, Red's lip twitched to a hopeful smile. "He'll wake, then? We did it?"

Eammon's lips pressed together, strange-shaded eyes alight with some layered emotion she couldn't quite read. "We did it," he said quietly, pressing ahead toward the gate.

Red trailed after him, lips still curved. She'd helped. She and Eammon had healed Bormain, cleared him of shadow-rot. Maybe that meant they could heal the whole Wilderwood.

But the smile faded as fragments of memory slipped in, the things Bormain said while still riddled with darkness. A name, in particular.

Solmir.

The first time Bormain mentioned the youngest of the Five Kings, Eammon had passed it off as ravings. She'd left it at that, albeit uneasily.

But for the man to mention Solmir twice made it seem like more than ravings.

Lear gave them an appraising look when they reached the gate. Loreth stood next to him, a full canvas bag clutched in her hands. She passed it off to Eammon in a hurry before slipping into the crowd, shooting Lear a conspiratorial glance.

Eammon sighed. "I assume you heard."

"Don't think too ill of her." Lear cranked the lever that opened the wooden gate, the screech of hinges soft against the sounds of the bustling city. "An attempt to heal the shadow-rot is quite a lot to expect someone to keep to themselves. What's the verdict?"

"It worked." Eammon's voice sounded like his throat was raw.

The only sign of Lear's shock was the widening of his pale-blue eyes. "Well, shadows damn me." A chuckle as he looked from Eammon to Red. "All hail the Wolves."

Eammon didn't reply. He shouldered the canvas bag, full of Fife's requested supplies.

"You know you can always call on us, Wolf," Lear said, the humor gone out of his tone. "If you find yourself needing help."

"I appreciate it," Eammon said as he walked through the gate. "But I think things are beyond anyone else's help at this point."

Lear's expression went pensive once Eammon passed. "Watch him, Lady," he murmured to Red. "The Wolf and the Wilderwood twine together so, and the weakness of one is the weakness of the other. He looks like he's worn himself to frayed seams."

"He does that." Red watched the Wolf, a broad shadow against the distant forest.

Beyond the gate, Eammon stood stiffly, looking toward the northern horizon, away from the Wilderwood. Every line of his body seemed to strain forward, like he wanted to run in the opposite direction of the trees. But he couldn't. The roots around his bones might as well have been shackles.

Red gave Lear a tight-lipped smile. He nodded, cranking the gate shut, muffling the sounds of the Edge.

Slowly, she walked to Eammon's side. He didn't look at her, eyes still trained on the hills to the north disappearing into a haze of fog and fading sunlight. After a moment, he turned toward the forest. Above, the sky shifted toward twilight to match the Wilderwood's horizon, the two of them fading from blue and lavender to meet somewhere in violet.

Red followed him over the moss, fingers tapping nervously at the still-unfamiliar shape of the dagger on her thigh. "He mentioned Solmir again."

"I'm aware." His stride barely faltered.

"That's twice now." She paused, waiting, but he didn't offer to fill the silence. "It seems like more than a coincidence."

"Does it?"

The venom in his voice caught her off guard. Red stopped, yards away from the dark maw of the Wilderwood. "It *means* something. You know it, and so do I."

Eammon stopped walking, but stayed silent. A breeze ruffled his hair.

"I don't know if you're trying to protect me, or if you just don't want to bother telling me anything." Her hands curled and released, loose fists that held nothing. "But I can only help you as much as you let me, Eammon."

He'd half turned as she spoke, the line of his profile sketched dark against the trees and the encroaching edge of twilight—jaw rigid, a lock of escaped black hair hanging over his forehead. Red wanted to pummel him and pull him close at once, but settled for crossing her arms over her chest.

"In the old stories, Solmir was supposed to marry your mother." She said it softly, like she could stitch the story together even with uneven seams. "She ran to the Wilderwood with Ciaran instead, and Solmir ended up trapped in the Shadowlands with the other Kings. But there's more to it, isn't there?"

Eammon's sigh seemed to echo, to bounce off the trees at the edge of the Wilderwood. The battle within him was evident, to stay silent or to speak, but after one laden moment, the fists at his sides loosened, like holding them tight was suddenly too strenuous a task. A deep breath, and when the words came, they were threadbare. "He killed my parents."

They'd had so many conversations about grief. Here was one more. Her hand was on his shoulder before she had the conscious thought, before she knew she'd moved forward. She half expected him to flinch away, but instead Eammon sagged into the contact.

He spoke faster, like a dam had been struck and the river was waiting. "My mother always felt guilty that Solmir shared the Kings' fate. She didn't think he deserved it, said he'd been caught up in their schemes without an escape. They'd been friends, apparently, before they were betrothed." Eammon's teeth set sharp against the word *friends.* "I heard Gaya and Ciaran talking about it sometimes. When they thought I wasn't listening." He shook his head. "Nearly a century and a half of the same circular argument."

So nonchalant, the way he discussed centuries. His lifetime stretched over so many of hers, like the hundreds of years it took a sapling to fully grow—it made sense, when he was born to parents who made him shortly after they'd tangled themselves with a forest. Red had never thought to imagine Eammon as any different from the man she met in the library, not quite human, held in stasis by his strange relationship to the Wilderwood. But now, brushed in twilight, she could see a younger version of him. Eyes not so tired, shoulders not so rigid, unaware of the burden set to fall on them.

"Ciaran didn't want to release Solmir," Eammon continued. "Gaya claimed he'd been embroiled in her father's machinations against his will, but Ciaran didn't believe that. And with the Kings bound together the way they were, he didn't think it'd be possible to release only one from the Shadowlands, anyway."

A subtle change since he'd first decided to tell her the story, from *my parents* to *Gaya and Ciaran*, an artificial distance she wasn't sure he was aware of creating. Like he wanted a separation, like he wanted a gulf. Like being close was too painful.

She understood.

Red kept her hand on his shoulder, but her eyes flickered toward the border of the Wilderwood. It stood tall and dark and fathomless, a place for losing.

Eammon ran a weary hand over his face. "Gaya decided to try anyway. She opened a breach, and Ciaran felt it happen. He went after her." A pause, a heavy breath in. "By the time he got there, she was dead already. Consumed by the Wilderwood, to keep her from harming it further."

The tale was easy to pick up from here. The Wolf, carrying the forest-riddled body of the Second Daughter to the edge of the woods. Figures shrouded and made less real by myth.

Except that they were the parents of the man standing before her now. Except that he'd seen it all happen.

"I saw him carrying her." Low, expressionless, turned toward the forest that pulled him inexorably back into its darkness. "I followed him to the border. I heard what he said, but I didn't understand what it meant. It took me so *damn* long to understand what he meant."

Here his voice broke, but instead of shuddering, Eammon kept every muscle statue-still, like if he made himself less human the emotion couldn't catch up. When he spoke again, it was a murmur. "He lasted a year after that. A year on his own, the Wilderwood eating him away the whole time. Taking everything that made him anything close to human. Breaches opened. The forest was full of shadow-creatures, but the borders stayed closed and didn't let them out, like... like when something is about to die, and holds on all the tighter for it."

"It wasn't your fault." She spoke as quietly as he did, a whisper against the darkening sky and the waiting, hungry wood. "None of it was your fault."

He didn't respond, lost in the cadence of his own horror story. "And then he *died*," he said, as if it was still a startling end to the tale, all these centuries later. "He died, and in that moment, the borders opened, like that dead hand finally losing its grip. The shadow-creatures got out." A pause, a rattling breath. "It was all instinct, after that. Cutting my hand, putting it to the ground. The Wilderwood... resurrected, I guess. Grew in me. It hurt." His hand curled against his chest in memory of pain. "I've always wondered if it hurt me more or less than it did him. I can't come up with an answer. He wasted away beneath it, and I'm still here."

The last part was a whisper. They stood there, a man and a woman on the edge of the dark, both bent and shadowed beneath the weight of awful history.

"Then I was the Wolf," Eammon said quietly. "And until Fife and Lyra arrived, I was alone."

Red didn't know what to say. This story had haunted her whole life—he'd lived it, had to exist under the shadow of its happening and the ghost it left. She wanted to comfort him; every line of his body said he didn't want to be comforted.

"The forest was in so bad a state, getting a new Wolf didn't heal all the breaches." He'd gone back to neutral tones now. Tucking emotion away, burying it. "So some of the shadow-creatures that had escaped when the Wilderwood briefly died still lingered."

"Until Kaldenore came," Red said, piecing it together. "And the Wilderwood drained her to heal itself as best it could." Not good, not bad. But hungry. And desperate.

A broken sigh. "No ending here has ever been happy, Red."

He shrugged off her hand. He turned toward the Wilderwood. Red's fingers closed on empty space as he strode between the trees.

Alone. Determined, always, to be alone, even when she was standing next to him.

After a moment, she followed, light pressure fizzing over her skin when she passed the border. They moved through the fog in silence.

Eammon's hand shooting out of the gloom to seize her arm made her grunt in surprise. Red's boots tripped over the leaves, and she saw what he'd pulled her from—a perfectly circular piece of shadow-rotten ground, nearly hidden in the dim. It looked like a circle of spilled paint over the canvas of the forest, with no listing tree to mark its center.

A missing sentinel. A hole.

Eammon's lips pulled tight. The hand on her arm tremored.

Magic bloomed to Red's fingers, ready for use. "What do we do?"

"I told you before." Eammon shook his head. "There's nothing you can do, Red."

"There has to be *something*. Or are you just determined to leave me out of it?"

He froze, and that was answer enough.

Red drew her dagger. Eammon's grip went from her elbow to her wrist, lightning-fast, pulling her close enough that her nose nearly notched into his sternum. She didn't try to jerk away, but neither did she let go of the hilt, holding the blade sideways between their chests.

"No," he nearly snarled. "Not yours."

"It worked once—"

"And the Wilderwood almost had you." His voice was harsh, amber eyes burning, green encroaching where the whites should be. "I won't let it happen again."

"So I'm just supposed to let you bleed out, then? Give yourself over to the Wilderwood completely when you don't have enough blood left to satisfy it?"

A tremble in their locked-together hands. She couldn't tell which one of them it came from. "If that's what it takes."

The sound was quiet. If they weren't caught in fraught silence of their own, they wouldn't have heard it—a thin screech, like tearing metal. Red's teeth snapped together, a low, strange discomfort creeping up from her feet, through her bones.

Eammon's face blanched. His hand curled around the hilt of his dagger, the other still on her wrist. His eyes went to the pitted, rotten ground as he stepped slightly away from her, moving like prey in a predator's sight line.

The sound came again, louder. The surface of the pit undulated, something stirring beneath.

"Red." Nearly a whisper, and Eammon's eyes were wide. "Run."

The pit ruptured before she had the chance.

It was darkness solidifying, shooting upward. Different from that first night—not some formless thing cobbling a counterfeit body from bone and shadow. This *had* a body, a wrong and terrible one, a tube of black scales and clinging rot. The tearing-metal noise came from an open mouth, wide as Eammon was tall, ringed with layers upon layers of carrion-caked teeth. The thing wove from side to side, towering in the air, circular jaws gnashing at the twilight sky.

The eruption tossed her backward, the edges of her vision dark and hazy. Red didn't come fully back to herself until she felt Eammon beside her, ripping her dagger from her hand. Whether to use it himself or to keep her from it, she didn't know.

"*Go!*" He jumped to his feet, whipping around in front of her with his teeth bared, facing the thing that had wrenched itself from the breach. Not a shadow-creature, nothing so insubstantial—one of the other monsters the Shadowlands held?

It seemed taller now, like it'd pulled more of itself free of the hole. Eammon held both daggers in one hand and swiped at the palm of the other, twin slices across a dirt-crusted lifeline. "Red, *go*!"

She scuttled backward across the ground, boot heels churning up roots and rock. A scream hung in the back of her throat, one she wouldn't let loose, and her eyes couldn't leave Eammon. Power curled up from her center, blooming like a vine, nearly solid. Nearly a weapon.

Eammon slammed his sliced hand to the shadow-churned dirt. The monster's sharp teeth came down, and he backhanded it away, the desperate movement sending blood drops flying. Where they fell, the darkness on the ground healed for a moment, but it was like rain on a house fire, too little and too weak. The thing roared.

Red stopped, hair tangled in branches, teeth set and chest burning. It wasn't fear that drummed her heartbeat, not anymore—it was *anger*, anger to see Eammon bleeding himself dry, anger that he had to.

Shatter-edged magic climbed through her veins like ivy.

Every movement was unthinking instinct. Red stood, arched her fingers, and the Wilderwood arched with her, synced to her movements. With a snarl, she thrust her hands forward, the taste of earth in her mouth and green in her veins, gathering every bit of magic she could from the thin thread of it winding through her frame.

The forest followed her lead.

That tearing-metal scream reached a crescendo as vines wrapped the beast's awful length, squeezing until the gore-caked sides split, opened. The creature whipped from side to side, tangling in reaching branches, ripping itself on thorns grown long and sword-sharp until it fell with a sound like a thunderclap, pieces of it breaking away as it hit the ground, stinking of decay. The parts that landed in the shadow-pit sank slowly down; the parts that landed outside the ring of darkness sat like lumps of meat. Unattached to the whole, rot set in quickly, eating through the flesh like acid.

One more screech, one more thrash, and the monster was gone.

Slowly, Red straightened her fingers, and as she did, the Wilderwood sheathed its weapons. Thorns shrank, branches bent back, vines slithered into the underbrush. The forest settled and was silent.

The shadow-pit still marred the ground, but nothing rippled beneath it. Next to the edge, Eammon slumped on his knees, eyes wide. But then he looked to her, and pushed himself up, and walked across the forest floor like he was a compass needle with her as north star.

Her whole body felt numb. Red nearly swayed toward Eammon's waiting warmth, caught herself. "What *was* that?"

"I told you to run." His bloody hand raised, like he might touch her, then fell away empty. "You don't know what could've happened, you could—"

Red grabbed his sliced hand, jerked it toward her so he would follow. "And leave you alone? You keep asking me to do that, and I *won't*, Eammon."

His eyes on her mouth, his non-bloodied hand curling to touch her cheek, like his body couldn't keep up with his words. "It's for your own good."

"I won't," she murmured again, and there was so little space between them that she barely had to move to press her lips to his.

One beat of surprise, both of them frozen. Then they melted together, easy as water running downhill, as breath pulled into waiting lungs.

One of Eammon's hands gripped her hip, the other coming up to cup the back of her neck. She pulled his bottom lip between her teeth like it was something she could claim; he made a low noise in his throat, arm cinching around her waist, pulling her so close there was no room for light between. Red's fingers sank into his hair, pulling it loose from its knot to sweep softly against her wrists. When her nails brushed his scalp, his breath hitched.

Red pressed as close as she could, something deep and desperate pulling at her. She'd kissed and more than kissed, but never with this *need*—like they were two pieces fitting back together, like her edges were meant for his hollows. His fingers dug into her hips, the ground fell away, then her back pressed against tree bark. Her only lucid thought was sharp disappointment when his mouth briefly left hers, and savage satisfaction when it came back.

Then—a harsh breath against her collarbone as Eammon straightened. "No."

Confusion pushed through the warm muddle of her thoughts. Her feet were on the ground again, and she had no memory of how it happened. Her lips felt tender, his blood was in her hair. Around them, the growth of the forest seemed to arch in their direction, the edges of ferns and leaves greening.

Eammon's jacket lay on the ground; he bent to pick it up, his back to her. His hand hung by his side, the palm still lacerated, but his fingers bent in and outward, casting off the memory of her skin.

"Why?" Her throat felt tight, only enough space for one word.

He looked back, just once, eyes full of guilt and something else. "Trust me."

Eammon swung his jacket over his shoulders, ran a hand through his mussed hair, and turned to march into the Wilderwood. Cheeks burning, Red followed. They stayed carefully apart, and silent.

Later, Red stood at the door to the tower, frowning up into the open windows.

Neither she nor Eammon had spoken when they reached the Keep, though they'd stood in the foyer a moment, silent and watching.

Eammon had turned away first, headed toward the library, and Red had watched him until even his shadow was gone.

She'd taken her bag of new clothes up to their room. There were two gowns, a few shirts, and thick leggings, and as Red packed them into the drawer, she'd made up her mind.

Now, standing at the tower door, she still wore Eammon's shirt.

That first time the mirror had shown her Neve kept tugging at her thoughts, the strange conversation she'd overheard—something about escape, something about weakening. She couldn't shake the notion it might have something to do with the Wilderwood.

Shoulders set, Red pushed the door open.

The stairs were dark and cold, the room above colder still. Red's breath fogged as she walked to the mirror against the wall, its surface matte and gray.

She yanked a hair from her braid, touched with dirt from their earlier battle, tangled from Eammon's hands. Red wound the strand around the whorls of the frame, sat back on her knees, and waited.

For a heartbeat, nothing. Then, that silver shine, that roll of smoke, that feeling of pressing up against a window. The mirror showed one clear figure in a blurred landscape.

Neve.

Her twin sat on a bench, staring at something in her hand. A flower, large as a dinner plate. A twitch of motion, and the flower wilted, petals sagging, brown decay threading through them.

Neve dropped the bloom, peering at her palm. Crystals of frost clung to the edges of her fingers, and across her hand, a slash bisected life and love and heart lines, not quite scabbed over. The veins in her wrist shaded dark before clearing, quick enough to almost be a trick of the light.

Even in the suspended state the mirror left her in, Red's stomach dropped. Something about Neve's hand—the cold, the bleeding line—echoed her own magic. An inverse, a dark reflection.

"The more trees we pull out of the Wilderwood, the more power we can harness from the Shadowlands. And the weaker the forest's hold will become." The voice was as blurry as the figure it came from, barely clear enough to make out the words. Red could see only a flash of white, a smudge of auburn.

"And she should be able to escape?" Neve glanced at her companion. "The Shrine is full of these experiments, Kiri, and yet my sister still isn't here."

"That is not our only goal, Neverah." Exasperated, like this had been repeated over and over. "And we should exercise caution. If she comes—"

"*When* she comes."

No response.

More smoke, and the mirror was flat and gray again.

Red's breath burned when she pulled it in, like she'd been sprinting rather than sitting. When she stood, her knees creaked against the cold.

The curl of unease in her gut had been right. Neve was the reason for the missing sentinels. She wasn't quite sure how, not positive of the mechanics, but what she'd seen was enough to know it was true.

Her sister was still trying to bring her home. And she was killing the Wilderwood to do it.

Red stumbled from the tower on numb legs. She pushed open the door to the Keep, staring blankly ahead, mind stuttering over plans that came together and broke apart.

Neve.

Lyra strode from beneath the broken arch of the dining room, a steaming bowl and a crust of bread in her hands. She arched a slender brow. "You look like you've seen a ghost."

It felt like she had. "Where's Eammon?"

"Your room, I think." Lyra took a bite of bread. "Fife says thank you for getting sweet bread instead of the usual. In his words, it tastes more like food and less like a brick."

"He should thank Loreth." Red gave Lyra a tiny smile before mounting the stairs, doing her best not to run.

In their room, Eammon leaned over a book on his desk, brow in hand, fingers stained with ink. He looked up when she topped the stairs, eyes underscored by dark circles.

The sight of him was enough to scatter her thoughts again. The kiss she'd pushed to the back of her mind rushed forward, memories of hands and mouths and warm, ragged breath. He gripped the pen like he'd gripped her hair, the line of his body bent over the table like he'd bent over her.

It made it harder to tell him she had to leave.

Red cleared her throat. "Is this what you're always doing in the library?"

"Mostly." He put down his pen, pushed his hair away. A streak of ink marred his forehead. "I'm translating from old Meducian."

"For *fun*?"

"We all have our own ideas of fun, Redarys."

She quirked a smile at that, though it fell before she could finish the curve. "Why'd you bring it up here?"

His eyes pinned her in place. "You rarely come to the library when I'm in it."

Heat curled low in her stomach.

Eammon took a deep breath, leaned forward like he might stand. "Red, I—" A wince interrupted him as his hand moved carelessly across the desk, leaving a trail of that thin, sap-like blood.

Worry eclipsed the warmth, worry and the memory of the mirror. Her voice came bare and fumbling. "I have to go back."

Eammon froze. Then his eyes pressed shut, and he sank back into his chair, resignation tightening the line of his jaw. "I understand. You should—"

"No, you *don't* understand." The words cracked, graceless. She wanted to tell him it had nothing to do with that kiss, but it wasn't quite the truth. It *did* have to with that kiss, but not the way he thought. Not in any way that even resembled regret. "You think I wouldn't have left before if that's what I wanted? You think I wouldn't have tried to run already?"

"You came here because you had no choice." He said it to the desk, to the paper now crumpled in his hand. "Because you were forced to. I should've made you leave the minute you—"

"I came here because I thought I had to save the people I loved from myself. I came here because I thought the power I had was something evil. You showed me it wasn't, that it's not good or bad, it just *is*." She swallowed. "I've known the whole time you wouldn't stop me, Eammon. Every moment I have spent here, I've chosen to."

He said nothing. But his fist closed tighter, like he had to restrain it from reaching.

Red sank to the edge of the bed. "I looked in the mirror." Changing course, leaving all the reasons for staying and leaving and choices hanging in the air. "It was just a hunch, to see if Neve might have something to do with . . . with what's been happening."

His brows lowered.

"I was right. She's the cause of it. The missing sentinels. I don't know how, but it's her."

"That's impossible."

"The mirror showed me the truth before, it's showing me the truth now. I have to find out what she's doing, see if I can stop it. And maybe if she sees me, sees I'm fine, she'll reverse the damage somehow." Her fingers knotted in the hem of his shirt she wore. "I have to try, especially if I can't do anything else. If you won't let me do anything else. The last thing I want to do is leave you alone, but—"

"I've been alone a long time." Low, roughened. Almost pleading.

She bit the corner of her lip like she could still taste him on it. "But you don't have to be."

A moment, iron-heavy, glass-fragile. Finally, Eammon looked away, shattering it into something that didn't shine so brightly. "When will you leave?"

"A few days. I'd like to practice some more first. Make sure I have my power under control." She swallowed. "Getting married helped, but it seems like I can only make it do what I want when... when I'm close to you."

Something unnamed flickered in Eammon's eyes. "Is that so?"

"From my observations, yes."

There was a challenge in the gaze they shared—each daring the other to talk about it. To attempt naming the warmth between them.

"We'll practice tomorrow, then." Eammon jerked his chin toward the bed. "But first, sleep."

He broke eye contact, turning toward his crumpled blanket against the wall. Even with the fire, the air was cold, and a shiver rolled through his shoulders.

"You don't have to sleep all the way over there."

Eammon's spine locked.

Red hadn't meant to speak the thought, and she blinked hard, hands tightening on her sheets. Too late to take it back, and Eammon's shoulders kept ratcheting up, the intention to flee in every line—

"I mean," she said quickly, "if you want to pull the blanket over by the fire, you can. It's cold. No sense in freezing."

She cursed herself silently, sure she'd shattered everything they'd built—whatever it was they'd managed to piece together—with her careless want. After the way he'd stopped their kiss, the way he'd kept such careful distance, she wasn't sure where she stood with him anymore.

There's not much of me left to give to another person, he'd said. After today, she wasn't sure how to tell him she'd take what she could get. Wasn't sure when the knowing crept up on her, somewhere between their odd marriage and magic lessons and a swapping back and forth of saving each other.

Maybe, if she could go to Neve—if she could find out what her sister was doing, find out how to stop it, hem the frayed edges of their sisterhood—after, she and Eammon could figure out what this was. What it could be.

Eammon's head turned in that way he had, just enough to fix her in place with one eye. Then he grabbed the edge of his blanket.

He pulled it between the bed and the fireplace, closer to the latter than the former. Red busied herself with climbing beneath her covers, aware of his every movement—how he shifted his head to find a comfortable angle, how his long, scarred fingers folded on his chest.

"I'm coming back," Red said to the ceiling, because it was the only thing she could fit her tangled emotions to. "I don't want to stay in Valleyda."

Eammon didn't respond. Slowly, she drifted, eyes closing, time stretching languid.

"Maybe you should," Eammon murmured in the dark.

Chapter Twenty-Two

He was gone when she woke, blanket crumpled, a note in his messy script perched on the desk. *Tower.*

Red dressed quickly—her leggings, his shirt, because old habits weren't easy to break—and ran her fingers through her hair, working out tangles but leaving it loose. Gingerly, she walked down the stairs, concentrating so she wouldn't slip on their moss-blunted edges. Lavender light bathed the tangle of branches and stone that used to be the corridor, made it almost beautiful.

When she reached the tower, shivering in the morning chill, Eammon leaned against a carved windowsill with a mug in one hand and a book in the other. He didn't acknowledge her, other than flicking his eyes up from the book, but his grip on the mug tightened.

He'd poured her a cup, even added cream. Red lifted it to her lips as she slid into the chair. A lone tree branch sat in the middle of the table, twigs curled like claws. Bands of silver paint had been hastily drawn where the twigs split off from the limb's main shaft. "Art project?"

His book snapped closed; Eammon tucked it beneath his arm. "Not quite." When he lifted his cup to his mouth, his shirt rode up, exposing a line of pale, scarred skin.

Red took a gulp of coffee too quickly and burned her throat.

Eammon sat his now-empty cup next to the branch and jerked a thumb toward the painted silver bands. "The paint is there so we can see how much the branch grows. A benchmark for your progress."

"*That* can't grow." Red took another sip, more carefully this time. "It's dead."

"So was that thornbush yesterday," Eammon countered.

The mention of *yesterday* made their eyes dart away from each other.

She'd thought they could ignore it. She'd thought if they pretended it didn't happen, it would fade into the background, a moment of weakness they'd grow beyond.

Foolish of her.

"I saw the thicket," Eammon said, his voice steady even as the tips of his ears burned. He strode to the mantel and shelved his book, keeping his back to her. "We passed it right before we saw the missing sentinel. It was dead, dried out, and it obeyed you anyway." The muscles in his shoulders moved as he crossed his arms. "Even in death, things stay tied to the Wilderwood."

His voice was low, roughened with emotion she couldn't parse with his face hidden. Tentatively, she touched the branch, nearly expecting it to spider-crawl over the table, but it remained still.

The silence tugged at her until she raised her narrowed eyes to his still-turned back. "Some direction would be welcome here, Eammon."

She hadn't meant to say his name. Even in irritation, it felt like too much in her mouth, too intimate after what they'd shared and the way he'd pulled away from it.

Kings, she wanted to kiss him again.

He turned, finally, something molten flickering in his eyes, halfway between anger and fevered heat. "You did well enough on your own yesterday."

He had to stop mentioning yesterday, damn him. He said it like a challenge.

Red leaned back in her chair, arms crossed. "I told you. It works better when we're close."

"Exactly how close do you need me, Redarys?"

It stopped her for a moment, mouth parted, possible answers roaring through her head like flames with fresh kindling. She settled for "Closer than that."

They stared at each other across the room, the air between them warm and waiting. With a ragged sigh, Eammon moved closer, until he stood just out of reach. "Better?"

She wanted to say no. She remembered him yesterday in the forest, kissing her like she was warmth in winter before pushing her away, and by all the Kings and all the shadows, *that* was the closeness she wanted.

But she nodded and turned to the tree limb.

Her power wouldn't cooperate. Trying to grasp it felt like trying to hold hands with water. Red couldn't make it bloom, couldn't do anything but chase it fruitlessly. With a frustrated growl, she opened her eyes to the still-dead branch, fingers curling on the wood of the table. "It's not working."

"It worked just fine before."

"You were closer before."

She clenched her teeth shut as soon as she'd said it, but it hung like an ax and couldn't be taken back. Eammon said nothing, though she could hear his breath, the rattle of it in and out of root-tangled lungs.

"Is it emotional?" The attempt at brusqueness fell flat and made his voice only rougher, stoking the heat in her stomach. "The closeness you need, I mean. Or…or physical?"

"Both." Red closed her eyes, knowing this was giving in, knowing she didn't care. "Both seem to help."

Her eyes stayed closed, but the atmosphere around her shifted as he moved forward, warm and charged as the air before a thunderstorm. A breath of hesitation before he brushed away her loose hair, put his warm hand on the nape of her neck.

"I won't be there." He said it like an apology. "I can't always be there, Red."

She knew it. He was tied to this damn wood, mired in it. The sentinels trapped him as well as any shadow-creature, any wicked king, and he wouldn't be there in Valleyda to calm her chaos with his closeness. The more Red practiced control, the more she might be able to re-create it without him, but that wasn't what this was about, and they both knew it.

This was about stalling. About taking the closeness they could get.

"Being here now is enough," Red murmured.

The tips of his fingers curled against the roots of her hair.

The power in her center gathered and steadied, like this was what it wanted all along. It was simple to grasp it now, simple to turn it to her will.

The branch on the table had a muted golden glow when she opened her mind to the Wilderwood, stars behind clouds. Just enough for her piece of it, that thin thread winding through her, to connect to and command. As she arched her fingers, she saw it grow, the twigs stretching past their painted beginnings.

When her eyes opened, the branch was somewhat bigger, though not by much. Maybe an inch of space had appeared between the silver bands and the main bough.

Eammon moved abruptly away, taking his fingers from her neck, striding toward the window. He ran one hand through his unbound hair before shoving them both in his pockets. "There," he said, almost in a rush. "It's done."

Red bit her lip, mind churning fire-laced thought. His mouth on her throat, her hair in his hands, tree bark against her back as he pressed against her center. He'd thought it a mistake, but she hadn't, and now she was leaving. Even though she was coming back—*dammit*, she was coming back—she'd still heard that finality in his voice last night. The thing he'd murmured when he thought she was asleep.

Maybe you should.

It angered her, that he had room for doubt, to think she'd want to linger anywhere that wasn't close enough to see that faint scar on his cheek. Room to think they were the same people who'd faced off in a library on her twentieth birthday what felt like lifetimes ago, room to think the space between them hadn't fully and irrevocably changed.

Red stood, her chair scraping backward across the floor. "I can do more."

He stiffened.

"I'm capable of more than that. You know it." Red propped her hips against the edge of the table, fingers curling into the wood, and the next words were plea and invitation and challenge all at once, rough with want. "Help me do more."

His turning seemed to take ages. Eammon's arms fell from crossed to hang by his side, fingers already curved like they held something. The first step was tentative, then he strode across the room like it was a battle march, face determined. His hands hit the table on either side of her hips, tensed enough for her to trace the tendons.

"Are you sure?" It was strained, tightly reined in. It begged an answer.

"It worked yesterday, didn't it?"

"You called the Wilderwood before I kissed you."

Her fingers skimmed across his cheekbone, the nail tracing that thin white line. The first mark she'd left on him. "But not before I wanted you to."

A tiny, rueful smile flickered at the corner of his mouth, but his eyes were all hunger as his fingers slid up the small of her back, slipped beneath the fabric of his shirt she still wore. She traced the outside edge of his ear, his jawline, stubble rough under her fingers. The hand not on her back cupped her face, thumb running a half-moon over her cheek, scarred palm against her throat.

"Am I close enough?" The space between his mouth and her pulse was paper-thin.

Red tugged his hair, tipping her head so her lips barely brushed his. "Not yet."

Yesterday was a kiss born of fear and desperation and relief. Forgetting it wouldn't be easy, but it would be *possible*—a momentary slip, a lapse in judgment, easy to dismiss.

This was different. This was deliberate. It would unravel the bonds they'd made of necessity and turn them irrevocably to something else. His eyes burned into hers, looking for benediction.

When Red pulled him down, his mouth opened on a sigh.

Eammon's tongue swept her lip, slow, purposeful. Red made a helpless noise in her throat, pressed farther into his chest. Her fingers dug into his back, pulling him as close as she could, searching for empty places she could fill as one scarred hand skated over her rib cage, her hip. The other cupped the side of her neck like it was something too fragile to let go of, something he was afraid to lose.

His thumb pulled against her bottom lip, opening her mouth for another, deeper kiss. "Now?"

"Not yet." She arched into him as the coffee cups clattered to the floor, greedy for more of his touch, resentful of the fabric between them. "Closer."

A low laugh, rumbling against her throat. "Try, first." They were reduced to snatches of words, mouths eager for other things.

Red caught his lips again even as she bent her fingers in the vague direction of the branch. Flaring golden light behind her eyes, a momentary glimpse of the two of them as tangled roots—his beacon-bright, hers a thin candle-flame, fed by his closeness.

A rustling noise beside them, and neither looked toward it. Her fingers tangled in his hair, pulled his mouth back to hers.

Her power redirected itself as Eammon pressed against her, as heat built between them and their breathing grew ragged. She could feel the Wilderwood around them, *in* them, blooming upward. The rush of roots in the ground beneath the tower, the stretch of branches toward the open windows, the forest drawn to her as she was drawn to him. Bonds, slipping off. Whatever had held it shackled ebbed away, grip loosening, letting the Wilderwood creep closer—

Eammon froze, hands on the bare skin of her waist beneath her shirt. His fingers dug in, and he kissed her, once more and fiercely. Then, releasing her like a burning ember, he pushed away, breathing hard.

Red reached for him, just for a second. But he'd turned, back to her, and she let her hands fall empty. "Eammon?"

"Give me a minute." His hand scrubbed through his hair, made it stand up at odd angles. "Just…just give me a minute, Red."

Slowly, her magic recoiled, shrinking back down into her hollows. As her pulse slowed its thundering, she noticed the windows.

The greenery growing on the outside of the tower had bloomed into a riotous, anachronistic spring. Thick, woody vines nearly covered the gaps in the stone, blocking out the lavender light of the Wilderwood with huge white flowers and verdant leaves. Tendrils of roots spilled over the windowsill, stretching toward the table where she sat, studded in tiny blooms.

As Red watched—as Eammon stood with his back to her, shoulders moving with his breathing—the new growth slowly shrank back. The root tendrils retracted, slipping back out the window, away from her. The white blooms closed. The leaves dropped away from the vines as they disappeared, back to their proper places, leaving gaps of sky in their wake. The movements were rhythmic, matched to Eammon's breath.

He'd said that holding the Wilderwood used all his concentration. And now, kissing her, distracted from that singular purpose—it'd slipped, the magic escaping the careful cage he kept it in.

"I'm sorry." His whisper was a cut. "I thought I could... it doesn't matter what I thought. This was a mistake."

Red crossed her arms, hunched over them like she could hide, make herself smaller. The three-fold scar on her stomach, his wound she'd healed so long ago, twinged for the first time in weeks. Somehow, *sorry* hurt more than *mistake* did.

Something brushed her arm. Red glanced to the other end of the table. The branch she'd directed her magic at was huge, the silver-painted bands at least a foot away from the central bough. Green leaves sprouted from the ends of the twigs, summer-verdant.

She must've made a noise, because Eammon turned slightly, worry in his face like he thought he might find her crying. His eyes widened when he saw the branch.

"Told you I could do more." Her voice was hollow. The tears he worried for hung in her throat and grew sharp.

Dark hair feathered over Eammon's shoulders as he hung his head. He ran a scarred hand over his face. "I wish things could be different. But they just... they can't. I can't hold it back from you if I..." He trailed into silence. Took a breath. "Keeping the Wilderwood from coming for you takes everything I have," he said, the words clipped and measured. "All my concentration, all my strength. Everything. There isn't anything left. And the forest is so tied in me, so close to the surface..." A short, sharp gesture to the encroaching growth around them. "When I get close to you, it does, too. And I won't let it trap you here, Red. I *won't*."

There's not much of me left to give to another person.

There's not much of me left.

He'd told her to trust him, yesterday, when he broke off their kiss and went about his business as if it never happened. But instead they'd pushed, breaking through the thin barriers they'd set up between themselves. The pieces were too jagged to put back together.

Whatever they'd just shattered, it was the only thing they could have.

Red slipped off the table. "I wish things could be different, too."

She ducked down the stairs so he couldn't see the tears start.

Chapter Twenty-Three

Red closed the Keep door with more force than necessary, pressing her back against it like a barricade. Her tears had been short-lived, thankfully, a benefit of living a life that gave her little opportunity to spill them. Still, her face was blotched and her eyes felt heavy.

The front door pushed open, Fife and Lyra tumbling in. She was laughing, a palm pressed to her stomach, and Fife's hands flew as he shaped some story in the air, the most animated she'd ever seen him. Red stood quiet, watching. Things between them were complicated, Fife had said, but it was clear they loved each other uniquely. Simply.

It made her chest ache.

Fife held a canvas bag similar to the one they'd brought from Asheyla's yesterday, the top drawstring half open and spilling a length of scarlet. When Lyra caught sight of Red, she hurriedly grabbed the fabric and stuffed it back in the bag. "Red!"

She pasted on a smile, rubbed at her eyes, and hoped the dim light would be enough to obscure the vestiges of tears. "Back from the Edge?"

"Picking up the last of the supplies." Lyra opened her own canvas bag, pulling out a bottle of wine to wag in the air. "Valdrek claims this isn't watered. I'm inclined to believe him, since you and Eammon saved his son-in-law." She said it nonchalantly, but curiosity flashed across her delicate features, and she looked at Red like she saw everything she'd tried to hide behind a false smile and quick-scrubbed eyes.

Red looked away. "What's in the other bag?"

Fife glanced at Lyra, an unspoken conversation. "Well, he's not here to give it to her," Fife finally said. He offered Red the bag. "Your cloak."

Their behavior seemed odd, for it to be nothing but her mended cloak, but Red didn't have the energy to think too hard about it. She took the bag and slung it over her shoulder without looking inside. "Thanks."

Another wordless glance between Fife and Lyra. "Eammon around?" Fife asked as he turned toward the dining room, disappearing beneath the arch.

"We'll find him later. He's probably translating until he's cross-eyed again." Lyra gave Red a gentle look, one that invited confidence if it was needed. "You can come with us, if you want. I'm making Fife brew tea."

Red bent her mouth to a semblance of a smile but shook her head. "Thanks anyway." Mud and blood spattered Lyra's leggings, and the edge of her *tor* looked like it'd been hastily wiped down. "Did you run into something?"

"A few more shadow-creatures." Lyra huffed a laugh, but it was thin. "It was a good thing Fife was there. He spotted one before I did. Managed to toss a vial of blood at it before it made itself a body."

"I didn't know he patrolled, too."

"It's not really patrolling, I guess." She shrugged, a shade of sadness flitting across her dark eyes. "He just wants to see if there are any weak spots."

Like the villagers, pressing forward from the Edge. So many people caught in the Wilderwood's tangle, so many people wanting to escape.

Red chewed on the corner of her lip, thinking of the conversation she'd overheard the day of the mirror, the day she found out about Isla's death. How Eammon said she could leave if she wanted. How he and Fife and Lyra were too bound to the Wilderwood for it to be an option. "*Are* there weak spots? Truly?"

The vials of blood in Lyra's bag clinked together as she shifted on her feet. "Honestly? I don't think so. Not on the Valleydan border, and not weak enough to let us out. The Wilderwood has its teeth in too deep." A pause. "I don't think Fife really believes he's going to find anything. But hope, you know? It's like a boot that won't break in. Hurts to walk in it, hurts worse to go barefoot."

Red knew hope and its burn like she knew the scent of Neve's hair, the pattern of scars on the back of Eammon's hands. "Would you *want* to find a weak spot, if it was there to find? Would you leave?"

It sounded deceptively simple, for how layered a question it was. Lyra's long eyelashes flickered down to brush her cheeks as she sighed. "I don't know. The world...it's been so long since I was in it, and it would be so different, and who knows what would happen to us once we left the forest, and I...I just don't know." She rubbed at her forearm. "The Mark is what binds us here, not the borders, so even if we found a weak place it'd probably be useless. But if we did, and it let us go..." Her hand dropped. "If Fife went, I would, too. We stay together, him and me."

The ache in Red's chest sharpened.

Another tiny smile. "The tea is a standing invitation," Lyra said, turning toward the dining room to join Fife. "Just let me know, and I'll bully Fife into baking something, too."

Red gave her a halfhearted smile, then mounted the stairs. Their voices were a hush as she climbed up to her and Eammon's room, carrying the bag with her mended cloak.

The bed was rumpled, just as she left it. Red sat with a sigh, dropping the bag, burying her face in her hands.

She should leave. That was the plan, wasn't it? Go back to Valleyda, stop Neve, do what little she could to keep the Wilderwood strong. Still, the idea of leaving Eammon didn't sit well. She might be hurt and angry—and sad, and embarrassed, and a whole host of other emotions she couldn't even name—but leaving him felt *wrong*, strange-shaped and rough-edged in her chest. Not just because of what she felt for him, but because of the power and connection they shared, the ties that bound them to the forest and each other. She was meant for the Wilderwood, and abandoning it tore at her, almost physically.

He wouldn't stop any of them from leaving. She knew that. If she could go to Valleyda and stay there, if Lyra and Fife could find a weak spot in the Wilderwood's defenses and slip free, Eammon would all but chase them out. Send them away while he withered in the shadows.

Determined to suffer alone.

Shaking her head, Red loosened the drawstring of Fife's bag. A glint of gold shone among the scarlet; frowning, she pulled the mended cloak from the bag, breath catching in her chest.

Her cloak was more than mended. It was remade.

A changing forest spread from crimson shoulder to crimson shoulder, embroidered in golden thread—summer on the left, trees lush-leaved, autumn and winter in the center, with those leaves falling, and flowering spring on the right. The trees ran from branch to root, knotting in intricate loops, before becoming an image of a wolf leaping toward the hem.

Red pressed her knuckles against her lips until she could feel her teeth behind them. A bridal cloak.

It was an ancient Valleydan wedding tradition, one she never thought she'd take part in. The bride would wear a cloak embroidered with depictions of her new spouse's lands and estates, a symbol of the new home they would build. Generally, bridal cloaks were white and embroidered in silver. But her cloak was still scarlet, the thread golden, rare and rich.

The symbol of her sacrifice, made into something that represented the new life she'd made. A future sewn together from the tatters she'd been left with.

She could still feel the bruise of Eammon's kiss on her mouth.

Red pulled off her clothes and climbed beneath the cloak. Heedless of the time, whether dusk or day or midnight, Red let the warmth of her bridal cloak and the scent of leaves and libraries lull her to sleep.

She woke alone.

Groggily, Red pushed away the heap of blanket and cloak, swept back her unkempt hair. Someone had set a fire in the grate, blazing merrily, but Eammon's blanket was still folded between the bed and the hearth. Her eyes narrowed.

If he expected to avoid a goodbye, he was mistaken. Red wouldn't go quietly. Damn his reasons, he couldn't kiss her like that—*twice*—and expect her to go quietly.

Her clothes lay in a heap on the floor; she pulled them on, boots and all. After a moment, she slung her new bridal cloak over her shoulders.

She was halfway to the stairs before her legs buckled.

The thorn-and-leaf darkness of a vision closed in immediately, this time an encroachment of forest that drove her to her knees. Red gasped, fingers pressing into her temples, deep-green magic blooming out of her chest to weave through her veins.

The connection between her and Eammon flared to life, even stronger than it had the day with Bormain.

Hands, again. Scarred and rough, sinking into the dirt. Veins running emerald, bark closing where skin should be. A forest between bones reached for a forest outside them, because this body had given everything else, and the barrier between man and wood was almost gone.

Her throat—*Eammon's throat*—gagged up dirt. Sentinels grew around him in a perfectly circular ring, bone white and clear of rot. One stood taller, a strange, rectangular scar across its bark, like something had been stripped from it. And around its roots, a tangle of something gleaming—

The vision was gone, perception wrenched back into her own body. Red's heart jackknifed against her ribs.

Eammon had done…something. Bled himself out, until only magic was left.

And the Wilderwood was taking him over.

She skidded down the stairs without a thought for trying to find Fife and Lyra—there was no time, not when Eammon was…was *unmaking*, unraveling. Red shoved open the door to the Keep, ran to the gate, pressed her hand against the iron. It opened to her touch, like it recognized her now.

The path was unknown, but her feet seemed to point toward Eammon, and she trusted the instinct. Red ran through the Wilderwood, and the beat in her veins and the prayer in her mouth was *hold on, hold on, hold on.*

She heard him before she saw him. Eammon's labored breathing was echoed by the forest, the two of them heaving in sync. A ring of white trees before her opened on a clearing with the Wolf in its center. His lashed and bloody back caught the violet light, a man-shaped bruise on the world.

"Eammon!" His name snapped from her tongue like a whip crack, but he didn't seem to hear. His head bowed so far forward his hair brushed the dirt, arms sunk in soil to the elbow, sweat gleaming in twilight. The sentinels bowed toward him, reaching, needing, worship and sacrifice at once.

Red's knees hit the ground next to him, hands running through his hair with a tenderness her racing heart and screaming breath belied. She didn't bother asking for an explanation. There was clarity in the way his veins burned emerald, the rings of bark closing around his arms, the whites of his eyes now wholly green around amber irises. Whatever vestiges of humanity he'd managed to salvage over centuries running out as forest ran in, because he was the only one to hold it, and one was no longer enough.

Must be two. The memory echoed, but it seemed to come more from the shard of magic she carried than her own mind.

"What can I do?" A snarl heralded the memory of his usual answer, but when she spoke it was a plea. "Don't say *nothing*."

"It's the only way." Sediment fell from Eammon's hair as his head shook. His voice echoed, layered and resonant. "This is the only way to hold it, if I don't want it to take you."

Red dug her fingers into his temples, made him look at her. "It's *not*. I'm not letting it take you from me, Eammon."

The golden afterimage of the Wilderwood bloomed over her vision when she touched him, double-exposed. He'd spent himself to the last, magic and blood, but the forest needed more. Was taking more.

Green veins stood out in Eammon's neck, tendons like ridges of root. "Only way." Greater distortion in his voice, rustling leaves in autumn wind, stronger than she'd ever heard it before. "Either it takes me, or it takes you."

"That's a price I'm not willing to pay." She gripped his jaw, forced his green-haloed eyes to hers. "I'm not leaving you to this. You don't leave me either, Eammon. Don't you *dare*."

His full lips pressed together. His eyes stayed on hers as tiny leaves edged at their corners.

Must be two. That memory again. An urging.

She wrapped her hands around his shoulders, a strange echo of their embrace in the tower. A tug at her twining magic, but it slipped from her grip. It was the Wilderwood, a small shard of it lodged in her, and the Wilderwood didn't want to obey.

All the pieces he'd given, all the blood he'd spilled, and it still wasn't satisfied.

"No." She didn't know she'd spoken aloud until it hissed from between her teeth. "You can't just keep *taking*, shadows damn it! First the Second Daughters, and now him? They didn't belong to you, and neither does he! None of us *chose* this!"

Her voice had risen until it was a scream, echoing in the trees, feral as a hunting-sound from some wild thing. And as it left her throat, the Wilderwood...paused. Something vast and unknowable, a consciousness that barely fit the definition of such a thing and adhered to no morality she could understand, stopped and turned to her and *regarded*.

Choice.

Quieter than she'd heard the Wilderwood speak before, more contemplative. A fall of leaves from a now-dead branch, fluttering to the ground.

Red didn't have time to try to parse it out, no time to argue with a forest and hope it understood. The magic in her pulled toward Eammon, her thin thread of power wanting to follow, to go meet the rest of the Wilderwood as it flowed into him, remade him.

The forest, reverting into its nexus. Taking Eammon and leaving itself in his place. Scouring the borders between man and forest until there was no delineation.

But it would need all of itself to do it. Including the part of it that lived in her.

Red clamped down on her magic with every bit of strength she could muster, that small piece of the Wilderwood that had made a home in her.

And she *tore*.

It hurt. It ripped at her veins like thorns, like taking a stem and splitting it in half. It hurt the Wilderwood, too—she could hear it, a shriek in a voice of leaf and branch, vibrating her bones. Guilt soured her stomach, guilt for harming the thing they were meant to save.

Kings and *shadows*, it always came back to guilt.

But it worked. Red tugged at her shard of Wilderwood magic like she was trying to pull up a weed by the root, diverting its flow, keeping it from running into Eammon. A small amount, but it was enough to keep the forest from seeping into him. To keep him as close to human as he could be.

It fought against her, the pain of it making her eyes water, making her feel like every vein ran with coals. But Red held on, refusing to let go, caging the bit of forest within her the same way Eammon had caged his all these years.

And then, it stopped. Stopped, and held silent for a moment that hung heavy.

The atmosphere shifted. The *Wilderwood* shifted, a ripple in the roots beneath her feet, a shimmer in the leaves.

The weight of an inhuman realization. Something, finally, understood.

Red's small piece of the Wilderwood ceased trying to run out of her, settled back into the places she'd made for it. It didn't speak again. But she had a strange sense of something decided.

And whatever it was, it meant the forest would leave Eammon be. For now.

Slowly, Eammon and the Wilderwood untangled, as much as they were able. Root tendrils seeped out of his arms, back into the ground, leaving bloody gashes in their wake. He shuddered, coughing up dirt against her knees. Two circles of bark braceleted his wrists, showed no sign of fading—another permanent change the forest left, like that extra inch of height, like the green threads in the whites of his eyes.

But he was her Eammon again.

Red slumped next to him, her forehead falling against his.

A moment, and Eammon shifted away, though the movement felt heavy, unwilling. "How'd you find me?"

"Vision." Her hands shook without his skin to steady them. "How did this happen?"

He stood, knees watery. "I healed them all."

It took her a moment to catch his meaning. When she did, her eyes widened, going from his face to the bloodless, green-tinged slashes on his palms, his arms, his chest.

Every gap where a sentinel should be, gone. And when he'd run out of blood, he'd called forest. Called the Wilderwood's magic until it nearly crowded him out.

"Why?" she asked hoarsely. "Why would you *do* that?"

He didn't look at her. "So when you return to Valleyda, you have no reason to come back."

Red's cloak weighed on her shoulders like stones. "No," she said, because it was the only thing her mouth could shape. "No, that doesn't make sense. I have to come back, you need—"

"I don't need you." It would've been cold, had his voice not shaken. "I took care of the Wilderwood on my own for a century. I can do it again, I can take it without falling. I can be stronger."

Stronger than Ciaran. Stronger than the man who'd started this long string of death and roots and rot, whom the forest had drained when he was left alone.

"I gave it what it needed. Cut deep enough, deeper than I thought I could. I can be enough alone." Eammon's hands curled, the slashes in them bloodless, dripping only sap and edged with green. "This proves I was only being weak."

"And what happens when it needs that again? Eammon, it almost had you. It almost *took* you, made you…" She didn't know what it had almost made him, not really. Something that wasn't human, but he hadn't ever been one, had he?

A monster, maybe.

"It took *them*," he said. "Every Second Daughter. It only left me because it knew it needed someone living." He held up his hand, flexed his blood-and-sap-covered fingers. "I can live. No matter what it makes me."

"Stop it. You can't just—"

"There's nothing *for* you here, Red!" Eammon loomed like the trees around them, shadowed and severe. "Your sister is stealing the sentinels so you can escape, right? So do it. Escape." His hand cut through the air as he turned away. "Be free of me with a clear conscience."

"Free of you? Is that what you think I want?" She swallowed, then tugged at the edge of her cloak, pulling it around so the twilight caught the golden embroidery. "Is that what *you* want?"

A muscle in his back tremored under the dirt and sap-like blood. Eammon looked at the cloak, something deep and unfathomable in his eyes, then turned his face away. "It doesn't matter what I want."

"What are you doing?" It sounded broken, it sounded like a plea, but she had no more steel left for it.

There's nothing for you here.

Eammon still faced the trees, as if the sight of them shored his resolve. "I am trying," he said, almost a prayer, "to do what's best for you."

"Horseshit." Frustrated tears blurred her vision; Red savagely wiped them away. "*Horseshit.* You don't get to decide what's best for me, Eammon."

He flinched.

"Why?" It came out shivery, the ghost of a question she'd been asking for weeks. "Why do you insist on being alone when I am *right here*?"

His answer came quiet. "Alone is safer for both of us."

"You can't just—"

"I *killed them.*"

It was snarled through bared, wolf-like teeth; he'd turned like a predator. On instinct, she took a step back.

"The Wilderwood drained the others because I didn't hold it back." Fierceness was in every line of his frame, but he couldn't hide his eyes—they were lost, they were hollow, they were glad she'd backed away. "I let myself be weak, I didn't bear it alone, and it killed them. Shadows *damn* me if I let it happen to you."

Red's head shook, a slow, sorrowful back and forth.

His hand cut toward the mass of gleaming white at the base of that tall sentinel with the scarred bark. The thing she'd seen in her vision, when she peered through his eyes, the thing she'd been too panicked to examine closely. Now her gaze followed his hand, and the shapes were impossible not to recognize.

Bones. Bones tangled in roots, in vines. Three rib cages, three skulls, a chaos of others she didn't know the names for.

What was left of the Second Daughters.

Eammon's voice was hoarse and rasping. "Don't you want to escape now, Red?"

Chapter Twenty-Four

Air was a slippery thing, too thin to hold in her lungs. Red's hands opened and closed on her cloak. He'd told her what happened to the others, to Kaldenore and Sayetha and Merra, but *seeing* it struck her cold, an icy chill of fear that ran from her temples and slowly down her spine.

Eammon turned away, shoulders a hunched ridge. "Go." He rubbed a weary hand over his face, smearing blood. "Please, go."

"No." Red grabbed Eammon's hand, laced her fingers tightly with his, pressing their palms together and daring him to pull away. "Tell me what happened to them. *Exactly* what happened, no more half answers." Her nails bit into his skin, and she thought of myths and how they made terrible things somewhat easier to bear. "Tell me the story, Eammon."

That stiffened him further, made his jaw clench and his eyes arc away from her, to the waiting Wilderwood beyond their ring of cleared ground. "I warned you before. None of the stories here have happy endings."

"I don't care about happy endings. I care about you."

His breath rattled in and out of his lungs. She thought he'd pull away, but instead his hand relaxed into hers, like he didn't have the energy to resist. When he finally spoke, the words were clouds of fog, with the low, measured cadence of a remembered tale.

"I'd been the Wolf for nearly ten years when Kaldenore came. By then I'd figured out how to use blood to keep the forest mostly together, when... when it wanted to take more than I was willing to give. Got the idea from Fife and Lyra." He faced the tree line, away from her, but the memory of Ciaran's awful death still drew tension into his shoulders. "I didn't know what to make of it, not at first. But then I remembered what I'd heard Ciaran say, and Kaldenore showed me the Mark, told me how it called her north." Shame lowered his tone, made his head dip farther, black hair obscuring his face. "I should've sent her back, but the Wilderwood... it already had her. It'd tangled itself in her when she first crossed the border."

The thorn on her cheek, the drop of blood, fanged sentinels chasing her through the fog. "Like it tried to do to me."

Eammon jerked a nod. "I didn't know how to stop it. Not then."

He'd done it for her, though. Shackled the forest through white-knuckle, all-consuming concentration, keeping the wild thing leashed.

Rustling in the leaves around them, almost like a sigh.

"Kaldenore didn't last long," he said hoarsely, barely a breath in the chilly air. "The Wilderwood was desperate. It drained her quick."

"And once it did," Red murmured, "you were alone with it again."

"I was alone with it again." Bitterness laced his voice, bitterness and shame and exhaustion. "I still didn't fully understand what had happened, not really. But I started to put the pieces together—the bargain, how it'd been worded so there would be Wardens even if Ciaran and Gaya died. Worded so it would pass on."

His voice cut on their names, but it was deliberate. Cutting was better than breaking.

"After that, I started experimenting. Giving the forest more blood, letting in more magic. Trying to hold it on my own. But then Sayetha arrived."

Red's fingers twitched, phantom sympathy for a woman she

didn't know. Kaldenore's sickly elder sister had served only a year as Queen before dying childless, and Aida Thoriden, the oldest daughter of the next House in line, already had one daughter before she took the throne. Queen Aida learned she was pregnant with Sayetha within weeks of her coronation.

"I tried to keep the same thing from happening to her that happened to Kaldenore." Eammon's voice was barely a breath, only audible for the silence of the forest around them. "But I wasn't strong enough. The Wilderwood drained her, too, in the end."

A second rib cage, a second skull. Red tasted copper—she'd bitten too far into her lip.

Eammon still faced the trees, still wouldn't look at her. Dirt patterned the bloody skin of his arms, almost delicate in the dim light. "After Sayetha, I did everything I could, studied whatever I could get my hands on, trying to keep it from calling Second Daughters, or at least from killing them once they came. Merra arrived, eventually, but I was able to keep the forest from her. For a while."

Death piled around the Wolf, corpses of those he couldn't save. Those the desperate Wilderwood tore through, bent only on its own survival, on the task set before it and the strength it needed to carry through.

She wanted to scream at it. Wanted to kick the sentinels until they were bloody, wanted to burn them all to the ground.

"It was my fault. I grew complacent." He shook his head, a fall of dust scattering over bare, still-sweaty shoulders. "I stopped concentrating, after she'd been here awhile. She lived her life and I lived mine, friendly but distant. I thought it could be enough. Maybe the Wilderwood would be content with only her presence and my blood. But it wasn't." A snarl in his voice. "It was just waiting for me to slip."

When they'd kissed in the tower, pressing desperately together, the Wilderwood had seen an opening. Seeping in the windows, growing slowly toward her. And Eammon had noticed, and pushed

Red away, knowing that whatever longing they felt could never fully be acted on. Because it would be a distraction, pulling him from the constant work of keeping the Wilderwood shackled. Because bringing her closer to him meant bringing her closer to his hungry forest.

Everything in Eammon was for the Wilderwood—all he *was*, down to the bone and blood. Everything in his life was oriented around making sure he never slipped again.

Oriented around keeping her safe from the thing that had taken so much of him.

"It came for Merra, and she couldn't take it." Still, his voice cadenced like a tale, like he could keep himself at arm's length from his own history. "She tried to…to cut it out. Died before I could stop her."

Third skull. Third rib cage. Third set of bones, fed on by vines and white trees.

"Cut it out?" The question was a bare breath, shaky and quiet.

That made him turn, finally, his green-and-amber eyes fierce in his dirt-streaked face. "It won't happen to you. I won't let it."

But she couldn't leave it at that, not with the bones in the corner of her vision and his blood tacky between her fingers. Not with the plucked string in her heart, vibrating a frequency she almost knew.

"Tell me what it does to them," Red whispered, even though she knew the answer. A dying man and a root-threaded body, the myth that hung over both their heads. "Please."

Eammon freed his hand from hers, gently, and ran it over his face, eyes cast away like he was looking for answers in the starless sky. "It isn't immediate. The Wilderwood doesn't mean for you to die."

Around the clearing, the white sentinels stood silent and still. Listening. That decision made in an unfathomable, inhuman mind, solidifying.

"The forest needs an anchor." Eammon crossed his arms, hiding the new bracelets of bark on his wrists. "That's what it's after."

An anchor. A living seed, a nexus for it all to stem from. Him, holding it all alone.

Must be two.

Red's palms itched to touch him again, to find a friction to his skin. "An anchor," she repeated. "Like the way it anchors in you. But it needs more than that. *You* need more than—"

"Stop it, Red." It sliced through the air, knife-cold and just as sharp. "Stop. It's not for you." A ragged sigh, another pass of his bleeding hand over his face. "None of this should be for you."

"Why not?" Her voice shook with anger, with bewilderment, with something else. "You want me to just leave you here? Go back to Valleyda and forget about all of this, leave you to bleed into a forest until there's nothing left and you become... whatever it wants you to become? And what about after that, if you can't hold the Shadowlands closed anymore even once it takes all of you? How do you think this ends, Eammon?"

"I don't know." He said it quietly. His softness, always a contrast for her edges. "I don't know how it'd all end, and I'm nearly past caring. But I'd know I tried to keep you safe. I'd know I did my best to keep you from going down with me."

"You act like this is a punishment. You didn't choose this any more than I did. This isn't your *fault*."

"It's my fault you're here. It's my fault they died. I wasn't strong enough, so the Wilderwood kept calling Second Daughters. Kept taking them." He said it all evenly, matter-of-fact, but his eyes still burned and his hands kept twitching to fists, like he wanted to hide the scars on his palms.

So she took his hands. Wove her fingers with his. Held them so tight her knuckles blanched, so tight she could feel his scars like lace pressed against her skin. "It's not going to take me," she said, a low whisper. "And I won't let it take you."

It almost put a name to the thing growing between them, that declaration. But the name was too vast and too fragile, something that might break them to acknowledge now.

"I'm trying to protect you," he murmured. "Red, I'd let the world burn before I hurt you."

"It would hurt me to leave you here." Prayer and confession. "It would hurt me to leave you all alone."

His sigh shuddered on the end. Red tugged at his scarred and bloodied hands. "Let's go home."

They walked back silently, hands tightly clasped, nearly sealed together by sap and blood. The Wilderwood stayed quiet, preternaturally still. Red still had that sense of slow, unknowable thought, churning deep in the forest, rolling over what it'd heard, what it'd seen.

Choice.

She thought she heard the word again, murmured in thicket and bower, but no leaves dropped and no moss withered. Like the Wilderwood whispered it into the thin thread of its magic she carried, something for only her to hear.

When they reached the Keep, Red climbed the stairs to their room with Eammon's arm wrapped around her, providing what little support she could when the top of her head came to only his shoulder. She led him to the bed, despite his noise of protest. "You need it more than I do."

Eammon looked at her from under the fringe of his hair, something unreadable in the twist of his mouth.

She wanted to kiss the look away. She didn't.

The cloak spread over her like a blanket as she stretched out on the floor. She fingered the embroidery, the gold wolves tangled in tree roots near the hem. "This is beautiful."

Eammon was silent long enough that she wondered if he was

already asleep. "I hope you don't mind," he said finally. "If you just want the plain cloak again, Asheyla can—"

"No." Fierce and final. "It's perfect."

Another pause. "You deserve a real bridal cloak," Eammon murmured into the ember-lit dark. "Even if it's only a thread bond."

Warmth rose in her fingers, curled in her middle. "It's just as binding as a marriage, you said."

There was a question in it, one that recalled mouths and hands and other ways to bind a marriage. Things he wouldn't let happen, because it would be a distraction from his task of keeping the Wilderwood in check, and would spell an end for them both.

His inhale was sharp. He caught her meaning. It was cruel to say it, maybe, cruel to let that heat suffuse her voice. But he'd had room for doubt, earlier, room to think she might not come back. She needed him to know she would. That whether he could answer this want or not, she would always come back.

"Just as binding." His voice was strained.

She wasn't sure how long they both lay there, staring up into the ceiling, painfully aware of the shape of the other. When Red finally dropped into sleep, her dreams were burning.

Valleydan Interlude VII

The sunlight in the gardens hurt Neve's eyes after so long in the Shrine. Unthinkingly, she lifted her hand to shade her face. Blood smeared over her cheek, the new slash in her skin tugging with a slight but aching pain.

With a curse, she rubbed the blood away, then peered at her palm. She'd taken care to slice herself in different places every time; thin, precise cuts of Kiri's dagger. They never seemed to completely heal.

Stealing pieces of the Wilderwood was bloody work.

Bleeding on the branches pulled at the rest of the tree they'd been cut from, made them fall away from the forest to appear instead in the cavern of the Shrine. They grew strange and inverted, resisting, but they came. There were at least a dozen now, an unnatural forest encased in rock, growing from stone and watered with blood.

And if you offered the blood, you received the magic, sharp and cold as daggers of ice. Magic from the Shadowlands that left frost on your fingers, darkened your veins. Felt like winter slithering around your bones.

Magic she'd finally stopped denying herself.

She'd resisted, for a time. This strange power was never her objective—Neve didn't care about anything other than weakening her sister's prison, making a way for her to return. But the more she bled for it, the more it tugged at her, shadowed and seductive. Promising control, at least over this one thing.

At the end of it all, she couldn't make Red run, and now she couldn't make her leave the Wilderwood. But she could wrench power from it. Here was something that rested entirely in her grasp, and the more time went on, the more foolish it seemed not to wield it.

With a touch, Neve could wither a flower. A flick of her fingers could turn a leaf from green to brown, and sometimes it seemed like shadows grew longer when she drew near them, like they were waiting for her command. The delicate tracing of darkness in her veins took longer to fade away each time she used it.

And Red was still gone.

Guards were stationed in the village nearest the border, watching for her return. Kiri said they had to be cautious—even if the bonds holding Red to the Wilderwood loosened enough for her to escape, they might not let her free entirely, and there was no way to know how she might be altered by them. But nothing emerged from the edge of the trees.

Frowning, Neve gestured at a green bush by the path. Cold across her fingertips, veins running like ink. The leaf curled in on itself, brown and brittle, before dropping to the path.

Kiri emerged from the shadows of the Shrine, blue eyes avid as she deftly wrapped her bleeding palm. She always cut deep, gave more blood than necessary. Neve didn't think it gave her any more magic than it gave the rest of them. She thought Kiri just enjoyed bloodletting.

Other priestesses filtered silently into the gardens behind Kiri, bandaging their own wounds. Around each neck, a branch-shard pendant, white bark brushed with subtle shadow.

The new High Priestess reached up with copper-smeared fingers, lightly touched the matching pendant at her neck. Her eyes fluttered closed, a brief moment of calm, before opening again. A slight smile crossed her face, untouched by any sharpness, only seen in these brief moments when the blood was fresh.

Neve's own pendant was still in the drawer of her desk. She hadn't touched it since that day she accidentally marked it with her blood, the day she had that overwhelming sense of being watched. Kiri seemed irritated by this quiet rebellion at first, but didn't push. Arick, who for reasons unknown to her had never received an odd necklace of his own, seemed almost...relieved.

But the other priestesses still wore theirs, each pendant produced by Kiri after they'd made their first blood offering, wielded the magic of the Shadowlands for the first time. Neve didn't know where she got the wood; it wasn't from any of the trees now crowding the Shrine. She didn't ask.

News of the changes in the Order had trickled slowly across the continent. Not the concrete details, but how they were doing more to free the Kings than just sending Second Daughters, how the candles in the Shrine had changed from scarlet to shadowy gray. Neve had braced for backlash, but it turned out Kiri was right. Whatever Valleyda decided, the other Temples fell in line, especially as the rumors of what they'd done in Floriane Harbor spread.

None of them knew the full scope of what was happening here—Neve didn't even know how one would begin to explain it—but some priestesses from other countries were curious enough to come to Valleyda, to be part of the movement. The Order was still smaller than it had been before banishing dissenters to the Rylt, but its growth was slow and steady.

One of the priestesses exiting the Shrine carried a bloodstained cup—Arick's daily contribution. Neve had never known him to be squeamish, but recently he'd either sent his sacrifice with a priestess or brought the cup himself, rather than offering straight from the vein. It still worked. Blood was blood, and Arick's was what had woken the branch shards in the first place, made them able to draw the white trees out of the forest.

"The Consort Elect will arrive shortly to observe the new arrival," Kiri said, coming level with Neve. "Are you planning to stay?"

She wasn't. Neve was headed to the garrison, where she would ask Noruscan, her captain of the guard, if he'd received any reports from the Wilderwood. Kiri knew this. Still, she asked, like she was daring Neve to come up with a different answer.

"I'm retiring for the evening." Neve turned away, headed down the path. "Tell Arick to meet me in my chambers, when you're finished."

She needed to talk to him. Arick was uncharacteristically cautious about Red, too, warning Neve that the woman who returned might not be the woman they'd lost, that the binds of the Wilderwood were difficult to untangle. The way he spoke about her was almost cold. It made Neve wonder why he was doing this, sometimes, when she had the energy to wonder such things, but Red and Arick had always been a complicated equation. The threads binding them all were wound in inextricable knots.

She was halfway down the path when Kiri spoke again. "We made you a Queen for many reasons, Neverah. You seem to only think of one."

Her footsteps faltered, stopped.

"Not just to bring Redarys back." Kiri's voice snapped on Red's name. "Not just for revenge against the Wolf. For the restoration of our *gods*. I begin to worry that you might falter in your work should your sister reappear."

Would she? Neve didn't know. But the cold magic coiled in her palms felt like reassurance, like safety and control, and that would be hard to give up. "That won't happen."

"I certainly hope not." A pause, and Kiri's voice slanted low. "Perhaps we were too hasty, in the making of your reign. In the making of *you*."

The words recalled a familiar idea, a dark shape in a dark room Neve kept carefully closed off. It haunted the corners of her mind when she couldn't sleep, a shadow of a thought that wouldn't leave her alone.

So Neve didn't think. Instead, she strode to the priestess. She touched Kiri's arm and let all that strange, dark power go.

It had been an accident, the first time she did it, touching the back of Arick's hand to ask him to pass the wine. Cold had sparked between them, like recognizing like. It was enough to make him yelp.

She'd tried to apologize. He'd shaken his head. "Nothing to be sorry for." His fingers had twitched on the stem of his wineglass. "You've taken to this in ways I couldn't have imagined, Neverah."

Her cheeks had flushed, inexplicably. Neve turned to her own wine, but she'd felt his eyes on her, glinting with an emotion she couldn't read.

Now she meant the release of this cold magic to hurt. And the hiss of breath between Kiri's teeth said it did.

"You didn't make me." Neve curled her fingers like claws. Frost crusted her palms, her veins inked black. "Whatever else you've done, you didn't make me."

Blue eyes narrowed. "I gave you power, Neverah. Don't forget that."

"You showed me where it was. I took it myself." Her grip tightened. "There was no giving, there was only taking."

She let go of the priestess's arm. A bluish handprint was left behind, like frostbite.

Kiri covered the mark with her other hand. "Don't presume to take too much, Your Majesty," she murmured. "This is bigger than you. Bigger than your sister. And even if she does return, she'll be tied to the Wilderwood in ways you don't understand. If you want her back—fully—you need me."

It worked a shudder through her spine, to know Kiri was right.

"We'll see." Neve turned sharply on her heel, pulling the hood of her black cloak over her head, and left the High Priestess behind.

The garrison was nearly empty. Half the fighting force was in Floriane, guarding against the eternal threat of uprising, and more were at the border of the Wilderwood, watching for any sign of Red's return. It was probably foolish to leave the capital so lightly guarded.

Neve flexed her hands. The grass growing through the cracks in the cobblestones browned as frost limned her fingers. Not so lightly guarded after all, perhaps.

Noruscan waited near the door, like always. Neve peered up at him from beneath her hood—a poor attempt at disguise, but enough for the short distance. "Anything?"

"Not today, Majesty." There was a note of relief in his voice, and it set her teeth on edge. They'd always feared Red, thought her more relic than girl, proof that the world was wider and more terrifying than they'd prefer it to be. A flicker of that same fear twisted to Neve now.

Part of her liked it.

"When she comes," Neve said, an echo of how she always responded, "bring her to me."

The commander nodded, just like he always did.

Her errand complete, Neve swept toward her rooms. She hadn't moved when she became Queen—sleeping in the same place Isla died didn't sit well with her. Dinner was already waiting on a cart before her desk. When she took meals at all, she took them here.

Someone else waited here, too. Forearms braced on his knees, head bowed.

Raffe.

Neve's pulse jumped. She couldn't remember the last time she'd seen Raffe. These days were a blur of bleeding and planning, little food and less sleep. Her hands went to her hair, the hollows of her cheeks—she didn't spend a great deal of time looking in mirrors these days, but she knew she didn't look well. She hadn't thought to care until now.

"Forgive me for intruding," Raffe said, still looking at his hands.

"You aren't intruding." She pressed her back against the door, spine straight against the rush of feeling the sight of him brought. Sorrow, heat, shame.

They stayed like that, anchored in opposite corners. Neither of them knew how to navigate the space between.

Raffe sighed as he stood, a sound deep enough to drown in. His eyes went to her cut palm, then away. "Spending time in the Shrine again?"

Neve closed her hand to a fist. The edges of her cut stung. "Order business."

Raffe made a low noise in his throat. Tentatively, like he thought she might rebuff him, he took a step closer. When she didn't object, he closed their distance and took her hand.

He tilted her palm back and forth, even though they both knew he could see nothing in the dim light. This was just an excuse for touch.

"I'm worried for you," he murmured.

And Neve couldn't dispute it. Couldn't tell him not to worry, couldn't pretend there was nothing to worry about.

So instead, she kissed him, because Kings and shadows *damn* it, maybe one thing could go the way she wanted it to, if only for a moment.

Raffe never did anything by halves, and kissing was no exception. By the time he pulled away, making space for fears and misgivings to come rushing back, Neve was breathless, hair mussed and lips bruised.

Raffe tilted his forehead against hers. "Whatever you've done," he whispered, "it's not too late to undo it."

"I can't." Had she thought of undoing it? Maybe, deep in the night, when the darkness of unwanted thoughts loomed too large to ignore. "Raffe, I have to do this. If it can free Red—"

"Red isn't *here*." His whisper was fierce, and Neve pressed her forehead farther into his, like she could drown it out. "You can't bring her back. She's *gone*."

Her fingers dug into his back, and she kissed him again, not gently. A kiss to swallow things. For a moment, he let her, then he broke away, his fingers winding in her hair.

"Neve." He pulled back enough to look in her eyes. "There is nothing you could do to make me stop loving you, no matter how terrible. You know that, right?"

The word was a thud in her heart, heavy and light at once. The first time he'd told her, and it was under the pall of *this*.

Kiri's words echoed in the garden—*perhaps we were too hasty in the making of your reign.*

When she spoke, it was barely sound. "What do you think I've done, Raffe?"

"I have truly awful timing, don't I?"

Raffe released her, stepping back like she was a coal that could burn. Neve turned in a whirl, nerves and inexplicable guilt twisting in her stomach.

Arick stood in the doorframe, a smile with no warmth on his face. The look in his eyes wasn't anger, exactly, but they held a strange light as he looked from Neve to Raffe. "It's good to find you here, Raffe. I've been meaning to speak with you."

"It's been a while." Raffe lifted his chin. "You've been busy."

"Both of us have." Arick dipped his head toward Neve, indicating the other half of *both*. "Kind of you to help your Queen relax."

Moonlight reflected on Raffe's bared teeth, but it was Neve who stepped forward. "Arick. Don't."

He stopped mid-stride, a momentary flicker of surprise on his face. The bright moonlight gave his eyes a strange blue cast. "Apologies."

Fraught silence. When had it become like this with the three of them? Furtive and secret and harsh, when it had been easy once?

Neve swallowed against a bladed throat.

"You said you needed to speak with me," Raffe said finally. "Speak."

Arick's grin was lazy, but his eyes were sharp. "What are you doing here?"

A beat of surprise. Then Raffe sighed. "Look, I understand that you and Neve—"

"Not that." It didn't sound entirely true, like there were waiting emotions that had to do with the kiss he'd interrupted, but Arick wasn't addressing them now. "What are you doing in Valleyda, Raffe?"

Raffe's eyes narrowed.

"You've known all there is to know about trade routes for years now. Your family is eager to have you home." Arick shrugged. "Don't you want to see them?"

No answer at first, Raffe's eyes flickering between Arick and Neve. "Of course I do," he said quietly. "But I wanted to be here for Neve, after...after everything."

"You've certainly done that." Arick was so different lately, but the three of them had known one another long enough that she recognized his pain when she heard it.

Her puzzled gaze darted to him, made shadowless by the wash of moonlight. He looked almost as taken aback by that pain as she was.

Raffe looked to Neve, swallowed hard. "We'll speak later. Remember what I said, Neve." He spared one final glance for Arick, then walked out. The door closed behind him.

Neve slumped into her desk chair, forehead in her palm.

There was something almost unsure in the way Arick held himself, lingering in the center of the room. The discomfort looked odd on his frame, usually languid and nonchalant. "You should eat."

"Not hungry."

He didn't press. From the corner of her eye, Neve saw him cross his arms. "What was he asking you to remember?"

A strange slant to his voice, as if he both wanted and didn't want her to answer.

She didn't. Instead, she asked a question of her own, giving words to the dark thing in her head, the suppositions that kept her awake. "Arick, what happened to my mother?"

A moment of lead-heavy silence. "Why would you ask that?"

And that was an answer in itself.

Neve's head sank lower. A low, pained sound escaped from behind her teeth. She should've known. Isla's sickness, how it came on so fast...she should've known.

The worst part was that a piece of her had. Had recognized that something strange was happening, and ignored it, because it got her closer to what she wanted.

Her sister, home. Some Kings-damned *control*.

She heard Arick's footsteps cross to her, felt the shift in the atmosphere as he reached out a hand. He didn't touch her, as if he knew that would be a bridge too far, but she felt his desire to. A deep, begrudging ache to comfort.

"And the High Priestess?" She stared at her hands, interwoven like vines, bloodlessly clutched. "Her, too?"

"Yes."

Not twists of fate. Not proof she was right. Murders. "Who else knows?"

"Only Kiri." A pause. "Kiri killed them both."

Kiri, with her disapproving mouth, her smugness. There from the beginning, orchestrating the fall.

She heard him swallow. "My plan didn't include so much death, but it...it served its purpose. I didn't tell you because it wouldn't have made a difference." His hand finally moved, landing lightly on hers. It was cold, but she didn't pull away. "We do what we have to do."

An echo of the night after Isla died. Not the night everything changed, but the night they crested the hill of it and began careening down the other side. She'd set the wheel in motion, and now she had to hold on until the end was reached.

A deep breath. Numb lips. "We do what we have to do."

All this death had to pay for something.

"You are an extraordinary woman, Neve." He used her shortened name so rarely these days. Every time he did, it came out like something he wasn't sure he was allowed to say. "You've risen to every challenge, you've held up under burdens no one should have to bear. You are a better Queen than this place deserves." His thumb twitched slightly, like he wanted to run it over her knuckles. He didn't. "You are too good for this."

Neve looked at Arick, confusion and uncertainty freezing her in place. In the silver light through her window, his eyes looked almost blue instead of green.

He squeezed her hand, once, before dropping his. "It will be over soon." Then Arick bowed, and slipped out into the dark.

Chapter Twenty-Five

She woke with her spine at odd angles and her neck aching. Red sat up with a disgruntled sound, rolling her shoulders. On the bed, Eammon's deep, even breathing was just shy of a snore.

A smirk pulled at her mouth. She'd have to tell him the issue persisted.

Firelight combed golden highlights through his black hair, his face softened in sleep. She studied its angles, for once not hardened by exhaustion and teeth-clenching control. There was a slight scar through one dark eyebrow. Stubble shaded his jaw, a tiny nick from a careless razor right below his chin. It heartened her, strangely, to see a mark not made for the Wilderwood.

And to think, she'd once thought the Wolf too severe to be handsome.

Red pushed his hair off his forehead. He sighed, still asleep, moving the angle of his chin so his lips brushed her palm. The root-tendril Mark stood out against his pale skin, swirling to half-way down his forearm, up past his elbow. Last night, she'd been too preoccupied with saving him from the forest to concentrate on the shape of his chest, the breadth of his bare shoulders. All things she'd noticed before, obviously—it was impossible not to—but not this close, not since the night she healed him.

The sheet pooled around his waist where he'd kicked it down

in the night, and the faint blush of those three scars glanced across his abdomen. Her hand was half reaching to touch them before she pulled it back.

No. She couldn't. *They* couldn't.

The dining room was empty when she went down the stairs, and so was the kitchen. A battered kettle hung over a banked fire, and she poked it into flame before scouring the shelves for tea leaves. She half hoped she wouldn't find them, one more thing to stall the inevitable.

Red had to leave. She had to go to Valleyda.

It had been foolish to put it off as long as they had. Only a day, but she should've left the moment she realized what was happening. The only reason she hadn't was because she didn't want to leave him. He'd let himself be a distraction, let her use him as procrastination; stalling the inevitable just as much as she was. She didn't know whether she wanted to hit him or kiss him for it.

Both, probably.

The pot whistled. Red jumped and pulled it off the hook, too quickly. A burn stung across her knuckles, and she looked at it for a moment, thinking of Eammon, how he always insisted on taking her hurt.

She resolved not to let him see it.

Red was on her second cup of weak tea when Lyra walked through the broken arch of the dining room, pulling leaves from her hair. Her *tor* clattered to the table as she sat across from Red, wrinkling her nose at the teapot. "I hate this stuff."

"It's all I could find." The blade's edge was dark, smeared with Lyra's blood and something like sap. "What happened?"

"More missing sentinels." Lyra pulled a cloth from her pocket and rubbed it along the *tor*'s edge. It didn't do much other than spread the muck around, and she quickly abandoned the endeavor with a low curse. "Cut up a few shadow-creatures, but I couldn't do anything about the holes. My blood won't touch them anymore. Doesn't do a damn thing."

More holes. He'd healed them all, nearly given up himself to do it, only for more to appear mere hours later. "Eammon healed them all last night. All the breaches." Red sighed. "Didn't take long for new ones to open."

The other woman's eyebrows flicked up, a thoughtful expression on her elfin face. Lyra set her *tor* aside. "Self-martyring bastard." Despite her earlier protestation, she tugged over the teapot and poured herself a cup. Then she sat, peering at Red through the steam as it wreathed her dark curls. "Do you want to help him?"

"Of course I do." The question was unexpected, but the answer was so automatic that Red didn't have time to be caught off guard.

Lyra settled in her seat, legs crossed and tea cupped between her palms, watching Red like she was weighing something in her mind. Finally, her dark eyes closed, long lashes sweeping her cheeks. "He's kept it from you. You know that, right?"

She did. In Red's mind, bones wrapped around the base of a tree, tangled with vines.

"He's done it for so long, and I don't think he'll stop. Especially not now." Lyra sighed, sipped her tea. "I don't know how it works. Not fully. The way the Wolf and the Wilderwood tangle together and how they come apart. But I know that if anything is going to change, Red, it will have to be you that does it."

Choice. A memory of rustling leaves and cracking branches, forest sounds shaped to a word.

"If I knew what you had to do, I'd tell you. Even though Eammon would hate me for it. But I don't." She placed her chipped teacup on the table, next to her *tor*. "Something about this is different, both with you and with the Wilderwood. Something more than Eammon holding it back. And you're the only one who can figure it out."

Their eyes locked across the table. Red nodded.

Another beat of silence, then Red pushed back her chair, stood. "Do you want bread?"

Lyra shook her head. Red grabbed two slices—one for her, one for Eammon. A letdown of a parting gift, after he'd given her a bridal cloak and the tangled thread of his history. She trudged up the stairs like stones were tied around her feet.

Eammon sat at his desk, clothed now and mostly scrubbed of blood and sap, though a streak of green-threaded burgundy still slashed behind one ear. He'd bound his hair, messily, and was fully absorbed in an open book. Red craned her neck to see what he was reading, but she didn't recognize the language.

"It's rude to read over someone's shoulder," he muttered as he turned a page.

She tried to quip, but he was close enough to reach out and touch, and that fact filled her mind like fog in a jar. Instead she took a piece of bread and placed it on the page. He gave an affronted snort before picking it up, taking a bite with his eyes still tracking over words.

Red sat on the bed and watched him, cataloging his movements. His finger brushed back and forth over the corner of the page while he read it, then dipped behind to turn. His foot bounced beneath the desk. Hair fell over his forehead, and he pushed it back, only for it to fall again.

"I'm leaving today," she whispered.

The line of his shoulders went rigid.

Her chest was a cage for things she couldn't trap into language. The only words that seemed right were too vast, too heavy. A frailty would be wrought by them, and Red couldn't afford to be frail now.

So instead, she repeated herself. "I'm coming back."

He took a shuddering breath, closed his book. "Think about it, Red. You don't—"

"Stop." Red stood, went to stand in the tiny gap between him and the desk. "We aren't having this discussion again. I'll stop Neve, get her to reverse whatever damage she's done. And then I will be right back here, Wolf, and you'd better be prepared to tell me what I have to do to save you from these damn woods."

He finally looked at her, their eyes almost level, heat in the green and amber. His sigh was ragged.

"Eammon?" Fife's voice, calling up the stairs. "Lyra's back. Another one is gone."

It froze him, turned all that heat in his eyes to something cold and resigned. Eammon's hands clenched his knees, gaze shifting away from hers to the middle distance beyond. He spoke without moving. "When do you leave?"

"Now." No use putting it off. No use hoping he'd touch her. He held himself carefully away, even after everything, after two kisses and three skulls and countless words they locked behind their teeth.

Eammon nodded. "I won't keep you, then." He stood and walked toward the stairs, leaving her alone.

Lyra and Fife were as skeptical of her plan as Eammon was.

"Your *sister* is the reason the sentinels are disappearing? She's hell-bent on killing the Wilderwood, so you're just going to go present yourself to her?" Fife's brow arched. "And I'm the only one who thinks this sounds like a bad idea?"

"What she's doing is for me. I have to find out what it is, a way to stop it. She's trying to bring me home."

"It would appear she's been successful."

"I'm not *staying*." It came out almost a hiss, and it took Fife aback—his crossed arms slackened, and a line drew between his brows.

Red closed her eyes, took a breath. "I'm coming back, Fife."

His reddish hair caught the dim light as his incredulous gaze swung from Red to Eammon. "And you're fine with this?"

"It isn't my decision." Eammon leaned against the staircase, feigning nonchalance, but his spine was rigid.

Fife's sigh deflated his shoulders. "I hope you know what you're doing." His eyes slid from Eammon to Red. "Both of you."

"*Fife.*" Lyra's tone was warning, though worry lived in the downward curve of her mouth. Her eyes flickered to Red's. "I can take you as far as the border. Make sure you don't get lost."

"Give me a moment." Red hurried up the stairs. "I forgot something."

When she reached their room, Red was out of breath. Her bridal cloak spread across the floor where she'd slept beneath it, the same colors as the fire in the grate. The embroidery glinted as she picked it up.

A pen lay on the desk, next to a haphazard stack of papers and books in languages she couldn't read. She tested the sharp end with her finger before dipping it in the inkwell.

Three days, she scrawled. *And then I want the bed back.*

Eammon's eyes slipped cursorily over the cloak when she came back down the stairs, settling on her face. He said nothing. Red pressed her lips together, hitched her bag on her shoulder.

Lyra glanced quickly between them before turning to the door. "At the gate, when you're ready."

Fife's mouth opened, but he closed it on silence. Lifting one hand in an awkward wave, he passed through the broken arch into the dining room.

Then she and the Wolf were alone.

Eammon was silent. He still half believed this would be forever—she could see it in the way his hands tightened on his arms, the work of his swallowing throat.

So many words caught between them, and *goodbye* was the only one he would say.

She didn't let him. "Three days." Red turned, pulled up her scarlet hood, and slipped through the door, leaving the Wolf in the shadows.

The *tor* glinted on Lyra's back like a sickle moon. She wove deftly through the Wilderwood, Red following close behind.

They walked a few minutes in silence before Red heard it. A slight but unmistakable *boom*, reverberating through the forest.

Another breach, opening.

"Shit." Lyra unsheathed her *tor*, pulled a vial of blood from the bag at her waist with a practiced motion. "We'll keep moving, but keep a close eye on the ground."

Red nodded, hands curled to claws. The thread of magic in her chest spiraled, ready for use.

They crept forward. Finally, the dark edge of a hole where a sentinel should have been stretched from a pool of fog.

At the edge of the pit, a tiny cyclone of leaves and twigs swirled. Lyra unstoppered the vial of blood and poured it out over the twisting column. With a whine, it broke apart, leaves fluttering to the ground only slightly touched with shadow on the edges.

"Got to it quick enough." But she still didn't sheath her *tor*. "Eammon will have to—"

The next one cobbled itself together quickly, like it'd learned a lesson from its slow-moving counterpart. A whirl of dead twigs and leaves and pulled-up bones, not bothering to make a humanoid shape, bursting up from the ground and hurtling toward them.

They both acted on instinct. Red curled her fingers, pulling at magic, sending vines whipping out from the underbrush. They passed through the half-formed shadow-creature enough to break it apart, slow it down, but it hurled itself back together in their wake.

Lyra was ready. Another unstoppered vial, poured along the edge of her blade in a graceful arc, then she launched herself at the shadow-creature.

The curved shine of the *tor* bit through the dim light, spinning blood and sap. The sword was an extension of Lyra herself, the curve of it like a dancer's arm as she twirled in the gloom. Red's vines kept whipping through the thing, breaking it into pieces, and Lyra went after each bit, slicing with her bloodied blade so the parts that made it fell uselessly to the forest floor. It took only seconds, then the shadow-creature was gone, nothing but a mess of rotting, dark-touched detritus on the ground.

They both stood still for a moment, breathing hard. Red straightened her hands, and vines slithered back into the underbrush. She swallowed the taste of dirt as her veins ran from green to blue again. It was the most successful wielding of Wilderwood magic she'd managed since helping Eammon fight off the worm-like beast on the way back from the Edge, but it didn't feel like much of an accomplishment. They couldn't close the breach, and as long as it stayed open, any victory was temporary.

A moment of silence, both of them waiting to see if the breach would birth something else. Then Lyra sheathed her *tor*, not bothering to wipe it clean. "This breach is small. The shadow-creature won't have time to reanimate before Eammon can get to it. Hopefully." She turned, heading back through the forest again. "I would bloody it up, but I don't want to waste what I have. It wouldn't make a difference, anyway."

Red lingered a moment longer, staring at the pit of shadow, dark and rotten on the ground. Cursing softly, she spun to follow Lyra.

The trees thinned as they grew closer to the border. Thick fog served almost as a wall between the Wilderwood and the outside world, but shards of a blue sky shone through the haze. Valleyda, close enough to touch, and the only emotions Red felt were apprehension and preemptive homesickness.

Too soon, they'd reached the tree line. "Three days," Red announced, just as she'd told Eammon, like the Wilderwood could hear her and mark the time as well as he could. "This shouldn't take longer than three days. Then I'll be back."

The snatches of sunlight between the branches caught copper strands in Lyra's tight-coiled hair as she nodded. "Three days." She headed back into the fog, back toward the Keep. Back toward home.

"Look after him," Red murmured. "Please."

"Always have." Lyra looked over her shoulder, dark eyes honeyed in the dim. "Remember what I said."

Red nodded. Forest magic bloomed in her chest, waiting.

When Lyra was gone, Red faced the trees she'd slipped through on her twentieth birthday. With a deep breath, she slipped through again.

Daylight was a physical weight on her shoulders, a knife-shine in her eyes. For a moment she stood there, blinking, a woman in crimson on the edge of the world. Autumn painted the sky a crisp blue, and she caught the scent of bonfire smoke on the wind.

Behind her, a murmur. Red turned, peering into the shadows of the Wilderwood as it whispered in its strange language of leaf and thorn.

We will wait for your choice.

A branch broke away from a trunk, dried and desiccated as it tumbled to the forest floor. A thicket of small bushes withered, curled in like a dying beetle.

But we'll have him, if we must.

Her jaw clenched against the rattle of the words in her bones, the sharp-splinter piece of the Wilderwood's power she carried speaking into her hollow places. "Fuck you," she muttered.

The Wilderwood didn't respond.

She hurried down the grassy slope, toward the road and the village beyond. Her lungs buzzed, like the air outside the forest was different from what she'd been breathing, and it made her head too light.

When Red reached the road, she stopped, squinting. A tall, spindly structure stood at the edge of the village, just close enough to make out. A guard tower.

Red allowed herself only a moment to puzzle over it, mind overtaken by practical concerns. It was half a day's ride by carriage to the capital, and she didn't have money for a horse. Walking would—

A high, sharp whistle interrupted her thoughts, loud enough to make her wince. Distant shouts rang around the hills, a sound like thundering hoofbeats. A cloud of dust rose near the guard tower.

Panic dropped her stomach, but it was momentary. The tower must be watching the Wilderwood—there was nothing else to see in this direction. Which meant they'd seen *her*, which made it pointless to hide.

Instead Red stood at the turn of the road, chin tilted upward, scarlet cloak on her shoulders. She didn't cringe away when the band of riders reached her, out of breath, swords drawn.

One of them pointed his blade in her direction, overbright in daylight she wasn't used to.

Red raised her hands in a posture of surrender. "I understand your alarm, but—"

"Don't come any closer." The blade shivered, broadcasting his shudder.

"Hold." Another guard, with the silver stripe of a commander across his shoulder, held up his hand. He leaned forward, frowning at Red's face. "I know you."

"You should."

His gaze followed the folds of her cloak, then widened. "Second Daughter."

She wasn't in a position to be particular. Still, Red's lips lifted, teeth glinting in unfamiliar sunlight.

"Lady Wolf," she corrected.

Chapter Twenty-Six

She didn't protest when they tightened cuffs around her wrists. Red schooled her face into calm as the guards clustered, murmuring, casting worried glances her way.

"It looks human."

"Of course it does. If you think that *thing* is the Second Daughter, or whatever it called itself, you're a fool. The Second Daughter is long dead. The Wilderwood holds nothing but monsters."

A scoff. "You believe those stories?"

The first guard jerked a thumb at Red. "I do *now*."

"Calm yourself, Coleman. You sound like a maid at a Harvest campfire." The commander was roughly handsome, with broad cheekbones and a coppery beard. He stood between Red and the rest of the soldiers, eyeing her contemplatively. "The Queen did warn us to watch for her."

"The *Queen*, Noruscan? She's half mad—"

The leader—Noruscan—caught the speaker across the mouth with the back of his hand, the movement nearly nonchalant. "That's quite enough."

The other man made a surprised noise as blood trickled from his lip. He shot a venomous glance at Red, as if it was her fault.

Noruscan looked her curiously up and down, like she was a statue. A relic. Red's stomach sank at that look, the sting of it doubled after so long without.

The commander's gaze turned to the Wilderwood behind them, tall and dark, and the sight of it seemed to settle some internal debate. "We'll take her to the High Priestess."

Red's brows pulled together. The Neve she knew—the one she'd seen in the mirror, desperate for her return—would want her sister sent straight to her. "Are those your orders, Noruscan?"

The use of his name made the commander recoil, stepping closer to the clustered soldiers.

"Don't *talk* to it, man," the guard with the still-bleeding lip and shaky sword-arm cautioned.

The captain peered at her, assessing her threat, then grabbed her arm. Shackles pinched into her skin, but Red didn't fight. The last thing she needed was to inspire that shaky guard to a moment of bravery.

"You'll ride with me." Noruscan pulled her over to his horse. Before boosting her into the saddle, he reached for the ties of her cloak.

Red twisted from his grip, instinct moving her more than thought. "No."

"How do you think the capital will react, if you are who you claim?" His face was stern lines, his eyes dark with something that wasn't quite fear, but skirted close to it. "They sent you to a monster, and the monster gave you back. How will that look, Second Daughter?"

Her pulse thrummed steady against her shackles. As much as it set her teeth on edge, he was right. She couldn't afford to broadcast her presence to the whole kingdom, and the scarlet bridal cloak would draw undue attention. "Will you return it?"

A moment of hesitation, his ruddy brows low. But he nodded.

Red slipped the heavy fabric from her shoulders, swallowing hard. When Noruscan settled behind her in the saddle, he placed the cloak almost gently in her lap. She twisted her fingers in it as they galloped away.

Two hours' hard riding, and the gates of the capital shone on the horizon.

"Hide that," Noruscan said as he sawed on the reins, turning the horse toward the gates. He tapped a fist on her bridal cloak.

His tone held warning. *Hide it or we'll take it from you.* Red balled the cloak in her hands as well as she could, tucking the embroidery on the underside.

When they reached the guard tower, Noruscan rode close, pulling up Red's shackles so they caught the sun. "Thief from the outer villages," he barked.

The lie made her lips twist, but Red stayed silent. Cooperation seemed her best option here, the surest way to get to Neve.

The guard waved a lazy hand, and the gates opened.

Noruscan's horse cantered toward the palace. As soon as they crossed into the courtyard, he dismounted, helped her down cautiously. One of his hands brushed the bare skin of her arm, and he pulled back quickly, like her touch might burn.

They were terrified of her. Once, that might've hollowed her out, but now Red just wondered how she could use it. Hands still shackled, she shook out her cloak, clumsily fastening it around her neck.

The battalion marched her into the Temple, flanking either side, hands on their blades and eyes pointed away. They entered the hallway that led from the palace gardens, all marble and glass, but stopped at a simple wooden door instead of going all the way to the amphitheater. Noruscan waved a hand to dismiss the others, but he followed Red inside, closing the door behind them.

The far wall was a window, looking out on the gardens and letting in bright, airy light. A lone priestess sat at a desk beside it. She stood slowly, folding her hands into her sleeves. Dust motes like light shards twisted lazily around her red hair.

A new High Priestess, then. Red frowned. It shouldn't have been a surprise—the other had been getting up in years. But a new High

Priestess coupled with what she'd seen in the mirror made her hackles rise.

The Shrine. Whatever they were doing, it was in the Shrine.

"Your Holiness." Noruscan bowed. Red stayed upright. "She claims to be the Second Daughter."

Calculating blue eyes flickered over Red. "Does she, now?"

"She came from the Wilderwood," Noruscan said quickly. "But she hasn't shown any signs of... of abnormality."

Red straightened her shoulders, trying to make eye contact, but the bright light of the window left the High Priestess's face in shadow. "How would you like me to prove it to you, Your Holiness?" Then, because subtlety was something she'd never been good at, "If you'll take me to the Shrine, to pray and pay my respects, I'm sure I could answer any questions you have."

"Don't trouble yourself." The priestess moved into the light, hands held loosely by her sides. A strange pendant lay against her breast, a piece of white wood touched with threads of darkness. Red's eyes narrowed at it.

The priestess noticed. Long-fingered white hands picked up the bark shard, dangled it in the shaft of sunlight. "Familiar, I'm sure. Twisted up in you like rot in a corpse."

"I don't know what you mean." But the splinter of magic in her, the shard of the Wilderwood, twined and bloomed around her bones.

The High Priestess—Kiri, Red remembered now, the name she'd heard Neve say in the mirror—flicked the corner of a cold smile, letting the pendant drop back against her chest. Slowly, she approached, close enough that Red had to fight the urge to step back. The priestess's gaze was searching, like if she looked hard enough she could see *into* Red, into the hollow places between her organs.

"You arrival might derail us," she said, nearly speaking to herself. "But perhaps you'll be a useful pawn."

Red's brow furrowed, genuine confusion eclipsing the manufactured kind. "I don't understand—"

But before she could finish, Kiri's hands shot up, crooking into tortured shapes, and icy cold slammed into Red's body.

Red's own hands rose, like the invasion was something she could fight off, but all the power she'd learned to control was nowhere to be found. Whatever the High Priestess was doing, lacing ice through her veins, seemed to make her own power wither and hide, canceled out. It felt like being crushed, ground under some cold heel—the Wilderwood's magic, taken and inverted, crawling through her as if searching for something.

It made a twisted sort of sense. Freeing Red would've been cause enough for Neve to weaken the forest, but not the Order. They had to have more of a reason, more of a reward.

This cold, awful magic must be it.

When the icy onslaught was done, Red was on her knees. She didn't remember falling. Breath rattled in her lungs, and her throat felt thorned with frost. Blood dripped from her nose to pool on the marble.

From the corner of her eye, she saw Noruscan flinch.

The veins on the High Priestess's wrist were ink-dark, wet with crystals of melting frost. One long finger dipped into the blood on the floor, brought it to the light.

"Scarlet," the priestess whispered. "Only scarlet." Sunlight flashed off bared teeth. She looked to the commander. "Leave us."

Noruscan slid his gaze between them, almost regretful, before turning toward the door. It closed with a sound like a sepulcher.

When Red wiped her mouth, her hand was shaking. "I just want to see Neve." The tremble in her voice wasn't artifice. She felt like she'd been turned inside out, every secret thing beneath her skin bared to terrible light. "Just take me to the Shrine, and let me see Neve."

She had to see what was in the Shrine. She had to see what Neve had done, and figure out how to fix it.

Especially if it birthed this power, this twisted darkness that made her weak, made the Wilderwood in her recoil. What would it do to Eammon, if it did this to her?

Kiri eyed the blood on her finger. "You'll see the Queen when I deem it safe." She stood, wiping a red streak on her white robe. "There's something there, some remnant of the forest's binding. You're just hiding it. Rest assured it will be found."

"I don't understand." Red sat back on her heels. "I'm *here*. You weakened the Wilderwood for me. Isn't this what you were working toward?"

"Stupid girl. This is so much bigger than you and your foolish sister." The High Priestess circled like a carrion bird. "You've served one purpose. Perhaps you'll serve another. It's not for me to decide."

Red swallowed. Neve and Kiri had two different perspectives on what was happening here, she was sure of it. Their methods might align, but their objectives didn't. At least, not completely.

She hoped.

"Neverah is beginning to understand," Kiri continued thoughtfully, almost to herself. "She knows she needs me to disentangle you fully." A thoughtful pause. "Something could always go wrong. She wouldn't know."

A shiver worked its way down Red's spine.

"Red?"

The High Priestess's hands, once again crooked in preparation for cold magic, instead disappeared into her sleeves. Stumbling to her feet, Red whirled toward the door.

Neve, thinner than Red remembered, black hair held by a silver crown. Neve, rushing toward her, hands outstretched. Neve, solid and real.

"I did it." Neve wavered on her feet, her face a mix of joy and awe and, almost, fear. "I did it."

Red collapsed into her like a rag doll, breathing her sister's rain-and-roses scent, clutching her like someone returned from the dead. "Neve," she murmured, and couldn't make herself say anything else. "Neve."

"I knew it." Neve's arms held her with strength their thinness belied. Tears ran warm onto Red's brow. "I knew you'd come back. I knew you'd escape."

The word *escape* coiled uneasily in her stomach, but Red ignored it. She pulled Neve closer, letting her spine go crooked, letting the tears gathered behind her eyes fall into her sister's hair.

It was almost enough to make her forget why she'd come.

Neve leaned away and tucked Red's hair behind her ear. She wound their fingers together, turning toward the High Priestess. "Kiri. I hope you've greeted my sister properly."

Something odd in her voice, something hidden. The High Priestess bent another slight edge of a smile. "As properly as time allowed," she said. "I'm sure we'll get better acquainted."

Neve tightened her fingers around Red's. "Quite." She shifted on her feet. "You'll tell the others, then? Let them know that all our work has come to fruition?"

An unreadable expression flickered across Kiri's features. "Not full fruition," she said quietly. "Our work is not yet done. Majesty."

The honorific was clearly an afterthought, meant to convey more in tone than words. Red's brow arched.

"I'm aware, Kiri," Neve murmured, something dark flickering in her eyes. "But let me enjoy one victory before we plug away at another, please."

Apprehension tempered Red's joy at seeing Neve again, the reason she was here staring her stark in the face. Neve against the Wilderwood. Neve caught up in schemes Red didn't entirely understand.

Her sister was warm beside her, the scent of her hair familiar and comforting. Still, when Red blinked, she saw Eammon's dirt-streaked face, saw green-and-amber eyes.

"Come." Neve pulled her toward the door. "I'll have dinner brought to my chambers. You look exhausted."

Right before the door closed, Red glanced over her shoulder. Kiri's face was calm, but her clenched jaw spoke of something deeper than displeasure. Her eyes met Red's, blue and cold enough to burn, then the door slammed shut.

Chapter Twenty-Seven

Red's cloak drew all the attention she'd feared and more as they moved through the halls. Servants and nobles alike stopped to peer, then outright stare as they recognized her. The Second Daughter, returned from the Wilderwood.

Neve paid no mind, tugging Red along by the hand like the girls they'd been before, not the Queen and the Lady Wolf. She gestured to a passing handmaiden. "Have dinner brought to my rooms, please. For three."

The handmaiden gaped even as she nodded. "Queen Neverah... and, um, your... Redarys..."

"My sister has returned." Neve's voice was achingly sincere. "Well and whole."

Well and whole. Red tried to smile, but the pressure of these familiar halls was almost a physical weight. The atmosphere buzzed over her skin, a frequency at odds with the rhythm of her heartbeat, like Valleyda itself recognized she didn't belong anymore.

The handmaiden's mouth worked soundlessly. "That's... that's wonderful." She could have exchanged *wonderful* for *terrifying* without altering her tone.

Neve didn't notice. "Tell Arick to meet us." She swirled away in a froth of skirts and silver.

"I'm not particularly hungry," Red said, pulled along behind her. "I was wondering if maybe we could go to the Shrine, before dinner?"

That made Neve stop. She turned, brows knit. "*You* want to go to the Shrine?"

Neve had always been the cunning one, and Red only blunt. She shrugged. "It's been a long time."

Her twin's dark eyes narrowed, the corner of her bottom lip disappearing between her teeth, and Red thought of that strange exchange in the Temple. Kiri and Neve, united in whatever they were doing to the Wilderwood.

She'd known this wouldn't be as simple as showing her sister she was fine and asking her nicely to stop, but now that the reality stared her down, Red's spine felt like a sapling buried under frost.

Neve stared at her a moment longer. "Not now," she said finally, turning to hurry down the hallway. "Tomorrow, maybe."

She didn't know how to do this. Red was no stranger to keeping secrets from her sister, but the careful modulation, the hemming of truths—they weren't things that came naturally, especially not now. Part of her wanted to spill the whole story, to spell out the history and what was happening and how Neve had to stop. But then she thought of what she'd seen in the mirror, of Kiri's words only moments ago, about plans and fruition and how Red was only part of it. The path here was complex, littered with traps, and putting a foot wrong could bloody them both.

The best plan seemed to be to get to the Shrine. To see exactly what Neve had done.

More courtiers and servants passed them by, more wide eyes and shapeless whispers. Red's shoulders hunched toward her ears, like she could make herself smaller.

"They seem surprised." Red wasn't sure what reaction she'd expected. She wasn't sure what *anything* she'd expected. All her thoughts were bent only toward stopping the disappearing sentinels, toward helping Eammon. Now it felt like she was stumbling along to keep up, everything rushing and tangling too quickly to make sense of.

"Of course they do." Neve pushed open the door to the same rooms she'd had since they moved from the nursery. "They thought you were dead." Her voice was brittle. "But we knew you were alive. Arick and I knew."

Arick. His name should've been a comfort, but instead disquiet curled around Red's spine. When she tried to remember his face, it was still the shadowy thing that had come for her at the Keep's gate, and her memories of his body had narrowed to only his possessive hold on her wrists the night of the ball.

The sunlight through the window highlighted the hollows in Neve's cheeks, the jut of her collarbone. Her hands went to the silver circlet, all but wrenching it from her hair; she set it on the dressing table and rubbed at her forehead as if it pained her. Shadow pooled along the circlet's curve, warping the room's reflection. It was similar to the one she'd worn as the First Daughter, but more ornate—delicately filigreed, inset with tiny diamonds. Red remembered Isla wearing it, and the thought was a lurch in her chest.

"I'm so sorry," Red murmured. "Neve, I'm so sorry you had to go through it alone."

Neve's distorted reflection in the circlet went rigid. "It was..." Her mouth worked like she might say more, but nothing came out. She tucked a stray lock of black hair behind her ear as she folded into the chair at her desk. "It was difficult."

The chambers had a sitting room off to the side that Neve never used; Red pulled over one of the heavy, brocaded chairs to sit next to Neve's desk instead. For a moment, they sat in silence, two sisters and the ghost of a mother. Neve looked at the carpet instead of Red, a slight indentation in her skin where the circlet had weighed heavy.

"I'm glad to be Queen." She said it like a confession. "I don't think

I'll ever stop feeling guilty for that." Her spine straightened, eyes raising. "But you're here now. I saved you. That makes it all worth it."

It made Red's skin feel too small, this declaration that she needed saving. *She knows she needs me to disentangle you fully.*

"How did you do it?" Kings, she could barely keep her face schooled to mere curiosity, could barely keep the accusing edge from her voice. Here was her sister, whom she loved down to her bones, but the air between them was thick with secrecy and things misunderstood. "How did you weaken the Wilderwood so I could..." She couldn't finish it. *Escape* wouldn't hold its shape on her tongue.

Neve's dark eyes flickered up from her pale, knotted hands, a line between her brows. Like Kiri before, her gaze was searching. As if she was looking for something in Red, some abnormality hiding just out of sight.

The moment passed. Neve blinked, and the calculating light in her eyes went out, replaced instead by relief. "It doesn't matter." A smile, more brilliant for how pale and wan she looked otherwise. "You're here now. Whatever else we have to do to make sure you're safe, we'll do it."

Red shifted nervously.

Neve put a reassuring hand on her knee, mistaking the reason for her discomfort. "There's no need for worry, Red. The Wolf can't reach you here, and we'll root out the rest—"

"I'm not staying." It came out sharp, and she knew she should've swallowed it the moment it left her mouth. But there was so little truth between them, it was almost unbearable.

Maybe her own honesty could wrench some from her sister.

Neve's brow knit, uncomprehending. "If you'd rather go to one of the other holdings, I can arrange that, too. I understand not wanting to be in the capital."

"No." Red winced. This could only sound graceless. "Neve, I... I'm going back to the Wilderwood."

Disbelief fell like a shadow, dimming Neve's eyes. "What?"

Red didn't know where to go from there, how much to safely share, and she hated it. "I came back because I wanted to see you. Because… because I wanted to know what you were doing." She didn't say because she wanted to *stop* it, unsure if she could admit that or not, unsure what Neve might do. "But I want to go back. Eammon—"

"Eammon?"

"The Wolf. His name is Eammon. Gaya and Ciaran's son." A pause, a deep breath. "Neve, so much is different than—"

"Stop." Quiet, but with enough gravitas behind it that Red's teeth clicked shut. Neve's hand was up in the air between them, a slight tremble in her fingers. She took a deep breath of her own, let it out with her eyes closed. "You're on good terms, then. Good terms with the Wolf. Good terms with the Wilderwood."

The cold in her voice sent heat to Red's cheeks, an inverse reaction. She reeled truth back into her mouth; it was obvious Neve didn't want to hear it right now. "You could say that," she murmured, nervously tugging at the hem of her cloak.

The movement drew Neve's eye. For the first time, her twin took stock of the cloak, mouth drawing tighter. "That isn't the one you left with."

The embroidery pressed against Red's skin, grounding. "Not technically, no."

Silence, silence, a well of it they couldn't fill. Then Neve's voice, tremulous: "What have you *done*, Red?"

She'd asked herself the question, more than once. She'd married the Wolf of the Wilderwood. It was a massive, frightening thing, and one she'd do again in a heartbeat.

"Nothing I didn't want to," she answered quietly.

Her sister's hands knotted tighter, knuckles blanched white. Across the room, the ornate mirror shone them back at themselves. Golden and dark, reflections of each other.

Neve's eyes pressed closed. "Don't worry." It was a murmur, a reassurance for herself as much as for Red. "We expected...not *this*, but something. We'll fix it."

"What do you mean?"

But whatever answer Neve might've given was interrupted by the opening door.

Servants pushed in a dinner cart to Neve's forgotten sitting room, enough food for five people with place settings for three. They were in and out in silence, staring wide-eyed at Red's cloak, avoiding her face. As they left, a lone figure filled the doorframe.

"The prodigal returns," Arick said.

He stood straighter, was a trifle thinner. He'd taken to wearing his hair differently in the time she'd been gone, curling long over his collar. Red stood, though her legs felt stiff, forcing a smile and pushing Neve's strange behavior aside, something to be dealt with later. "Hello, Arick."

Smiling, he pushed off from the doorframe, met Red in the center of the room, and folded her in his arms. The embrace felt oddly clinical, so unlike what they'd shared before. Arick smelled different, too. Maybe he'd switched cigars, or his valet had stopped packing mint leaves in his pockets. She couldn't name this new scent, only that it was cold.

"You look well, Red." Arick's hands rested on her shoulders, and the part of her that remembered the alcove wanted to squirm away. Gloaming light through the window dimmed the edges of things, but she didn't miss the searching way his eyes flickered over hers. "Or should I call you Lady Wolf? That's the title you gave Noruscan, I heard."

Neve made no sound behind her, but Red still glanced over her shoulder, like the jolt through Neve's spine rattled hers, too. Her twin froze for half a moment before going to her sitting room, sinking to the couch.

"Just Red is fine," Red murmured.

The corner of Arick's smile sharpened. He released her shoulders and crossed the room to stand next to Neve. She visibly relaxed at his presence. One hand feathered over her forearm, a light, reassuring touch.

Tentatively, Red took the seat across from them. "Is Raffe joining us?"

The name made Neve stiffen. "No."

"Raffe returned to Meducia." Arick opened a pot on the cart. His eyes flashed as he glanced at Red, and for a moment, they didn't look green. "Pheasant, Red. Your favorite."

The scent made her stomach growl. It'd been a long time since breakfast in the Keep. "Seems a strange time for him to leave."

She couldn't imagine Raffe abandoning Neve so soon after her coronation. Not when every line of her frame spoke of struggling, not when their feelings were so clear. When Raffe and Neve were in the same room, the only time their eyes weren't on each other was when the other was looking.

The fact that he was gone made the unease in her stomach crawl up toward her throat.

Arick handed Neve a full plate; she took it listlessly. "He hadn't been home in so long," he said, with a brief, hard laugh. "Can you blame him, wanting to be there instead of freezing Valleyda?" He filled another plate and held it out to Red.

She took it, balanced it on her lap. "I suppose not."

"You just missed him," Neve said. "He left three days ago."

"I hate I didn't get to say goodbye."

Neve's eyes shuttered and turned back to her plate. She picked up her fork but never brought it to her mouth.

Arick glanced at Neve with genuine worry, but when his gaze came to Red, it was cold. He glared at her like he felt her guilt, like he wished for more of it.

She didn't know how to move here, didn't know how to act. The frames of these relationships had twisted in her absence, subtly changed in ways she couldn't make any sense of.

Red ate quickly and without tasting. She took a gulp of wine—Meducian, of course, and going to her head in one swallow. She'd grown used to the watered-down stuff Eammon bought from Valdrek.

Eammon. Every thought of him delved in like a thorn.

Night fell beyond the window, and guttering candles cast the only light. It muted the angles of Arick's face, made them nearly unrecognizable. "Surely you have adventures to regale us with, Red." He sipped his wine and sat back in his chair, casting his face in shadow. "What terrible things have you seen in the Wilderwood?"

Red took another unladylike gulp. "It's not all terrible."

"I suppose you wouldn't think so." This from Neve, still and quiet. She'd barely picked at her food.

Red's own tasted like ashes. She set her plate aside.

Arick rested a steadying hand on Neve's knee, just for a moment. "Tell us about it, then, if it's not so terrible after all." Candlelight gleamed over his teeth. "Is it less frightening, once the Wilderwood has you?"

More. But Red couldn't say that, not with Neve right there. Neve, scared and trying to help, even though her help only whetted a blade.

And something about the question seemed strange. Leading.

"It's always twilight." She let her voice slip to storybook cadences—tell the beauty, take out the teeth. "The walls of the Keep have moss on them. There are trees big as houses. And fog, always fog."

Neve watched her through wide, dark eyes. A bittersweet shard of memory, the two of them as children listening in rapt attention to a tale of the Wilderwood, illustrated on window glass. Something contracted in Red's chest.

"And what's *he* like?" Arick's gaze tracked over her cloak, mouth quirking. "It's unprecedented for a Second Daughter to return. Did you hate each other that much?"

"No." It cracked out of her, too sharp to be nonchalant.

Arick said nothing, face still shadowed, but she could see his grin. Next to him, Neve's teeth worked at her lip.

Weariness piled up like stones. Between the wine and her long, strange journey, it was an effort to keep her eyes open. Red couldn't string together the niceties of excusing herself. "Where would you like me to sleep, Neve? I'm sure my old room is being used for something else."

"It's not." Neve's eyes were almost shy. "It's exactly as you left it."

Red chewed the corner of her lip.

As if it was a cue, Arick stood. "Kiri asked that you meet her at the Shrine, Neve." A muscle flickered in his jaw, eyes momentarily flinty. "I'll accompany you, of course."

Finally. Red straightened expectantly.

"In a moment." Neve's gaze flickered to Red, then away, standing with Arick's proffered hand. "I want to get Red settled first."

"I'd be happy to go to the Shrine with you." Too eager—Arick's face darkened. Red shrugged. "Whatever it is you have to do there. So we can spend some more time together."

Far from encouraged, Neve's eyes fluttered closed, a weary blink that sank her shoulders. "No. Not right now." Straightening, shaking off whatever pall had fallen over her. "Besides, I'm sure you're exhausted."

Red knew a lost argument when she saw one. She nodded. "Tomorrow, then."

A quick glance between the Queen and her Consort Elect. "Tomorrow," Neve agreed.

Turning, Arick sketched a bow at Red. "Lady Wolf." Then he was gone, disappeared into the dark maw of the hallway.

Neve led the short way to Red's room next door. Nothing had

changed from the morning Red left. Her nightgown was still crumpled in the corner.

The wood of her old wardrobe was painted white and silver, so different from the scratched thing in the room she shared with Eammon at the Keep. Neve gestured to it. "All your clothes are there. Anything you might need." She crossed to the corner and picked up the discarded nightgown. "I *did* have them change the bed linens, at least, so you should be comfortable."

The air between them felt heavy, like something waited in it. "I was telling the truth, Neve," Red finally said, standing awkwardly in the center of the room that no longer felt like hers. "I came back to Valleyda because I wanted to see you."

Neve made a mirthless sound. "You say it like it's some great journey rather than just returning home."

"This isn't home anymore."

The nightgown in Neve's hands fluttered, the only tell of the tremble in her hands. "I see." There were layers to her voice, a depth the two words didn't properly illuminate. But when her eyes rose to Red's, the shine in them was determination, not tears. She handed over the nightgown. "I'll see you in the morning. We can go to the Shrine then."

Neve nearly fled the room, skirts flashing around the doorframe. Red stood alone in Valleyda for the first time since she'd returned, and the air itself felt unfriendly.

The nightgown fit perfectly, but the fabric itched. Her bed smelled like roses, so different from the coffee-and-leaves scent she was used to now. Red was a warped puzzle piece, her changes nearly too subtle to see, but enough to keep her from fitting back into the place she'd left.

Still, she fell asleep nearly as soon as she closed her eyes, exhaustion pulling her down into the dark.

Chapter Twenty-Eight

Red knew Eammon's movements by now, cataloged in moments of feigned sleep, observed through half-closed eyelids.

Whatever moved in this room wasn't Eammon.

The air smelled wrong, like flowers, like rain. The movement stopped, and something whispered, feminine and strange.

Teeth bared, Red shot up from the couch, fingers hooked like claws.

White walls, silver shine, and the terrified faces of three handmaidens. No forest. No Keep.

No Eammon.

The maid closest to her recovered, straightening with a conciliatory smile. She curtsied, but her eyes still held the sheen of cornered prey. Behind her, the other two clutched sheets to their chests and watched Red as though she might attack, some feral creature from the Wilderwood.

Well. They weren't entirely wrong.

Pushing tangled hair from her eyes, Red tried for a smile. It only seemed to frighten them more.

The first steeled herself to speak. "Morning, Lady Wolf. The Queen asks that you meet her in the gardens when you're ready."

Right. Today was the day she'd finally see the Shrine. See what Neve was doing and how she could fix it.

What would be left of them, once she did? What would be between them to pick up and put back together?

"Breakfast is on the table," piped up one of the others, like their courage was a collective thing. "And clothes in the wardrobe."

"Thank you." Red stood awkwardly, crossing her arms over her chest. The three of them gawked at her like a myth come to life, like they didn't quite believe she existed.

She hadn't missed this feeling.

Her cloak lay over the back of the chair they clustered around, and the dart of their eyes confirmed it was the subject of the whispering. Their gazes held a wordless conversation, then the one who'd spoken first turned to Red.

"We'd heard you came back with a different cloak," she said, voice steady despite her knotted hands. "An embroidered one. Like a bridal cloak."

Of course they'd heard. She'd paraded through the palace in it, told Noruscan to call her *Lady Wolf.* The seasoned court gossips must've put two and two together. Red gave one weary nod.

Three pairs of eyes grew even wider, something she hadn't thought possible. They looked at one another, somewhat at a loss, before one of the previously reticent handmaidens took a tiny step forward. "So you…you *married* the Wolf?"

Wolf and *monster* were interchangeable in her tone. Red stiffened, though not long ago she would've done the same. How unfair, the way history twisted.

"I did." Red headed for the wardrobe. The handmaidens moved as one, backing away like a school of fish.

The brave one spoke again. "Isn't he wicked?"

"No." Red pulled out the first dress her fist closed on. Forest-colored, embroidered in white thread that reminded her of scars. "No more wicked than any other man. Far less wicked than most."

Silence. Red didn't look at them, didn't want to see if the looks on their faces were surprise or disbelief or something in between. "You're free to go. I'm perfectly capable of dressing myself."

Skirts rustled through the door, but the brave one lingered beneath the lintel. When Red turned, she didn't flinch, eyes narrowed. "Did he tell you why the Second Daughters have to go to the Wilderwood?" she asked. "The truth?"

Some things were too hard to explain. Some things were too heavy for fragile belief to shoulder. And Red didn't have time to even try.

"Because the monsters are real," she said. "And even the Wolf needs help sometimes."

The handmaid's eyes widened. She curtsied, quick and clumsy, and disappeared through the door.

The blooming season in Valleyda was always short, summer truncated by northern cold, and things were generally more brown than green by the time autumn approached. Still, it was strange for the gardens to be almost wholly dead. Hedges were nothing but sharp bundles of twigs; flower beds held only dry grass. Even the hardier blooms that usually lived until the first snow were limp and nearly colorless.

Neve waited beneath a barren arbor. Tired shadows stood out beneath her eyes, but when she spotted Red, her mouth flickered a smile. "You look well."

She'd availed herself of the washbasin in Neve's room, wiping stray smudges of dirt from her jaw, working out the snarls in her hair. It was the first time in a long while Red had looked in a mirror for the purpose of seeing herself, and the changes were obvious. Her eyes weren't as hollow. Her mouth wasn't so thin. The line of her shoulders was crooked, like something weighed on them. It had reminded her of Eammon, and she'd had to squeeze her eyes shut for a moment.

Red dropped a mock curtsy. "It's been a while since I wore a dress," she said, picking at the embroidery on her sleeve.

"You *would* reappear dressed like a storybook huntsman." Neve shook her head, lips twisted in a wry grin. "I'm surprised no courtiers swooned at the immodesty."

"Immodest or not, dressing like a storybook huntsman is far more practical."

The grin vanished. "For traipsing through the Wilderwood, I suppose it is."

Her voice drew battle lines. Red wilted.

Neve turned to walk down the pathway, and Red fell in beside her, their silence as chilly as the autumn air. The twigs of a barren hedge scraped Red's arm as they passed. She could almost *see* the leaves withering, months of decay distilled into seconds. A strange scent tickled her nose, cold and somehow familiar. It plucked at her, something she should recognize, but she couldn't quite draw all of it together into a conclusion. "What's wrong with them?"

Neve's shoulders stiffened, but her voice was mild. "It's been a hard autumn."

Autumn had just begun, but Red didn't mention that. A leaf dropped from the hedge to the cobblestone path. She frowned, nudging it with her toe. It crumpled to dust, leaving a brittle skeleton ringed with dead lace.

"I know the gardens don't look like much," Neve said. "I should probably get someone to fix them. But no one passes through this way, really, unless they're on the way to the Shrine."

The mention of the Shrine seemed to tug at both of their frames, up straighter and away from each other. Silence fell between them, shining and brittle as springtime ice.

When Neve reached out and grabbed Red's hand, her palm was slick with sweat. "My intention was always to save you." The sincerity could slice. "Everything I've done, it was to save you."

"Neve, I told you." Red's voice sounded soothing, falsely gentle, and she hated it. Hadn't Neve spoken to her the same way, countless times? Like an animal struggling in a trap and only making it cut deeper? "I don't need saving. Eammon is a good man, and he needs me. I understand why you did it, but hurting the Wilderwood—"

"Hurts you." Neve's eyes had closed when Red said Eammon's name. Now they stayed that way, squeezing tighter. "Hurting the Wilderwood hurts you."

"Yes." Red wasn't sure what else to say.

"I should've expected this." Neve released Red's hand, slowly, like lowering something in a grave. "They tried to warn me the forest wouldn't let you go easily. It doesn't matter whether it's the son or the father, the Wilderwood made the Wolves monsters, and now he's tangled you in it, too."

"All Eammon has done is be bound to the Wilderwood for a bargain he had no part in." Red grabbed her sleeve, pulled it up so her Mark glared in the sunlight. "If that makes him a monster, what does it make me?"

No answer. The air between them all but vibrated.

Dark shadows deepened under Neve's eyes, her sigh stooping her shoulders. "You wanted to see the Shrine."

She'd nearly forgotten, in the rush of her anger. Red nodded, but she didn't pull her sleeve down. The tendrils of her Mark curled beneath her skin, stark and solid as ink.

"Come on, then." Neve started back down the path, drifting beneath thorny arbors that used to hold flowers.

She stopped just outside the arched stone entrance, looking back at Red over her shoulder. The swirl of emotions on her face was hard to parse—sadness and hope and fear and relief. "You should light a candle," she said softly. "You should pray."

"I don't want to pray."

A swallow worked the narrow column of Neve's throat. "Then do it for me." She disappeared into the dark.

Red closed her eyes, took a shaking breath. She could light a candle, if Neve wished it. No one but her would know she cursed the Kings as it burned.

She stepped into the Shrine.

Nothing was different. Maybe it'd been foolish of her to think this would be so easy, that whatever she needed to find and reverse would be immediately apparent.

But on second glance, there were subtle changes. Dark-gray candles flickered on the ledges of altars, at Gaya's marble feet. Red frowned—she remembered them being crimson. The darkness behind the statue, that second room with its gauzy curtain and sentinel shards, seemed somehow deeper than before. Like the cavern had grown larger.

And Neve was nowhere to be seen.

Apprehension crawled up Red's throat. She crept forward, between the carvings of Second Daughters and the Five Kings. "Neve?"

"Here." Her sister's voice rose from behind the statue, muffled by the curtain. It reminded Red of the day before she left. Neve rushing through the morning-lit archway, candle guttering and voice rasping, begging her one last time to run.

Red felt like running now.

Cautiously, she moved farther into the Shrine. She picked up the curtain, candlelight flickering over her hands as she lifted it away.

The cavern behind was massive, far larger than before. But that wasn't what set shock deep in her belly, what made her mouth fall open.

It was the sentinels.

Branches cut through the stone floor while rotting, shadow-dripping roots spanned the dark ceiling, a forest growing in the wrong direction. Scarlet stains marked the bone-white bark, smears like handprints.

Anchored in rock, watered with blood. Sentinels, but inverted, twisted, so the pent-up magic that made the Shadowlands could be freed. The Wilderwood taken and turned to horror, power tainted with the darkness it held back, ripped up and *harvested*.

Deep within Red's chest, her shard of the forest mourned, a soundless scream rattling her bones and making her muscles go numb.

She didn't know she'd fallen to her knees until the stone bit into them, a sharp ache that still held no candle to the pain reverberating from the Wilderwood. A high, keening noise echoed around her ears, she and the sentinels in chorus.

"See?" Kiri's voice was cold and clinical. Red saw her through tear-blurred vision, a slash of white skin and red hair against the sickly trees, the same colors as the bark and the blood. "I knew it'd be more apparent here, in our grove. The Wilderwood is in her still, Neverah, and if you want her back, we'll have to cut it out." Her eyes gleamed, fixed on Red like a predator's. "It will weaken the cursed forest further, losing its anchor. This could be a blessing."

Neve's face was drawn, but her mouth was a decided line, and agonized love shone in her eyes.

It made all this so much worse, that love.

"You can't." Red shook her head, though the movement was agony against the rioting, twisting thread of magic in her center. "Neve, you can't do this."

Shadow hissed as it dripped from the roots above their heads, liquid rot. With every drop that hit the floor, the veins in Kiri's and Neve's wrists flared black.

And Neve didn't answer.

A glint of silver—Kiri drew a blade from within her sleeve.

She swept forward, blade held high, then slashed it down Red's forearm. Red had the mental clarity to roll away, to keep the knife from going deep, but the blade sliced enough of her to make her bleed. She clapped her other hand over it, Eammon's voice echoing between her ears—*don't bleed where the trees can taste it.*

Abruptly, the keening of the inverted sentinels silenced, like they'd all heard the slash.

Like they could smell her blood.

Kiri pried Red's hand from the cut, peered at it. "That can't be right," she muttered, the cadence veering out of sane rhythm, her voice jagging higher. "That can't be right! Every Second Daughter is bound!" She raised the knife again.

"Kiri!" Neve, her voice strained, like she'd had to call it up from some hidden place. Indecision was written into every line of her, her mind changing direction too quickly for her body to follow. Her hands outstretched, her eyes wide, darkness gathering in her wrists.

But Red didn't have time to figure out if this was what Neve wanted or if it had spiraled out of her control—she was listening to the silence of the inverted sentinels, and remembering Eammon's voice, and careening rapidly toward a plan.

Kiri raged on. "If I have to cut to your heart to find the damn roots, I—"

Red reached up, snatched the knife away too quickly for Kiri to react. Teeth bared, she ran the blade across her palm, nearly deep enough to see the gleam of bone. She'd done this only once, she didn't know how much blood she'd need. Then, with a snarling, animal sound, she slammed her hand to the floor. "Go on!" she screamed at the Wilderwood. "Isn't this what you wanted? Take me! Take what you fucking need!"

There was a moment of hesitation, as if the Wilderwood had to question itself, had to decide how to use what she was offering. The shard of it she carried, the seed of her magic, bloomed only to wither again in a parade of indecision.

And she knew, somehow, that this wasn't everything the

Wilderwood needed. That this was more complicated than a sliced hand on its roots. There was still a piece she hadn't quite grasped, a necessity beyond mere healing—a new factor in the tangled, complex equation of trees and Second Daughters. Something the forest wouldn't take unless she understood *exactly* what it was, what it would cost, and offered it anyway.

We will wait for your choice, it'd said as she slipped out between the trees. The decision it'd made, that night in the clearing. The Wilderwood had taken before, taken what wasn't its own, and it was never enough. It waited for her choice, and that choice must be made in full knowledge of what it meant, not in a moment of panicked desperation.

The seed of her magic coiled deeper, down and away from the forest outside. It would wait.

All of this in a torrent, a rush of knowledge from the shard of strange power she'd carried for four years. Red couldn't make sense of it, not now, so she just pressed her bloody hand to the floor hard enough to feel rock dust in her veins.

"Blasphemy." Kiri didn't go for the knife. She stretched her hands out, cold and darkness gathering in her veins. "Godless, heretical thing."

Red clenched her eyes shut, hand still pressed to the ground, and waited for that frozen, inverted magic.

But nothing came. Only a gurgle.

She looked behind her—Kiri, held suspended, Neve's hands clasped on either side of her throat. The same darkness she'd seen Kiri use gathered in her sister's hands, cold enough to chill.

"Neve?" Red's voice sounded so small.

Her twin's face was not apologetic. Darkness had overtaken the whites of her eyes, swallowing her irises in black; the veins below her lids ran inky. "I won't leave you," she snarled, showing her teeth. "I won't leave you to him, Red, but I can't... not like this."

Stillness. Red's hand still pressed to the ground, blood pumping out of her and into the twisted sentinels, and she and her sister stared at each other, veins lined in black and green.

Then, a rumble.

The roots in the ceiling vibrated, breaking through the rock that held them, scattering dust. Golden phosphorescence swirled under shadow-rotted bark, gathering the darkness like a bandage soaking up blood as the sentinels sank down from swollen, misshapen trees to the branches they'd been before. A drop of shadow froze before Red's face, shuddering in suspended motion, before reversing direction and seeping back into the roots above—inverted magic, righting itself.

It weakened Neve's grip, made the dark veins beneath her skin stutter. Her hands dropped, and Kiri, now freed from her frozen hold, rounded on her with a shriek.

"You won't stop this!" Kiri screamed it, eyes alight, everything in them mad and empty. "You won't keep us *godless*!"

She raised her hand to strike, gathering shards of that stuttering dark power, but then a rock fell from above, knocking her prone and out of sight. Neve disappeared in a cloud of dust, slumping sideways, her eyes rolling up in her head.

Roots pulled out of the ceiling, destabilizing it; the floor shuddered as the barren branches cutting through the rock shrank away. It sounded like an earthquake, it felt like an apocalypse. Red's vision dimmed at the edges, her cheek pressed against the breaking stone as her hand trailed blood across the floor. All she wanted was to rest, to lie still...

Another rock fell, landed on Red's uncut hand. She screamed as the bones shattered, but it was enough of a shock to make her move. Adrenaline helped her push the rock away, rise to staggering feet. Lurching, she tried to move toward where she'd last seen her sister. "Neve!"

No answer but breaking floor, no sound but cracking stone. "*Neve!*" A sob built in her throat, sharp as the bones in her mangled hand.

The ceiling wouldn't hold much longer. Larger pieces fell, cracking against the floor, and the doorway grew rapidly smaller as ruin piled around it. Swallowing another sob, Red dashed for the narrow opening, spilling past stone Second Daughters and burning candles, bloody and broken.

Her knees hit the cobblestones outside the Shrine. She tried to rise, failed. A scream hissed through her teeth, pain hitting her in waves.

"Redarys?"

Arick's boots filled her vision as he crouched in the autumn sun. His voice was harsh, jagged. "What have you done? Where's Neve?"

Red didn't answer. Instead, she focused on the cobblestones behind him. On what wasn't there. Her pain brought clarity, stripped the truth bare in her voice. "You don't have a shadow."

He paused. Then something sharp on her temple, and the world went black.

Chapter Twenty-Nine

Amber eyes and a soft mouth, dark hair between her fingers. Red was loath to wake, even as cold water dripped down her neck, stones digging into her back. But she roused, peeled her eyes open, pain fading in as dreams of Eammon faded out.

Damp rock walls, metal bars. A dungeon.

Logically, she'd known there were dungeons under the Valleydan palace, but she never remembered them being used. The ceiling began mere inches above her head, and a single guttering sconce provided the only light. Through the dim, she could barely make out another cell across a skinny, damp hallway. Masses of shadow lurked behind the bars.

Red dared a look at her hand. A mess of awful angles, everything bent the wrong way beneath her skin. The other hand, the one she'd sliced, was scarlet and angry and tacky with blood. Pain churned to nausea; she retched, but nothing came up.

Gritting her teeth, Red placed her lacerated hand against the wall. Behind it, she could sense the deep roots of growing things above—grasses and weeds threading through the dirt. A shuddering breath, and she bent her fingers slowly, tugging at the thin curl of her magic in her chest, seeing if she could manage enough to pull them toward her, just as a test.

The magic roused, barely. Enough to feel, not enough to use, not enough to affect the growing things beyond the wall. Her hand fell.

She squeezed her eyes shut, taking the thoughts pain shattered, piecing them together into the path that led here. Arick, asking after Neve. His boot on her temple. He'd brought her to a dungeon, where no one would think to look for her.

And he didn't have a shadow.

Desperation thrummed at the base of her throat. Red crooked her unbroken fingers again, coaxing fruitlessly at her splintered power.

"It's the walls."

Arick strode down the damp hallway, lit by guttering torchlight, hands clasped behind his back. He moved differently—before, Arick walked as if the world would wait on him, loose and languid. Now his posture was at almost-military attention. The dim light told her nothing about his shadow.

Red swallowed against a bone-dry throat. "What?"

He tapped his knuckles nonchalantly on the wall beside the bars. "This deadens magic. I'm not sure how, to be honest. Valchior was a hard ruler, and he didn't like for anyone to be better at calling power than he, back when it was free for the taking. Still doesn't." Another tap before he tucked his hands behind his back again, regal despite the damp. "In any case, he didn't share his secrets with the rest of us."

Her head ached, and his nonsense made it throb harder. "You *kicked* me."

"I did." He didn't seem sorry. "You hurt Neve."

Neve. Red looked up, hope sharp and sudden. "Is she alive? Did she make it out?"

Arick opened his mouth to answer, but another voice beat him to it. "No thanks to you."

A slender figure stepped into the transient light. Kiri. Two bluish handprints marked the sides of her neck where Neve had held her, made her voice a whispery rasp. "You've long outlived your usefulness, Second Daughter. Now you're nothing but a liability."

"Kiri." Arick's eyes were a colorless glitter. "Hush."

Red's whole body was a knot of agony. She searched Arick's face, looking for some kind of warmth, any echo of the man she'd known. But he watched her like an animal in a cage, observing her pain with nothing more than vague curiosity.

Behind him, in the half-illuminated cell, the mass of shadow shifted.

Red's eyes squeezed shut against the throb of her wounded hands. "Neve is alive." If she didn't phrase it like a question, the answer couldn't be *no*. "She's all right."

"Neve is safe." Arick's voice held a strange note of softness. "As safe as I can make her."

That, at least, brought a flood of relief. "Why am I here? What is this place?"

"A place for things that work against our gods." Kiri's lip lifted in a sneer. "Things like *you*."

Arick's jaw tightened.

"We'll save them." Kiri's eyes rose to the ceiling of the dungeon, mildewed and moldering, with the light of someone looking on holiness. Her hands rose to her chest like her heart was something she could cradle. "Now that you're here, now that we know you are empty and the Wolf stands alone. We've made the Wilderwood weak, their time is soon at hand. Our Kings will finally return, and our rewards will be great." Her unsound eyes turned to Arick, head bending to bow. "*All* of our Kings, in the flesh."

Distaste lived in the set of Arick's mouth, but he said nothing. Arick, who made it a point to think of the Wilderwood and the Five Kings as little as possible. Arick, who had no patience for things regarded as holy.

"You don't want the Kings back." Red shook her throbbing head. "Eammon told me—"

"Of course he did." Arick rolled his eyes. "The boy's just like his father, mistaking foolishness for nobility. I told Ciaran things would end badly when he and Gaya concocted their stupid plan. He never listened, either."

It slid around in Red's head, still, pain taking over the space she needed to parse all this into sense. But the mention of Ciaran stuck in her mind like a burr, and her eyes narrowed. Eammon's father, spoken of like a friend.

Or a rival.

"You're lucky the boy's improved his control," Arick continued. "He tried to hold the roots back from the others, but the Wilderwood had its way in the end. You're the first who's had a choice in the matter." His eyes narrowed. "You could've left at any time, saved your sister a world of heartbreak. There was never any Wilderwood in you at all, not enough to make any difference. You're rootless, Redarys. Nothing but bones and blood."

Arick crouched so they were level. Surely it was just the dim light and the haze in her head, but his eyes seemed strange, not quite the right color.

"You won't let yourself be saved." His not-quite-right eyes searched hers. "That's what he told me. Not by him, not by Neve. Determined to be a martyr."

"Let her be a martyr, then." Fervor in Kiri's voice, in her claw-like hands. "Her only use was to keep the Queen in line, but she couldn't even do that." She pointed to the handprints on her throat. "She went rogue, we need to—"

"*Kiri.*" Her name was a slap of sound, and the High Priestess dropped her hands like a cowed child. Her eyes were ice chips.

"We'll keep her here," Arick continued. A pause, and his tone softened. "Neve's already lost too much. I won't let her lose her sister, too."

It should've been comforting, but his face made it clear—Neve was the only thing saving Red. There was bitter, spiking irony to it.

"Besides," Arick murmured, almost to himself, "she could prove useful yet. I'll need total surrender from the Wolf for this to work." His eyes caught the light of the sconce, glittered cold. "He's familiar with bargaining."

"Arick." It was a whisper, a plea. Red's cracked lips tasted of copper. "I don't understand."

Behind Arick, the shadowy mass in the other cell moved. Groaned.

Kiri whirled, poised to strike, but Arick held out an open palm. "No." His eyes cut from the priestess to Red, considering. Then he shrugged. "Let her see. I tire of holding the illusion."

Arick's arm fell, and the lines of his face rearranged, seeping shadow like smoke.

Red blinked, sure her head injury affected her vision. But the drip and merge of his features continued, like water thrown over a still-wet canvas. A sharper jaw than Arick's, edged in a short, dark beard. Long hair, past his shoulders, somewhere between brown and gold. Pale skin, blue eyes. Handsome, in a cruel way.

Not-Arick rolled his shoulders, a slight smile picking up the side of his mouth at her horrified expression. Next to him, Kiri's teeth shone predator-bright. "Ask his name," she whispered, fierce and low. "Ask his name, and tremble for it."

The man grinned at Red. "I think she knows."

"Solmir." It came out hoarse, it came out sure.

The youngest of the Five Kings nodded. "Astute." He stepped to the side, waved a regal hand at the cell bars behind him. "But another desires an audience, Second Daughter."

The shadows coalesced, like he'd given them permission, and became a body. Familiar eyes blinked against torchlight. A familiar face, though grimed in blood and dirt. Arick's hands, covered in cuts, closed around the bars. "Red?"

Red tried to make a sound, tried to call to him, but all she could muster was one sob. Her bleeding hand pressed against her mouth.

"Arick," she murmured, tear tracks clearing dirt and dust from her cheeks. "Arick, what have you done?"

"What he had to." Solmir stood like a jailer, arms crossed and brows low. "He saw a chance, and he took it. We all do foolish things for love. To feel like we have a purpose." He nodded to Kiri, who picked up a battered cup from the floor, the edge rusty with old blood. "Go on and tell her, Arick. I'm sure she'll want the whole sordid tale."

Arick's eyes closed. He titled his forehead against the bars. "I bargained," he said quietly as Kiri picked up his hand, as she cut into it with a tiny dagger. "I went to the Wilderwood, I found one of the white trees near the border. It...leaned. Leaned over, like it was about to fall, like the ground around it was close to giving way. That's how I could touch it. Just one branch. Just barely." He shook his head, slowly. "It *hurt*, the hum, like someone'd stuck a whole sawmill in my ribs. But I got close enough."

"Why?" She shook her head, stars spangling in her eyes. "*How?* The Wilderwood doesn't bargain anymore, it's not strong enough."

"But the things in the Shadowlands are." It didn't sound like a boast. It sounded weary. Solmir leaned his back against the wall.

"A living sacrifice." Kiri smiled beatifically. "A living sacrifice, fresh from the vein."

Black and scarlet welled from Arick's palm, shadow swirling through his blood as it dripped into the cup.

"And once blood has been used to bargain with the Shadowlands," Kiri continued, "it can be used to invert the Wilderwood. The boy's shadow-tainted blood awakened the branches in the Shrine, set them to a nobler purpose. And all who offered more blood afterward reaped a harvest of power, just as promised to me in my long years of praying." Apparently satisfied, she shoved Arick's limp and bleeding hand back through the bars, rounded on Red. "You think you've won by defiling our grove, cursed thing? You know *nothing*. Five lives are—"

"Shadows damn us, woman, do you ever stop talking?" One long-fingered hand covered Solmir's eyes. Kiri's teeth snapped shut.

"That's why you don't have a shadow." Instinct made her hands curl despite her injuries, and a new wave of pain drove Red's teeth together. "You're *Arick's* shadow. And he's yours, when he has to be." She shook her throbbing head. "All this, and you aren't really here."

"Oh, I'm here." Solmir's hand dropped, eyes glittering. "Here enough."

"The white tree was easy to see." Arick spoke low and almost slurred, like he was recounting a dream. An exorcism, the whole bloody tale spinning out of him now that he'd started. "So pale against the rest, like bone." The hand Kiri had cut flexed open convulsively. The deep puncture wound in his palm blazed lurid scarlet, a black spot of rot blooming in its center, sending sickened tendrils through his skin. "I bled on it. Living sacrifice. Just like she told me."

Kiri smiled.

"And it...opened." Even now, Arick sounded horrified, like he couldn't believe what he'd done. "The branch reared back, like... like something *alive*, like a startled horse. There was this sound, this awful tearing sound, and a *boom*. And then *he* was there, standing right at the edge of the trees, shadows curled around him like chains. And he asked what I wanted, and what I would give for it."

"What did you want?" She knew. She asked anyway.

Arick didn't answer, but his head bowed lower.

"He wanted a way to save you." Solmir said it like it bored him. "And he said he would give everything."

Oh, Arick. Arick, telling her he loved her over and over, even when she never said it back. Arick, building a castle in the air where they could have a happy ending, mortaring it with blood and empty promises.

"At first he was just my shadow." Arick recounted the tale to the damp floor, like looking at Red hurt. "But then...when things..."

"He couldn't stomach it." Kiri swirled the cup of his blood under her nose like wine, breathing deep. "He couldn't handle when we realized they needed killing, the High Priestess and the Queen. So they changed places. One the shadow, one the man."

"I'll have you remember that you were the only one who decided they needed killing," Solmir murmured. "But once it happened, Arick wanted... distance from the situation."

Red could taste her heartbeat. Her stomach twisted on itself. "How could you?" It was a breath of sound, a wound in the air. "How could you do that to Neve?"

"It was *for* Neve." Solmir pushed off the wall, mouth a snarl. "Kiri may have overstepped, but this is what Neve wanted, whether she'll admit it or not. She was just as desperate to save you as Arick was. She would do *anything* for you, Redarys. You don't deserve a tenth of her love."

Red lunged at the bars, her unbroken hand smacking against the metal. She recognized the warmth in his voice, the shape of things it didn't say. "If you touched her," she rasped, "I'll kill you."

Solmir watched her with unreadable eyes. His hands turned to fists, then relaxed. "I didn't," he said, quiet enough to mask whatever emotion lived in it.

Behind him, Arick pulled in a shaking breath. "We just wanted to save you." His eyes rose, bruised and dark. "Especially once we learned what was coming. We just wanted to save you, Red."

"You can calm down the groveling, then." Now composed, Solmir propped his foot against the wall again. "Redarys saved herself."

Her teeth ground together. "I still don't know *what you're talking about.*"

"The *roots.*" Solmir rolled his eyes. "You haven't taken them, though it's clear you care for the Wolf. You're a practical woman, apparently. You've learned love isn't reason enough for ruin. You chose to save yourself."

Choice.

She thought of the Wilderwood in the cavern, that awareness that it needed more from her, something it would no longer deign to take. She thought of Eammon, straining under the weight of the sentinels as they came for her again and again, trying to finish something started long ago. She thought of bones at the base of a tree, testaments to all the Second Daughters who came before, drained by a desperate forest that hadn't yet learned its lesson. Hadn't yet learned that something taken would only wither, while something given might grow.

She thought of roots.

Solmir's lip curled. "The Wilderwood will fall. The Wolf will die. The Kings will be freed." He shrugged, eyes narrowed, voice rueful. "And everyone will get what they wanted."

Understanding came like the sudden bloom of a night flower, unfurling all at once in new light.

A choice had to be made, and here was hers.

"I'll take them," Red breathed.

Three pairs of eyes shot to her, confusion in each gaze, but Red paid no attention. Mustering up all her focus, all her will, she pulled at the thin thread of deep-green power in her center, made it bloom despite the deadening walls. It felt like it might kill her, every tug of blood through her veins a challenge, but still she pulled.

Red took a deep breath and pressed the edge of her sliced palm to the bone of her hip, pushing until the cut split farther and fresh blood seeped from her skin. With a pained gasp, she slapped her bloody hand to the floor of her cell.

Bleeding, and hoping with everything in her the trees could taste it.

"I want the roots," she said, voice bell-clear and carrying. "I understand what it means, and I want them anyway, because I am for the Wolf, and the Wolves are for the Wilderwood."

For a breath, the four of them froze in suspended silence. Then—a roar, a rush, as if a million stones overturned at once, as if something sped under the ground like some great beast flashing beneath the surface of the sea.

Roots, rushing from the north to flow into her waiting wound.

The floor cracked as the roots of the Wilderwood thrust up toward her hand, miles traveled in an instant at the call of her blood. The first press of it against the slice in her skin stung, but after that, the way the roots seeped in and curled around her bones felt like home.

The Wilderwood had finally learned, that night when Eammon almost lost himself to it. A Mark and words on a tree and invaded blood wouldn't sustain it anymore. It needed her to choose it.

To choose *him*.

And she had been, by slow increments, ever since she met him. Choosing the black curl of his hair and the rough texture of his scars, the way the corner of his lip lifted, just so, when she said something he thought was funny. How his brows lowered when he read and how right before he fell asleep he'd let out a long, soft sigh and *Kings* how his mouth felt on hers, how he clung to her like ivy against the stone walls of their Keep.

It was, in the end, the easiest choice she'd ever made.

The seed in her grew and grew, unfettered by anything because it was *hers*, hers by word and blood.

It was a quiet storm of root and thorn and branch, the deluge of the Wilderwood finally coming for her—not as a predator, but as a missing piece, grateful to finally fit against the splintered edges it had left. The thin tendril of power she'd been given four years ago sped out to meet the rest of itself, and when she breathed deep, she tasted loam, growing things, honey.

Arick, shadow-thin, threw an arm over his face. Solmir pushed off from the wall with his teeth bared. "Shadows *damn* you—"

His words were lost in the rush. The power in her center met the power outside, collided and *bloomed*, filling her with root and branch. It grew in the hollows of her lungs, climbed along her spine, vines wrapping organs and seeding in her marrow.

The darkness behind her eyelids was shaped like leaves. And when it cleared, she saw Eammon. Not just his hands, not just the world through his eyes—him, entire, almost something she could reach out and touch.

He jolted from his seat at the edge of their bed, like he saw her as clearly as she saw him. Amber eyes cycled through shock, and wonder, and finally terror as he leapt, hand reaching out to empty air, mouth shaping her name—

Then he was gone, and she glowed golden in a dungeon with the roots of the Wilderwood between her bones.

Red pushed out her hands, fingers crooked. The tiny roots of grass above them grew long, stretched toward her, spangling the ceiling with starburst shatters and sending rock dust raining.

Kiri tried to cower against Solmir, but he knocked her to the side, thrusting out his hands and shaping his fingers into claws. Shadows gathered, but Red was flush with the power of a whole, healed Wilderwood, and all she had to do was arch a hand in his direction. Golden light wrapped Solmir's fists, straightened his fingers, and he roared agony at the stone ceiling as it consumed his own cold magic, canceled it out.

"You'll abandon her." Solmir gritted his teeth, blue eyes glittering in Red's light. "You'll be trapped in the Wilderwood, forever. You're choosing him over her."

It made her heart feel too large for her ribs, made the beat of it against vine and bloom a painful thud. "If the Wilderwood falls and the Shadowlands break through, I'll lose them both."

"Then you have little faith in her." Still a snarl, but there was something sorrowing in it. "Neve takes to shadows better than you think."

Her lips peeled back from her teeth at that warmth in his voice again. Red closed her hand to a fist, jerked it sideways.

The light wrapped around Solmir's hands swept him in the direction Red willed it, bashing his head against a fallen rock from the ceiling. He fell next to Kiri and lay still.

Red's glow bathed the dungeon, though already the pain was starting, the roots pulling her toward the Wilderwood. The forest reeled her back like the roots in her body were a kite string. More dust spilled from the ceiling, the sound of breaking rock a discordant symphony.

Slumped against the wall, Arick looked half a corpse. His eyes were hollows, cheekbones knife-sharp. He winced away, like she hurt his eyes.

Red thrust out her hand. "Come with me!"

A stone fell from the ceiling and should have hit him; instead, it fell to the floor, like Arick was formed of smoke, like *he'd* become the shadow.

Arick shook his head. "I can't, Red." A tear slid down his cheek, cleared it of dirt. "I'm tied to him. I can't leave."

"Please." She reached through the bars like she could hold his bloody hand, knowing it was fruitless, begging anyway. "Please."

"Go, Red." Another fall of rock, another rain of dust. "You have to *go*!"

Sobbing against pain of two kinds, Red bent her fingers again. Grass roots wrapped around the bars, made impossibly strong by the magic of the Wilderwood. They split, rending from stone with an awful tearing sound, and she climbed through, squeezing between the wall and the already-fallen rocks on bare, bleeding feet.

Neve. She had to find Neve. Red closed her eyes, pelting blindly down the corridor as if the golden glow of the roots could guide her toward her sister. Pain lanced every limb, but she gritted her teeth against it. A grate up ahead filtered starlight onto the stone floor; Red scrambled through, leaking green-threaded blood from her unbroken hand, the other still a mess of agony at the end of her wrist. She emerged on an empty alley next to the palace walls, and tried to rush forward, searching for a gate, a way in.

A scream ripped from her mouth as the roots tightened around her bones, pulling her back in the opposite direction. Red strained against it, her pleading audible now. "Please, I have to at least tell her goodbye, please..."

The Wilderwood didn't answer, not in words. But she could feel its apology, feel it in the gentling of the vines around her spine, the bloom along her rib cage. Growing, and pulling her inexorably away.

Still, she struggled forward. Her vision blackened, and she fell to her knees on the cobblestones, a harsh sob in her throat. With as much care as they could, the sentinels reached their roots into her, curling around her organs, calling her back home.

Home.

Neve wasn't dead. Solmir claimed she was safe, and though she loathed the softness with which he said her sister's name, she believed him. Believed that he wouldn't hurt her, that he'd protect her, in his own twisted way.

And Red would know if Neve was dead.

Her head hung low. Red released one more wrenching sob. Then she turned and ran toward the Wilderwood.

Chapter Thirty

Red smacked the stolen horse's flank, sending it running back toward the village. She doubted he'd make it all the way back to the capital—he was a fine thing, and whoever found him bridle-less and wandering could probably use him more than some drunk lord could.

The forest in her bones had guided her through the city, invisible as any urchin in her bare feet and bloody dress. Pain still splintered through her limbs, but it was manageable, and lessened as she moved northward. The horse she stole from a tavern's hitching post, his rope carelessly tied. Riding under the deep-blue cover of sky and stars reminded her of sixteen and Neve, and she wept into his mane.

The Wilderwood was different. When she'd left—yesterday, only yesterday—it'd looked like the dead of winter, branches gnarled and bare, leaves gray on the ground. Now glimmers of autumn shone gold and ocher, seasons moving in reverse. In her chest, roots reached, stretching through the gaps in her ribs like she was water and air and sun.

It ached when Red turned toward Valleyda, pulling at the roots as they grew, but she did it anyway. She stood on the slight hill just before the forest's edge, the crossroads of two homes that were never content to share her.

Her eyes closed, tear tracks drying on her cheeks. Maybe if she stood here long enough, right at the edge of her world, Neve might sense her.

Maybe Red could will her reasoning into the earth, weave some kind of understanding into the air her twin would eventually breathe.

"I love you." An echo of the first time she'd disappeared between these same trees. Neve's promise that day had come true—they'd seen each other again. Red hadn't made a promise, not out loud, but this felt like it coming true, anyway. Her place had always been the forest.

One more deep breath of outside air, then Red slipped into the Wilderwood.

Trees stretched tall, branches spread in fanfare. The moss made a carpet for her bare feet. The sentinels speared up from the ground, tall and proud with no trace of rot around their roots.

A trick of the light made it almost look like they bowed.

The forest inside her stung as it grew, as it anchored. Above her, the sky faded from lavender to plum, and Red's breath hitched in her chest.

The Wilderwood soothed in a voice of rustling leaves. A vine grazed along the ridge of her shoulders in comfort.

"Red?"

Lyra picked through the forest deft as a fawn. "I thought you said three days?" There was something stricken in her voice, her manner.

"I got homesick," Red whispered.

Golden leaves crunched beneath Lyra's feet as she approached, brows drawn into a question she already knew the answer to. Tentatively, she laid her hand on Red's arm. Static rent the air, a sharp crackle like the atmosphere before a thunderstorm, and Lyra hissed as she pulled her hand back, dark eyes wide.

"Oh," she breathed, understanding distilled into one syllable.

Red's knees felt weak. "I figured it out."

Everything chased her, everything catching up. Adrenaline spiked in her middle, memories of Arick and twisted sentinels, Kiri's knife, Solmir's face. And Neve, Neve beyond her saving. Spots swam in her vision. "Where's Eammon?"

Lyra's face was unreadable. "Waiting for you." She eyed Red's hands, one sliced and bloody, the other clearly broken. "Those need to be seen to. Come on."

Red followed Lyra silently through the trees. It made a path for her, the Wilderwood, retracting roots and thorns. A fall of leaves fluttered to the ground.

One lighted in Lyra's curls. She plucked it out, turned it over in her hands. "*Kings*," she murmured, something awed in her voice. "It wasn't like this before. Even with... with the others."

"The others didn't have a choice." Red reached out with her cut hand and touched the bark of a sentinel as she passed. It was warm beneath her palm, soothing on the slices. "I did. Eammon made sure I did."

Lyra nodded. She opened her hand. The leaf fluttered to the ground.

When they reached the gate, he was waiting. He opened it before they reached the iron, running across the forest floor, eyes wide and mouth set and arms warm as they wrapped around her, tight enough to pick her up off the ground.

Eammon's fingers shook as he pushed her hair away from her face, traced her jaw. Red rested her forehead against his chest. Warmth bloomed, the forest in him welcoming the forest in her, a missing piece fitted into place.

"What did you do, Red?" Horror laced Eammon's voice, and when she looked into his eyes, it lived there, too. He pressed his forehead against hers, swallowing hard. "What did you do?"

Fife brought food and wine, but didn't linger, movements small and eyes unreadable. His voice met Lyra's when he climbed back down the stairs, murmuring low and indistinct.

Eammon sat at the foot of the bed, features shadowed by the

blazing fire behind them. Red's hands rested gingerly on her knees, one sliced and scabbed, the other broken. After taking the roots, the pain of them had been nearly forgotten, but now it was a struggle to keep her breathing even.

"They hurt you." Eammon looked at her injuries like he was cataloging each one, debts requiring restitution.

The forest in her chest rustled. "I'm here now. I'll be fine."

"You aren't *fine*." His eyes stayed on her hand, like he could intimidate it into healing, but the vehemence in his voice made it clear he was talking about more than broken bones and dagger cuts.

She touched his wrist, leaving a smear of her blood. "Eammon, I—"

His fingers closed over hers, cutting her off. She tried to pull away, knowing his intention, but warmth and golden light flared before she could. Eammon growled through gritted teeth as cuts opened on one hand, but he didn't pause, reaching for the other. A *pop*, and her bones righted even as his broke over them, the shift sharp against her skin.

Red flinched. She looked at Eammon expecting changes, new height or the whites of his eyes completely taken by green. But other than a faint blush of emerald along Eammon's veins, nothing happened. The bark braceleting his wrists remained, and the green-threaded veins around amber irises, but the Wilderwood wrought no more changes in him.

She'd taken half the roots, rebalanced the scales. Made him closer to man than forest.

His eyes widened, locked on hers. Then they closed, his jaw tightening against the pain he'd taken.

"Self-martyring bastard," she whispered.

A low grunt was his only reply. Eammon went to the desk with its scattered paper, rummaging for a bandage with his bleeding hand. When he found one, he turned his attention to his broken fingers.

Red turned her head and closed her eyes, not wanting to see him set the bones. Another low, strained growl, another *pop* that made her wince.

When she looked back, both his hands were wrapped. He spoke to them rather than her. "You shouldn't have done this. Without the roots, the Wilderwood would've let you go."

"And it would've taken you." The image of him half subsumed in forest was as easy to recall as a recent nightmare. "It needs two, Eammon. You can't carry it all alone, not forever. I couldn't leave you to—"

"You should've left me to *rot*." Eammon did look up then, eyes fierce. "You know what happens." His voice was hoarse, the last word barely sound. He turned away on it, like he didn't want her to see him break.

"It won't happen this time." She knew it, knew it as sure as she knew the shape of his mouth. "This time it's different. I *chose* to take them, knowing the consequences."

"It doesn't matter."

"It does." Gently, she stood from the bed, crossing the room to stand behind him. They didn't touch, and he didn't turn, but every line of him attuned to every line of her. "Eammon, I took the roots because I lo—"

"Don't." A whisper, low and rough. "Don't."

Her lips pressed together, closing the confession behind them.

They stood silent. Eammon's jaw trembled with the effort of keeping it clenched. Finally, he pushed back his hair with his bandaged fingers. "Tell me what happened."

It sent everything careening back, all the emotion she'd cried out as she rode here on a stolen horse. Red's breath shook, a tremor that started in her voice and traveled down her hands. "They have Neve. They have my sister, and now I can't get to her, and I chose it and I wanted it but *shit* they have her, and I—"

"Shhh." His bandaged palms cradled her face, all the ways he held himself apart coming undone at the sight of her crying. "We'll figure something out, Red, I promise you. We'll find a way."

Slowly, she quieted, under the run of his fingers through her hair and the library scent of him in each breath. She felt the moment he stiffened again, when his touch fell away from her and he took a small step back.

But he kept holding her hand. And that gave her enough stability to take a deep lungful of Wilderwood air, and start from the beginning.

Eammon stayed still and quiet through her story, until she recounted Kiri cutting her. Then his teeth ground hard enough for her to hear it over the flames in the grate.

Her voice faltered when she reached the dungeon. "Can you feel it when a new breach happens?"

Confusion knit his brows. "Used to, back when I'd first become the Wolf. Not anymore."

"Arick...Arick made a breach. More than a breach. He bled on a sentinel, opened the Shadowlands." A pause. "He bargained with Solmir."

Silence. Even the fire seemed to deaden its crackle. Eammon's breath scraped harsh, every muscle tensed, new blood staining the bandage on his hand holding hers.

Haltingly, Red told the story. Arick and his terrible bargain, his blood waking the sentinel branches in the Shrine and pulling them away from the Wilderwood, Solmir taking his place. Eammon barely moved. He didn't speak. It was more unsettling than if he'd raged.

"He thought I hadn't taken the roots because I didn't want them." Red darted a look at Eammon, unable to stop the angry tightening of her lips. "He thought you'd told me everything."

The snarl on his face faded to something softer, sadder. "I was afraid if I told you everything, you *would* take them. You'd try to help me." He snorted at the floor, eyes hidden behind his unbound hair. "I was right."

"Of course you were." He knew her well, her Wolf. "Eammon…" She faltered, remembering how he'd reacted when she almost said it before. "I chose this. I chose you."

"You shouldn't have." His voice was a whisper. "I wasn't strong enough to save them, Red. Even after the Wilderwood had them, I tried to hold the worst of it back, to keep the full weight of it away. It still drained them, every time." A shuddering breath. "What if I can't save you?"

"That's what you don't understand. I'm saving *you*." Tentatively, the hand he wasn't holding reached up to cup his cheek. "Let me."

Eammon had held himself tense the whole time she talked, but when she touched his face, all the rigidity faded. His mouth parted, his amber eyes glowed. "Kings." He cursed like one might call for mercy, and his eyes closed as her thumb brushed his bottom lip. "Kings and *shadows*, Redarys."

"You didn't let me finish, earlier, and this feels important to say." Her fingers hooked on his jaw, fierce in their gripping. She said it almost stern, almost like a challenge, daring him to contradict her again. "I *love you*, Eammon."

He shuddered an exhale.

"I'd like to kiss you," she breathed, "but not until I know how you feel about what I just said."

His laugh was sweeter for being unexpected, though quiet and rueful. One of his hands wrapped around her waist, pulling her closer; the other came up to card through her hair. "Of course I love you." There was fire in his touch, fire in his eyes as they burned into hers. "That's why I'm so afraid."

"We can be afraid tomorrow," Red murmured.

And then his mouth was on hers, warm and sweet and tasting of honey, and there was no fear in his hands on her skin, no fear in the feel of his lip between her teeth. His hands cupped her jaw like this was something to protect, something holy, and his tongue pushed at hers before his mouth went to her throat, covering the rapid rhythm of her pulse. She gasped, low and ragged, and they were on the floor, hands fumbling with laces until nothing stood between. He stared at her a moment then, lying on the wooden floor of the tower room with her hair loose and tangled, the ring of her Bargainer's Mark stark against her bared, flushed skin.

The Mark was larger, now, like a representation of the forest blooming in her bones. The ring of root just below her elbow sent tendrils curling away in both directions, reaching from the middle of her forearm to the curve of her shoulder, patterning her skin like lace.

Eammon ran his fingers over it, barely a touch, eyes wide and wondering as they drank her in. "Shadows damn me, you're beautiful," he muttered, then he kissed the Mark, lips brushing the sensitive crook of her arm, tracing up to her collarbone.

She tried to arch up and bring him back to her lips, but Eammon's hand found her other shoulder, pushed her gently back to the floor. "Don't. I've wanted this too long to rush it."

"Is that an order?"

One brow arched over a burning amber eye. "Would you like it if it was?"

"Yes."

He laughed, the warmth of it drifting over her skin. "Good to know." Kisses on her shoulders, her sternum, the curve of her breast, back up to her throat, leaving her breathing shallow and her pulse ragged.

"I wanted it," she murmured against his lips when he reached her mouth again. "The roots, the Mark, I wanted it all."

"I believe you." Another deep kiss, one that made her writhe. A wicked grin. "But I'll let you prove it."

Red drew a hand over the jut of his hip, tugging him toward her, lips curved just as wicked as his voice had been. He made a low sound, fingers tangling in her hair, tipping up her chin. Teeth caught her neck, something that should have hurt but didn't, pulling a moan from her throat and making her hips sway toward him as his mouth went lower. He grinned against her skin as his palms skated over her, his knee between her legs, her back arching off the floor in a wordless plea for more. More of this, more of what they'd been running from for so long now. She wanted to feel every single scar he carried and know them by heart.

Eammon paused, firelight shadowing the dips and hollows of his chest, arm cradling her head. Red squirmed toward his warmth, trying to touch as many surfaces of him as possible.

His thumb traced a light half-moon over her temple. "You're sure?"

"I'm sure." Her fingertip traced his swollen lip, and he shuddered. "Always am, with you."

He surged over her, a tide that swept them both away. The roots of the Wilderwood pulsed, growing deeper, twining together like the Wolves on the floor.

Chapter Thirty-One

At some point, they moved from the floor to the bed, and though Red's limbs ached when she woke, it was due to something more pleasant than hard floors. Eammon's skin was warm beneath her cheek, his arm bent behind her neck and palm resting on the crown of her head. His breath came deep and even, but when she turned to kiss his shoulder, he still made a low, pleased sound and pulled her closer.

Red propped her chin on the scarred plane of his chest. Eammon's overlong hair stuck up at odd angles, mussed from her fingers. His face was soft with sleep, the permanent line between his brows smoothed. Lightly, so as not to wake him, she traced it with a finger.

The Wilderwood, coiled around her bones, pulled marginally tighter. Red squirmed against the ache. Nothing about anchoring a forest within your skin was comfortable, especially as it grew and settled in.

Another twinge, enough to make her wince, and a faint sound through the open windows. A sigh, shaped by fluttering leaves and the stretch and bloom of branches.

Brow furrowed, Red carefully extricated herself from Eammon. He grumbled but didn't wake, burrowing his head farther in the pillow. She picked up the first item of discarded clothing she touched on the floor—his shirt—and pulled it over her head, arms wrapped around her chest as she crept to the window.

Autumn blazed in the Wilderwood. Scarlet and gold, a swath of sunset colors more vibrant than any she'd seen in Valleyda. Fog still rolled over the ground, but now it seemed ethereal, soft rather than sinister. Fallen leaves carpeted the forest floor, but the ones still clinging to the tree limbs were blushed with green, like autumn was moving backward, slowly blooming into summer.

For a moment, Red was too wrapped up in it to heed its pull. She and Eammon had made the Wilderwood whole, finally brought it balance. The beauty of it made her breath catch.

But there was one thing more to do, and the forest urged her forward.

Red pressed her lips together, the chilly air through the window raising goose bumps on her skin. She looked over her shoulder at Eammon, still sleeping.

Let him sleep, she thought. *You can lay bones to rest yourself.*

And there was something right in it. Something right about Red being the one to try, however falteringly, to give the other Second Daughters peace.

She pulled a pair of leggings from the wardrobe, stuck her feet in her boots. She went to grab her scarlet cloak before remembering it was still in Valleyda. One shaky sigh, that she'd left it there, but a marriage was more than a cloak. As for the other reasons she'd kept it—the claiming of who she was, *what* she was—she didn't need a cloak for that anymore, either. She knew it in her bones, she wore it in her eyes instead of on her shoulders.

The note she'd left for Eammon about wanting the bed back still sat on his desk, like he'd carefully placed it right back where he'd found it. Red flipped it over, scrawled new words. *I'm in the clearing.* Then, with a wry twist of her mouth: *Wolf-things.*

The sky was pale lilac instead of lavender, like it strove for daybreak, and the Wilderwood stood in silent reverence as Red moved through it. The path to the clearing where she'd saved Eammon wound through the forest outlined in golden leaves; her boots crunching over them was the only sound.

The sentinel with the Second Daughters' bones clustered around its roots stood taller than the others, its branches already green-leafed. The scar on the bark was still there, where something had been cut away. She'd put together what it meant—this was the tree where Gaya and Ciaran made their bargain. Where they became Wolves. Whether the other Second Daughters had been drawn to the tree to die or their bones appeared there through some strange Wilderwood magic, she wasn't sure. But it seemed fitting.

The site felt holier than the Shrine ever had.

Three skulls sat at equidistant points along the sentinel's trunk. Kaldenore, Sayetha, Merra. Three women the Wilderwood had taken and drained in desperation. Three women Eammon had tried to save.

The growth around the skulls had vague bone-shapes, as if parts of the Second Daughters had become forest as they lay here. Roots twined through gaps in rib cages, flowers bloomed on vertebrae. Red pressed her hand against her stomach, wondering if that's what it looked like beneath her skin.

Leaves rustled, an isolated breeze sending a whirl of gold that ruffled her hair. There were no dearly bought words in it—they were beyond that now, she and the Wilderwood—but Red understood all the same.

"Fear makes us all do foolish things," she breathed.

Beside her boot, a thin stem poked through the ground. It grew slowly, blooming until a wide white flower touched Red's palm.

Red brushed her fingers over the petals. She didn't speak, but she nodded, and that seemed enough for the forest.

She felt him before she saw him, her body attuned to every movement of his. Eammon stepped slowly forward until he stood beside her, staring at the bones wreathed around the tree. He brushed a finger over the flower, then clasped her hand.

"This will never happen again," he said, low and fierce.

Another fall of leaves, another creaking twig. The Wilderwood's acquiescence.

Moving on instinct, Red stepped forward. Eammon squeezed her hand once before letting go, a silent mourner watching her benediction.

Red laid her hand on the first skull. Kaldenore, she somehow knew. She'd attended only a handful of funerals, and never paid close attention to any of them. So when Red spoke, it was simple. "Be at peace," she murmured. "It's over."

Almost without thinking, she pulled forward the golden forest magic within her. So easy to do, now, like flexing her finger or arching her back. It flowed through her palm, into what was left of Kaldenore. Washing the horror away, drowning it in light.

When her eyes opened, her hand touched dirt. The skull had sunk into the ground, the Wilderwood soaking up the last of the woman who'd been its sacrifice. Obeying Red's word to finally lay these bones to rest.

She moved through the others, giving them the same blessing—Sayetha, then Merra. When Merra's skull was gone, she walked back to Eammon, blinking against the burn in her eyes. He wrapped his arms around her, surrounding her in his paper-coffee-leaves scent, and when her breath broke on the end, his embrace only tightened.

"Eammon!"

Lyra pelted through the autumn-bright forest, grinding to a halt with her hands on her knees. Her breath was a harsh whistle, and worry etched in her flawless face. "Fife met me at the gate and told me to come find you. Someone's at the Keep."

Eammon's fingers tightened around Red's. "The forest let someone through?"

"Well, yeah." Her thin fingers gestured wryly at the autumn glow around them. "He said his name was Raffe."

Raffe and Fife had no idea what to do with each other. When Red threw open the door, out of breath from her headlong sprint through the forest, the two men stood on either side of the staircase, eyeing each other warily. Fife held a wooden spoon across his chest like a shield, dripping soup, but the fierce light in his eyes made it look sinister rather than ridiculous. Raffe's hand hovered over the hilt of a dagger at his belt.

Red's brow climbed. "Raffe?"

He looked surprised to see her at first, attention diverted from Fife's dripping spoon. But then Raffe grabbed her shoulders and pulled her into a rough hug. "Did he hurt you?"

"No, of course not." She backed up, confusion creasing her forehead. "What are you—"

"I'll thank you to keep your hands off my wife." Eammon filled the doorframe, eyes flaring like embers.

"Shadows damn us, I'm perfectly fine. On *both* counts." Red pushed Raffe's hands from her shoulders. "Eammon, this is Raffe. A friend of mine from Valleyda. Raffe, Eammon." She paused. "The Wolf."

"I gathered." Raffe's fingers twitched toward his dagger hilt. When he spoke, it was almost a snarl. "What have you done with Neve?"

Her arms went slack. "What do you mean?"

"She's *gone*, Red."

Red blinked. The room seemed to fade in and out of focus, the edges of things muddied and misty.

Neve. The panic from last night, the storm of emotions Eammon had helped soothe away, came rushing back. She and Eammon would come up with something, she had to believe it, because what else could she do? But now, with Raffe's tired, worried eyes boring into her, helplessness in his face…

Her knees felt watery.

"You came all the way to the Wilderwood to make accusations?" Eammon put a steadying hand on Red's shoulder, like he could tell she was a breath away from drowning. His jaw was a harsh line in the dim light. "The Queen isn't here."

"That's what I told him," Fife said darkly. He brandished the soup spoon in Raffe's direction. "He wouldn't listen."

"She's not in Valleyda, not in Floriane. She's *gone*, and the only thing she's talked of since Red left is getting her back." Raffe looked at the Wolf's hand on Red's shoulder with burning eyes, and a snarl bent his mouth. "Isn't one sister enough?"

"*Raffe.*" Her own voice cleared the fog in her head. Red drew herself up under Eammon's hand. "I promise you, she isn't here. Tell me what happened." Her voice shook. "Please."

Raffe's eyes tracked from Red to Eammon, the calculation in them clear. "He might have her hidden away." Distrust sharpened his voice to a razor-edge. "He's the *Wolf*, Red, and no matter what he's told you—"

"I know who he is, Raffe."

"He isn't…" Raffe stepped forward, mouth pulled tight, but something beyond her caught his attention. Anger bled away to incredulity, then wonder.

Lyra stood in the doorframe, *tor* drawn, backlit by autumn light that made a corona of her dark curls. Her eyes narrowed at Raffe, mouth somewhere between a smirk and a snarl. "Please continue," she said, polite as any courtier. "If I want you to stop talking, you'll know."

Raffe's eyes were round as moons. His mouth worked, like he'd forgotten how to form words. Slowly, he raised his fist to his forehead, and it took Red a moment to remember where she'd seen the motion—a traditional greeting, from one Meducian noble to another.

"Plaguebreaker," Raffe murmured. "You look…damn me, you look just like the statue."

Fife and Eammon darted glances, their faces identical masks of guarded acceptance. Whatever had just occurred to Raffe, it wasn't a surprise to them. But there was a new tension in their frames, prepared to jump to Lyra's defense at the slightest provocation.

A beat, and Lyra sheathed her *tor*. She balled a fist, raised it briefly to her forehead, then crossed her arms. "I didn't know that story was still told."

Red's brow furrowed. Plaguebreaker…like the myth of the Plague Stars, a whole constellation winking out at the moment of miraculous healing. And the band of root around Lyra's arm, and Fife's answer when she asked what Lyra bargained for: *Her story is longer and more noble than mine.*

"Not everyone knows it." Raffe sounded half entranced. "But there are those in Meducia who remember you, who revere you as much as or more than the Kings. The altar is still there, in the cliffs by the harbor. They leave you gold coins and pray for healing from illness." He shook his head. "My father brought some, once. When I was young. I was sick, and after he prayed, I got better."

Lyra's lips twisted, face unreadable. "I doubt I had anything to do with that."

"Still." He took a tentative step closer. His head arced toward the floor, like he might bow, then he thought better of it. "How did you do it? How did you stop the plague?"

Lyra's eyes shone honey brown in the candlelight, arms tightening across her chest. "I bargained," she said, voice clipped and measured. "My brother…" One hitch in her breath, barely noticeable, before she swallowed and went on. "My youngest brother became infected. So I bargained. Bound myself to the Wilderwood in exchange for a cure."

Raffe's face was unreadable. He looked from Lyra to Eammon and back, glanced around the Keep. "And you live here," he said slowly. "With the Wolf. In the Wilderwood."

"With us." Fife took a small step forward. The spoon in his hand didn't look foolish at all anymore.

Lyra shrugged. "There are worse places to be." A slender brow arched. "And since you're asking," she added, "the Queen isn't here."

Raffe's gaze flickered between Lyra and Eammon. His eyes closed, briefly, and the tension in his shoulders went slack, like his anger had been the only strength in his spine. "Then I have no idea where she might be."

The floor was solid beneath her, but Red felt like she was falling. Eammon's hand on her shoulder was all that kept her upright, a counterpoint to the chaos in her head. Neve was gone. Red had left her, pulled away by the roots in her bones, and now she was gone. Her throat felt like she'd swallowed needles.

"What happened?" Eammon asked.

Raffe sank to a seat on the bottom step, denting the moss. "No one has seen her in the palace since yesterday morning." He sounded hoarse, like the words were too heavy for his throat to lift. "Not since the incident in the Shrine. The rumor was that the Second Daughter was there..."

"You thought I took her." Red's voice was harsh.

Raffe didn't nod, but the tightening of his clasped hands was a sentencing. "I didn't..." He stopped, started again. "I knew she was doing something that affected the Wilderwood. And I knew—"

"Then why did you leave her?" Red didn't realize she'd advanced a step until the weight of Eammon's hand fell away. "If you knew what was happening, how could you leave her?"

"You think it was my choice?" Raffe snapped the word, like he could break it between his teeth. "It wasn't. The Order sent me away."

"And you *let* them?"

"Arick all but forced me out." Despite the blade of his tone, there was sadness in Raffe's face. Arick had been his friend, too. "He said I had nothing to gain by getting embroiled in Valleydan politics, and he said it like a threat. I rented a room in the city, kept an eye on things as best I could. It's all I could do." He ran one hand helplessly over his shorn hair. "It wasn't enough."

Red took her grief and buried it deep, something to be dealt with later. For now, her mind whirred through possibilities, solutions.

One clicked.

"I know how to find her." She spun on her heel, toward the back door. "Come with me."

Chapter Thirty-Two

The mirror was propped against the same wall where Eammon had first left it. Red half expected the glass to be clear, the healing of the Wilderwood reflected in its relic. But the surface was still matte and gray, touched by the subtly sinister twist of smoke. Maybe it would take time to heal, or maybe it was something that would always look foreboding.

Red swallowed. She wasn't sure which option disconcerted her more.

"This...shows you Neve?" Apprehension made Raffe's voice brittle. He'd balked at the sight of the tower, wrapped in vine and branch, bursting with as much golden autumn as the rest of the Wilderwood. Now he held himself carefully, arms crossed so he didn't touch anything.

"Gaya made it so she could see Tiernan." Red untied her braid, shaking her hair over her shoulders. She pulled out one strand, hesitated, then tugged a few more. Neve might be harder to find this time.

"And it works?"

Eammon's eyes flickered from Red to the mirror, the same nervousness she felt etched into his face. "Mostly."

"Strange magic," Raffe murmured.

"An understatement." Despite his nonchalance, Fife held himself stiffly against the stair railing. Lyra had gone to the Edge to tell Valdrek what was happening, to finally make good on his promise of help if the need ever arose. Red knew Fife would be nervous until she returned.

With one last reassuring look at Eammon, Red wound the strands of her hair through the mirror's frame and sat back on her heels, waiting for the smoke and shine, waiting for her sister.

When the vision finally came, it was blurry, even more than usual. Wherever Neve was, it was dark. She lay on her back, unmoving but for the slight rise and fall of her chest. Indistinct shapes flickered around her, but Red saw a flash of an auburn braid and a white robe, and someone tall with a face like smeared paint, shifting between one thing and the other.

Kiri and Solmir.

As she concentrated, the darkness above Neve slowly coalesced to a night sky, midnight blue, scattered with stars. Valleydan countryside sky. A line of deep violet split the horizon—the edge of the Wilderwood.

Slowly, Red came back to herself, relief making her breath shudder. "She's alive. In Valleyda, but near—"

The words choked off into a scream of unexpected pain. It flashed down her spine, the roots around it twisting, branches spearing across the inside of her skin. Eammon's eyes flashed, his hand reaching out as he tried to come toward her, but his knees buckled before he could, hitting the floor with a muffled groan.

"What are they doing?" Raffe's voice, somewhere between shock and fear.

"The roots," Fife breathed, face blanched.

Outside, a low keening noise, a gathering wind, and a crack of falling branches. The autumn colors muting, fading, winter seeping in again.

Eammon was on his knees, fist pressed against his side, jaw an agonized ridge. He tried to move, but another slice of pain lanced through them both, turned his forward motion into a fruitless spasm. Something cut away, something *taken*.

Raffe backed against the wall, wide-eyed. "What *happened*?"

"Wilderwood." With teeth-baring effort, Eammon lurched toward Red, pulling her up with a steady hand despite the pain. His palms ran over her arms, looking for wounds. "They've taken more sentinels."

It felt like a hundred knives, the way the forest skittered in her chest, the way it fought to close itself around the unimaginable tear—dozens of sentinels, ripped away at once. Her veins were a rush of sap, her heartbeat clattering against stretching branches, all of it agony.

At the bottom of the tower, the door banged open, footsteps rushing up the stairs. Valdrek topped the rise, Lyra behind him, both of them out of breath. "What is going *on*, Wolf? The Wilderwood was open when we entered, then an awful—"

He stopped cold, eyes wide as they took in Red's and Eammon's drawn faces and what they must mean. "Kings and *shadows*."

"Apt." Eammon's lips were white. He steadied Red against him.

"They're doing it," she murmured. Words in a dungeon, before she took the roots—*the Wilderwood will fall, the Kings will be freed*. "Solmir is freeing the rest of the Kings from the Shadowlands."

Outside, the Wilderwood's keening had subsided, but the silence it left was almost worse. They'd left the tower, unsure how its magic-heightening influence might be affected by such violence done to the forest. Red leaned against Eammon, all but limping. Eammon walked tall, but pain lived in the line of his mouth.

Raffe pushed open the door to the Keep, and Red nearly collapsed on the bottom step of the staircase, teeth clenched against the sting of so many missing sentinels. Eammon leaned against the banister, his fingers white-knuckle on the newel post.

Lear had accompanied Valdrek and Lyra, and took a place near the wall, armed to the teeth with weapons that should've been ancient, glinting in the light of the burning vine. His blue eyes were sad and tired. "When I said you could always ask for help, Wolf, I was thinking more about finding material to rebuild the Keep, or maybe getting your input on crop rotation. Not the whole damn Wilderwood collapsing."

"We were halfway here before it started." Lyra, voice low, fingers on the hilt of her *tor.* "Everything was fine, then all of a sudden, it…*tore.*"

"It sounded like the trees were screaming." Valdrek shook his head. "I've never heard the forest make that sound before."

"We have to go to the border," Raffe said from the shadow of the staircase. "We *have* to, if that's where he has Neve."

"The Wilderwood won't let us out. Not now that I have the roots, too." Red stood, though the effort drove her teeth together. "You'll have to find her, Raffe."

He nodded.

"Eammon, Fife, Lyra, and I can go as far as the tree line," she continued. "Raffe will go look for Neve, and we'll heal whatever breaches are close until he finds her."

Eammon shook his head, slightly, like the movement hurt. "Solmir is *there*, Red. You can't get that close—"

"My *sister* is there." It was nearly a whisper, though part of her wanted to scream it. "There's no time. We have to go *now.*"

He shut his mouth against further protest, chin dipping forward as if the weight on his shoulders had increased tenfold.

Valdrek's eyes flickered over them. "So of the five of you," he said slowly, "only one can leave the forest." He pointed to Raffe. "I assume you came in during the brief period where the Wilderwood seemed to have its shit together."

"It opened the border," Red said softly. "When I took the roots, when the Wilderwood was healed, the Valleydan border opened." It made her throat ache, to think of how close they'd been. How briefly everything had been balanced, only to be knocked sideways again.

A pang of longing twisted Valdrek's face, just for a moment. "Well," he said, looking to Lear, "we'll come, then, and try our luck."

"It won't let you out." Eammon's words came strained.

"Maybe not. But the Wilderwood is held by two now, and differently than before."

"It should just be me and Raffe," Eammon argued. "Even if it did let you through, there's too much risk—"

"We owe it to everyone in the Edge to make an attempt. And if the forest *does* let us out, and there's a part we can play in healing it, we have to try." Valdrek shrugged. "You're getting our help, Wolf, whether you like it or not."

Red stood, covering Eammon's hand with her own. She glared up at him. "No more keeping yourself alone," she hissed. "You asshole."

Worry lit his eyes, but Eammon turned his hand over under hers, laced their fingers together.

Lear chuckled, but it was a hard thing. "Maybe we'll even kill this Solmir fellow. That would be enough to have a ballad written, eh? Killing one of the Kings?"

Firelight gilded Lyra's curls as she stepped forward. "We're going, too."

Behind Lyra, Fife crossed his arms, Bargainer's Mark standing out in sharp relief against his freckles. He gave one confirming nod.

Eammon's eyes were shadowed hollows. He looked to Red. She squeezed his hand.

"Let's go, then," he murmured.

Every tree in the Wilderwood was thorn-jagged and winter-sharp. The leaves on the ground were gray and skeletal, leached of autumn color as if months had passed instead of minutes. Above their heads, the sky mottled like a bruise.

The hilt of the dagger strapped around Red's thigh brushed her wrist. Knives glittered in the shadows of Eammon's coat. She wondered if they'd be able to use them. She wondered if what they went to face was something that could be fought. Kiri could be killed, and so could Solmir while he was on this side of the forest—she assumed—but if the rest of the Kings came through…

Heal the breaches, rescue Neve. She kept it up like a litany, this recitation of the two things she knew they could do.

"Do we have a plan?" Lyra murmured. Her *tor* was a crescent of silver in the dark. With every step, the bags at her and Fife's waists clinked, filled with vials of blood.

"Stop him." Eammon didn't pause in his unflagging pace.

"He's mine." This from Raffe, walking behind them and thus far silent. He turned his eyes from the ground to Lyra, dark and glittering. "If Solmir is there, even if he's where you can get to him, he's mine."

She nodded, once.

Silence fell, broken only by the sound of boots over leaves.

The pain of the torn sentinels had flagged to a dull ache. Still, Eammon walked stiffly at the front of their strange procession, like every movement taxed a limited store of energy.

Red picked up her pace until the back of her hand brushed his. Eammon hadn't touched her since they left the Keep, when they'd rushed upstairs for weapons. Then he'd pulled her to him, kissed her like he could impart some protection through the weight of his mouth.

"Whatever I have to do, I'll do it," he whispered. "Whatever I have to do to keep you safe."

Red traced his scars. "I love you." Her mouth quirked halfway to a smile, then fell. "I'm for the Wolf."

His thumb had brushed over her lower lip. "I'm for you."

Now there was no softness in him, like he'd spent it all in that moment. Eammon was harsh angles and sharp edges, and he moved with vicious intent.

"I'm sure, if you ask nicely, Raffe will bring him past the border and let you have a turn." The words were toneless, hollow. She said them because there was nothing else to say. Because *it will be fine* sounded too much like a lie.

There was no humor in his eyes when they met hers. "I won't let anything happen to you."

Red grabbed his hand. He let her.

Up ahead, the trees thinned, rising twisted from the ground. Their small war band stopped, motion arrested by shock.

The border of the Wilderwood was a wasteland, trees scattered and broken, those that still stood contorted into tortured shapes. Pits of rotten earth pockmarked the ground—one directly before them, the edge of another visible in the shadows to the left. The sky split in a sawtooth line, plum-dark twilight crashing into indigo, scattered with stars like the glass from a broken window.

Beyond, in the flat and empty expanse of northern Valleyda, a tightly clustered copse of white trees grew, maybe half a mile from the border. Twisted roots stretched up to the sky, tangling and matting together in an impenetrable ring, while thicker branches slashed through the ground below—another inverted sentinel grove, growing upside down. Between the bleached-bone trunks, nothing stirred.

Red recoiled. The Wilderwood within her did, too.

"There." Raffe was beside her, bared teeth a flash in the dark. "She'll be there." He jogged over the burned earth toward the grove with no hesitation.

Valdrek stepped up to the broken border, Lear beside him. As he tentatively stepped over the line, Red felt a tugging in her chest, like a frayed string snapping. The forest, letting them go, knowing that holding its borders wouldn't help it now.

"Well." Valdrek turned back, surprise and a tired, sorrow-tinged joy in his eyes. "The world feels much the same on this side. Good luck, Wolves." He started over the hills after Raffe, Lear following behind.

Lyra stood with her *tor* in her hand, a loose readiness to her frame like she was set to spring. "No shadow-creatures yet," she said, eyes scanning the broken edge of the forest. "I can't decide if that's comforting or not."

"The Shadowlands have more important things to let loose." Eammon kept his voice steady, though his jaw was a clenched line of pain. His eyes flickered to Red. "I'm going to scout the edge of the forest with Lyra. You and Fife stay here. Don't come any closer to the border until I call for you."

"Is that an order?" Half a joke, an attempt at lightness to lift the iron feeling in her chest.

Eammon huffed, half a laugh for half a joke, fingers tightening on hers. "If you want it to be."

"Eammon—"

He tucked her hair behind her ear, scarred palm brushing her cheek. "Let me do this."

Gently, he untangled their fingers. Gently, he brought her hand to his lips. Then he was gone, off into the ruin their forest had become.

Fife stepped up beside her as Eammon and Lyra moved quickly away. "Foolish of us," he said, trying for the usual brusque tone he took with her and falling short.

She arched a brow.

He shrugged. "Falling in love with reckless idiots."

Red gripped Fife's fingers, briefly, then let them fall.

A flutter of movement caught her eye, in the opposite direction of Eammon and Lyra. Something white, hidden in shadows, right at the edge of the Valleydan border. Eyes narrowing, Red took a lurching step forward. "Do you see that?"

"See what?"

Another flutter of white. In her vision, Neve had been wearing white.

That was enough to make her run.

"Red!"

But she didn't pay attention, hurtling toward that flicker in the shadowed trees. Maybe Neve had woken from her strange trance, come to the edge of the broken forest—

"Come," said a voice from the shapeless darkness behind the tree. It was quiet, quiet enough for the voice itself to be indistinct.

"Neve?" Red called, everything in her focused on saving the sister she'd left behind.

No answer.

"*Redarys!*" A scream this time, a scream to scrape a throat bloody. Eammon, calling for her. The Wilderwood in her chest sliced and burned, a warning against being so close to the edge, but Red clenched her teeth and kept going. Her boots skidded in the dirt as she reached the tree, putting out a hand to sling herself around it.

From the shadows, Kiri grinned.

Red tried to backtrack, but her lungs ached so badly, and the falling forest anchored in her hurt so much. Her fingers fumbled against the hilt of her dagger, too panic-numb to find a grip, and then Kiri's hands were around her throat, pressing hard.

"More trouble than you're worth," the High Priestess hissed, eyes glinting madly in the collision of stars and twilight. "You don't deserve to see our gods returned."

"*Red!*" She felt the slither of roots over her ankles, the piercing of the Wilderwood in her chest as Eammon tried to garner its broken pieces into power.

“Say goodbye to your Wolf.” Kiri’s hands tightened on Red’s neck. “He’ll be joining you soon enough.”

Then—hands wrenching at the priestess’s arms, opening her fingers to let air back into Red’s lungs. Solmir cursed mildly, grabbing Red’s arm in a bruising grip and pulling her toward the ragged tree line.

Distantly, over the sound of her gasps, Red heard running footsteps, heard Eammon’s bellow.

“More trouble than you’re worth, maybe,” Solmir muttered, hauling her by her arm so her feet fell out from under her and her knees slid in the dirt, “but more useful alive than dead.”

Red opened her mouth to curse, to shout for Eammon. But Solmir pulled her over the border, and every fiber, every nerve exploded in burning, all-consuming pain. All thought of anything else washed from her mind in the flare, her scream reverberating through the Wilderwood.

The trees bowed in mourning.

Chapter Thirty-Three

Red's knees skimmed over the dead grass of a late Valleydan autumn as Solmir wrenched her forward. Her chest felt like a broken cage, roots reaching for home—if she looked down, surely she'd see branches breaking through her skin, rimed with viscera, her body made a sepulcher. An awful keening echoed in her head, and she didn't know where it came from, in too much pain to know if her mouth was open or her vocal cords in use.

Vines tried for her ankles, for Solmir's, but they were weak and skittering, made brittle by a dying forest. Branches clustered, reached as far as they could before snapping back like a spent bowstring. "Red!" Eammon's scream scoured his throat. "*Red!*"

Valdrek and Lear stopped in their careful prowling through the field, Eammon's voice cracking through the still night air. Raffe broke into a run, disappearing into the twisted grove. Valdrek cut his hand at Lear, gesturing for him to follow the other man. As Lear disappeared between the trees, figures in white shimmered into view, like they'd been hidden in the center of the grove until this moment.

Priestesses. Five of them that Red could count, through the strange, shivery clarity that hovered above her pain. Something about the number seemed portentous, awful in a way she couldn't quite put together yet.

She thrashed in Solmir's grip, but he held on vise-tight. Kiri walked beside them, smooth and unhurried, hands tucked primly into her sleeves.

A strained roar—Eammon, lurching across the Wilderwood's border, pain blanching his face and raising tendons in his neck. His dagger slashed out, but Solmir jerked easily away. Kiri stepped aside with a small sound of distaste, as if Eammon was a minor inconvenience, a gnat that needed swatting.

Another lunge, but something snapped Eammon back, as if he'd hit an invisible wall. His neck twisted toward his shoulder, so far it looked like it might break, and Red's scream had nothing to do with the way Solmir threw her aside like a cloak he'd grown tired of wearing.

"It's to be this, then?" He sounded nearly weary. "Pointless heroics?"

Teeth bared, Eammon launched at him. One punch landed on the King's chin, the grind of Solmir's jaw audible as his head snapped up. The dagger in Eammon's fist flipped sideways in his grip, then slashed out, opened Solmir's arm.

But Solmir just stood there. Like he was waiting.

Eammon tried to lash out again, when a spasm racked through his whole body. His spine locked, bent almost backward. Strained silence, like he was holding it back, then an agonized scream burst from behind his teeth.

Vines slithered from the Wilderwood and hooked around Eammon's arms, his ankles, his boots leaving runnels in the dirt as they dragged him backward. He called Red's name through a throat that sounded razored, fought himself forward, but the Wilderwood pulled his thrashing body back and back and back, toward the border of the ruined forest.

Something almost like pity lit Solmir's face. "It's too tangled in you to let you go," he said quietly. "The Wilderwood protects itself first."

"Like what happened to my mother?" Eammon snarled, straining against the border and the Wilderwood's hold. Vines wound around his legs, branches bent like fingers on his shoulders. Gentle, but inescapable. "When she tried to open the Shadowlands for you?"

Solmir's eyes were unreadable. "Exactly."

Kiri was halfway to the twisted grove now, a smear of white against the night-colors of the field. Something glittered in her hand. A dagger.

And another glint of silver, closer—Valdrek. Slowly, he crept toward the Wilderwood, keeping low to the dark ground between the twisted grove and the edge of the forest. His sword was drawn and at the ready, his eyes trained on Solmir's back.

Satisfied that Eammon was held, Solmir turned to Red, eyes admonishing. "Things would've been over and done by now if it weren't for you." Solmir shook his head. His long hair shifted in the night breeze, and the moonlight caught the raised ridges of small scars on his brow, equidistant and deliberate looking. "If you'd stayed in Valleyda, he would've given up."

"He wouldn't." Red tried to push up from the ground, but her body wouldn't obey. "He didn't give up before me. He wouldn't give up after."

His expression was one she hadn't seen him wear before, no longer anger or boredom or contempt. It was almost sorrow, and she hated him for it.

Something shot past his head—Lyra's *tor*. She and Fife had joined Eammon at the edge of the Wilderwood, as unable to leave it as he was. Lyra's face was a snarl, her teeth bared.

"That was foolish." Solmir sighed. "Once the Kings arrive, you'll want a weapon."

The Kings. Five of them, including Solmir. Five priestesses in the grove. And Kiri, headed toward them with a knife in her fist.

"Keep her from killing them!" Red yelled to whoever would listen, craning her head back just in time to see Kiri slip between the inverted trees. "You have to keep her from killing them!"

Her voice, hoarse from pain, might as well have been a whisper. But still, it was enough to make Solmir turn, enough to make his eyes scan the tall grass. Enough to make him notice Valdrek, crouched and waiting for an opening.

Valdrek didn't hesitate, once he knew he was caught. The silver rings in his hair glinted as he leapt, roaring, swinging wildly.

Almost casually, Solmir lifted his dagger and punched the hilt against Valdrek's temple.

Eammon lunged against the Wilderwood, shouting, but it held him fast. Red tried to get up, tried to struggle toward Valdrek, but something that felt like a wall of ice slammed her back down.

Tears trailed into her hair, her back pressed flat to the ground. It was the same cold Kiri had attacked her with in Valleyda, that made her organs feel iced and her throat rimed in frost, but stronger and heavier, born of years in darkness rather than blood on branches—Shadowlands magic, all that power twisted up into a prison, leaching into him as he served his sentence. The same magic he'd tried to use against her in the dungeon, and this time she wasn't full enough of golden light to fight it back.

Pain still roared through her, agonizing, contorting her muscles as the Wilderwood fell and fell. She cried out, though her mouth tried to clamp around it.

"It's not so tangled in her as it is in you." Solmir spoke casually, voice pitched to carry over the yards between him and Eammon as if it was a tavern table. "The forest in your Lady is new, easy to uproot. You know how to fix this. How to stop her pain."

"No!" Red arched up off the ground, nearly in half, craning so her eyes could meet Eammon's. "*No.*"

A rumble, a deep reverberation that make her teeth clatter together. Red tried to aim her blurry eyes toward the grove, just enough to make out a white-robed figure falling to the ground, trailing scarlet.

The first priestess, dead. Four to go.

"She'll die if you don't." Solmir gestured toward the grove behind them, the distant horror happening on its roots. As he did, another priestess fell.

Two down.

"Bringing them through—what they've become—will kill the Wilderwood and everything attached to it. It's been part of you too long, Eammon. There's no way for you to escape it." Solmir's hand touched Red's hair, lightly, and she flinched away as much as she could, when her body was a battleground for the rip of the roots and the cold weight of shadowed magic. "But she can."

Eammon's chest heaved. His eyes shone above the agonized rictus of his mouth. Fife had pulled Lyra away, had an arm wrapped around her shoulders as they stood and watched in horrified, helpless silence.

"Why?" Eammon's voice sounded shredded. "Why bring the rest of them through? They brought you down *with them*! They're the reason for all of it!"

Solmir's eyes were like chips of ice. For a moment, his mouth worked, like he might actually offer an explanation. But then he shook his head, almost defeated. "Because it's inevitable. Their return is inevitable." A pause, his voice growing serrated edges. "And the longer they have to prepare, the worse it will be."

Another bone-rattling rumble, shaking the earth. Then another, louder.

Four down.

Across the gulf of the border, Eammon's eyes bored into hers, a promise burning in amber and green. *I'd let the world burn before I hurt you.*

She read his intention, like she could read everything with Eammon. Red set her teeth, snarled at him. "No—"

Eammon's head wrenched to the side as he pulled the Wilderwood out of her, as the forest within her body uprooted. He roared agony at the sky, and she realized that wasn't the whole of it, what he'd said about the world burning.

He may let the world burn, but he'd let himself burn with it.

Red screamed, digging her fingers in the dirt. "Give them back! Damn you, give them *back*!"

The Wilderwood didn't listen. She coughed up bloody leaves, knots of roots. Desperately, she thought of stuffing them in her mouth and swallowing them back down, but it was useless. She was nothing but human again, nothing but bone and organ and blood.

The branches and roots and vines around Eammon tensed once, like a closing fist, then opened. A spasm, bending his spine, and Eammon fell to his knees, shuddering. Tendons stood out like tree roots in his neck, his shoulders, visible through the ripped fabric of his shirt. His fingers clawed into the ground as golden light, dim but visible, pulsed through his veins.

"Give up, Eammon," Solmir muttered, not paying attention to Red at all. This was between the King and the Wolf. "Give *up*."

And after a moment, the Wolf lay still.

The world froze, poised on a knife's edge. Fife and Lyra stood like statues, tear tracks gleaming on Lyra's cheeks.

A moment of stillness.

A choice, made.

A *surge*.

The forest rose up behind Eammon like a wave, a cresting tide of root and branch and vine and thorn. The sentinels arched toward him, stretching sharp white fingers. They pierced his skin and flowed inward, turning to light, making star-tracks of his veins, gold-to-green. The Wolf was corpse-still, but the things that made the Wilderwood pumped into him like rain to a river. It came and came, a wave breaking against his back, a forest seeping back to seed.

Then Eammon stood.

He pulled himself to his full height, then higher, topping seven feet, eight. His eyes changed as his shadow grew longer on the ground, the whites around his amber irises turning to pure, bright emerald. Ivy wreathed his wrists, a garland of it growing in his too-long black hair as swirls of bark armored his arms, as branches like antlers grew from his forehead.

All those small changes—the splinters the Wilderwood left when he used its magic alone, the pieces of himself he'd given up, everything he'd tried to stop by offering his blood—it was all just a ghost of this.

A forest made a man made a god.

Eammon—what had been Eammon—turned his strange god-eyes to Red, cowering in the dirt, and she understood. He'd finally given up. Given up on being man and forest, given up on the impossible binary of bone and branch. He'd pulled all of it into him, the shining network of the Wilderwood crowding out everything of who he'd been before.

This time, he'd let it take him over. He'd given himself up, to save her. And those inhuman eyes held nothing of the man she loved.

Red's sob tasted like blood.

A low, rueful laugh rolled from Solmir's mouth. "Wolves and their sacrifices."

A final *crack*, like the earth itself sundered. In her tear-blurred vision, Red saw the fifth priestess fall, Kiri's knife glinting blood-tinged light before she darted into the grove. At the same moment, Lear threw himself out from between the trees, landing in an unmoving huddle. Shadows burst from the ground around the twisted sentinels, a ring of writhing darkness.

Solmir made that strange shape with his hand again. The shadows rolled over the ground like a black tide, flocked to him like birds, making mad skittering noises. They built Solmir up, made him taller, surrounded him in darkness.

Grinning, seething shadows, he beckoned.

And the Wilderwood—*Eammon*—charged forward with a roar.

Chapter Thirty-Four

The Wilderwood was no longer a forest. It had uprooted itself, taken a different form. Its boundaries were the boundaries of Eammon's body, wreathed in thorn and vine. Eammon was gone, and the Wilderwood stood in the shape of a man in his place.

When he ran toward Solmir, the earth shook.

Red crouched, no longer pressed down by cold magic, sorrow and horror drying her mouth. The forest-god still looked like Eammon, still had his angular face and dark hair. But the way he moved was alien, fog shifting through branches, leaves twisting in wind. He was golden light to Solmir's shadow, and both were terrible.

Eammon—what had been Eammon but wasn't anymore and, *Kings*, she was going to lose it—cracked his fist into Solmir's jaw. Bark and leaves burst from the contact, Solmir's head snapping sideways even as a sharp, exulting grin curved his lips.

"You could've had such a peaceful death." Solmir wiped blood from his mouth with the back of a shadow-gauntleted wrist. "Wolves die easier than gods do."

Lyra stood at the edge of the forest, eyes wide and disbelieving. Then, snarling, she rushed forward and snatched her *tor* from the ground, no longer held back by the border of a Wilderwood that wasn't there. Fife followed her with no hesitation. Trees still stretched behind them, but they were different—the colors muted, the sky above star-strewn, the colors of night instead of twilight.

Just a forest, like any other forest. Everything that made it the Wilderwood was in Eammon now.

The bodies of the priestesses lay in white-robed, scarlet-stained huddles between the inverted sentinels in the twisted grove, their blood leaking onto the roots. Kiri was nowhere to be seen. Lear had roused, inching away from the trees with a gash in his forehead that dripped steadily into his eyes.

The gulf of shadow that ringed the grove grew wider and wider, darkness eddying into the air like smoke. The earth around it rumbled, the rattling of a locked door.

A door that would soon be forced open.

Eammon's hands shot forward, and trunks erupted spear-sharp from the ground. They passed through Solmir like he was smoke, darkness curling away and curling back. Solmir's fingers crooked, and shadows shackled around Eammon's arm, twisting it behind his back. A roar, a sound like cracking branches, like a forest burning. When Eammon wrenched free of the shadow's grip, dark burn marks scored his skin.

Despite the emptiness in her chest, the knowledge that every trace of the Wilderwood was gone from her, Red's fingers still curled into claws. She shot up from the ground, stumbled toward the warring gods.

It wasn't shadow that threw her back. It was a vine, blooming, wrapping her waist to set her gently but firmly down. Inhuman eyes she didn't know peered at her, in a face she'd kissed. There was no recognition in them.

She stayed still on the ground, every breath feeling like a swallowed knife.

A slight form, rushing over the ground. Lyra, *tor* gripped in her fist and teeth glinting moonlight. The blade sliced through Solmir's shadow-sheathed leg, a blow that should've left a stump, but his body dissipated and came together again. Sneering, he batted Lyra away, sending her flying. She landed next to Red and was still.

"*Lyra!*" Behind her, Fife screamed it full-throated. His dagger was in his hand as he turned to Solmir, dwarfed by his shadow-wreathed height.

"Fife, don't!" Red crawled to Lyra, put shaking fingers against her neck. Her pulse was light but steady, her breath shallow but there. "It's pointless!"

She could see in his snarl that he knew it, and also that he didn't care. Solmir hurt Lyra, so he'd hurt Solmir, an easy equation. But it couldn't be now. A strangled roar, and he sheathed his dagger, rushing over to where they lay.

Behind him, Eammon and Solmir raged on, oblivious, a cosmic battle in microcosm.

"She's alive," Red said as Fife stumbled forward, moving her hand on Lyra's pulse so his could replace it. "She's breathing."

A sob of relief as he felt her heartbeat, his head bowing low enough for sandy-red curls to brush Lyra's forehead. Made clumsy by fear, Fife pulled off his jacket to tuck it around her, like it could be a shield.

Then sat frozen, eyes glued to his now-bared forearm.

To what wasn't there.

"The Mark." He stopped, swallowed. Then, gently, he pushed up Lyra's sleeve. Brown, unmarked skin where the Bargainer's Mark had been, gilded in starlight and unblemished by roots.

His eyes met Red's, wide with wonder and no small bit of fear.

A weight on her shoulders, a heavy regard that pricked the skin of her neck. Red looked over her shoulder, throat tight, knowing what she'd see.

Eammon—*not Eammon*—gazed at her with luminous green-and-amber eyes for half a second, almost puzzled. Then the heavy gaze went to Fife. One nod, perfunctory and business-like.

"Shit." Fife's hand closed around his forearm.

The forest-god turned back to his battle, the whole pause taking barely a breath. Jagged branches grew from his fingers, sweeping for Solmir's face.

The dark giant Solmir had become didn't try to dodge. The branches swept through him like he was shadow, and he coalesced back into form in their wake.

Shadow.

Red's mind tripped over the thought, then latched. When she'd seen Arick outside the Shrine, Arick who was Solmir, there'd been no shadow on the ground behind him. And Kiri's words in the dungeon—*one the man, one the shadow.*

Five priestesses lay dead, five lives to free five kings. Solmir, already half here, should be condensing into flesh, should be using the sacrifice to manifest fully in this world. But still he held on to the connection with Arick, staying the shadow as long as he fought Eammon.

As long as Solmir fought Eammon, Arick would stay the man.

Fife crouched between Lyra and the war between shadow and forest, hand on his dagger. When he spoke, it was with his characteristic bluntness. "I don't know what your next move is. But I'm staying with Lyra."

"I'd never ask you to do anything different."

Still brusque, but with affection in it. "I know."

Red knew what had to happen now. But it was a heavy weight in her middle, one she didn't want to look at too closely. Not until it was clear there was no other choice.

The choice would have to be made quickly. Eammon couldn't fight a shadow forever.

She pushed herself up on shaking legs. "I'm going to the grove."

Fife met her eyes. Nodded.

Red took off running.

Lear met her at the edge of the sweeping shadows ringing the grove, swiping blood from his face. "Tried to stop them." He waved his scarlet-streaked hand to the priestesses' bodies, nearly hidden in writhing darkness. "Kept begging them to run. None of them listened, and the redhead knocked me a good one before I could try to pull them out." The wound in his forehead dripped into his eyes; he wiped the blood away like it irritated more than pained him. "I didn't go any farther before the shadows sprang up, but Raffe is still in there."

"I have to go find him." Even with all the Wilderwood spilled from her, the grove still felt repellent. Something that should never be under the sky. "I have to find my sister."

Concern lit Lear's eyes. "If she's in there, I don't know what exactly you're going to find."

"Me either." Red swallowed. "But it's our only chance of stopping this."

Lear nodded. Then he inclined his head in a short bow. "Good luck, Lady Wolf."

Before she could lose her nerve, Red ran forward, leapt over the furrow of growing shadow, and landed inelegantly next to the corpse of a priestess.

The grove was blanketed in silence, blocking out the roar of gods outside. The ground was dark but solid, even as it rumbled. Still, she could almost feel the fault lines forming beneath her feet, cracks something could seep through.

The sentinels bowed inward, ashamed. Red put her hand on a trunk like she could offer comfort. There were more of them than she realized, growing only inches from one another, the white of picked bones.

It gave Kiri plenty of places to hide.

The snap of a twig was Red's only warning as the High Priestess lurched from behind an inverted sentinel, swiping wildly at Red with a bloodstained dagger. She ducked away, the slash catching only the fabric of her sleeve.

"Should've killed you before." Kiri's voice sounded ravaged, like she'd been screaming for hours. "Can't do anything to stop it now." Another wild swipe, weighed down by blood-soaked robes. "Our gods are coming, and you'll—"

A hollow *thunk*, a hilt on her temple. Eyes rolling back, Kiri slumped to the ground.

Behind her, Raffe sheathed his dagger.

His fingernails were torn and bloody. The hilt of the dagger was pockmarked, chipped, like he'd slammed it repeatedly against a rock. "Took you long enough."

Outside the grove, a muffled roar. He turned toward it with an arched brow, only mildly interested, then nodded at the body of the priestess near the edge of the trees. "How long do we have?"

"Not long. Eammon—" His name burned in her throat, made her swallow past a lump that felt bladed. "He's keeping Solmir occupied, but he can't for much longer."

Another roar, another shudder of the ground, like it was the back of some slow-waking beast. Raffe nodded, then headed through the bone-like trees. Silently, Red followed.

The grove opened on a clearing with two things in the center. Arick, face caught somewhere between shame and resignation.

And a coffin.

It looked made of smoky glass, like shadows frozen in ice, but the figure inside was clear. Dark hair, closed eyes, face the same color as the bone-pale trees. At the edges of her body, veins ran black, and the threads of darkness continued past the bounds of her skin—down the stone sides of her grave-slab, down into the rotten ground with its twisted branch-roots churning through the earth.

Neve, tied to this inverse Wilderwood. The process of bringing the sentinels into the cavern had taken weeks, but with a willing sacrifice so close at hand—and unconscious—Kiri and her Order had grown a new grove in moments.

And anchored it within her sister.

A low, keening noise escaped Red's throat. Next to the coffin, Arick's eyes squeezed shut.

"I can't move it." Raffe's voice was flat and emotionless, all feeling wrung out. "I pushed, but I was afraid I might hurt her." His voice didn't break, not exactly, but it wavered on a thin thread.

The bottom of Neve's coffin—a coffin and Neve in it, her mind couldn't fit the words together—looked fused to the ground, grown from the thatching white branches cutting through the rotten earth. Slowly, with the same fear Raffe had, Red stepped forward, making sure not to step on any of the dark lines connecting her sister to the grove. This close, she could see the shadow running through them, beating like a pulse.

Nausea churning her stomach, Red knelt, touched her fingers to one of those black veins.

Darkness behind her eyes, like her vision had been ripped away. A nightmare blur of images—a wide gray sea, something beneath it flashing innumerable teeth. A huge, scaled carcass, the size of a mountain and just as still. Wrong-shaped skulls in carrion piles. A thin, bony figure, a rotting floral wreath on its head, chained to a rock. Four monolithic men on monolithic thrones, shrouded in white, crowned in iron spikes. Next to them, a fifth throne, empty.

Red jerked her hand away, breathing hard, sweat on her brow. In her coffin, Neve didn't stir.

"He promised." Her teeth wanted to shred the words; her nails bit into her palms as she stood on unsteady feet. "He *promised* she would be safe."

"She's alive." Raffe said it like he'd been repeating it to himself over and over. "She's...she's *like this*, but she's alive."

Outside the grove, another roar ripped through the quiet. Soon Solmir would tire of being the shadow to Arick's flesh, even if it gave him an advantage against Eammon. Soon he would let himself be made whole by the priestesses' sacrifice, and the rest of the Kings would come to join him.

And the Wilderwood—Eammon—would die.

It was time for choices. She could see only one.

"Arick." Her voice was hoarse.

At his name, Arick's eyes closed tighter. "I'm so sorry," he said quietly. "We were all just trying to save you."

"Come here." Tears choked her. "Come here, please."

A pause, then a lurch as he moved over the darkened ground. Red fought to keep herself steady against her childhood love's broken stance and the sure knowledge of things vast and terrible stirring beneath her feet.

She reached up when he came close enough to touch, gently laid her fingers on his bloodied face. "I know you didn't mean for this to happen."

"No. But I didn't care what was going to happen, not then." There was shame in it, just barely. "I only wanted you safe."

Red's lips pressed white. All of them loved like burning, no thought for the ashes.

"I *am* safe." Her hand left his face, fell to her dagger. She tried not to think on it, tried to let her body work without her mind's direction. "I love Eammon, and he loves me. That's safe."

Another roar ripped through the grove. "Do you love what he's become?"

"We've both been monsters," Red whispered. "I'll love him, whatever he is."

"You loved me once. You never said it, but you did." Arick's dry throat worked a swallow, eyes still pressed shut. "Didn't you?"

"I did." It was barely a whisper, this gentle thing that existed beyond truth and lie. Her fingers closed around the dagger hilt. "Not the way you wanted me to. But I did."

His eyes opened. "Do it quick, then."

Near Neve's coffin, Raffe was silent. When Red looked at him, his eyes shone, but his mouth was a tight line.

Arick bowed his head, and after a moment, he knelt before her. She wanted to grab his shoulders, force him up, but she stood frozen, her hand on her dagger and him like a supplicant at an altar.

"Blood to open," Arick murmured, a last rite. "Blood to close. My blood brought Solmir here. My blood inverted the Wilderwood. A living sacrifice." His eyes rose to hers, and the peace in them, the *relief*, was somehow worse than fear would've been. "This only ends when the sacrifice is no longer living."

Her fingers trembled, sweat-slicked and sliding off the hilt. She'd known this was the answer. But now, when she could see his eyes… "I can't."

"I tried to do it myself, in the dungeon. It never worked. I can't do it alone." Gently, Arick reached out, closed his hand over hers. Together, they drew the dagger. He settled the blade against his throat. "You have to do it, Red. Let me save you this time."

Tears slipped down her cheeks. The earth beneath her rumbled as she knelt, too, putting them level.

Arick pressed his lips to hers. She let him. "Find a way to get him back," he muttered against her mouth. "You deserve to be loved, Red. You always did."

His hand dropped, pleading in his eyes.

Red kissed his forehead, squeezed her eyes shut. She held the dagger still, but she felt Arick push himself forward, heard the soft sigh and felt the warm blood as it dripped, then sheeted. When he dropped to the ground, she dropped with him, forced her eyes open so she could see his.

He raised a hand. Tucked her hair behind her ear, just like he used to do before, when they lay like this. Then a light went out, and his mouth slackened, and he was still.

Red heaved one, racking sob.

The shadows at the edge of the grove paused. The roaring outside went silent.

On her grave-slab, beneath the shadowy glass of her coffin, Neve pulled in a ragged gasp.

Red shot up at the sound, sodden with Arick's blood, rushing to Raffe's side. Raffe used his dagger hilt, but Red just used her fists, punching at the glass, not stopping even when she felt her knuckle split, the crack of something fracturing beneath her skin.

But the glass held, and below it, Neve's eyes opened.

She looked at Raffe. Then she looked at Red. Her face was expressionless, someone who didn't know if they were awake or asleep.

"Neve." It rasped from Red's throat. She lashed out at the glass again, leaving a bloody streak. "*Neve!*"

Neve didn't respond. Slowly, dream-like, her gaze turned to her arms, to the black lines emanating from her like external veins. If they horrified her, she didn't show it, expression curious as her opposite hand reached out, brushed over one of them. It pulsed at her touch, and she shivered, like it was cold.

A moment, stretching long. Neve's hand fell. She closed her eyes. Then, lip pulling up in something like a snarl, she closed her fists.

The dark veins shuddered. With a sound like a nest of vipers, they... *retracted*, pulling out of the grove and back into Neve. The air hummed as Neve reclaimed the magic that had been spooled out of her, the darkness that had used her like a seed. It flowed into her like a tide of shadows, swirling over her skin. A sound at the edge of Red's hearing, almost like a sigh.

And the grove *ripped*.

The twisted sentinels crashed sideways, breaking and melting as the ground opened up. Red scrabbled against the sides of Neve's coffin, trying vainly to shove it out of the collapsing grove. Raffe pushed with her, but neither of them could make it budge. The coffin sank into the dark-churned earth like it was quicksand.

Red screamed. Outside the grove, she heard an echoing bellow, one of tree and leaf and thorn.

"Red!" Raffe grabbed her hand, hauled her away from the rapidly growing hole. "Red, we have to get out of here!"

"We can't leave her!"

"We don't have a *choice*!"

The earth ate at the sides of Neve's coffin, covered it in dirt and dark. One glimpse of a gray-scale world with a shadow-eaten horizon, and she was gone.

Raffe hauled her away, beyond the ring of churning dirt, like a hurricane burrowing into the earth. The only solid ground left in what had been the grove was where Arick's body lay. Now that body was twitching, changing, becoming something different.

The flesh and the shadow, brought together again. She was almost sorry when the body finally looked like Solmir, alive, because it meant she'd have nothing to bury.

"You don't understand!" he screamed, wild eyes finding Red's. "You don't understand, they're still—"

A shadow curled around his throat and into his mouth, gagging him, the grave he'd escaped from eating him alive.

A shuddering *boom*, a spray of dust and rock, and the grove was gone. The door was closed.

With Neve on the wrong side.

Chapter Thirty-Five

The tall, dying grass itched through Red's dirty clothes. She sat silently next to Fife, both of them looking down at Lyra. Time had passed in an uncounted blur, and every time she blinked, all she saw was dirt closing over Neve's face.

Lyra's breathing was steady, her heartbeat sound. Still, Fife cradled her wrist in his lap and kept his fingers closed over it, counting up the signs she was alive, if not awake.

"Neve isn't dead." Raffe sat with them on his knees. After the grove had disappeared, he and Red had drifted toward Fife and Lyra, the four of them drawn together by loss like they could band against it. "I know she isn't dead."

"She's alive." Red's lips barely moved, her eyes stayed fixed on the waving grass. "Just... trapped."

"We have to bring her back." Raffe's face was tearstained, his jaw a hard line. He'd pressed his hands into the dirt, like he could dig his way to the Shadowlands. "What do we do?"

"I don't know," Red answered. "I don't know."

Silence. Then, Raffe swore, standing. "That's not good enough, Red." He stalked away through the dead grass, and all she could do was watch him go.

When the grove disappeared, it had taken the corpses of the priestesses with it. But Kiri's body, not dead, still slumped in the grass a few feet away. Her chest shallowly rose and fell, her blood-crusted hands curled into claws. Red knew she should feel anger, revulsion. All she could dredge up was pity.

"I'm sorry," Fife said quietly, still watching Lyra. "I'm sorry about your sister."

Red opened her mouth but found no sound. She'd left Neve, again. Left her in a coffin, and let that coffin be pulled into the Shadowlands. Failed her, again.

She bit her lip against its trembling.

Fife's swallow was audible. When he looked up, his eyes sparked, determination in the line of his mouth. Gently, he placed Lyra's limp wrist in Red's lap. "Stay with her," he said. "There's something I have to do."

He got up, walking with purpose toward the tall, antlered figure at the edge of the forest. Red's instinct was to close her eyes, to block him from her sight. But she took a deep, ragged breath and made herself watch. Made herself look at what Eammon had become.

What had replaced him.

The line of the forest-god's profile was unchanged as it turned toward Fife's approach, still angular, shadowed by dark hair. He only watched the other man for a moment before his newly green gaze fixed on Red.

There was no light of love in it. Barely recognition. Every beat of her heart was a pained rattle against her rib cage.

Too much. Red looked back down at Lyra. Her sleeve was still pushed up where Fife had checked for the Mark, her skin still unblemished. When Eammon had taken in the Wilderwood, *become* the Wilderwood, he'd let them go. Released them from the bargains they'd made.

Bargains. The word stuck in her head, bent her thoughts around itself.

Her hand closed over her own sleeve, where her Mark had been.

She knew it wasn't there anymore, but she didn't have the bravery to look. Instead, her eyes tracked to Fife, still striding toward the forest-god, and she knew exactly what he was going to do.

The same plan she was forming, both of them hoping it would be enough.

Her legs were coltish when she stood, stabbed with pins and needles. She felt guilty leaving Lyra alone, but the plain was peaceful now that the grove was gone, and nothing would bother her here. Stumbling, Red made her way over the field, hand still clutching her empty arm.

They were aches of two different kinds, Neve and Eammon, pulling at her heart. If she saved one, could she save the other? She remembered the glow of the Wilderwood in her bones, light to hold a shadow. The same shadow that trapped Neve now. The two people she loved the most, the two people she had to save. Light and shadow, snared together, horrific and beautiful and each *taking* something from her.

If she became something horrific and beautiful, could she take it back?

She stopped a few feet away from Fife and what had once been Eammon. The shorter man glared up at the god who was the Wilderwood with fire in his eyes. The Wilderwood looked down a crooked nose with minor curiosity.

His nose was still crooked. Still him, in there somewhere, lost in all that magic, all that light.

"You took my life once, bound it up for someone else. Take it back." Fife pushed up his sleeve, bared his arm. "Give me the damn Mark, and heal Lyra. Make her..." He trailed off, swallowed. "Make her whole."

The god cocked his head. "You wanted your freedom," he said musingly, in a voice that held echoes of leaves falling and branches creaking in wind.

"All I want is her," Fife replied.

A pause. "I understand." There was something almost puzzled in that layered, forest-laced voice. The god understood Fife's desperate want, his willingness to do anything to save someone he loved, but didn't quite know why.

Red bit her lip.

An emerald-veined palm reached out, fingers closing around Fife's arm. Fife gasped, just once, then gritted his teeth. When the god's hand dropped, a new Bargainer's Mark bloomed on Fife's skin.

Behind them, on the ground where Lyra lay, there came a deep breath, stirring the grass.

No words, just a sharp nod. Then Fife turned, all but running to Lyra. The freedom he'd wanted so badly, finally earned and then traded away.

The Wilderwood watched him go. Then green-drowned eyes turned to Red.

She wondered if she should approach like a supplicant, if she should kneel. Fife hadn't, but Fife's bargain had been more straightforward than Red's would be.

She did neither of those things. Instead she stepped forward, looking up at him with her teeth set and her eyes narrowed, the same determination she'd once shown him in a library with a torn red cloak and a bloody cheek.

His shadow fell over her, and the form of it on the ground was a forest, the trees tall and straight. Antlers of alabaster wood sprouted from his forehead; ivy curled around his brow. His strange eyes peered down at her, amber surrounded in green, holding flickers of recognition. Like he knew her shape, but not the space she should occupy.

The Wilderwood had known her, and Eammon had known her. But when they were brought together, one made the other and indistinguishable, they'd become something new. Something that had no context for Second Daughters, no memory of embroidered cloaks and hair wrapped around bark. It was enough to make her falter, just for a moment.

Red drew herself up. Even before, she'd barely reached his shoulder, and now she had to squint to see his face.

When he spoke, his voice was vine and branch and root. "Redarys?" He said it like something forgotten, like he was straining to remember.

Red pitched her voice to carry, but still it came out small. "I've come to bargain with the Wilderwood."

Silence. Something clouded his eyes, sorrow stretched to god-proportions and made unfamiliar.

In a move that might've been tentative, he stretched out his hand. Red placed hers in his green-veined palm. His scars were still there.

"What is it you wish?" Resonant, vibrating her bones.

She wished he'd never had to see his parents die. She wished the scars on his hands were from farming or blacksmithing or childish recklessness rather than cuts made to feed a forest. She wished that maybe they could've met differently, a man and a woman with no magic, no grand destiny, nothing but simple love.

And she wished to save Neve. She wished that this man she'd loved who'd become a god she didn't know could reach down and pull her sister up from the shadows—the shadows Neve had chosen, in the end. A reclamation, a redeeming Red didn't know the particulars of, but somehow, deeply, understood.

That same deep understanding let her know that simply bargaining to save her sister wouldn't work. Her time tied to the Wilderwood gave her instinctive knowledge of its limitations, let her know you couldn't just wish to pull someone from the Shadowlands. That door was closed, and opening it would take more than bargaining, would scour her heart in ways she couldn't fathom yet.

There was so little she could do. But she could save Eammon. And maybe, together, they could find a way to save Neve.

"Give him back to me," Red whispered.

The god cocked his head, regarding her through those eyes that were at once strange and familiar. The mouth she'd kissed parted. The hand that had been on her body tensed, and she felt everything, everything, a current of what they'd been running through them both like marrow through a bone.

"And what are you prepared to give?" he asked her in a voice that still held traces of Eammon's, hidden in layers of thorn and leaf. "To bargain for a life requires binding."

Red took his hand, pressed it to her heart, beating rabbit-rhythm. "I was bound once. Bind me again."

The Wilderwood, golden and shining, looked at her through Eammon's eyes.

"I love you, Eammon." She pressed his hand harder, like she could imprint the knowledge on his skin. "Remember?"

And as roots spilled from his hand into her, she saw that he did.

A rush of golden light poured from Eammon's fingers, finding holds in the gaps between her ribs, the hollows of her lungs. The network of the Wilderwood split itself neatly in two, roots stretching through her veins, blooming along her spine. It gave her itself, entire, making her the vessel instead of just the anchor, half a forest in her bones.

She gasped, and it tasted like green things, like Eammon. She heard his deep breath like an echo, felt as the Wilderwood melted away and left her Eammon in its place.

Mostly her Eammon. Mostly the Wilderwood melted away. But part of it wasn't gone—it was in *her.* Wolves and gods, the lines between them not as firm as they'd once been.

Her eyes opened, and the world looked different. The colors brighter, like a freshly painted canvas. Her skin fizzed, and when she looked down at their clasped hands, she gasped.

A delicate network of roots pulsed visibly under her skin,

spanning from right below her elbow to the middle of her hand. They swirled like ink, deep green against white. Her Mark, altered to represent the bargain she didn't make as well as the one she did.

Her eyes rose to Eammon's. He was still taller than before. Bark still sheathed his forearms, a thin halo of green around his amber irises, and two tiny points poked through his dark hair. They'd changed, both of them, crafted out of human and into something that could hold the whole of the Wilderwood between them, not just its roots.

But those eyes knew her. And when she met his mouth with hers, it knew her, too.

Behind them, where the Wilderwood used to be, there was only a plain forest. Autumn colors filtered through the trees, crowned with red and yellow leaves. It shone with the memory of magic, but there was none. All the power—the sentinels, the network that held back shadow—lived in her and Eammon.

She kissed him again, brushed her fingers against the forest-colored thrum of his pulse, and it felt like home.

Lyra's voice cut through the golden shimmer they'd slipped into, a pocket of reality that ignored all others. "Godhood looks good on you, Wolves. Or should I call you the Wilderwood, now? Collectively?"

"Please don't," Eammon groaned.

Red turned, her smile sheepish. Lyra had an arm slung around Fife's waist, keeping her upright. Her grin was tired but genuine, and she moved with only a slight limp. Next to her, Fife was quiet, eyes guarded.

His sleeve was rolled down, Red noticed.

"You'd know about godhood," she said lightly to Lyra, stepping back from Eammon but keeping their hands knotted together. "*Plaguebreaker.*"

Lyra grimaced. "Not exactly the same, I don't think."

"Close enough," Eammon rumbled, voice still holding a touch of that strange resonance. His eyes cut to Fife. The two men shared an unreadable glance.

Breaking away from Fife, Lyra rolled up her sleeve. Her brow arched, looking from Red to Eammon. "Unless I spilled a great amount of blood during the hour I was unconscious, I don't think this should be gone." A slight waver in her voice. "And what happens now, if I'm not tied to the forest anymore?"

Eammon shrugged, the movement a ripple of wind through treetops. "You lived long within the Wilderwood. You'll live long outside it, too. Things once tied to magic don't lose it easily." His voice went softer, the flutter of a leaf to the ground. "Now you can make up for lost time."

A grin picked up her mouth, elfin features brightening as she rolled her sleeve back down. "Well, then. I certainly plan to."

Fife glanced at her sidelong and was silent.

On the hill behind them, Valdrek was waking up. Lear helped him stand on shaky legs, face a horror of blood from his head wound, though he seemed in good enough spirits. Eammon squeezed Red's hand before crossing to the two men, conversing in low tones.

In the dry grass, Kiri still slumped unconscious, not stirring though her chest rose and fell. Next to her, Raffe looked down at the fallen priestess with undisguised contempt, arms crossed over his chest. "I'm putting her on the first ship to the Rylt," he said as Red approached. "Shadows damn me, I'll not show up with a catatonic High Priestess *and* tell them their Queen is missing. I'll be dead before winter."

Red pressed her lips together. The roots on her arm glimmered a faint gold.

"If Floriane gets wind of her absence, it will be chaos. And Arick…" Raffe shook his head, pointedly not looking at her when his voice wavered on the name. "Clearly, you have other obligations, what with becoming the vessel of the whole damn Wilderwood—"

"She's still my sister, Raffe." It came out harsher than she meant, and around her feet, the edges of the dry grass blushed verdant green. "I will find her," she whispered. "I don't know how, but I will find her, and I will bring her back. That is my *obligation*."

He looked at her through narrowed eyes, taking in the Mark, the dead grass now turned green. Slowly, he nodded.

Red pointed her fingers at Kiri. Long grass braided itself into ropes and encircled the priestess's hands and feet, steel-strong. Raffe picked her up before Red could ask if he needed help, turning toward the village with her deadweight across his shoulders. He didn't look back.

She watched him until the flare of the sun blocked him from view, then went to join the others.

"So that's it, then?" Valdrek's voice was somewhat slurred, and his eyes seemed slightly distant, but other than that he seemed no worse for the wear. "The Wilderwood can't hold us back anymore, because the Wilderwood is... *you*."

Eammon shrugged. "More or less."

"So we can return." A smile picked up Valdrek's mouth, eyes gaining more focus. "Kings and shadows damn me."

"Not everyone will want to." Lear ran the hand that wasn't steadying Valdrek over his bloodied forehead. "Some will stay. Some won't know how to live in a whole world again."

Valdrek shrugged, gently shaking off Lear's hand to stand on his own strength. "I think it's a thing that can be learned." He turned toward the forest. "No time like the present to find out, after we share the good news!"

Lear rolled his eyes, but it was good-natured. With a nod, he followed Valdrek into the trees.

Then it was only the four of them, as it had been at the Keep. There was some measure of distance among them now, a space carved by change and violence, and for a moment they were silent.

"We can go anywhere," Lyra murmured. Fife's lips tightened, but

Lyra didn't notice. She cocked a brow at Red and Eammon. "*You* can go anywhere. How convenient, to carry the Wilderwood around inside of you."

"*Convenient* may be an overstatement," Eammon muttered.

Lyra grinned. "While I understand the *going anywhere* part, in principle," she said, "I find that I would like to sleep in my own bed tonight." Turning, she caught Fife's sleeve. "Come on. Give the gods a minute."

Fife followed her into the forest, still quiet, though right before they reached the tree line he slipped his hand down her arm and tangled his fingers with hers.

Then they were alone.

Eammon grasped Red's hand, and she leaned into his shoulder. Exhaustion weighed her limbs, and worry for her sister, and confusion over what might come next.

But for now, just for a moment, Red let herself feel content. She let herself feel done.

Her twentieth birthday felt like lifetimes ago. Red's lips twisted in a wry smile. "Remember when we first met?"

Eammon turned to run his fingers through her hair, tiny strands of ivy now threaded in the dark gold. "When you bled on my forest," he said, "or when you burst into my library?"

"I was thinking of the second one," Red answered. "When you told me you didn't have horns." She reached up, tapped the small points that pressed through his dark hair, remnants of his antlers. "Ironic."

He laughed then, and it sounded like wind through branches. Mouths met, warm and hungry, and he picked her up and swung her around, a fall of autumn-colored leaves chasing them.

Then he set her down, and rested his forehead on hers. They breathed the same air, the Lady and her Wolf, and for the moment it was all either of them wanted.

"Let's go home," Eammon murmured, and hand in hand, the Wardens walked through their Wilderwood.

Epilogue

Red

Strands of golden hair wrapped the mirror like rays around the sun. Blood streaked the frame, rusty against the gilt, and a pile of fingernail clippings rested on the wooden floor before it, the edges ragged from where she'd bitten them off. Red sat on her knees, hands balled in her lap, eyes wide and staring into the black surface, trying to will it into silver.

Show me my sister. Show me.

But the mirror was blank and flat.

Red raised her fist like she might strike it, might splinter the placid surface that refused to reveal Neve. But her fingers flexed out instead, and a low, pained sound rolled from her throat. Her hand fell back to her lap. Red closed her eyes.

"Nothing?"

Eammon's voice, soft. He stepped up beside her, holding out a glass of wine. She took it, and his hand dropped to her shoulder, squeezed.

The alcoholic burn was soothing against the lump in her throat. "Nothing," she confirmed.

He sighed, looking at the mirror like he wanted to shatter it as much as she did. "We'll find her," he said, the same reassurance he'd been giving her for a week. "We'll find a way."

From anyone else, it would sound hollow. With Eammon, she knew it wasn't just words. He'd do everything in his power to help her find Neve.

But as days drifted past and they grew no closer, the comfort in that knowledge was wearing thin.

When Eammon offered her his hand, she took it. He pulled her up, brought her against his chest. A susurrus like falling leaves chased his heartbeat beneath her cheek.

"Come on," he said, lips brushing her forehead. "You could do with some time out of the tower."

With one last look at the mirror, Red let him lead her down the stairs.

They passed the gate, drifted into the forest hand in hand. The Wilderwood was in them now, but magic things didn't lose their natures easily, and the forest blazed autumn colors though the rest of Valleyda had descended into winter. It wasn't quite the eternal summer of the stories, but it seemed to suit them better.

The forest was quiet now, no more dear-bought words needed to communicate. But Red could feel it within her, a second, stranger consciousness running congruent to her own. A part of her held just barely separate, like looking at your hand in a mirror and seeing the minuscule ways the measurements were off.

Godhood was a strange thing.

They walked in comfortable silence until they broke the tree line, the walls of the Edge rising in the distance. The sounds of a city still clambered from within—Valdrek planned to lead a group of villagers into Valleyda in the next few weeks, but there were many preparations to be made before then. And Lear had been right, not everyone wanted to go.

Red's brow knit. "Does Valdrek need help organizing again?"

"Not quite." Eammon raised her knuckles to his mouth, kissed them. "I might have spoken to Asheyla," he said against her skin. "About a replacement for a certain cloak."

Her smiles had been few in the last week, but all of them had been because of Eammon. Red's lips curved as they met his, the spark of her hope rekindling in her chest.

They'd find Neve. They'd fix this. Together.

Fingers wrapped around the Wolf's, she let him pull her forward.

Neve

Gray. All she could see was gray. Gradients of it—light and dark, mist and charcoal—but all gray, only gray.

Except sometimes there was blue, peering down at her. The brightest blue she'd ever seen, surrounded by sweeping darkness, like long hair. She liked the blue. It was reassuring somehow.

Slowly, feeling came back into her limbs. She didn't remember much—silver and shouting, growing trees—but she knew that lying here, in a sea of gray and sometimes blue, wasn't what she was supposed to be doing.

It was a while before she realized she could move. First her arms, then her legs, pins and needles pricking up her muscles. Without thinking too hard about it, she raised her hands, pressed on the glass that covered her. It rose easily.

Raising her arms made her notice the dark shadows over her skin, like she wore sleeves of black lace. She frowned at them a moment. There was almost a *beat* to the threads of darkness, a second set of veins. It twitched at a memory, but she couldn't cobble the whole thing together.

In the quiet, it seemed like the darkness was in her head, too. Something crouched at the edges of her mind, together and yet separate.

Her legs swung over the edge of a stone slab. She sat up.

The room was circular. Four windows stood at equidistant

points, the sills carved with sinuous lines like wafting smoke. Above her was a painted night sky, stars and constellations all in shades of gray behind a hanging paper moon.

Beyond the windows, the world was gray, too. A gray forest, branches growing down while roots grew up, disappearing into a thick sky made of fog. As she watched, something moved through the upside-down trees—immensely large, sliding snake-like.

It made her feel like cowering and pulling the glass over her again.

"Hello, Neve."

Her head snapped around, wrenched from the upside-down forest to look at the man in the corner. His hands clasped between his knees, long hair falling over his shoulders. It was just as gray as the rest of this place, but if she looked closely, she could catch hints of brownish gold.

"You're awake." Blue eyes peered at her, fixing her in place. "I've been waiting."

The story continues in...

For the Throne

Book Two of The Wilderwood

Keep reading for a sneak peek!

Acknowledgments

If it takes a village to raise a child, it takes a metropolis to make a book. I owe so much to so many people who made it possible for Red and Eammon and the entire forest disaster crew to see the light of day.

First thanks goes to my husband, Caleb, who has gallantly dealt with me softly murmuring "Red and Eammon vibes" at every emo love song for nearly five years now and also made sure that I always had time to work on this book even when it was just something I was casually poking at, because he knew it made me happy. I love you, I love you, I love you.

First publishing-specific thanks goes to my indomitable agent, Whitney Ross. You have been not only an incredible advocate, but a wonderful friend as well. Thank you for seeing what this story could be and pushing me to get there.

To my editor, Brit Hvide—I'm still so amazed I get to work with you. Your guidance and enthusiasm (and patience with my brainstorming phone calls where I say "um" and curse a lot) have made this whole process so incredible.

And because I have been blessed with an embarrassment of riches where editors are concerned, a huge thanks also to Angeline Rodriguez! Working with you was an absolute blast, and I am so thrilled to call you a friend and colleague.

I've been truly, ridiculously lucky where writing friends (who become just best friends) are concerned. Erin Craig, you are my person. Thank you for reading, quite literally, every single draft of this book and never letting me give up on it. Bibi Cooper, I love you so much, and you are a source of constant joy. There is no one I would rather send nonsensical DMs to.

To my Pod—Anna Bright, Laura Weymouth, Jen Fulmer, Steph Messa, and Joanna Ruth Meyer. I don't have words to say what you all mean to me. I wouldn't be here without you.

To Monica Hoffman and Stephanie Eding, the mentors who plucked this manuscript out of contest slush piles when it was, frankly, a hot mess—thank you for teaching me how to revise and for seeing to the heart of this story long before it was really apparent.

Tori Bovalino, Emma Theriault, Claribel Ortega, Kelsey Rodkey, Saint Gibson, Kit Mayquist, Gina Chen, Em Liu, Sierra Elmore, Emma Warner, Meryn Lobb, Kelly Andrew, Suzie Sainwood, Paige Cober, Sadie Blach, Tracy Deonn, Rachel Somer, Jordan Gray, Morgan Ashbaugh, Diana Hurlburt—your support and friendship has meant the world and made the world bearable. To Layne Fargo, Roseanne Brown, Alexis Henderson, Shelby Mahurin, and Isabel Cañas, my PitchWars crew—I love you all, and I'm damn proud of us. And to the Guillotines, MK and Harry and Chris—you guys are absolutely brilliant, and I am so honored to be friends with you.

To Sarah Gray, Liz O'Connell, Ashley Wright, Chelsea Fitzgerald, Stephanie Sorenson, Leah Looper, Nicole Prieto, Jensie Trail—I have loved you all for so many years now, and I am so thankful to have your support and friendship and memes.

And of course a huge thanks to the entire Orbit team, who has been an utter joy to work with at every turn. You guys are amazing.

Lastly, thank you to all the readers who have been excited about this book from the beginning. Thanks for letting me tell stories.

extras

meet the author

Photo Credit: Caleb Whitten

Hannah Whitten has been writing to amuse herself since she could hold a pen, and she figured out sometime in high school that what amused her might also amuse others. When she's not writing, she's reading, making music, or attempting to bake. She lives in Tennessee with her husband and children in a house ruled by a temperamental cat.

Find out more about Hannah Whitten and other Orbit authors by registering for the free monthly newsletter at orbitbooks.net.

if you enjoyed
FOR THE WOLF
look out for
FOR THE THRONE
Book Two of The Wilderwood
by
Hannah Whitten

Chapter One

Neve

Out of the open window, something was moving. That wasn't so strange in and of itself—she'd seen so much in the scant minutes she'd been awake, so much that her mind couldn't twist into the proper patterns. Words rang in her ears, made soft and rounded by a mind that wouldn't stop running in panicked loops. Her head felt thick, her body alien, understanding a flickering thing that eluded her grasp.

If she refused to listen, refused to treat this like it was real, maybe it wouldn't be.

Darkness slithered in Neve's head, cold through her veins. She clenched her fists.

Patient words, repeated again, drumming into her brain despite her best efforts: "Do you understand why you're here?"

His voice was so smooth, so conciliatory. Like a physician to a newly awakened patient. It was uncanny, really, that she'd never realized he wasn't Arick. Whatever they'd used to switch places made his voice *sound* like Arick's, but the cadence was all wrong. From Arick, everything had the rhythm of a joke. From Solmir, nothing did.

Solmir. Her mind skittered away from the name, one more thing that made no sense.

But that wasn't quite true, was it? It made too much sense, and therein was the problem.

Kings, what had she gotten herself into?

"I didn't want it to come to this, Neverah." Her full name again. She remembered how odd the shortened version sounded coming from him in those last few months. A false closeness they hadn't quite earned yet, and part of her had known it even then. "Things…veered out of my control. Wildly."

He sat behind her from where she stood at the window and looked on the gray world. His wooden chair made up one of four pieces of furniture in this spare tower room. Two chairs, a table…her coffin.

There was a fireplace next to Solmir, but it was empty. The room was circular, marked by four windows, their sills carved with sinuous lines that reminded her of smoke. Nothing on the walls, but that gray paper moon hung from the central point of the dark-painted ceiling, spangled with drawn-on constellations she recognized. The Two Sisters, the Plague Stars.

And all of it, everything, gray.

Neve didn't look at the man—the *god*—behind her. She concentrated on the thing outside the window instead, a monster that seemed easier to understand. A distant mottled side, like the body of a snake in half molt, winding through inverted trees.

A gray beast, a gray forest, everything gray but her captor's eyes. They blazed blue, and she could nearly *feel* them boring into her back, willing her to turn. Willing her to acknowledge what was happening here, to remember what she'd done.

What she'd done.

So much to remember, so much to parse. Darkness running out of her like a second set of veins, power in them pulsing like a heartbeat. Power that she pulled in, power that she chose to make part of herself.

Red's face. Red and Raffe, screaming at her from beyond the smoky glass. Neve left them, Neve *chose* to leave them. What else could she deserve, she who by her own selfishness had nearly unleashed an apocalypse? She'd resigned herself to shadows, and here they were, shaped like a man and a tower and a gray world filled with gods and monsters.

Their religion had no concept of an afterlife, but she'd twisted so many of those holy pieces already, made them fit what she wanted. Maybe she was dead, maybe this was a punishment created specifically for her.

For her, and for him.

"In the end, I had no choice." If Solmir noticed that she was close to panic, that all his patience did nothing to soothe her speeding heart, his tone didn't indicate it. It stayed even and placating, it made her want to rip out his tongue.

The thought, such unexpected violence, tugged at her veins, pulled at something in her head. All the shadow she'd pulled within her spun and writhed beneath her skin; the darkness crouching at the edge of her thoughts was set to pounce. Not her thought, not her action—something different, lurking in her like a waiting predator.

Her hands had curled to claws, and she didn't have to look down to know her veins ran tar black.

"I thought I had no choice." He said it quietly, like this was a confession. Still facing the window, Neve bared her teeth. He'd get no absolution from her. "You were weak. You'd let in too much shadow, given too much over, and when you fought Kiri in the Shrine…you were gone, after that. You wouldn't wake up. I thought anchoring you to the magic of the grove might heal you." She still didn't look at him, but she heard the faint sound of his loose long hair shifting over his shoulders as he shook his head. "I didn't expect you to—to take it all in, when your sister came to save you."

Sister. Neve closed her eyes.

"But that could work for us." Hope was an incongruous thing here. It sounded so out of place. "I thought I would have to try the same plan again—wait for another opportunity, when we're rapidly running out of time. But with you here and Red on the other side, there might be another way."

That was enough to make her finally look at him, whipping around from the window. He leaned forward in his chair, elbows braced on knees, hands clasped between them. It was strange to see someone you'd been close to for months in a body different from the one you knew. Solmir's long, straight hair fell over his shoulders, obscuring most of his face. A row of tiny scars marked his hairline, small in the center of his forehead, growing larger as they tracked to his temples. He wore thin silver rings on nearly every long finger, and the liquid shift of his hair revealed a matching silver ring in his right earlobe.

He raised his eyes to hers. Blazing blue, bluer than any sky or ocean she'd ever seen.

She wanted to speak. She had every intention. But seeing him there, a fairy-tale god made her villain, kept her vocal cords from working.

He could read on her face what she wanted to say, though. "We have to end them." A whisper, like even now he was afraid they might be overheard, in this wide prison-world that held only beasts. "They're amassing power, Neverah. They have been for centuries. They want the world they were cast out from, and they will unmake it before they let it go on without them."

And there it was. The reason for all this. The motivation behind everything they'd done, he and Kiri, using her and Arick's grief as a catalyst for their own cosmic plans.

She wanted to spit at him. She wanted to cry. All Neve did was pull in a deep, shaking breath.

"Connecting you to the shadow grove was never part of the plan," Solmir murmured. "Giving you... what I gave you... was never part of the plan. But I did both of those things to save you, Neverah. I don't expect you to believe me, but I did."

Did she believe him? Neither *yes* nor *no* seemed safe.

"The other option seemed too outlandish," he continued, speaking to his clasped, sliver-ringed hands, "too mythical. But I guess it's ridiculous for us, of all people, to discount a myth. Had I known the original plan would go so poorly, I would've been looking from the start."

So poorly, indeed. Neve remembered things in snatches, from before the smoked-glass coffin, before the shadow grove. The Shrine. Red, crouched like something wild, bloodied and listening to the trees. Pain in her head, then pain everywhere else, aching cold turning her inside out as she grabbed up more of that dark power than she ever had before, one last effort to save her sister from the inhuman thing she'd become.

But Neve had lost her humanity, too, in the end. Black lines, shadowed power, inverted trees.

There'd been pain, pain like unraveling, like someone had taken the thread at the end of her and sent her spinning. But then—a soft kiss on her forehead. A flare of *something*, deep in her, a lifeline her soul could wrap its claws around. And the pain was gone.

That's when she'd seen Solmir, Solmir-who-was-Arick, shimmering in and out of view like a mirage. When had she put together what had happened? Had someone explained it to her? She didn't think so. The power in her, cold and spangled with ice, seemed to do the explaining itself. Cold magic was its own end, threads of shadow spelling out what she should've seen the whole time: Arick wasn't Arick, what she thought she was doing wasn't the whole of it, and she'd shackled herself to a plan that didn't care if Red lived or died.

There was more to it than that. There had to be. But if all of it ended with Neve inhuman and dark in a world meant for gods, did the minutiae matter so much?

And what of Red? Shadows damn her, had Neve gotten anything she wanted, or had it all spun so far out of control that she'd lost everything?

Control. Kings and shadows, all she wanted was some *control*.

"Redarys is alive." It was almost like Solmir could read her thoughts, see her fear spelled out in her eyes. His own eyes flickered over her face, blue as an ocean in this sea of gray. A gust of cold breeze blew through the tower's open windows, ruffling the straight smoke-shine of his hair. "She and her Wolf, both. They're unharmed." A flash of dark emotion across his hatefully handsome face. "We'll need them, for this new plan to work."

Red and her Wolf. The monster she'd chosen.

All his talk of new plans, of finding something, and she had no idea what any of it meant. She was the prisoner of a King, and dark power flowed through her veins like blood, and Neve understood none of it.

She opened her mouth, unsure what would come out, and what did was "There's something outside."

His brows drew together, dark slashes over blue eyes. Solmir looked over his shoulder, flicking the shining sheet of his long hair behind his shoulder. It was brownish-gold, she thought. In the world above. She wasn't sure how she knew that; it was buried somewhere in the memories that spangled and wouldn't come together into a clear picture. It felt like intimate knowledge, here where there was no color but his eyes, that she also knew the color of his hair.

If she weren't so numb, if she didn't feel like a corpse who hadn't realized its death yet, Neve might've been sick.

Solmir peered out the window, at the slowly slithering mass in the inverted forest. Roots stretched toward the sky, up and up and up, farther than Neve thought should be possible. Eventually, they nearly disappeared, became faint enough that she could almost convince herself they were just strangely stratified clouds. Branches thatched over the ground like bridges built by madmen. In the window behind her, there was no inverted forest, nothing but an expanse of gray rolling ground and gray rolling sky. The roots were still slightly visible, miles up into the air, but they didn't extend down into trunks and branches. And other than that, nothing.

Nothing but them in this tower on the edge of nowhere. An eternity of gray and monsters beyond the door.

"A lesser beast," Solmir said, waving a hand at the slithering thing as he turned back around. "The Old Ones are deeper in the 'lands, tied to their own territories. They won't come this far out. And the Kings are tethered to the Sanctum."

He said these things like she should know what they meant. Neve shook her head. "Territories?" Her voice croaked, sounded like she'd swallowed a handful of nails. "Sanctum?"

"The gods trapped here have made their own places," Solmir said, as if it was an explanation and not just another string of words that made sense separately but not together. "They shaped the 'lands into kingdoms, carved it up. Not many of them are left, but the ones who are stay in their places. The Oracle is in the mountains, the Leviathan in the sea, the Serpent underground. And the Kings in the Sanctum." He gestured again at the creature beyond the window. "That's a lesser beast. There aren't many of them left. Lesser beasts are the only things that will venture this close to the edges of the Wilderwood, the only things stupid enough to think they can escape." He shrugged, fallen fully into the role of lecturing teacher, like that could distract her from the horror she was caught in. "Before, they could occasionally. But not now that the Wilderwood is healed and held by two Wolves again."

If he didn't stop mentioning Red, Neve was going to lose it. Her hands found the sinuously carved windowsill behind her and dug in, clawing like it could be a lifeline. Was Red looking for her? Was she gripped with the same desperation that had held Neve by the throat for the past months?

She didn't know. She didn't know.

Another stirring of anger in her heart, thoughts of violence. But this time, it wasn't against Solmir—it was against Kiri, against Arick, even—everyone around her who had let her do this. The veins in her arms ran darker at the thought.

What had happened to her?

"Nothing to be worried about." Solmir finally stood, clasped his hands behind him at almost military attention, like he'd taken every ounce of rawness she'd sensed from him before and tucked it carefully away. He stood a head and a half taller than her, built strong but lithe, face aristocratically handsome with an edge of cruelty—a knife-blade nose, sharp cheekbones, dark brows slashed over those infernally blue eyes. He looked cold.

So unlike Raffe.

Kings, her knees were going to give out.

"If it decides to die right outside our window," Solmir continued, still in that measured voice that said he could tell she was fractured, and was trying very hard not to make her break, "then, maybe I'll be concerned. The shadow-creatures it produces are a nuisance—all that trapped magic letting free when a soulless thing finally dissolves." His eyes narrowed at Neve, like he was taking her mettle. "They have some moments of semi-sentience, when they first get free. Mostly, they just try to break through to the world above. But now, they'd probably be drawn to the Kings. Build up their power."

There was something for her mind to latch onto, concrete in his sea of explanations. "You keep talking about the Kings like you aren't one of them."

It came out stronger, the first time she'd sounded like herself since she woke up. She sounded like a queen.

He had no right to look so stricken.

"You brought me here." Winter gathered in her closed fists, spangles of ice in her veins as her sluggish thoughts caught up with her heart, alchemized emotion from her tired body. "You tricked Arick, and you tried to kill my sister after telling me you could save her, and you *trapped me here with you.*"

The last word was nearly a shout, her hands raised and

clawed. Black lines shivered over them, her veins made snakes of shadow, ice crystallizing on her fingers. But he didn't back away. He didn't look frightened. He looked, instead, like he was weighing something in his mind, deciding whether one path or another would be easier to take.

When the decision was made, he shrugged. "I did." No denying, no attempting to mitigate the magnitude of what he'd done. "I did what I had to, Neverah. Had honesty been an option, I would've given it to you. But it wasn't." His brows drew together, chin tipping upward. "Yes, I brought you here. Yes, I trapped you. But I promise you this, on my life and on my blood: I will see you safely from here once our work is done."

On my life and on my blood. An ancient vow, one she'd only read in history books. It should've sent her thoughts skittering again, scattered from the center like beads from a snapped bracelet, but instead it was somehow bolstering.

"You and I are going to end this underworld," Solmir murmured, low and fierce. "We are going to burn it to the ground and take the Kings with it."

if you enjoyed
FOR THE WOLF
look out for
THE JASMINE THRONE
Book One of The Burning Kingdoms
by
Tasha Suri

The Jasmine Throne *begins the powerful Burning Kingdoms trilogy, in which two women—a long-imprisoned princess and a maidservant in possession of forbidden magic—come together to rewrite the fate of an empire.*

Exiled by her despotic brother when he claimed their father's kingdom, Malini spends her days trapped in the Hirana, an ancient, cliffside temple that was

once the source of the magical deathless waters, but
is now little more than a decaying ruin.

A servant in the regent's household, Priya makes the treacherous climb to the top of the Hirana every night to clean Malini's chambers. She is happy to play the role of a drudge so long as it keeps anyone from discovering her ties to the temple and the dark secret of her past.

One is a vengeful princess seeking to steal a throne.
The other is a powerful priestess seeking to save her family.
Their destinies will become irrevocably tangled.

And together, they will set an empire ablaze.

Chapter One

PRIYA

Someone important must have been killed in the night.

Priya was sure of it the minute she heard the thud of hooves on the road behind her. She stepped to the roadside as a group of guards clad in Parijati white and gold raced past her on their horses, their sabers clinking against their embossed belts. She drew her pallu over her face—partly because they would expect such a gesture of respect from a common woman, and partly to avoid the risk that one of them would recognize her—

and watched them through the gap between her fingers and the cloth.

When they were out of sight, she didn't run. But she did start walking very, very fast. The sky was already transforming from milky gray to the pearly blue of dawn, and she still had a long way to go.

The Old Bazaar was on the outskirts of the city. It was far enough from the regent's mahal that Priya had a vague hope it wouldn't have been shut yet. And today, she was lucky. As she arrived, breathless, sweat dampening the back of her blouse, she could see that the streets were still seething with people: parents tugging along small children; traders carrying large sacks of flour or rice on their heads; gaunt beggars, skirting the edges of the market with their alms bowls in hand; and women like Priya, plain, ordinary women in even plainer saris, stubbornly shoving their way through the crowd in search of stalls with fresh vegetables and reasonable prices.

If anything, there seemed to be even *more* people at the bazaar than usual—and there was a distinct sour note of panic in the air. News of the patrols had clearly passed from household to household with its usual speed.

People were afraid.

Three months ago, an important Parijati merchant had been murdered in his bed, his throat slit, his body dumped in front of the temple of the mothers of flame just before the dawn prayers. For an entire two weeks after that, the regent's men had patrolled the streets on foot and on horseback, beating or arresting Ahiranyi suspected of rebellious activity and destroying any market stalls that had tried to remain open in defiance of the regent's strict orders.

The Parijatdvipan merchants had refused to supply Hiranaprastha with rice and grain in the weeks that followed. Ahiranyi had starved.

Now it looked as though it was happening again. It was natural for people to remember and fear; remember, and scramble to buy what supplies they could before the markets were forcibly closed once more.

Priya wondered who had been murdered this time, listening for any names as she dove into the mass of people, toward the green banner on staves in the distance that marked the apothecary's stall. She passed tables groaning under stacks of vegetables and sweet fruit, bolts of silky cloth and gracefully carved idols of the yaksa for family shrines, vats of golden oil and ghee. Even in the faint early-morning light, the market was vibrant with color and noise.

The press of people grew more painful.

She was nearly to the stall, caught in a sea of heaving, sweating bodies, when a man behind her cursed and pushed her out of the way. He shoved her hard with his full body weight, his palm heavy on her arm, unbalancing her entirely. Three people around her were knocked back. In the sudden release of pressure, she tumbled down onto the ground, feet skidding in the wet soil.

The bazaar was open to the air, and the dirt had been churned into a froth by feet and carts and the night's monsoon rainfall. She felt the wetness seep in through her sari, from hem to thigh, soaking through draped cotton to the petticoat underneath. The man who had shoved her stumbled into her; if she hadn't snatched her calf swiftly back, the pressure of his boot on her leg would have been agonizing. He glanced down at her—blank, dismissive, a faint sneer to his mouth—and looked away again.

Her mind went quiet.

In the silence, a single voice whispered, *You could make him regret that.*

There were gaps in Priya's childhood memories, spaces big

enough to stick a fist through. But whenever pain was inflicted on her—the humiliation of a blow, a man's careless shove, a fellow servant's cruel laughter—she felt the knowledge of how to cause equal suffering unfurl in her mind. Ghostly whispers, in her brother's patient voice.

This is how you pinch a nerve hard enough to break a handhold. This is how you snap a bone. This is how you gouge an eye. Watch carefully, Priya. Just like this.

This is how you stab someone through the heart.

She carried a knife at her waist. It was a very good knife, practical, with a plain sheath and hilt, and she kept its edge finely honed for kitchen work. With nothing but her little knife and a careful slide of her finger and thumb, she could leave the insides of anything—vegetables, unskinned meat, fruits newly harvested from the regent's orchard—swiftly bared, the outer rind a smooth, coiled husk in her palm.

She looked back up at the man and carefully let the thought of her knife drift away. She unclenched her trembling fingers.

You're lucky, she thought, *that I am not what I was raised to be.*

The crowd behind her and in front of her was growing thicker. Priya couldn't even see the green banner of the apothecary's stall any longer. She rocked back on the balls of her feet, then rose swiftly. Without looking at the man again, she angled herself and slipped between two strangers in front of her, putting her small stature to good use and shoving her way to the front of the throng. A judicious application of her elbows and knees and some wriggling finally brought her near enough to the stall to see the apothecary's face, puckered with sweat and irritation.

The stall was a mess, vials turned on their sides, clay pots upended. The apothecary was packing away his wares as fast as he could. Behind her, around her, she could hear the rumbling noise of the crowd grow more tense.

"Please," she said loudly. "Uncle, *please.* If you've got any beads of sacred wood to spare, I'll buy them from you."

A stranger to her left snorted audibly. "You think he's got any left? Brother, if you do, I'll pay double whatever she offers."

"My grandmother's sick," a girl shouted, three people deep behind them. "So if you could help me out, uncle—"

Priya felt the wood of the stall begin to peel beneath the hard pressure of her nails.

"Please," she said, her voice pitched low to cut across the din.

But the apothecary's attention was raised toward the back of the crowd. Priya didn't have to turn her own head to know he'd caught sight of the white-and-gold uniforms of the regent's men, finally here to close the bazaar.

"I'm closed up," he shouted out. "There's nothing more for any of you. Get lost!" He slammed his hand down, then shoved the last of his wares away with a shake of his head.

The crowd began to disperse slowly. A few people stayed, still pleading for the apothecary's aid, but Priya didn't join them. She knew she would get nothing here.

She turned and threaded her way back out of the crowd, stopping only to buy a small bag of kachoris from a tired-eyed vendor. Her sodden petticoat stuck heavily to her legs. She plucked the cloth, pulling it from her thighs, and strode in the opposite direction of the soldiers.

On the farthest edge of the market, where the last of the stalls and well-trod ground met the main road leading to open farmland and scattered villages beyond, was a dumping ground. The locals had built a brick wall around it, but that did nothing to contain the stench of it. Food sellers threw their stale oil and decayed produce here, and sometimes discarded any cooked food that couldn't be sold.

When Priya had been much younger she'd known this place well. She'd known exactly the nausea and euphoria that finding something near rotten but *edible* could send spiraling through a starving body. Even now, her stomach lurched strangely at the sight of the heap, the familiar, thick stench of it rising around her.

Today, there were six figures huddled against its walls in the meager shade. Five young boys and a girl of about fifteen—older than the rest.

Knowledge was shared between the children who lived alone in the city, the ones who drifted from market to market, sleeping on the verandas of kinder households. They whispered to each other the best spots for begging for alms or collecting scraps. They passed word of which stallholders would give them food out of pity, and which would beat them with a stick sooner than offer even an ounce of charity.

They told each other about Priya, too.

If you go to the Old Bazaar on the first morning after rest day, a maid will come and give you sacred wood, if you need it. She won't ask you for coin or favors. She'll just help. No, she really will. She won't ask for anything at all.

The girl looked up at Priya. Her left eyelid was speckled with faint motes of green, like algae on still water. She wore a thread around her throat, a single bead of wood strung upon it.

"Soldiers are out," the girl said by way of greeting. A few of the boys shifted restlessly, looking over her shoulder at the tumult of the market. Some wore shawls to hide the rot on their necks and arms—the veins of green, the budding of new roots under skin.

"They are. All over the city," Priya agreed.

"Did a merchant get his head chopped off again?"

Priya shook her head. "I know as much as you do."

The girl looked from Priya's face down to Priya's muddied sari, her hands empty apart from the sack of kachoris. There was a question in her gaze.

"I couldn't get any beads today," Priya confirmed. She watched the girl's expression crumple, though she valiantly tried to control it. Sympathy would do her no good, so Priya offered the pastries out instead. "You should go now. You don't want to get caught by the guards."

The children snatched the kachoris up, a few muttering their thanks, and scattered. The girl rubbed the bead at her throat with her knuckles as she went. Priya knew it would be cold under her hand—empty of magic.

If the girl didn't get hold of more sacred wood soon, then the next time Priya saw her, the left side of her face would likely be as green-dusted as her eyelid.

You can't save them all, she reminded herself. *You're no one. This is all you can do. This, and no more.*

Priya turned back to leave—and saw that one boy had hung back, waiting patiently for her to notice him. He was the kind of small that suggested malnourishment; his bones too sharp, his head too large for a body that hadn't yet grown to match it. He had his shawl over his hair, but she could still see his dark curls, and the deep green leaves growing between them. He'd wrapped his hands up in cloth.

"Do you really have nothing, ma'am?" he asked hesitantly.

"Really," Priya said. "If I had any sacred wood, I'd have given it to you."

"I thought maybe you lied," he said. "I thought maybe you haven't got enough for more than one person, and you didn't want to make anyone feel bad. But there's only me now. So you can help me."

"I really am sorry," Priya said. She could hear yelling and footsteps echoing from the market, the crash of wood as stalls were closed up.

The boy looked like he was mustering up his courage. And sure enough, after a moment, he squared his shoulders and said, "If you can't get me any sacred wood, then can you get me a job?"

She blinked at him, surprised.

"I—I'm just a maidservant," she said. "I'm sorry, little brother, but—"

"You must work in a nice house, if you can help strays like us," he said quickly. "A big house with money to spare. Maybe your masters need a boy who works hard and doesn't make much trouble? That could be me."

"Most households won't take a boy who has the rot, no matter how hardworking he is," she pointed out gently, trying to lessen the blow of her words.

"I know," he said. His jaw was set, stubborn. "But I'm still asking."

Smart boy. She couldn't blame him for taking the chance. She was clearly soft enough to spend her own coin on sacred wood to help the rot-riven. Why wouldn't he push her for more?

"I'll do anything anyone needs me to do," he insisted. "Ma'am, I can clean latrines. I can cut wood. I can work land. My family is—they were—farmers. I'm not afraid of hard work."

"You haven't got anyone?" she asked. "None of the others look out for you?" She gestured in the vague direction the other children had vanished.

"I'm alone," he said simply. Then: "*Please.*"

A few people drifted past them, carefully skirting the boy. His wrapped hands, the shawl over his head—both revealed his rot-riven status just as well as anything they hid would have.

"Call me Priya," she said. "Not ma'am."

"Priya," he repeated obediently.

"You say you can work," she said. She looked at his hands. "How bad are they?"

"Not that bad."

"Show me," she said. "Give me your wrist."

"You don't mind touching me?" he asked. There was a slight waver of hesitation in his voice.

"Rot can't pass between people," she said. "Unless I pluck one of those leaves from your hair and eat it, I think I'll be fine."

That brought a smile to his face. There for a blink, like a flash of sun through parting clouds, then gone. He deftly unwrapped one of his hands. She took hold of his wrist and raised it up to the light.

There was a little bud, growing up under the skin.

It was pressing against the flesh of his fingertip, his finger a too-small shell for the thing trying to unfurl. She looked at the tracery of green visible through the thin skin at the back of his hand, the fine lace of it. The bud had deep roots.

She swallowed. Ah. Deep roots, deep rot. If he already had leaves in his hair, green spidering through his blood, she couldn't imagine that he had long left.

"Come with me," she said, and tugged him by the wrist, making him follow her. She walked along the road, eventually joining the flow of the crowd leaving the market behind.

"Where are we going?" he asked. He didn't try to pull away from her.

"I'm going to get you some sacred wood," she said determinedly, putting all thoughts of murders and soldiers and the work she needed to do out of her mind. She released him and strode ahead. He ran to keep up with her, dragging his dirty shawl tight around his thin frame. "And after that, we'll see what to do with you."

The grandest of the city's pleasure houses lined the edges of the river. It was early enough in the day that they were utterly quiet, their pink lanterns unlit. But they would be busy later. The brothels were always left well alone by the regent's men. Even in the height of the last boiling summer, before the monsoon had cracked the heat in two, when the rebel sympathizers had been singing anti-imperialist songs and a noble lord's chariot had been cornered and burned on the street directly outside his own haveli—the brothels had kept their lamps lit.

Too many of the pleasure houses belonged to highborn nobles for the regent to close them. Too many were patronized by visiting merchants and nobility from Parijatdvipa's other city-states—a source of income no one seemed to want to do without.

To the rest of Parijatdvipa, Ahiranya was a den of vice, good for pleasure and little else. It carried its bitter history, its status as the losing side of an ancient war, like a yoke. They called it a backward place, rife with political violence, and, in more recent years, with the rot: the strange disease that twisted plants and crops and infected the men and women who worked the fields and forests with flowers that sprouted through the skin and leaves that pushed through their eyes. As the rot grew, other sources of income in Ahiranya had dwindled. And unrest had surged and swelled until Priya feared it too would crack, with all the fury of a storm.

As Priya and the boy walked on, the pleasure houses grew less grand. Soon, there were no pleasure houses at all. Around her were cramped homes, small shops. Ahead of her lay the edge of the forest. Even in the morning light, it was shadowed, the trees a silent barrier of green.

Priya had never met anyone born and raised outside

Ahiranya who was not disturbed by the quiet of the forest. She'd known maids raised in Alor or even neighboring Srugna who avoided the place entirely. "There should be noise," they'd mutter. "Birdsong. Or insects. It isn't natural."

But the heavy quiet was comforting to Priya. She was Ahiranyi to the bone. She liked the silence of it, broken only by the scuff of her own feet against the ground.

"Wait for me here," she told the boy. "I won't be long."

He nodded without saying a word. He was staring out at the forest when she left him, a faint breeze rustling the leaves of his hair.

Priya slipped down a narrow street where the ground was uneven with hidden tree roots, the dirt rising and falling in mounds beneath her feet. Ahead of her was a single dwelling. Beneath its pillared veranda crouched an older man.

He raised his head as she approached. At first he seemed to look right through her, as though he'd been expecting someone else entirely. Then his gaze focused. His eyes narrowed in recognition.

"You," he said.

"Gautam." She tilted her head in a gesture of respect. "How are you?"

"Busy," he said shortly. "Why are you here?"

"I need sacred wood. Just one bead."

"Should have gone to the bazaar, then," he said evenly. "I've supplied plenty of apothecaries. They can deal with you."

"I tried the Old Bazaar. No one has anything."

"If they don't, why do you think I will?"

Oh, come on now, she thought, irritated. But she said nothing. She waited until his nostrils flared as he huffed and rose up from the veranda, turning to the beaded curtain of the doorway. Tucked in the back of his tunic was a heavy hand sickle.

"Fine. Come in, then. The sooner we do this, the sooner you leave."

She drew the purse from her blouse before climbing up the steps and entering after him.

He led her to his workroom and bid her to stand by the table at its center. Cloth sacks lined the corners of the room. Small stoppered bottles—innumerable salves and tinctures and herbs harvested from the forest itself—sat in tidy rows on shelves. The air smelled of earth and damp.

He took her entire purse from her, opened the drawstring, and adjusted its weight in his palm. Then he clucked, tongue against teeth, and dropped it onto the table.

"This isn't enough."

"You—of course it's enough," Priya said. "That's all the money I have."

"That doesn't magically make it enough."

"That's what it cost me at the bazaar last time—"

"But you couldn't get anything at the bazaar," said Gautam. "And had you been able to, he would have charged you more. Supply is low, demand is high." He frowned at her sourly. "You think it's easy harvesting sacred wood?"

"Not at all," Priya said. *Be pleasant*, she reminded herself. *You need his help.*

"Last month I sent in four woodcutters. They came out after two days, thinking they'd been in there *two hours*. Between—that," he said, gesturing in the direction of the forest, "and the regent flinging his thugs all over the fucking city for who knows what reason, you think it's easy work?"

"No," Priya said. "I'm sorry."

But he wasn't done quite yet.

"I'm still waiting for the men I sent this week to come back," he went on. His fingers were tapping on the table's surface—a fast, irritated rhythm. "Who knows when that will be? I have plenty of reason to get the best price for the supplies I have. So I'll have a proper payment from you, girl, or you'll get nothing."

Before he could continue, she lifted her hand. She had a few bracelets on her wrists. Two were good-quality metal. She slipped them off, placing them on the table before him, alongside the purse.

"The money and these," she said. "That's all I have."

She thought he'd refuse her, just out of spite. But instead, he scooped up the bangles and the coin and pocketed them.

"That'll do. Now watch," he said. "I'll show you a trick."

He threw a cloth package down on the table. It was tied with a rope. He drew it open with one swift tug, letting the cloth fall to the sides.

Priya flinched back.

Inside lay the severed branch of a young tree. The bark had split, pale wood opening up into a red-brown wound. The sap that oozed from its surface was the color and consistency of blood.

"This came from the path leading to the grove my men usually harvest," he said. "They wanted to show me why they couldn't fulfill the regular quota. Rot as far as the eye could see, they told me." His own eyes were hooded. "You can look closer if you want."

"No, thank you," Priya said tightly.

"Sure?"

"You should burn it," she said. She was doing her best not to breathe the scent of it in too deeply. It had a stench like meat.

He snorted. "It has its uses." He walked away from her, rooting through his shelves. After a moment, he returned with another cloth-wrapped item, this one only as large as a fingertip. He unwrapped it, careful to keep from touching what it held. Priya could feel the heat rising from the wood within: a strange, pulsing warmth that rolled off its surface with the steadiness of a sunbeam.

Sacred wood.

She watched as Gautam held the shard close to the rot-struck branch, as the lesion on the branch paled, the redness fading. The stench of it eased a little, and Priya breathed gratefully.

"There," he said. "Now you know it is fresh. You'll get plenty of use from it."

"Thank you. That was a useful demonstration." She tried not to let her impatience show. What did he want—awe? Tears of gratitude? She had no time for any of it. "You should still burn the branch. If you touch it by mistake..."

"I know how to handle the rot. I send men into the forest every day," he said dismissively. "And what do you do? Sweep floors? I don't need your advice."

He thrust the shard of sacred wood out to her. "Take this. And leave."

She bit her tongue and held out her hand, the long end of her sari drawn over her palm. She rewrapped the sliver of wood up carefully, once, twice, tightening the fabric, tying it off with a neat knot. Gautam watched her.

"Whoever you're buying this for, the rot is still going to kill them," he said, when she was done. "This branch will die even if I wrap it in a whole shell of sacred wood. It will just die slower. My professional opinion for you, at no extra cost." He threw the cloth back over the infected branch with one careless flick of his fingers. "So don't come back here and waste your money again. I'll show you out."

He shepherded her to the door. She pushed through the beaded curtain, greedily inhaling the clean air, untainted by the smell of decay.

At the edge of the veranda there was a shrine alcove carved into the wall. Inside it were three idols sculpted from plain wood, with lustrous black eyes and hair of vines. Before them were three tiny clay lamps lit with cloth wicks set in pools of oil. Sacred numbers.

She remembered how perfectly she'd once been able to fit her whole body into that alcove. She'd slept in it one night, curled up tight. She'd been as small as the orphan boy, once.

"Do you still let beggars shelter on your veranda when it rains?" Priya asked, turning to look at Gautam where he stood, barring the entryway.

"Beggars are bad for business," he said. "And the ones I see these days don't have brothers I owe favors to. Are you leaving or not?"

Just the threat of pain can break someone. She briefly met Gautam's eyes. Something impatient and malicious lurked there. *A knife, used right, never has to draw blood.*

But, ah, Priya didn't have it in her to even threaten this old bully. She stepped back.

What a big void there was, between the knowledge within her and the person she appeared to be, bowing her head in respect to a petty man who still saw her as a street beggar who'd risen too far, and hated her for it.

"Thank you, Gautam," she said. "I'll try not to trouble you again."

She'd have to carve the wood herself. She couldn't give the shard as it was to the boy. A whole shard of sacred wood held against skin—it would burn. But better that it burn her. She had no gloves, so she would have to work carefully, with her little knife and a piece of cloth to hold the worst of the pain at bay. Even now, she could feel the heat of the shard against her skin, soaking through the fabric that bound it.

The boy was waiting where she'd left him. He looked even smaller in the shadow of the forest, even more alone. He turned to watch her as she approached, his eyes wary, and a touch uncertain, as if he hadn't been sure of her return.

Her heart twisted a little. Meeting Gautam had brought her closer to the bones of her past than she'd been in a long, long time. She felt the tug of her frayed memories like a physical ache.

Her brother. Pain. The smell of smoke.

Don't look, Pri. Don't look. Just show me the way.

Show me—

No. There was no point remembering that.

It was only sensible, she told herself, to help him. She didn't want the image of him, standing before her, to haunt her. She didn't want to remember a starving child, abandoned and alone, roots growing through his hands, and think, *I left him to die. He asked me for help, and I left him.*

"You're in luck," she said lightly. "I work in the regent's mahal. And his wife has a very gentle heart when it comes to orphans. I should know. She took me in. She'll let you work for her if I ask nicely. I'm sure of it."

His eyes went wide, so much hope in his face that it was almost painful to look at him. So Priya made a point of looking away. The sky was bright, the air overly warm. She needed to get back.

"What's your name?" she asked.

"Rukh," he said. "My name is Rukh."